Mila ha_____ation, to pierc_____rolled façade h_____ even though she could see that he felt beneath the surface.

She wanted Jordan to feel the earthquake that was happening inside her, to know the emotions that spurred from the hole the quake had opened, and the only way she knew how to do that was to kiss him.

But as she sank into the kiss, she thought that she was a fool for being so impulsive, for letting go of the control she fought for around him. And then she stopped thinking, her body pressing itself closer to his as she tasted him. The same— he tasted the same. Of fire and home and pure man. Her anger turned into passion, and there was no sliding back into the heat that they had always shared. No, they jumped straight into the fire, greedily taking in each other, hands moving over bodies that had changed yet were somehow still the same.

When he lifted her from the ground she went willingly, her arms around him, refusing to lose contact with him…

Mila had done it out of desperation, to please through that controlled facade. He clung to even though she could see that he felt beneath the surface.

She wanted nothing to hurt she had wondered how he married once from the first time that happened, and the only way she knew how to do that was to close him.

But it was love that kept she the way to hold on to being an initiative, the telling her that the terrible ache he felt for around him, told from the deepest thoughts, her body, pressing herself closer to him as she tasted him. The same he tasted the same. Of her had hotter and pure taste, that sheer tumble into passion, and there was no stopping back into the bed that they had always shared. No, they jumped straight into the fire, greedily tearing at each other clothes, no time to even take that had ranged yet were somehow still the same.

What is What love from the ground, she went to finally her arms around him, refusing to lose contact with him.

A MARRIAGE
WORTH SAVING

BY
THERESE BEHARRIE

MILLS & BOON

First Published in Great Britain 2017
By Mills & Boon, an imprint of HarperCollins*Publishers*
1 London Bridge Street, London, SE1 9GF

© 2017 Therese Beharrie

ISBN: 978-0-263-92305-6

23-0617

Our policy is to use papers that are natural, renewable and recyclable products and made from wood grown in sustainable forests. The logging and manufacturing processes conform to the legal environmental regulations of the country of origin.

Printed and bound in Spain
by CPI, Barcelona

Therese Beharrie has always been thrilled by romance. Her love of reading established this, and now she gets to write happily-ever-afters for a living, and about all things romance on her blog at www.theresebeharrie.com. She married a man who constantly exceeds her romantic expectations and is an infinite source of inspiration for her romantic heroes. She lives in Cape Town, South Africa, and is still amazed that her dream of being a romance author is a reality.

To my husband, Grant, thank you for showing me what a strong relationship is. It's knowing that we can face whatever comes our way that helped me to write a relationship that survives after the unthinkable. You are my inspiration.
I love you.

And for the incredibly strong women in my family. Your courage in facing the most heartbreaking of losses inspired this story. Your determination in facing the future inspired these characters.
I hope it brings you a measure of comfort.

PROLOGUE

JORDAN THOMAS COULDN'T take his eyes off his event planner.

Well, he supposed he couldn't exactly call her 'his' when his father had been the one to hire her. But since he had inherited his mother's half of the vineyard—which he would have gladly traded to have her back—he figured his father's decision went for the both of them.

'Are you going to keep staring at her, or are you going to introduce yourself?'

His father, Gregory, barely glanced at him as he said the words. The serious tone Greg had used would have alarmed anyone who didn't know him—would have made him seem almost angry—but at twenty-seven years old Jordan knew the nuances of his father's voice. Greg was baiting him.

'I'm still thinking about it. I'm not sure I want to bother her an hour before the event,' Jordan answered.

When his father didn't reply, he sighed.

'Maybe you should call her over so that I can introduce myself, Dad.'

His father nodded his approval. 'Mila! Would you come over here for a second?'

The minute she started walking towards them, Jordan's heart raced. She was absolutely beautiful, he thought as he took in the perfectly designed features of her face. A small nose led to luscious lips, pink as a cherry blossom and which curved into a smile when she saw his father. The smile kicked his heart up another notch even though her brown eyes watched him carefully, surrounded by the fullest, darkest eyelashes he had ever seen.

He wondered idly if they were like that with help from cosmetic enhancements, but something told him that everything about her was natural. She made him think of the fields where his grapes grew in the vineyard—of the vibrancy of their colours and the feeling of home he always felt looking at it.

He didn't have time to ponder the unsettling thought when she stopped in front of them.

'Mila, you haven't had the chance to meet my son yet.' Greg nudged Jordan, and if Jordan hadn't been so mesmerised by the woman in front of him, he might have wondered at his father pushing him towards her.

But all thoughts flew out of his head the minute he introduced himself and she said, 'Mila Dennis,' and took his outstretched hand.

He'd thought there would be heat—a natural reaction to touching someone he found attractive. But he hadn't expected the heat to burn through his entire body. He hadn't expected the longing that curled in his stomach, the desire to make her his. But most of all he hadn't expected the pull that he felt towards her—a connection that went beyond the physical.

She pulled her hand away quickly, tucking a non-existent piece of hair behind her ear, and he knew she had felt it, too.

'It's lovely to meet you, Mr Thomas.'

Her voice sounded like music to him and he frowned, wondering at his reaction to a woman he hadn't even known for five minutes.

'Jordan, please. Mr Thomas is my father.' He shoved

his hands into his pockets and watched as a smile spread across Greg's face. Jordan felt his eyebrows raise.

'Actually, Mila doesn't call me that,' Greg said, and Jordan realised Greg's smile was aimed at Mila. It was a sign of affection that made their relationship seem more than that of employer/employee. It was almost...*familial*. Almost, because Greg didn't even share his smiles—a rare commodity—with his family. With his son.

He would have to ask his father about it, Jordan thought when Mila's lips curved in response. But then she looked at Jordan and the smile faltered.

'Well, I think it's best that I get back. We have hundreds of people coming today. It was a great idea to host a Valentine's Day Under the Stars event.'

'It was mine.' Jordan wasn't sure why he said it, but he wanted her to know that *he* was responsible for the idea that had brought the two of them together.

He had a feeling it would be significant.

'Well, it was a great one.' She frowned, as though she wasn't sure how to respond to him. 'I'll see you both a little later then. Greg...' She smiled at Jordan's father, but again it faltered when she turned her attention to him. 'Jordan...'

She said his name carefully, as though it was a mine-field she was navigating through. He watched her, saw the flash of awareness and then denial in her eyes, and something settled inside him.

'What was *that*?'

His father had waited for Mila to leave before asking, and Jordan turned to him, noting the carefully blank expression on Greg's face.

'I think I've just met the woman I'm going to spend the rest of my life with.'

Greg's eyebrows rose so high they disappeared under the hair that had fallen over his forehead. And then came another nod of approval.

'I *knew* you were a smart boy,' he said, and a warm feeling spread through Jordan's heart at what he knew was high praise coming from his father.

Meeting Jordan Thomas had unsettled Mila so much that she'd almost lost her headline act.

When she heard the commotion in the tent they'd set up behind the amphitheatre stage—and saw the sympathetic look Lulu, her assistant and long-time friend, shot her on her way towards the sound—Mila knew she was about to walk into a drama.

'Why would you do this to me on Valentine's Day?' Karen, the pretty singer that the whole of South Africa had been raving about since she'd won the biggest singing competition in the country, was wailing. 'You couldn't wait *one day* before breaking up with me? And right before a performance, too!'

Wails turned into heart-wrenching sobs—the kind that could only come from a teenage girl losing her first love—and Mila felt the telltale tickling of the start of a headache. She took in the chagrined look on Karen's guitarist's face and realised he was responsible for the tears.

She sighed, and then strode to the little crowd where the scene was unfolding.

'What's going on?'

'Kevin broke up with me!' Karen said through her sobs, and Mila wondered why she had decided that hiring a fresh young girl to perform at one of the biggest events she had ever planned—for one of the most prominent clients she had ever worked for—had seemed like a good idea.

And then she remembered the voice in the online videos she'd watched of Karen, and the number of views all those videos had got, and she sighed again.

'On *Valentine's Day*, Kevin?' Mila asked, instead of voicing the 'What were you thinking?' that sat on the tip of her tongue. Best not to rock the boat any further, she thought. Kevin, who looked to be only a couple of years older than the girl whose heart he had broken, shifted uncomfortably on his feet.

'Well, ma'am, there was this—'

He cut himself off when Mila held up her hand, affronted that he was calling her 'ma'am' even though she was only a few years older than him. Four, max. She'd also realised that whatever Kevin had been about to say would have caused Karen even more distress.

'Okay, everyone, the show is over. Can we all get back to what we need to be doing? Our guests are starting to arrive,' Mila called out and then waited until everyone had scattered, eyeing those who lingered so that they eventually left, too.

When she was alone with Karen, she turned and took the girl's hand. 'Have you ever been broken up with before, Karen?'

Red curls bounced as Karen shook her head, and Mila suddenly felt all the sympathy in the world for her.

'It sucks. It really does. Your heart feels like it's been ripped into two and your stomach is in twists. It doesn't matter when it happens—that feeling is always the same. Stays there, too, if you let it.'

Mila thought about when she had been Karen's age—of how moving from foster home to foster home had meant that she'd never had someone to tell her this the first time a boy had broken *her* heart—and said what she'd wished she'd known then.

'But, you know, the older you get, the more you realise that the less it meant, the less it will hurt. And, since Kevin over there seems like a bit of a jerk, I'm thinking you'll be over this in a week…maybe two.'

'Really?' The hope in Karen's eyes made Mila smile.

'I'm pretty sure. And, you know, the best revenge is to prove to him that it didn't really matter that much after all.'

'But how…? Oh, if I perform with him, he'll think that I've got over it. Maybe he'll even want me back!'

She said the words with such enthusiasm that Mila resisted rolling her eyes. 'Sure… Why not?'

She watched Karen run to the bathroom to freshen up, feeling both relieved that Karen was going to perform and annoyed that she didn't seem to have heard a word Mila had told her.

'That was pretty impressive.'

The deep, intensely male voice sent shivers up Mila's spine, and she turned slowly to face its owner. Jordan Thomas's eyes were the most captivating she had ever seen—a combination of gold and brown that made her think of the first signs of autumn. They made the masculine features of his face seem ordinary though she knew that, based on the way he made her feel distinctly female, he was anything *but* ordinary. Light brown hair lay shaggy over his forehead, as though he had forgotten to comb it, but it added a charm to his face that might have been otherwise lost under the pure maleness of him.

She took a moment to compose herself, and then she smiled at him.

Because she was a professional and he was a client.

And because she needed to prove that the effect he'd had on her when they'd first met had been a fluke.

'Thanks. All a part of the job.'

'Consoling teenage girls is a part of your job?'

The smile came more naturally now. 'When the teenage girl is the headline act at my event, yes.'

He shoved his hands into his pockets and the action drew her attention to the muscles under the black T-shirt he wore. Heaven help her, but she actually thought about running her hands over them before she could stop herself.

'It looks great.'

She blinked, and then realised that he was talking about the event. She nodded, and then peeked out of the tent to where people were beginning to fill the seats of the amphitheatre.

'It's come along nicely.' She noted that the wine stalls were already busy, and she could smell the waft of food from the food vendors. 'You should pat yourself on the back. It *was* your idea after all.'

She glanced back at him, saw the slow, sexy smile spread on his face, and thought that she needed to get away from him as she had almost fanned herself.

'It may have been my idea to host the event here at the vineyard, but I could never have arranged a concert *and* a movie screening in one night.'

'It pulls in fans for the concert and romantics for the movie,' she said, as she had to Greg Thomas so many times before. 'Who can resist either of those events—or any event, really—under the stars, with delicious Thomas Vineyard wines on tap, on the most romantic day of the year?'

His eyes sparkled, as though her words had given him some kind of idea, and then he smiled at her. A full smile that was more impactful than a thousand of his slow, sexy ones.

'I need to check everything one more time. If you'll excuse me?'

Jordan nodded, and then said, 'I'll find you later.'

She frowned as she walked away, wondering what on earth he'd meant by that.

When the movie was about ten minutes in, she found out.

He had come to her and claimed that there was a problem with the wine delivery for those who had pre-ordered boxes to take home with them. Like a fool she had followed him, her mind racing to a million different ways of solving the problem. Only when he led her through a gate past the Thomas house did it occur to her that there might not be an emergency.

'What is this?' she asked quietly, even though they were far enough away from the guests that no one would hear her.

'It's a picnic. Under the stars.'

A part of her melted at that—the pure romance of it made her feel as giddy as a girl on her first date. But it didn't change the way her heart raced in panic as she took in the scene in front of her.

A blanket was spread out overlooking the vineyard, and in the moonlight she could see the shadow of the mountains. For a brief moment she wondered what it would look like during the day, with its colours and its magnitude and the welcoming silence.

She shook her head and looked at what was spread on the blanket. A bottle of wine—she couldn't read the label, though she thought she saw the Thomas Vineyard crest—cooled in an ice bucket with two glasses next to it. A variety of the foods that she hadn't had time to taste accompanied the wine.

Although she really didn't want to, she found herself softening even more, her heart racing now for completely different reasons than a man expressing interest in her.

'Are you going to stay or run?'

She looked up at him, and though his words sounded playful, his expression told her otherwise.

'Are those my only two options?'

'I could offer you another.'

She saw the change in his eyes and her body heated.

'What would you do if I ran?' she asked, hoping to distract him.

'I'd run with you.'

She couldn't speak because the pieces that had been floating around in her head since they'd met—and the feelings that had become unsettled the moment he'd introduced himself—told her there was truth to his words.

'You did all of this to…to see if I felt the same way?'

'No.' He smiled, and tucked a piece of hair behind her ear. 'I did this to make you realise that you *did*.'

'Jordan, I—'

His lips were suddenly on hers, and she felt herself melt, felt her resistance—her denial—fade away. Because as his mouth moved against hers, her heart was telling her that it wanted to be with him. She ignored the way her mind told her she was being ridiculous, and instead ran her hands over the muscles she had admired earlier.

With one arm he moved everything that was on the blanket away and she found herself on her back, with Jordan's body half over hers. But she pulled away, her chest heaving as though she'd run a marathon.

'This is crazy,' she said shakily, but didn't move any further.

'Yes, it is,' he replied, his eyes filled with a mixture of desire and tenderness.

She raised a hand to his face, pushing his hair back and settling it on his cheek. He turned his head and kissed her hand. And in that moment, under the stars that sparkled brightly on Valentine's Day, she realised that she might have just fallen in love with a man she had only known for a few hours.

Even as her mind called her foolish she was pulling his lips back down to hers.

CHAPTER ONE

Two years later

JORDAN STOOD OUTSIDE his childhood home and grief—and guilt—crashed through him.

The house was like many he had seen in the Stellenbosch wine lands—large and white, with a black roof and shutters. Except he had grown up in this house. He'd played on the patio that stretched out in front of the house, with its stone pillars that had vines crawling up them. He and his father had spent Sunday evenings watching the sun set—usually in silence—on the rocking chairs that stood next to the large wooden door.

He turned his back on the house and the memories, and looked out to the gravel road that led to the rest of the vineyard.

Trees reached out to one another over the road, the colour of their leaves fading from the bright green of summer to the warm hues of autumn. From where he stood he could see the chapel where he'd married Mila just three months after they'd met.

He shook his head. He wouldn't think about that now.

Instead he looked under the potted plants that lined the pathway to the front door for the key he knew his father had kept there. When he found it he began to walk to his father's house—except that wasn't true any more. He clenched his jaw at the reminder of the new ownership of the house—the house he had grown up in—and the reason he was back, and turned the key in the lock.

He heard it first—the crackling sound of fire blazing—and he set his bags down and hurried to the living room where he was sure he would find the house burning. And slowed when he realised that the fire was safely in the fireplace.

He turned his head to the couch in front of the fire, and his heart stopped when he saw his ex-wife sitting in front of it.

'What are *you* doing here?' he demanded before he could think, the shock of seeing her here, in his child-hood home, forcing him to speak before he could think it through.

She jumped when she heard him, and shame poured through him as the glass of wine in her hand dropped to the ground and the colour seeped from her face.

'Jordan… What…? I…'

In another world, at another time, he might have found her stammering amusing. Now, though, he clamped down the emotions that filled him and asked again, 'What are you doing here, Mila?'

Her fingers curled at her sides—the only indication that she was fighting to gain her composure. He waited, giving her time to do so, perhaps to make up for startling her earlier.

'What are *you* doing here?' she asked him instead, crossing her arms and briefly drawing his attention to her chest. He shook his head and remembered how long it had taken him to realise that she took that stance when-ever she felt threatened.

'You want to know why *I'm* here? In *my* father's home?'

'It's not your father's home any more, Jordan.'

His heart thudded. 'Is that why you're here? Because you'll own part of this house soon?'

She winced, and it made him think that maybe he wasn't the only one unhappy with his father's will.

'No, of course not. But I do live here.'

'What?'

The little colour she had left in her face faded, but her eyes never left his. If he hadn't been so shocked he might have been impressed at her guts. But his mind was still very much focused on her revelation.

'I live here,' she repeated. The shakiness in her voice wasn't completely gone, but the silken tone of it came through stronger. The tone that sounded like music when she laughed. That had once caressed his skin when she said, 'I love you.' The tone that had said 'I do!' two years ago as though nothing could touch them or their love.

How little they had known then…

He pushed the memories away.

'I heard that. I want to know why,' he said through clenched teeth, his temper precariously close to snapping.

'Because your father asked me to move in with him after…after everything that happened.'

The reminder of the past threatened to gut him, but he ignored it. 'So after we got divorced you thought it would be a good idea to move in with my father?'

'No, *he* did,' she said coldly, and again shame nudged him for reasons he didn't understand. 'He wanted—he *needed* someone around when you left.'

'And you agreed?'

'After his first heart attack, yes.'

Her words cut right through to his heart, and he asked the question despite the fact that everything inside him wanted to ignore it. 'His first? You mean his *only*.'

Something flashed through her eyes, and he wondered if

it was sympathy. 'No, I mean his first. The one that killed him was his third.'

Jordan resisted the urge to close his eyes, to absorb the pain her words brought. He wondered how he had gone to his father's funeral, how he had spoken to the few friends Greg had had left, and was only hearing about this now.

But then, was it any wonder? a voice asked him. His father had always kept his feelings to himself, not wanting to burden Jordan with them. An after-effect of *that* night, Jordan thought. But there was a part of him that wondered if Greg hadn't told him as punishment for Jordan leaving, even after his father had warned him that it would destroy his marriage—which it had. After Jordan had decided that limited contact with his father during the year he'd been gone—grief snapped at him when he thought that it had actually been the year before his father's death—was the only way he would be able to forget about what had happened...

'Why didn't you tell me?' he asked, determined not to get sucked in by his thoughts.

'He didn't want you to know.'

It was like a punch to the gut—and it told him that his father wanting to punish him might not have been such a farfetched conclusion.

'He told you that, or *you* decided it?'

Mila's face was clear, but when she spoke her voice was ice. 'It was Greg's decision. Do you think your father's friends would have kept quiet about it for *me*?'

She waited for his answer, but it didn't come. He was too busy processing her words.

'He didn't want you to come home until *you'd* decided to.'

'You should have called me,' he said, his voice low, dangerous.

'If you hadn't been so determined to put as much distance between us as possible—if you hadn't let it cloud your judgement—you would have *known* that you should have come home even though I didn't call you.'

Her voice was a mirror of his own thoughts, and if her words hadn't pierced his heart Jordan might have taken a moment to enjoy—perhaps a better word was *admire*—this new edge to Mila. But he was too distracted by the emotion that what she'd said had awoken in him.

Had his desire to escape the pain of his marriage blinded him to what he should have known? That he should have come home?

'So you're back because of the will?'

Her question drew him out of his thoughts—drew his attention to her. He took a moment before he answered her.

'Yes, that sped up my return to Cape Town. But I'm here for good.'

Jordan watched as her left hand groped behind her, and he moved when he realised she was looking for something to keep her standing. He caught her as she staggered back, his arm curved around her waist. His heartbeat was faster than it had been in a long time, and somewhere in the back of his mind he wondered if he'd really wanted to stop her from falling, or if he'd put himself in this awkward situation because...

He stopped thinking as he looked into those hauntingly beautiful eyes of hers that widened as they looked up at him. The love that had filled them a long time ago had been replaced by such a complexity of emotion that he could only see surprise there. And caution.

Her brown curls were tied back into a ponytail, making her delicate features seem sharper than they'd once been. But maybe that was because her face had lost its gentle rounding, he thought, and saw for the first time that she'd lost weight. Pressed against hers, his body acknowledged that her body felt different from what he remembered. The curves he'd enjoyed during their marriage were now more toned than before.

He wished he could say he didn't like it, but the way his body tightened told him that he would be lying if he did. The lips he had always been greedy for parted, and his eyes lowered. Electricity snapped between them as he thought about tasting her, about quenching the thirst that had burned inside him since they'd been apart...

They both pulled away at the same time, and again Jordan heard the smash of glass against the floor. Pieces of a wine bottle lay mingled with pieces of the glass Mila had dropped earlier, and Jordan belatedly realised that he'd knocked it over when he'd moved back.

'I'll get something for that,' she said, hurrying away before he could respond. But she didn't move fast enough for him to miss the flush on her face.

He stared at the mess on the floor—the mess they'd made within their first minutes of reuniting—and hoped it wasn't an omen for the rest of the time they'd spend together.

Mila grabbed the broom from the kitchen cupboard, and then stilled. She should take a moment to compose herself. Her hands were still shaking from the shock of seeing Jordan, and now her body was heated from their contact.

She hated that reminder of what he could do to her. Hated it even more that he could *still* do it to her, even after everything that had happened between them.

Why had he touched her anyway? She hadn't been going to fall—she was pretty sure about that. It had just been the prospect of him staying—her stomach still churned at the thought—that had shaken her balance. And then, before she'd known it, she'd been in his arms, feeling comfort—and something else that she didn't care to admit—for the first time since the accident that had ruined their lives.

She took a deep breath and, when she was sure she was as prepared as she could be to face him again, she returned to the living room.

And felt her breath hitch again when she saw him standing there.

He was leaner now, though his body was still strong, with muscles clearly defined beneath his clothing. Perhaps there were more muscles now, whatever excess weight there had been once now firm. His hair was shorter, though it was still shaggy, falling lazily over his forehead as though begging to be pushed aside. And then there was his face...those beautiful planes drawn into the serious expression she was becoming accustomed to.

'We need to do something about the house,' he said when he saw her, and moved to take the cleaning items away from her.

But he stopped when he saw the expression in her eyes—the coldness she had become so used to aiming at him to protect herself from pain—and she bent to pick up the pieces of glass.

'I'll be leaving in the morning,' she said, grateful that he couldn't see her face as she tidied up.

The idea of going back to the house that reminded her of all that she'd had—and all that she'd lost—made her feel sick. But what choice did she have?

After Jordan had left, she hadn't been able to be alone in the place where it had all happened. So she'd escaped to their beach house in Gordons Bay for a few months, before Greg had asked her to move in with him. But the divorce meant that she no longer had any right to stay there, and since she had been renting before they'd got married the only thing she had was the house she'd lived in with Jordan. It was in *her* name after all.

But what did that matter when she couldn't bring herself

to *think* about what had happened there, let alone *live* there and having to face the memories over and over again...?

'That wasn't what I meant,' he said.

Sure that she had got to all the pieces of glass that could be picked up by hand, she stood. 'Not the *only* thing, maybe.'

She wondered how she could speak so coolly when her insides were twisted. But then, she was used to saying things despite her feelings. How many times had she bitten her tongue or said the thing people wanted to hear instead of saying what she really thought? The only difference now was that she was actually being honest.

'Fine.' The word was delivered through clenched teeth. 'There is something else. Did you put him up to the ridiculous conditions of his will?'

Anger whipped through her, and she barely noticed her hand tighten on the dustpan.

'No, Jordan, I didn't. I don't want to own a house with you, and I don't want to plan an event with you.'

I just want to move on with my life.

He didn't say anything immediately. 'I don't want that either.'

'But we'll have to.'

'Because you want your half of the house, the vineyard?'

'Because if we don't you'll lose your half of both, too.'

He didn't deny her words, though she knew by the way his face tightened that he wanted to. It wasn't so much at the truth of what she said, but at the fact that it *was* the truth. How could Jordan explain the fact that his father had left his house—and his share of the vineyard—to *both* his son and ex-daughter-in-law? For someone who valued logic as much as Jordan did, having no explanation for something this important must be eating at him.

'I'm going to contest the will.'

The part of herself that Mila had felt softening immediately iced.

'Based on what?'

'On anything I can find. I won't just accept this.'

And yet you just accepted it when I told you to give me space.

'And if I *don't* succeed in contesting the will…will you…will you sell your shares to me without any of the conditions?'

Pain sat on her chest at the question—the one she knew he'd wanted to ask since he had arrived—and forced words from her lips. 'Yes, Jordan. If that's possible, and if that's what you want, I'll do it.'

Unspoken words filled the air—memories of when he had said much the same thing to her at the end of their marriage—and she closed her eyes against them. When she was sure her emotions were in check—when she was sure that she was strong enough to look at him—she did.

And realised how different he was from the man she'd known…and loved.

She hadn't noticed any of it when she'd seen him four months ago at his father's funeral. He hadn't looked at her then, she thought, too consumed by the grief of losing his only surviving parent—the man who had raised him—despite their complicated relationship. Or maybe because of it. She wasn't even sure he knew she had only gone to the church and graveyard, not being able to bear spending time socialising after the death of the only man she'd ever thought of as a father.

After losing the last of the family she had.

Suddenly she felt incredibly weary.

'I think it's best if I go to bed now,' she said, as the shock of seeing him finally caught up with her.

'Wait,' he said, and took her arm before she could walk out of the room.

She looked down at his hand as heat seared through her body at his touch, and quickly moved away. She didn't want to think about the physical effect he had on her. The emotional one was already too much.

He cleared his throat. 'I've arranged for a meeting with Mark Garrett in the morning. To see if I have grounds to contest. Since you're willing to sell, I was hoping you would come with me.'

Her eyebrows rose. 'You've made an appointment with your family lawyer? The executor of your father's will?' When he nodded, she said, 'And you're only telling me this now? When it's beneficial to you?'

He looked at her, those golden eyes carefully blank of emotion. 'I didn't think you needed to be there.'

'Because my inheritance doesn't concern me, right? No, it's fine. I get it.' She shook her head when he opened his mouth to respond. 'You've been making decisions for the both of us since we got married. Why stop now that we're divorced?'

She didn't wait for a response, but walked past him, hating the way her body longed to be held in his arms.

Hating the way her life was once again in turmoil because of Jordan Thomas.

Mila got up at five in the morning, her muscles hard with tension after a restless night. She got dressed and did the thing that always helped to keep her mind busy—she cooked. First she made a batch of scones and then muffins and pancakes. When that was done she scrambled eggs, made bacon and toast, and eventually, as the sun peeked through the kitchen windows, put on the kettle for coffee.

'What's all this?'

The deep voice startled her, even though she knew he was there. She supposed she had already grown so used to being alone in the months since Greg had been gone—her heart ached at the reminder—that anyone's presence, let alone that of the man who unsettled her most in the world, would have frightened her in the quiet of the morning.

'Food,' she said, and wiped her hands on her apron. She stilled, thinking that it made her look nervous. 'I'm going to take it down to Frank and Martha's.'

Frank was the kind-hearted man who'd helped manage the vineyard after Greg had taken ill and Jordan had moved away. She had a soft spot for him and, since cooking was something she did to keep herself calm, often took food to Frank and his wife, Martha's house on the Thomas property to share with the workers at the vineyard during the day.

Though now Mila supposed she should offer some to Jordan. Except that would make it seem as if she had got up that morning specifically to cook for *him*. Just as she had when they were married. So she wouldn't offer him breakfast, but would wait until later to pack up the food and let him get breakfast for himself.

Satisfied with the decision, she asked, 'What time is the appointment?'

To avoid his gaze, she turned to make herself coffee. But she stopped when she realised she was about to take out *two* mugs, her mind already making his as he liked it. So she turned back to him and folded her arms, ignoring the way the sight of his hair, wet from a shower, made her body prickle.

'Eight thirty.'

'In less than an hour,' she confirmed, proud of the fact that her voice wasn't as shaky as she felt. 'I'll go and get ready.'

She nearly ran out of the kitchen, but acting normally was eating at her strength. The last time she had been in that kitchen with Jordan she had been pregnant and happy, with the only true family she'd known—her husband and her father-in-law—around her.

The loss of it all was a physical pain.

She bided her time so that she didn't have to have breakfast with him, only coming out when they had to leave. Her eyebrows barely lifted at his choice of transportation—a sleek blue car she knew was a recent and expensive model—but her heart thawed when he opened the door for her.

The trip was silent and tense, but she consoled herself by repeating that it would be over soon. If she signed her share of the vineyard, of the house, over to Jordan she would be able to move out and move on. It would mark the end of the worst and best years of her life and, though her heart was nostalgic for the best, the worst was enough that if she could, she would sign the papers right there in the car.

When Jordan gave his name to the receptionist at the lawyer's, they were shown into an office where Mila spent another ten minutes of tension with Jordan while waiting for the lawyer to come.

'Good morning, Jordan... Mila.'

Mark spoke softly to her and she gave him a small smile. She had only met him twice—once when she'd signed a prenuptial contract, and again after Greg's death when Mark had come to give his condolences and to drop off her copy of the will. Both times he had been kind, and she'd appreciated that.

Jordan barely waited until Mark was seated before he asked, 'What was going on in my father's head when he made this will, Mark?'

Mark gave him a wry smile. 'I think you would be a better judge of that than me.'

When Jordan didn't return the smile, Mark nodded,

apparently realising Jordan was only in the mood for business.

'Well, you've both read Greg's will by now. It's actually quite simple in its conditions—which I know you both must find hard to believe, considering what it's asking of you. You already own half of the Thomas Vineyard, Jordan, having inherited your mother's share of the property when you were twenty-one. Greg's half has been left, as he states in his will, to his son and his daughter-in-law, on the condition that you both work together to plan an...'

Mark paused and took a closer look at the will.

'An Under the Stars event. Instructions have been left regarding the nature of the event—which, again, both of you will have read—and this event has to take place no later than two months after the last of you received a copy of the will.'

'I received mine two weeks ago,' Jordan interrupted, looking at Mila for confirmation of her date.

'I probably got mine a week before that,' she said, and wished her heart wouldn't beat quite as hard.

'Which would mean that we have just over a month to plan this. *If* we do,' Jordan said, his voice masking all emotion.

'Honestly, Jordan. I don't see you having a choice if you want to keep the vineyard solely in your family. If you don't plan the event, your father's share of the vineyard will be auctioned off and the proceeds will be divided between the both of you.'

'Excuse me, Mark?' Mila said, ignoring the way her stomach jolted as Jordan's eyes zoned in on her. 'The will says that I've been left half of Greg's portion as his "daughter-in-law," right?' When Mark nodded his head, she continued. 'So, since Jordan and I aren't married any more, won't that give Jordan grounds to contest the will?'

And leave me out of it?

Mark's eyebrows rose. 'When did you get divorced?'

'About a year ago.' Jordan spoke now, and his eyes were hopeful when Mila lifted her own to look at his face.

She knew that she shouldn't take it personally—if Greg's will could be contested they would both get what they wanted—but her heart still contracted.

She diverted her attention to Mark, saw him riffling through the papers in front of him, and felt concern grow when he lifted one page, his face serious.

'Is there a problem?' she asked.

'I'm afraid so.' Mark looked at them both and laid the page back down. 'Before we send the beneficiaries copies of a will, we check all the details we can for accuracy. Your marital status was one of them and, well...' He gave them both an apologetic look. 'According to the court records of South Africa, the two of you are still very much married.'

CHAPTER TWO

The silence that stretched through the room was marred only by their breathing.

Jordan tried to use it to compose himself, to control the emotions that hearing he was supposedly still married had drawn from him. But then, how could he compose himself when he knew there had to be some mistake?

'I could check again,' Mark said, when Jordan told him as much, 'but I'm afraid the chances of there being a mistake are quite slim.'

'But I signed the papers.' Jordan turned to Mila. 'You did, too.'

Her eyes, slightly glazed from the shock, looked back at him from a pale face as she nodded her agreement. He fought against his instinct to hold her, to tell her that everything would be okay. It wasn't his job any more. Unless, he realised as his mind shifted to their current situation, it *was*.

'With which law firm did you file the papers? I can have my assistant call them to ask them about it.'

'With *this* law firm,' Jordan said, his voice calm though his insides were in a twist.

Mark frowned. 'Do you know which lawyer?'

'With *you*, Mark. As you're my family lawyer, I filed the papers with you.'

His patience was wearing thin. All he'd wanted when

he'd come back was to sort out his inheritance. Once that bit of unpleasantness was done, he would be able to run his family vineyard.

It was the only way he knew to make up for the fact that he'd left without dealing with any of the unresolved issues with his father. To make it up to his mother, too, he thought, remembering the only thing she had asked of him before she'd died when he was five—that he look after his father.

He forced his thoughts away from how he had failed them both.

'I think there's been a mistake of some kind.' To give him credit, Mark was trying incredibly hard to maintain his professionalism. 'I remember you asked me to draw up divorce papers. But when I met your father to set up his will last year he said that the two of you were choosing to separate—not divorce.'

'Wait—Greg set this will up *last year*?' Mila's voice was surprisingly strong despite the lack of colour in her face. 'When exactly did he do it?'

'August.'

'That was a month after his first heart attack. And two months after I signed the divorce papers.'

'Did they have my signature on them?' Jordan asked, wondering where she was going with this.

'Yes, they did.'

'So you would have been the one to file the papers with Mark?'

If Jordan hadn't seen her looking worse than this once before—the day of her fall—he would have worried about how muted she had become.

'I didn't feel entirely comfortable with that...'

Something in her eyes made him wonder what she meant, but he decided now wasn't the right time to think about it. Not when he saw that she was struggling to keep her voice devoid of the emotion she couldn't hide from him.

'So we are still married,' he said flatly.

'No, no—I was going to drop them here after I'd signed, but then Greg asked me whether I would feel better if *he* did it. Because Mark was *your* family lawyer,' she said quickly, avoiding his eyes—which told him she was lying.

It only took him a moment to realise that she was lying about the reason she'd let Greg take the papers, not about his father's actions.

'Did you follow up with Dad?' he demanded, his anger coating his real feelings about the fact that his father had been there for Mila when he hadn't been. Or the fact that his father had been supportive at all—especially to someone who wasn't his son. Was it just another way Greg had chosen to show Jordan how wrong his choice to leave had been?

'Did *you*?' she shot back, and Jordan stared at her, wondering again where the fire was coming from.

'No, clearly not.'

There was a pause.

'I think that, all things considered, we should probably postpone this meeting until a later point,' Mark said, breaking the silence.

'I don't think that's a good idea with the time frame we're working with, Mark.'

Though denial was a tempting option, Jordan knew that he had to face reality. And it seemed the reality was that he was still married.

'Could you please give us a few moments to talk in private?'

'Yes, of course.'

If he was perturbed by being kicked out of his own office, Mark didn't show it as he left the room.

The minute the door clicked closed, Jordan spoke. 'So,

my father was supposed to give the papers to Mark, who was supposed to file them. And since none of that happened, I think Mark's right—we are still married.'

'Yes, I think so…'

Her eyes were closed, but Jordan knew it was one of the ways she worked through her feelings. Closing herself off from the world—and in those last months they'd shared together closing herself off from *him*—so she could think.

The silence stretched out long enough that he became aware of a niggling inside his heart. One that told him that there was still hope for them if they were married. He didn't like it at all—not when that hope had already been dashed when Mila had accepted the divorce.

He had filed for divorce because he'd thought that it was what she wanted—she hadn't called, hadn't spoken to him once after he'd walked out through the door to a life in Johannesburg. He'd taken it as a sign that she wanted the space she had asked him for to be permanent. And so he'd thought he would make it easier for the both of them by initiating the divorce, half expecting her to call him, to demand that he come home so that they could fix things.

But he'd realised soon enough that that wasn't going to happen—when had she demanded anything from him anyway?—and he'd figured that he had done the right thing. Especially since *he* had been the one to make the decision that had caused the heartbreak they'd suffered in the first place.

'Your father spoke to me about a reunion between the two of us.'

He turned his head to her when she spoke. Her voice held that same music he had heard the first time they'd met.

'In his last few months. He wanted us to be together again.'

She opened her eyes, and Jordan had to brace himself against what the pain he saw there did to him. Against the anguish that disappointment was the last thing his father had felt about him.

He cleared his throat. 'I suppose that gives this situation some meaning. He wanted us to plan an event like the one where we met. He knew that still being married would mean we would have to bend to his will. Unless we can show that he was unfit when he made it.'

'I don't think that will work.'

She shook her head, and he wondered why she kept tying her hair up when those curls were meant to be free.

'He was completely sane—his heart attacks had nothing to do with his ability to make rational decisions.'

'What's rational about *this*?'

She lowered her eyes. 'Nothing. Of course, nothing. But making an emotional decision isn't against the law.'

'It should be.'

'Maybe.' She looked at him stoically. 'But he isn't the first person to do that in this family, so I think we can forgive him.'

Jordan found himself at a loss for words, unsure of what she meant. Was she talking about when she'd asked him to go, or the fact that he had left? Regardless of their meaning, her words surprised him. She hadn't given him any indication that she regretted what had happened between them… But then again, she wasn't exactly saying that now either.

But still, the feeling threw him. And because he didn't like it, he addressed the situation at hand.

'It doesn't seem like we're going to get out of this before our time is up, Mila.'

'Out of this…? You mean out of our marriage?'

Why did the question make him feel so strange?

He cleared his throat. 'Yes. The divorce—the one we thought we had—was supposed to take six weeks, and that's as much time as we have to make sure the will's terms are met. So...' he took a deep breath '...what would you say about putting the divorce off until we've planned the event, and then we can take it from there?'

She briefly closed her eyes again, and then looked at him, her expression guarded. 'Why would I do that?'

'What do you mean?'

'Exactly what I said.'

Her guard had slipped enough for him to see a complexity of emotion that reflected the complexity of their predicament.

'I lose in this situation either way. If I help you, we'll get the inheritance, sure, but I would still have to sell my share to you. So what do I get out of this besides spending time with the man I thought I would never have to see again?'

It took him a moment to process what she was saying, and even then he found it difficult to formulate an answer. 'You'll get money. I'll pay you for the share of the vineyard my father left you.'

'Money? *Money?*' She pulled her head back as though she had been slapped. 'I can't believe that we're still married.'

Her words felt like a slap to him, too, but the shame that ran through him at his own words made him realise that maybe he'd deserved it. He was surprised that she had said it—she would never have done so before—but that didn't make it any less true.

'I'm sorry, Mila, I didn't mean that.' He sighed. 'This has been a shock to me, too.'

She nodded, though the coldness coming from her made him wonder if she really did accept his apology.

'You know money isn't an incentive for me,' she said after a few moments, her voice back to being neutral. 'Especially since selling you my share of the vineyard would mean that I lose the only thing I have left of someone I thought of as family.'

His heart ached at that because he understood it. But the logical side of him—the side that didn't care too much for emotions—made him ask, 'If you didn't want to sell your share of the vineyard to me, why did you say you would?'

'I didn't say I wouldn't sell. I just want you to understand what I'm giving up so that you won't say something so insensitive again.'

He was beginning to feel like a schoolchild who was being taught a lesson. 'What *do* you want, then, Mila?'

'I want—' Her voice was husky, her face twisted in pain. But it disappeared almost as quickly as it came, and she cleared her throat. 'I want to sell the house and the car—everything, really, that was a part of our life together.'

Pain flared through him, and the only way he knew how to control it was to pretend it didn't affect him at all. 'Why?'

'To get rid of everything so that I can move—' She broke off, and then continued, 'Move away.' She said the last two words deliberately, as though she was struggling to formulate them. 'I haven't been able to sort things out since you left. The past year I've been busy. Looking after Greg, planning some events and...'

Getting over you, he thought she might say, and he held his breath, waiting for the words. But they didn't come.

'Your help would be useful so that by the time the vineyard is yours, I'll have something to move on to.'

'Where will you go?' he asked when it finally registered that she wanted to move away.

She raised her eyes to his, and they brimmed with the emotion he thought he carried in his heart.

'I'm still working on that part.'

Hearing her say that she was leaving was more difficult than he could have imagined. He couldn't figure out why that was when he had done the same thing.

'Are you sure you're not sacrificing more than I am?'

She smiled a little at that. 'I'm sure.'

Her smile told him all he needed to know. That he needed to help her so he could help himself. Once this was all over he would have the vineyard his parents had owned and would be able to live up to the promises he'd made to them. Maybe he would even be able to make restitution for the decisions he'd made during his short marriage and finally find some peace.

'So if I agree to help you deal with everything from when we were married, you'll agree to plan the event and then sell your inheritance to me?'

'Yes.'

'And then we'll file for divorce again?'

'We?'

The hope he thought he'd extinguished earlier threatened to ignite again at the uncertainty in her voice. But then he remembered that *he* was the one who had filed for divorce the first time, and she was probably just checking whether that would be the case again.

'You,' he clarified. 'We might as well even the score since we have the chance.'

He could have kicked himself when he saw the way her eyes darkened. He wasn't entirely sure he blamed her since his words seemed callous even to his own ears. But despite that, she nodded.

'I guess we have a deal.'

CHAPTER THREE

THEY DROVE BACK to the house in silence.

Jordan's presence was already turning Mila's life upside down. He reminded her of the things she'd failed at. Of the things she had wanted since she'd realised as a child that she didn't have a family in the way her classmates did.

Her entire class had once been invited to a party and she had begged her foster mother at the time—a perpetually exhausted woman who'd spent all her time catering to her husband instead of the children she'd been charged with caring for—to let her go.

When she'd got there Mila had seen for the first time what a real family was. She'd seen her classmate's parents look at their child with love, with pride. Had watched them take photos together while the rest of her class played on the grass. Had seen the easy affection.

She had spent that entire afternoon watching them, wondering why no one else was when this family was clearly doing something out of the norm. But when Mila had been the last to be picked up, she'd seen the way the other parents had treated their children. She'd realised that *that* was normal, and that *she* was the one with the special circumstances.

Her longing for family had started on that day, spreading through her heart, reminding her of it with every beat. Since she had lost her child, those beats had become heavy with pain, with emptiness. And it would only be worse now that Jordan was back.

Since he was back for good, she would have to leave the house she'd been staying in for almost a year. Though she'd known she couldn't stay there for ever, she *had* hoped for more time than she'd got. Not only because she didn't know where she would go—again, the thought of returning to the house where she'd lost their baby made her feel nauseous—but because it had come to feel like the home she'd never had. But then, Mila had also hoped for more time with Greg—especially since she'd finally managed to pierce that closed-off exterior of his...

But that was the least of her concerns now that she'd found out she and Jordan were still married.

It was the hope that worried her the most. Hope had been her first emotion when she'd heard the news, and it had lingered until Jordan had brought up filing for divorce again. It reminded her of how receiving those papers for the first time had destroyed her hope for reconciliation. And rightly so. She shouldn't be—wasn't—interested in reconciliation, however easy it might be to get lured back into the promise of a life with Jordan.

But that wasn't what he wanted, or he wouldn't have left so easily. And that, she told herself, was exactly why she needed to protect herself from him. That was why she had accepted Jordan's suggestion that *she* be the one to file the divorce papers this time. She needed to remind herself that their life together—at least in a romantic sense—was over.

She didn't want him to know how difficult things had been for her since he'd left, even though she had almost told him about it in Mark's office. About how selling their possessions had nothing to do with moving away and everything to do with moving on. But because she couldn't bear to expose herself to him she'd lied instead. Though now that she thought about it perhaps moving away *was* the first step to moving on…

Either way, she needed his help. She couldn't go back to their house—she would never think of it as hers, even if it was in her name—alone. She couldn't face it by herself. And she *had* to face it. She had spent long enough grieving for the family she was sure she would never have now. She knew the loss of her son would stay with her for ever, but she was determined to make something out of her life. To prove that she would have been a worthy mother…

'Do you want to talk about how everything will work?' Jordan asked, almost as though he knew that she'd been thinking too much and wanted to distract her.

'You mean how we'll plan the event?' she asked, and looked out of the window to the vineyards they were passing.

Stellenbosch had always felt like home to her, even when she hadn't had a home. The minute she had driven down the winding road that offered the most beautiful sights she had ever seen—the peaks that stood above fields and fields of produce, the kaleidoscope of colours that changed with every season—a piece had settled inside her. That had been the first time she had visited the Thomas Vineyard.

'That's part of it, of course. But I was speaking about all the details. Like where you're going to stay, for example.'

She sighed. She had told him that she would leave Greg's house that morning, and when she'd said it she'd thought it was the best way to force herself to face going back to their house. But her deal with Jordan meant that she could delay that a little longer, and immediately the ball in her chest unravelled.

Though that didn't mean she could stay at the farmhouse.

'I can still leave today.'

She could stay at a bed and breakfast, she thought, forcing herself to ignore the pain in her chest. She didn't need to be thinking about how leaving would sacrifice her only connection to Greg—to the memories of family and the love she'd never thought she deserved. She also didn't need to remember that she'd spent little time working since the accident, which meant her bank account was in a sorry state.

'You don't have to,' he said stiffly, and she turned to him.

'What do you mean?'

'It might make more sense for us to stay together.' Jordan's eyes were fixed on the road. 'We have six weeks to sort this event out. Being in the same space will make it a lot easier.'

There was Mr Logical again, she thought, and unexplained disappointment made her say, 'I can't stay in the house with you there, Jordan.'

She saw him frown. 'Why not?'

Because there's too big a part of me that wants to play house with you again, she realised.

'It's too complicated. This whole thing with us still being married...' Her head pounded at the knowledge and what it meant. 'It's a lot to deal with. It would probably be best if you and I lived separately.'

He didn't respond as he turned onto the gravel road that led to the house that would soon be theirs. She used the time to remind herself that she had been at a standstill for a year. She couldn't keep letting the tragedies in her life *or* her dreams for a family hold her back. It was time to move on, and living with Jordan—even if it *was* practical, considering her current financial situation—didn't seem to be the way she would do it.

But then she thought about the deal she had made with Jordan—about how he was going to help her sell all the things from their marriage if she helped him—and she began to wonder if living together and planning the event *was* the way she was going to move on.

As though he knew her thoughts, Jordan repeated, 'I think you should stay. We're planning an event that will happen in the next six weeks. We need to get your house and your car sold—things that might take a lot longer than six weeks—but we can start now. And we can definitely get everything in the house sold before then.'

Which should help her financial problems, she thought.

'Handling all of it will be a lot easier if we could do it from the same place,' he said again.

It made sense, she thought, but cautioned herself not to make a hasty decision.

'I'll think about it,' she said, even though the rational part of her told her she should say no. 'But I'll stay here until I've made a decision.'

'Okay,' he responded politely, and though she didn't look at him, she frowned at his acquiescence.

The Jordan she knew would have pushed or, worse, would have made the decision for her. Was he giving her space just so he'd get what he wanted? Or was it genuine? She couldn't decide, but he had pulled up in front of the house now, and her attention was drawn to the raindrops that had begun to fall lightly on the windshield.

They made a run for the front door.

'Where you'll be staying isn't the only thing we should talk about,' he said, once they were inside the house.

Mila turned to him when she'd taken off her coat. The light drizzle had sprinkled rain through his hair, and her fingers itched to dust the glittering droplets away.

Another reason I should stay away from you.

'Yes, I know.'

She moved to the living room and started putting wood in the fireplace. It had become a routine—a ritual, almost—

and it comforted her. Perhaps because it was so wonderfully normal—so far from what she'd grown up with. 'We need to talk about the event—about how we're going to plan something I did in six months in just over one.'

She saw a flicker in his eyes that suggested that wasn't what he was talking about. She supposed she had known that on some level. Which was why she had steered the conversation to safer ground. To protect herself. Now she just had to remember that for the entire time they spent together...

'Is it possible?' Jordan asked, watching Mila carefully. Something about her was different, and it wasn't only her appearance. Though as she sat curled on the couch opposite him—to be as far away from him as she could, he thought—the cup of tea she had left the room to make a few moments before in her hand, he could see that the old Mila was still there.

His heart throbbed as though it had been knocked, and he found himself yearning for something that belonged in the past. His present—*their* present—involved planning an event to save his family's vineyard. And his family no longer included the woman he had fallen so hard for, despite every logical part of him...no matter what his heart said.

'It's going to be difficult,' she conceded, distracting him from his thoughts.

'What do you think we should start with?' he asked, deciding that the only way he could focus on their business arrangement was by talking about business. But then she shifted, and the vanilla scent that clung to her drifted over to him. Suddenly he thought about how much he had missed it. About how often he'd thought he'd smelled it—had felt his heart racing at the thought that she'd come to find him—only to realise that it had been in his imagination...

'Well, the conditions of your father's will stipulate that we try to replicate the original Under the Stars event as much as possible. But, considering the season…' she looked out at the dreary weather '…I'm not sure how successful that will be.'

As she spoke she ran a finger around the rim of her cup. It was a habit for her—one she reverted to when she was deep in thought. Once, when he'd teased her about it, she'd told him that one of her foster mothers had hated it when she'd done it. The woman had told her that she was inviting bacteria, and that Mila shouldn't think they would take her to the doctor if she got sick.

It was one of the rare pieces of information she had offered him about her childhood, and she had meant for him to be amused by it. But instead it had alerted him to the difficulty of her past. Since he knew how that felt, he had never pushed her for more information.

'I don't think he thought this through,' he said, to stop his thoughts from dwelling further, but only succeeding in shifting them to his father.

'No, I don't think so either,' she agreed. 'He meant well, but in his head this idea was romanticised. We would do an event together, just like the one where we met, and it would remind us of how we felt that first night.'

The dreamy look on her face made his heart accelerate, and for the first time Jordan wondered if his father had been right. But nostalgia wasn't enough to save a broken relationship.

'And then he'd have facilitated our reunion through his death,' she ended, the expression he'd seen only moments before replaced by sadness.

His heart ached. 'He always said he wanted his death to mean something.'

'Especially after your mother's,' she said softy.

His eyes lifted to hers, and the sympathy he saw there stiffened his spine. 'Maybe.'

He didn't speak about his mother's death. He had been five when it had happened and he had spent most of his life till then watching her suffer. Because she hadn't done anything about her cancer soon enough. Because she had chosen *him*.

The memory made him think about whether his father *had* designed his will as a punishment for Jordan. To get justice, perhaps, for the fact that Greg had always blamed Jordan for her death. Something Jordan had only found out years after his mother had passed away. It would be the perfect way for his father to make his death 'mean something,' Jordan thought, especially since Greg had made his will *after* Jordan had left to cope with the loss of his son, of his wife. It was something he knew Greg hadn't approved of, despite the fact that although Greg had been there physically, in all the ways that had mattered, Greg had done the same after Jordan's mother had died…

Jordan lifted his eyes and saw that Mila was watching him in that way she had that always made him think she saw through him. He only relaxed when she averted her gaze.

'We have six weeks to do this—which means that the event is going to happen in winter. And this rain suggests that the weather has already made a turn for the worst.'

He was grateful for the change in subject. 'It also means that the grounds in the amphitheatre won't be suitable for the public.'

'Actually, I don't think that will be a problem. When your father got sick, he couldn't take care of the vineyard as well as he'd used to. So we minimised operations. We closed up the amphitheatre since we wouldn't be using it, and concentrated our efforts on the wine.'

'How did you do that? The area is huge.'

She shrugged. 'I had a connection with a tent and marquee supplier, and he designed one for us. I'll take you to see it tomorrow, if you like…' She trailed off. 'You know, I could probably get him to customise the design so that the top of the marquee is clear. That way the event would still be in the amphitheatre—'

'And still be under the stars,' he finished for her.

'Why do you look so surprised?'

'I'm just…' He was just *what*? Surprised to see her throw herself into a task like this when he couldn't remember the last time she had shown interest in anything?

'I'm good at my job, Jordan,' she said flatly when he didn't continue.

'I wasn't saying that you weren't,' he replied.

The look she shot him burned through him, and he found himself bristling in response. It simmered when he saw a slight flicker in her eyes that made her look almost vulnerable, and he wondered why he couldn't tell what had caused her reaction. He should know her well enough to be able to… Except he didn't, he realised in shock.

'I'll draw up a list of everything that needs to be done and give you a copy once I have,' she said tightly as she stood, and Jordan could see that tension straightened her spine. 'We can discuss things then.'

She walked to the door and grabbed her coat.

'Where are you going?' he demanded, anger replacing the shock of only a moment ago.

'Out,' she replied, and slammed the door on her way out, leaving him speechless.

The woman who had walked out through that door— who had got angry at nothing and left before they could deal with it—was *not* the woman he had married. *Or was she?* a voice mocked him, and briefly he wondered if he was angry at Mila for seemingly acting out of character, or at himself for not knowing his wife well enough to be able to tell.

The thought spurred his feet forward, and he was out the door before she could get far.

'Mila! Mila, wait!'

Her steps faltered, but she didn't turn back. He stopped with enough distance between them that she wouldn't feel crowded, but so she could still hear him.

'Why are you upset?'

She turned and pulled her coat tight around her, determination lining her features. 'I didn't like that you looked surprised about me being good at my job.'

It took him a moment to process her words—especially since he was surprised that she had actually chosen to answer him.

'I wasn't surprised that you're good at your job. I *know* you are.' He watched her, hoping for some indication that she believed his words, but her face was carefully blank. 'You took the spark of an idea I had with the first Under the Stars event and turned it into something I'd never dreamed of. *And* you made it a success. Of course you're good at your job.'

'I *did* do all of that,' she said after a moment. 'I *am* good at my job.'

'Yes, you are,' he reiterated, and thought about the vulnerability he'd thought he'd seen in her eyes earlier. 'But are you trying to convince me of that, or yourself?'

She folded her arms in front of her—but not before he saw her wince. She *was* trying to convince herself, he thought, and wondered how she could even doubt it.

'Don't pretend like you know me.'

Because he was suddenly worried that it was true and he *didn't* know her, anger stirred inside him again. 'It goes both ways, Mila.'

'What?'

'You assumed that I thought poorly of you because of one look you misinterpreted. If you knew who *I* was, then you would have known that couldn't be true.'

'Then tell me the real reason for your surprise.'

Her arms fell to her sides and he watched her straighten her shoulders. As if she was preparing for battle, he thought. But he couldn't answer her question. It would open the door that both of them seemed happy to keep closed—the one that protected them from their past.

When he didn't respond, she shook her head. 'That's what I thought.' She sighed. 'You know, maybe I jumped to the conclusion that you thought I wasn't good at my job because you never told me that I was. But then, we didn't have that kind of relationship, did we?'

She walked away, leaving him wondering what kind of relationship they *had* had.

CHAPTER FOUR

MILA WALKED DOWN the gravel road to the amphitheatre, Jordan beside her, and some of her tension eased. It was home, she thought as she looked at the road shaded by trees, their leaves brown and gold as though they didn't know whether to mourn or celebrate the coming winter. The grass around them had begun to lose its colour, too, though there were still patches that seemed to be fighting to remain as green as in spring.

When she made it through the trees she was standing at the top of a slope that led to the vineyard on the one side, and to the amphitheatre on the other. She had sombrely told Jordan that she would take him there that morning, and thought she needed to get over herself. She'd spent most of her time since their argument thinking about why she'd been upset—the *real* reason, not the one she had made up.

Because as soon as she'd given herself time to think it through—with Jordan's words still in her head—she'd realised her reaction the previous day *had* been because *she* was doubting her skills. It wasn't just about her job either. Jordan's return had reminded her of her failures—at being a wife. At being a mother.

Her heart hiccupped and she laid a hand over her chest, hoping to comfort herself.

Losing her baby when she was barely six months pregnant had only succeeded in amplifying her insecurities. Insecurities that stemmed from growing up without hearing anyone tell her she was good at something—at anything. She could see now that it had led to her believing that she wasn't good *enough*. Certainly not for Jordan when she'd first met him, since he'd had everything she hadn't had in her childhood.

Love, a family, a home.

A little voice had reminded her of that throughout their marriage. It was part of the reason she wished Jordan had told her he was happy with her. Or that he was proud of her. Or that she was a good wife.

But then, they'd never shared things like that during their brief marriage. She had just accepted what he'd said because she'd been afraid to speak up in case it upset him. She hadn't wanted to risk him realising that their relationship was too good to be true. That she wasn't the right person for him.

Now she saw no point in keeping her thoughts to herself—he'd realised all that anyway. And perhaps that had been the reason for Jordan's surprise—she was no longer meek Mila who didn't speak her mind. What had that got her? Nothing but a heart broken by the loss of her husband and her child.

'Nothing beats this view,' Jordan said quietly from beside her, and her heart pounded when she turned and saw him looking at her. But then he nodded towards the vineyard, and she mentally kicked herself. *Of course* he wasn't talking about her—especially since things between them were still tense.

She turned her attention to the vineyard to hide her embarrassment at thinking such a silly thing, and took in the clash of different shades of red and brown. Fields of the colours together was a picture she would never forget—even when it was years in the future and she no longer had any reason to be a part of the Thomas Vineyard. She could see the dam just beyond the fields, large and beautiful, and behind it the hills that made the vineyard look surreal.

Walking the vineyard with him felt like old times. Despite how difficult things were with them now, when they had walked past the chapel where they'd got married, Mila's heart had longed for the people they'd been then. It didn't help that the weather had turned from the rain of the previous day to bright sunshine. It reminded her of her wedding day, almost two years ago.

It had been cold, true to the season, but the sun had been shining just as it was today, as though the gods had approved their union. A fanciful thought, she realised now, indicative of the person she had been then. The person who had fallen in love at first sight and married three months later.

The fact that their wedding anniversary was a few weeks away pained her, and she tried to ignore it. Her mind reminded her that she and Jordan hadn't been together long enough—physically or emotionally—for them to celebrate their *first* anniversary. Now, on their second, they'd be together physically, but emotionally...

'It's more beautiful than I remember,' he said, and she almost smiled at the sincerity in his voice.

'It's become a bit like home to me in the past year,' she murmured, deep in thought, and then her stomach dropped when she realised what she had said. 'Because of Greg,' she added hurriedly, hoping it would make her words seem less like a revelation.

He didn't answer her, and when she looked over he had a blank expression on his face. How was it possible that the tension between them could become worse? she wondered, her insides twisting.

'I have memories of every part of this place,' he said, his face pensive now. 'This is where I last saw my mother. This is where my father raised me.'

Mila frowned. Had he just willingly mentioned his mother? His reaction the previous night when she'd said something about her had been what Mila was used to. A quick brush-off, an unwillingness to respond. She had wanted to know about his mother so badly when they were dating, when they were married, but she'd never had the nerve to push beyond Jordan's resistance. Since she didn't really want to offer information to him either, she'd convinced herself that it didn't matter. That one day, while they watched their children play in front of the house, he would tell her about the woman who had died when he was five, and she would hold his hand and tell him that it was okay.

But that day would never come now.

Jordan turned towards the amphitheatre and she followed him, and then she stopped, her eyes widening when she realised what going to the amphitheatre meant. Why hadn't she realised this earlier, she thought in panic, when she could have done something about it? *Before* she had suggested it, for heaven's sake!

'Are you coming?' Jordan asked her, and she exhaled shakily, forced her legs to move and her mouth to respond.

'Yes…yes, I am.'

'This is great,' Jordan said when he saw the white marquee that covered the amphitheatre. The edges were pinned down between the trees that surrounded the area, and it had done its job for the most part, he noted. Though water ran down the steps, the seats and the stage were still dry, along with most of the ground. It would do for their event, he thought.

'Whose idea was it to do this? It was smart.'

He took the steps as he asked the question, and was about halfway down when he realised Mila hadn't answered him. Nor could he hear her following. When he turned back to look up at her his heart raced at her expression. Her face was white—and so was the hand that clung to the railing that ran down the middle of the stairs. He could see her chest heave—in, out…in, out—and his first instinct was to run to her side and make sure that she was okay.

But somewhere at the back of his mind he realised what was happening, and a picture of her at the bottom of the stairs at their old house, lying deadly still, flashed through his mind.

This is what you left behind, a voice told him, and a ball of grief and guilt drop in his stomach.

Careful to keep his expression blank, even as his heart thrummed, he walked up to her and slid an arm around her waist. She didn't look at him, and he could feel her resistance, so he waited until her hand finally gripped the back of his jacket. Slowly they made their way down to the bottom of the stairs, and with each step the ball of emotion grew inside him.

'Thank you,' she said through tight lips when they got to the bottom, but he could hear the shakiness in her voice—felt it in her body before she stepped back from him.

'Since the accident?' he asked.

She lifted her eyes briefly, and then lowered them again as she straightened her shoulders. 'Yeah. It's not impossible to do. It just takes longer.'

He didn't know what to say. How could he say anything at all? he wondered with disgust. He knew the loss of their son had hurt them both—Jordan lived with it every day, no matter where he was. Every moment of his life since that day still held glimpses of what it would have been like if his son had been alive—images of them as a family in the home where he and Mila used to live crushed his heart each time.

But the reality was that he *wasn't* a father. And, yes,

he had complicated emotions about it—dashed hopes, a broken heart—but his body was fine. Though his heart pained, he could go down a flight of stairs without thinking about the fall that had led to a placental abruption and a premature baby who couldn't survive outside the womb. *His* mind, though still dimmed by grief, wasn't addled by a fear of stairs.

Seeing Mila's reality, seeing the effect losing their baby had had on her, gutted him. The shame and guilt he already felt about the loss of their child pierced him. And the anger—the tension Jordan felt at the fact that Mila hadn't turned to him—flamed inside him.

'Why didn't you tell me?'

She slanted a look at him. 'About…?'

She was giving him a chance to back down, he thought briefly, but he wouldn't do it.

'About the stairs. Is there anything else you're still struggling with?'

'That isn't your business any more, Jordan,' she replied easily, though he could tell that the conversation was anything but easy for her.

'You're my *wife*, Mila.' It didn't matter to him that they had both signed divorce papers and had only found out they were still married the previous day. 'I have a right to know.'

'No, you don't,' she said tersely. 'You gave up that right when you walked out. When you sent me divorce papers. When you didn't come home.' There was a brief pause. 'I'm your wife in name only.'

'You asked me to leave.'

'You should have known you needed to stay!' she shot back, and hissed out a breath.

His eyes widened at the show of temper and his heart quickened at the sight of her cheeks flushed with anger. She still took his breath away, he thought vaguely, and then his mind focused on her words.

'Is that what you really wanted?' he asked softly.

She pursed her lips. 'I don't want to talk about this, Jordan. What's done is done.'

'Clearly it isn't done. Tell me,' he begged. It had suddenly become imperative for him to know what he had walked away from. And whether she had wanted him to walk away at all.

'You made a choice to leave, Jordan.'

She looked up at him, her eyes piercing him with their fire. It wasn't a description he would have used of her before. And perhaps before he wouldn't have found it quite as alluring. But it suited her, he thought.

'We all have to live with the decisions we made then. For now, we need to focus on getting this event done.'

His jaw clenched and tension flowed through his body with his blood. She made it seem as though he had left easily—as though he had *wanted* to leave.

'I left because you asked me to. Why are you punishing me for it?'

She watched him steadily, and for a brief moment, he thought he saw her soften. But it was gone before he was sure, and then she answered him in a low voice.

'You're fooling yourself if you think you left because I asked you to.' She stopped, as though considering her words, and then continued, 'You left because you couldn't handle my grief.'

He felt his blood drain. 'Did my father tell you that?'

Mila frowned. 'Why would you think that?'

Because that was exactly what his father had accused him of in one of their last conversations before he'd left, Jordan thought in shock. After Jordan had told Greg he was leaving—that Mila had asked him to and that he was going to Johannesburg to focus on getting their research institute started—his father had accused him of leaving because Mila's suffering had reminded Jordan of his mother's suffering. And that that meant Jordan was in the same position that his father had been in.

He had ignored the words when his father had said them—had believed the two situations had nothing in common—and had refused to think about it afterwards. But hearing those words come from Mila now brought the memory into sharp focus. But, just as he had then, Jordan shut down his thoughts and feelings about it.

'Do you think your contact would actually be able to make a customised marquee?'

He saw her blink, saw her adjust to his abrupt change in topic. She opened her mouth and closed it again, and then answered.

'Yes, I think he would.'

Her voice was polite. No, he thought, *controlled*.

'I think the more appropriate question would be if he'd be able to do it in such a short period of time.'

She took her phone out and started typing, changing the tone of their conversation. The tension was still there though, he realised, noting the stiff movement of her fingers.

'If he *is* able to do it we'll have solved one of the major problems of this event.'

'I'm sure the others won't be quite as bad,' he said, and walked up the steps to the stage.

He needed space from her, even though she was standing a far enough distance away that her proximity shouldn't have bothered him. The stage was clear of the usual clutter events brought, he saw, with only the large white screen used for movies behind him.

'It's not going to be easy,' she warned. 'We'll have to see if the same food vendors are available, *and* we'll have to find out if Karen can perform…' She trailed off, as though the thought frightened her, and he felt the release of the tension in him at the memory of Mila dealing with the teenage singer.

'Won't *that* be fun for you?'

'I can't wait,' she said wryly. 'We might have to consider someone else if she isn't available. After that, the hardest part is going to be getting people to come. Karen—or whoever we get to perform—will have a huge impact on that, but it's still going to be a challenge.'

'Social media will help,' he said, and walked down the stairs to where she stood. She was taking pictures, and he realised that with the marquee the space was different from what she'd worked with before. 'We can have Karen post something closer to the time. It could even be a pop-up concert.'

'That won't work,' she disagreed. 'Doing that would put us at risk of overcrowding or riots. Of course we can have her post about the event, but we need to sell tickets. That's the only way we can know how many people to expect.'

If he'd thought she wouldn't be insulted by it, he would have complimented her on her professional knowledge. But he'd learned his lesson the previous evening. He hadn't been around before to see her in action, but his father had complimented her often enough. Now Jordan could see why.

'Was it hard work the first time?'

She glanced over at him. 'Yes, but for different reasons. We had to start from scratch then. Design it, figure out what would work, what wouldn't. Now we don't have those problems, but we're working from a blueprint. Which means we're confined. It also puts us at risk of making a loss.'

'Well, regardless of that, we're going to have to plan this.' He stuck his hands into the pockets of his jacket. 'Maybe it's a good thing I wasn't here the first time.'

'Marketing wine in American restaurants does sound more exciting,' she said easily, and his heart knocked at hearing her attempt something remarkably close to banter. Perhaps they should stick to work, he thought.

'Well, seven of the ten restaurants I visited now carry our wines, so I *was* working. Besides, if I'd been here, we probably would have been married a lot earlier—' He broke off, cursing himself for not thinking. He almost saw Mila's walls go up again.

'This event is going to take a lot of work,' she said instead of addressing his slip. 'I might have to give Lulu a call...'

Her face had tightened, and Jordan wondered what he didn't know about Mila's only real friendship.

'Have you spoken to her recently?' he asked, watching the emotions play over her face.

'Now and then,' she answered him. 'Not nearly as often as I should have.'

The admission came as a surprise to him—and to her, too, it seemed.

'I think we've seen all we need to here.' she said quickly. 'The stairs...they're easier going up.'

It was a clear sign that she didn't want any help from him, and he had to clench his fists at his sides to keep himself from doing just that as he watched her painstakingly climb the stairs.

Why couldn't she just ask for help? he thought irritably, and then stilled when a voice asked him why she should need to ask at all.

CHAPTER FIVE

MILA HEARD THE door to the house slam and closed her eyes. Clearly Jordan hadn't returned from their trip to the amphitheatre in a good mood. Not that *she* was feeling particularly cheerful herself. She had let him bait her into lashing out, into revealing things she didn't want him to know.

It was only because she had been feeling particularly vulnerable after hesitating at those stairs. She had always hated that reminder of her accident—any reminder, really. But as she had stood in front of those steps, her heart in her throat, she had hated that the most. Because every time she thought she would be able to take a step she was reminded of the sensation of tumbling to the ground. Pain would flash through her at the memory of lying at the bottom of the steps, her breathing staggered, waiting for someone to help her.

She blamed that feeling for the accusation she had hurled at Jordan from nowhere earlier. She had never intended letting that slip—the *real* reason she thought he'd left—but her tongue no longer seemed to obey the 'think before you speak' rule she had always played by.

Heaven knew she was tired of taking all the blame for him leaving—yes, she *had* asked him for space, but that had been said in grief, in pain. She hadn't meant it, but when he'd packed his bags she hadn't been able to bring herself to ask him to stay. She had wanted him to—every fibre in her being had urged her to stop him—but she had also wanted him to *want* to stay. She had wanted him to refuse to go, to tell her that he needed her, to acknowledge that they needed *each other* to get through the heartbreak of losing their son.

But he hadn't, and she had been forced to admit to herself that their make-believe life—the one where they were playing at being a happy family and where she was a worthy wife—was never *really* going to be her life. Jordan hadn't had any reason to be with her before she had lost their baby, so why would he bother with her now, when she'd proved that she wasn't capable? When she'd proved that she was broken, especially during her grieving?

He must believe that, too, or he would never have asked her if Greg had told her that. Jordan must have said it to Greg at some point, in confidence, and the stunned expression she'd seen on his face must have been because Jordan had thought Greg had broken his confidence…

Hurt beat at her heart, but she set her shaking hands down on the lists of the things she needed to do and the notes from the phone calls she had made at the kitchen counter.

'Hey,' he said, and the deep voice made her heart jump in the same way it had when they'd first met.

She turned and saw the amicable expression on his face. Had she been mistaken about his mood? Perhaps not, she thought as she looked in his eyes.

'Hi,' she replied, determined not to let her emotions get in the way of amicability. If he could do it, so could she. 'You were gone for a while.'

'Yeah, I bumped into Frank and we talked about the vineyard. I got us some food, too.'

She could tell from his voice that something was bothering him, and while her heart wanted to ask him about it, her head told her to keep to the game they seemed to be playing.

'That was nice of you,' she said measuredly, and took the pizza from him.

It had already gone cold, she saw when she opened the boxes, making her wonder if he'd gone somewhere else after picking the food up. But she was distracted when she saw he had got her favourite pizza, and she had to force herself not to be swayed by something as simple as that that only indicated his memory.

'Frank couldn't have told you all that much,' she said, and took out two oven trays to warm the pizza on. 'You two spoke about the place quite often while you were gone.'

'Did he tell you that?'

She looked back at him, and was suddenly struck by how attractive he was. He'd taken off the red winter jacket he had on that morning, and now she was being treated to the sight of the muscles he sported almost lazily under his long-sleeved top. Even his light blue jeans highlighted the strength of his lower body.

She swallowed, and told herself to answer him instead of staring like a fool. 'Frank's mentioned it, yes. But he told your dad first, and Greg told me. I think he thought that if I knew you'd kept in touch, *I'd* get in touch with you.' She closed her eyes briefly as soon as she realised she'd said it. It was being in this kitchen with him, she thought, and desperately changed the topic. 'Do you want to eat now?'

'I'd like to take a shower first, but that shouldn't take too long.'

There was a pause, almost as if Jordan had wanted to say something else and then decided not to. She glanced at him and saw an unreadable expression on his face. That in itself told her something was bothering him, but still she refused to ask him. That wasn't supposed to be her job any more.

'This is different,' he said, abruptly changing the topic.

She followed his gaze and for the first time since Jordan had first brought her to his father's house she saw the brown cupboards and cream countertops. But since that was the part of the kitchen that *hadn't* changed, she knew he was referring to her new additions.

'I thought a little colour might cheer the place up.' She didn't add that she'd hoped it would cheer his father up, as well. Greg had always been a man of a few words, and often she'd thought that it was because of sadness. He hadn't ever spoken much about his wife—like father, like son—but when he had she'd seen that Greg had loved and missed her. And then in his ill health and missing Jordan, his sadness had become grumpiness and sometimes even meanness.

Jordan was watching her when she looked up, a complicated expression on his face, and she wondered if he realised what she hadn't said after all.

'I knew it would be something like that,' he said, and it sounded forced. 'I would never have pegged Dad as a fuchsia kind of guy.' He nodded his head to the curtains and matching utensils that were scattered across the counters.

She smiled a little, felt her guard ease a touch. 'I think he grew fond of it after a while. Though at the beginning he made all sorts of noises.' The smile widened. 'And then he started seeing how the colour lightened up the place, and how the art helped me, and he got much better then.'

The walls were covered with her mosaic artwork—something her doctor had once suggested she do to keep herself busy during a postaccident, postbaby check-up—and she was quite proud of it. It made her remember the simple things she had taken pleasure in before her life had been destroyed.

'How did it help you?'

He said the words so quietly that at first she didn't

register what he'd asked. And then she realised that her guard was down, and her shoulders stiffened in response. *It shouldn't be this easy to slip up in front of him*, she thought. Not when slipping up meant talking to him about the time she was trying to move on from. Not when it meant him prodding her about it *again*.

'It just gave me something to keep busy with while I recovered,' she said firmly, and then turned to put the oven on and slide the trays with the pizzas into it.

She took her time with it, and it didn't take long for Jordan to get the picture. After a few moments, she heard the shower being turned on and she sighed with relief.

He was getting under her skin, she thought. He had always been able to do that to her, from the moment she had first taken that glass of wine from him two years ago. She'd forgotten all her insecurities then—had slipped into those enticing eyes of his and had believed that they would last, that she could be someone he wanted. Someone he needed.

The past didn't matter now, she thought, checking the pizzas. She had been young and completely in love then. Now she knew better. She could protect herself now—she *would* protect herself, regardless of how easy it seemed to be to slip up in front of him. Whether it was out of anger, or out of familiarity, she would control it.

A sharp pain snapped her from her thoughts, and she looked down to see an angry welt spread across her hand where she had reached for the oven tray without a mitt. She rolled her eyes as she ran the hand under cold water, blaming her silly thoughts for distracting her, but grateful that she had only used one hand instead of both, as she usually did.

Once the pain had subsided to a throb, she saw the welt was threatening to blister and rushed to the bathroom to get the first-aid kit and the gel she knew would soothe the burn.

She realised too late that Jordan was still in there, and barely had the chance to move back before the door opened. A cloud of steam followed a muscular body precariously covered by her white-and-pink towel out of the room.

'I'm so sorry! I was just—' She felt her face redden as she tried to avert her eyes from Jordan's half-naked body.

Except every time she tried, her eyes moved back to him of their own accord. She had been right when she'd thought his body was more muscular than she remembered. His broad shoulders were more defined, the muscles in his chest and abs sculpted so perfectly that she wondered if it were possible for her insides to burn, as well. Then she cleared her throat and told herself that she had seen him like this before. There was no reason to panic.

She took a deep breath. 'I'm sorry, I just need to get the first-aid kit.' She gestured to her hand and was quite proud of the way she'd managed to put words together in the calm tone her voice had taken.

Which all went out the window when he immediately walked to her and took her hand in his.

'What happened?'

'I…I burned myself.' Her mind was whirling at the feel of her hand in his, at the contact between them—however minimal. But her heart was the problem—it was thumping at a rhythm she thought she couldn't possibly sustain, merely because of his proximity.

'Still a clumsy cook, I see. Even when you're just heating pizza,' he said softly, and then he led her into the bathroom.

She had no choice but to stand there as he reached for the first-aid kit. He pulled out the soothing gel and spread it gently over her burn, and the heat went from her hand to the rest of her. His body was still warm from the shower, and she could smell his body wash—the same kind he'd used before they had broken up. The same kind that had thrilled her each time she had smelled it.

And suddenly her heart and her body longed for him with an intensity that had her backing away from him.

'It's fine, thanks. I'll finish this up in the kitchen.' She grabbed the kit and almost ran back to the kitchen, not caring if he saw.

All she cared about was putting some distance between them so she could try and convince herself that he *wasn't* affecting her.

'Did you manage to call Lulu?' Jordan asked Mila when he'd finally got his body back under control.

He hadn't expected her to react like that after seeing him in a towel. The look she had given him before she had bolted had been filled with the desire that had marked their entire relationship, and his body had acted accordingly. But that was over now, he told himself, and he was making an effort to forget it. Except that all of a sudden he was noticing the curve of her neck, the faint blush of her cheeks...

'I did,' she replied, her voice husky, and he thought that maybe she wasn't as recovered as she pretended to be. 'She's coming over to the house tomorrow.'

Something in her voice made him forget about the curls that had escaped the clip she'd tied her hair back with. He looked up, saw the shaky hands that handed him his pizza and a glass of wine, and something pulled inside him.

'You're worried.'

'About seeing her?' She picked up her glass and plate, walking past him on her way to the lounge.

He followed, saw that she took one couch, and sat on the other. He didn't need another reason to be distracted by her. He watched as she broke a piece of pizza from the rest, but didn't lift it to her mouth.

'No, I think that's going to be fine,' she said, and lifted her head with a defiant smile.

But he could still see the uncertainty, and he knew that she was pretending. He just didn't know for whom.

'Do you really?'

'Yeah, of course. I mean, we've spoken in the last year.'

She was desperately trying to convince him—or perhaps again convince herself.

'Then why are you worried?' he asked again. 'And don't tell me you aren't because I can see that you are.'

'Honestly, it's nothing,' she replied, picking at her pizza, and he had to force himself not to be annoyed by her denials. He had to force himself not to push her just because he wanted to know. Because he wanted to help.

So he didn't answer her, biting from a slice of pizza that he didn't taste, chewing mechanically, waiting for her to speak. Her hands grew busier, and soon there was a pile of cheese on her plate and her pizza base was nearly bare. Still, he waited, because he could see it unnerved her, and perhaps it would do so enough that she would open up to him.

'I have to apologise.'

The words came out of nowhere, and Jordan felt a short moment of pride that his patience—a trait that maybe he needed more of—had paid off, before reacting to her words.

'Why?'

'I haven't…kept in touch with her like I should have. Not after the baby.'

She didn't look at him, and concern edged into his heart.

'You were in a difficult place.'

'And that's when you're supposed to *turn to* your friends, not push them away,' she said hotly, and then lifted a hand to her mouth as though she was surprised at her own words.

He could believe that, since it was the way he felt, too. Did she mean she shouldn't have pushed *him* away either?

'Maybe Lulu should have understood,' he replied carefully.

'Maybe,' she repeated. 'Maybe I expected her to.'

They were talking about the two of them, he knew, and yet he couldn't bring himself to speak plainly.

'You would have had to say it. How else would she have known?'

'Because she's my friend.'

You were my husband.

'She should have known.'

You should have stayed.

'People don't just know things, Mila,' he said with anger, the only emotion he was ready to accept. 'You have to tell them.'

'Because saying things means so much, right?' she replied calmly.

But he saw the ice in her eyes and he knew the calm was just a front.

'Like when you say things like "until death do us part"? That means you can never go back on it?' She raised her eyebrows, waiting for him to reply.

Just beneath his anger, he felt the guilt. When he had left he *had* gone back on his word. But he wouldn't have if she hadn't done it first.

'You said it, Mila. You have to turn to your friends when you need them, not push them away. *You* were the first one to go back on your word.'

Her eyes widened, and it seemed that for a moment the ice melted as a tear fell down her cheek. She wiped it away and stood.

'This was a mistake. Pretending we could do something as simple as having a meal together without getting into some kind of argument.' She slammed her plate onto the coffee table. 'Neither of us may be innocent in what happened between us, but don't for one moment think I went back on my word. *I* lost our baby. *My* body failed us. So when I asked for space I was racked with guilt. I was *devastated*. But you didn't even fight. You left like it was the easiest decision you ever made.'

'It was the *hardest* decision I ever made,' he shot back, setting his plate next to hers and standing, too, his body riddled with tension, with emotion. 'But it was better for me to focus on my work, on something I could control.' He frowned at the unexpected admission, and shook his head. 'It was the best decision, Mila.'

'For who, Jordan? You or me?'

She wiped at another tear and it pierced his heart.

'This is so silly. I'm going to bed. I'll see you in the morning.'

He couldn't bring himself to ask her to stay—knew that if he did he needed to say something other than the accusations that were coursing through his mind.

When he heard her bedroom door close he flopped down on the couch, thinking about her words. She'd wanted him to stay. The realisation was a blow to his heart that he didn't know he could recover from, and the niggling in the back of his mind—the niggle that had always made him doubt his decision to leave—finally gained ground.

He *had* believed that he was doing the right thing for her. But her words now made him wonder if it had been only for her, or for him, too. His own words seemed to prove that it had.

He thought about how relieved he had been to focus on something he could control, to focus on his work. Unlike the day when Mila had fallen and he'd had no choice but to sign the forms approving the emergency C-section. Unlike the subsequent loss of his son that he'd been unable to do anything about, just as he had been able to do nothing about Mila's grief and suffering.

He froze as his father's accusation about why he'd left played back in his head. For the first time he considered it. If Jordan *had* left Cape Town—had left the wife who'd needed him—because it reminded him of his mother's illness, then Jordan *had* been running. When Mila had asked him for space to deal with the tragedy of losing their child he had run away. From her pain…from his. Because he hadn't wanted to see her suffer—emotionally or physically—as his mother had. Because he didn't want to watch on, helpless, as his father had.

Pain stabbed through him and he rested his head in his hands. Were those the *real* reasons he had left?

CHAPTER SIX

MILA WOULD HAVE liked a day to ignore the world and lick her wounds. To ignore the fact that the tension between her and Jordan was making her feel ill. She knew that she was causing it—that if she could just sit back and agree as she had during their marriage, she wouldn't be in the situation she was.

But words kept pouring from her mouth as if she had no control over them. Maybe because she'd realised control didn't *do* anything. Jordan had still left, even though she had done—and said—everything she'd *supposed* to. She had managed to alienate her best friend—her *only* friend— even though she had always gone out of her way to make sure everyone liked her. To make sure she would always have someone who wanted her.

But when the doorbell rang the next morning she knew that she wouldn't be able to wallow. Not only because she had to meet Lulu, but because the meeting was only a part of what she needed to do for the event.

She'd made some progress—Karen's manager had told her that he would run the event by the singer and confirm after that. Her marquee contact had agreed to the customised design, his complaints about the short timeline quelled by the generous amount of money she'd offered. And on her to-do list that day was getting in touch with the food vendors and checking their availability for the next month. That and Karen would determine the date of the event, and once that was confirmed she would be able to start the marketing process.

Before she could get to that list, though, she needed to face Lulu.

Her hands were shaking as she made her way to the front door. She took a deep breath before she opened it, and then she smiled.

'Hi!' she said, and her eyes swept over Lulu.

Her first thought was that Lulu hadn't changed all that much. Her face was still oval shaped, her hair cut close to her head. Her brown skin was smooth, her light brown eyes careful as she looked at Mila. Her second thought was that none of that mattered when there was something massive that *had* changed.

'You're pregnant...' Mila said through frozen lips, and her heart sped up. Her breath threatened to speed up, too, but she saw the reserve in Lulu's eyes change to concern and forced herself to control it.

It was just one of those annoying reactions she'd had since losing her baby—like the stairs. She was strong enough to deal with the reaction her body had to seeing Lulu pregnant. Strong enough for the emotional one, too. So she ignored the heartache, the emptiness, and clung to the genuine excitement she felt for her friend.

'Congratulations!'

She pulled Lulu into a hug, ignoring the distance that had grown between them since her fall. She also ignored the way the swell of Lulu's belly made her feel incredibly empty.

'How far along are you?'

Lulu squeezed Mila quickly and then pulled back. The concern still gleaming in Lulu's eyes was almost eclipsed by the reserve that had now returned. 'Thank you. I'm twenty-eight weeks. I wasn't sure if I should come because of…'

Her voice grew softer as she spoke, and Mila knew exactly what Lulu was saying.

'Well, I'm glad you came. Please come inside.'

Lulu walked past her and Mila closed her eyes for a second. Lulu had kept her pregnancy from Mila for more than six months because she had been afraid of the way Mila would react. What did that say about her? she thought, and her heart felt bruised at the knowledge. She had never meant for her tragedy to keep her friend from telling her the happy news. It meant Mila had more to atone for than she'd originally thought.

'Is there anything I can get you? Some tea or coffee?'

'Um…no, thank you. I can't stay too long,' Lulu said, and Mila realised that she wouldn't have time to beat around the bush.

She watched Lulu gingerly lower herself onto one of the couches, and briefly thought that she remembered that perfectly. But she shook her head and decided she wasn't going to go down that path.

Instead, she spoke. 'Look, I know things between us aren't like they used to be. Our work has suffered because of…everything that happened to me…and now that I know you're pregnant I feel even worse about not taking on more so we could get commission—'

'I'm not interested in our work, Mila,' Lulu interrupted, her pretty face tense. 'Our *friendship* has suffered.'

Hearing Lulu say that made Mila feel worse. 'I know. I…I should have called.'

'You should have,' Lulu agreed. 'And you shouldn't have pushed me away at all. We've been friends for almost a decade.'

'I know,' Mila said again, and felt herself dangerously close to tears. It was almost the same conversation she had

had with Jordan the previous night. And it was time she admitted the truth of it to herself.

'I just...' She stopped. Took a breath. Tried again. 'I couldn't deal with it. I didn't want people around me who would remind me of the things I'd failed at.'

Lulu didn't respond, and Mila didn't look up to see what her friend's face might tell her. She didn't deserve the benefit of the doubt, she thought harshly.

'How would Jordan and I have done that?' Lulu asked finally, with a slight hitch to her voice that told Mila she was hurt. Her heart panged.

'I wasn't a good enough wife or a good enough mother, Lulu. Can't you see that?' Mila was suddenly desperate to make her understand. 'I should have taken it easy, like Jordan asked me to...' She faltered, but then continued, 'I didn't want Jordan around to remind me of how I had failed.'

'Even if that made sense—which it absolutely does not—why did you push *me* away? I wanted to be there for you.'

A trickle of heat ran down Mila's face. 'I know you did. But I didn't deserve someone around who wanted me to feel better about myself.'

'Oh, Mila...'

Lulu walked to where she was standing and pulled Mila into her arms. On autopilot, Mila returned the hug, too busy thinking about what she had just revealed to her friend—to herself—to be really present in the moment.

'You deserve everything. Happiness...love.' Lulu pulled back, her eyes teary. 'You *are* good enough. You just need to give yourself permission to believe that.'

Though she wanted to, Mila didn't waste her breath on asking how she could do that.

'I'm a mess,' Lulu said suddenly, wiping at her eyes. 'Pregnancy hormones are *very* real.'

'Yes, they are,' Mila replied, smiling, but then the smile faded. 'I'm sorry about everything, Lulu. I shouldn't have… Well, I should have let you be my friend.'

'Yeah, you should have.' Lulu watched her for a moment. 'Friends are *there* for one another, Mila. I don't know how after almost ten years you still don't know I'm not going anywhere.'

Because for almost double that time I didn't have anyone to show me what that meant.

But she simply repeated, 'I'm sorry.'

'Apology accepted,' Lulu said, and then sat down again. 'So—tell me the other reason you called.'

A genuine smile crept across her lips. 'How did you know?'

Lulu gave her a look that had Mila's smile spreading.

'I want to start working again. Seriously, this time. Again, I'm sorry I let the ball drop with all the events we should have been doing—'

'Oh, I've been doing them anyway,' Lulu interrupted. 'You have?'

Lulu shrugged. 'It didn't seem right to let things fall apart just because you needed some time to recover. So I've been responding to emails from the website and I forwarded you some so that you'd have something to do.'

Another smile crept onto Mila's face. 'You've been *managing* me?'

Lulu let out a small laugh. 'Yes, maybe I have. But it's meant that your business hasn't fallen apart.'

'Like my personal life, you mean?' The smile on Mila's face faltered before she reminded herself that she needed to move on. 'Thank you, Lulu. That means more than you know.'

'It wasn't a big deal. All the details, including the financials are in this binder.' Lulu reached into her bag—puffing just a little, since it was on the floor—and handed

Mila the file. She took it, but didn't look inside. She trusted Lulu, and knew everything would be in order.

'I already have our next event,' Mila said, and explained about the event they needed to plan, the timeline and what she'd already done.

She absorbed Lulu's shock at the details, and was immensely grateful when Lulu didn't comment on the fact that she was doing the event with Jordan…or the fact that they were still married. At least that was what she thought.

But after they had spoken about the event in more detail, and just as Lulu was on her way out, her friend said, 'You know, I was with you when you met Jordan *and* when you found out you were pregnant. I saw how happy both of those things made you. How happy being a family made you. Maybe finding out you're still married is a sign for you to try again. A second chance.'

Mila ignored the hope, the fierce desire that sprang up inside her at Lulu's words. 'That's not going to happen.'

'Why not? You still love him. I know you do. And you've always wanted a family, so…' Lulu trailed off.

'That doesn't matter any more, Lulu,' Mila said firmly. 'I just want to move on with my life. Focus on my work. Be a good aunt.' She tried to smile.

Lulu shook her head. 'If that's what you really want, I'll support you. But just make sure it *is* what you really want. And do me a favour?'

Mila looked up at her.

'Give yourself permission to think about what you want *honestly.*'

'Yeah, I will,' Mila responded, and then took the time to enjoy having a moment with the only person who had made her feel loved since she was sixteen.

No, that's not true, she thought, and heard Lulu's words about Jordan, about family, echo in her head.

Was a second chance possible?

No. She clamped down on the thought. She couldn't
go down that path. Not if she wanted to survive the task
they'd been given.

CHAPTER SEVEN

JORDAN WAS RETURNING from his morning run just as Lulu came out through the front door.

'Hey!' she exclaimed when she saw him, and Jordan grinned, remembering how much fun she had always been.

She and Mila had been a bundle of light together. It bothered him to see how much of that light had dimmed in Mila, he thought as he saw her, too, and his smile faded.

'You look great, Lulu,' he said, focusing his attention on the pretty woman in front of him. And then he saw that she was pregnant and his heart clenched. He suddenly became aware of the way his lungs struggled for air, the way his shoulders felt heavy with grief. He cleared his throat. 'Congratulations.'

'Thanks,' she said softly, and he saw the flash of concern in her eyes.

Because he didn't need it, he forced out, 'You finally managed to find someone who deserves you?'

'Yeah—still my husband.'

She smiled at him kindly and then turned back to Mila, who was watching their exchange with wary eyes.

'Let me know how this afternoon goes. Like I said, most of the vendors will be there. And I'll track down those who aren't.'

'Thanks.' Mila's eyes warmed as she looked at Lulu. 'I'll see you soon.'

They both stood and watched as Lulu walked to her car, and waved at the sound of her horn. When she was no longer in sight Jordan felt his legs go weak, and he walked forward to the chair that stood next to the front door.

'Hey…' Mila crouched down in front of him, and as his heart palpitated and he fought for a steady breath, she took his hand and squeezed. 'Look at me. *Look* at me, Jordan,' she repeated when he didn't respond the first time.

He lifted his eyes.

'You're going to be okay. Just keep breathing.'

She repeated it until finally he could feel his heart falling back into the uncomfortable rhythm it always had around her. He pulled his hand away, embarrassed at his reaction. She stood up, but his hope that she would leave it alone and go inside faltered when she took the seat next to him.

'So it happens to you, too?'

He looked over at her, but she was staring out to where the trees lined the driveway.

'I don't know what you're talking about.'

'Your lungs feel like they don't work any more and your heart feels like it's beating to keep the entire world alive.'

She still wasn't looking at him and he eased. He didn't know why he had reacted to Lulu in that way. He had seen other pregnant women before. Why had this one been any different?

'It's happened to you?' he said hoarsely before he could stop himself.

'Yeah, plenty of times.' She paused. 'It almost happened with Lulu today.'

'Why didn't it?'

'I didn't want her to think I wasn't happy for her.'

He nodded. He understood that. And perhaps for the first time he found himself opening up the door he had locked his feelings about his son's death behind.

'I don't know why this is different.'

'Because she's someone you know. You care about her,' she answered softly. 'It hits harder when it's closer to home.'

'Yeah, probably,' he agreed, but something told him there was something else, as well.

'I know what I said, but it doesn't mean that you're not happy for her.'

He knew she was looking at him, so he nodded, but didn't respond. Pieces were settling in his mind from where he had locked them away. And then he spoke almost without realising it.

'You're right. When I saw Lulu there was a part of me that was happy for her before the doom and gloom set in.' He realised now where the reaction had come from, and for some reason felt comfortable with saying it out loud. He didn't care to examine why.

'And…?' Mila prompted softly.

'And I felt bad about it because when we found out *you* were pregnant…' he couldn't quite believe he was saying it '…I was terrified.'

'What?' The shocked tone of her voice had his heart accelerating.

'Of course, I was happy, too. But I was scared.'

'You never told me that.'

'You were so happy. I didn't want to spoil that.'

'I was scared, too, Jordan.' She let out a little laugh when he looked at her. 'I didn't know the first thing about being a mother. About being in a family.'

His mouth opened in surprise, but before she could see it, he asked, 'Why didn't you tell me?'

'Because *you* were so happy.' She smiled over at him. 'I didn't want you to think I couldn't do it.'

Something bothered him about her answer. It reminded

him of the time she'd thought he was telling her she wasn't good at her job.

'I never thought that,' he said. 'I knew you were going to be a wonderful mother.'

'You would have been a wonderful father, too.'

'Maybe,' he replied.

Or maybe he would have been as emotionally unavailable as his own father had been. He frowned, but didn't ponder it any more. Not when he was thinking about how nice it was sitting with her. The grief he'd felt at seeing the chairs where he'd spent so much time with his father for the first time after Greg's death had faded, and he knew it was because of Mila. She was the only person besides his father that he wanted to be there with.

The realisation unsettled him.

'Why were you scared?' She interrupted his thoughts. 'I mean, I know becoming a parent is scary in general, but was that the only thing?'

No, he thought, but he couldn't bring himself to say it when he was only just beginning to realise the effect his parents had had on him. Like the fact that part of his fear over becoming a parent was because of the way his father had treated him as a child—fear that he would turn out just like that.

'Yeah, that's all.'

He looked over at her and saw that she didn't believe him. Saw the flash of hurt in her eyes because of it, felt the nudge in his heart. And still he couldn't formulate the words.

'It didn't seem like things went poorly with Lulu,' he said instead, hoping for reprieve.

'They didn't,' she replied in a measured tone, and he closed his eyes when he realised he might just have undone the progress they'd made. In their *working* relationship, he clarified to himself.

'So, you guys are friends again?'

'We were never *not* friends, it seems. She's even been doing events for me while I've been…away.'

'That's great,' he said lamely, and felt helpless as the tension seeped back in between them. Silence came with it, giving him enough time to berate himself for spoiling the tentative truce that they'd been starting to forge.

But he couldn't tell Mila why he hadn't told her everything. She didn't know that side of his father, and he didn't want to taint her memories of Greg by telling her about the angry person his father had been in Jordan's youth. About the remnants of that time that had marred his relationship with his father right up to Greg's death. And now Jordan would never get the chance to fix it, or to make up for the past year when he hadn't been in touch…

'Lulu told me about a food fair that's happening this afternoon.' She broke the silence. 'It's at the Johnson High School in town—and most of the vendors who were there for the original Under the Stars are going to be there. I'm leaving in an hour. You can come, if you like.'

'I'd like that very much. I'll go get ready,' he said softly, grateful that she was still trying to be amicable despite his reluctance to open up to her.

As he headed to the bathroom for a shower he thought about it. He hadn't told her much about his childhood. Their relationship had been such a whirlwind at the beginning, and he'd fallen in love with her before he'd known what was happening. And then they'd got married, just three months after meeting—Jordan couldn't remember *ever* making such an impulsive decision—and Mila had fallen pregnant a few months after that.

Things had been so anchored in the future for them that they hadn't considered their past. They hadn't considered how the way they had grown up and how the people in their lives might have an impact on their relationship.

It made him realise that there were pieces between them that had been broken long before they'd lost their child. They hadn't even been able to share the way they'd felt about having a baby, for crying out loud! Each of them hadn't wanted to offend the other with their real feelings. That wasn't a healthy relationship.

The conversation they had just had was the first open one they'd had since they'd met—at least about their pasts. Did that mean things were changing for them? Did he *want* them to? He couldn't deny how being with Mila reminded him of how much he had felt for her. Maybe *still* felt for her…

No! He shut that train of thought down as the water hit his body. There was no point in exploring that now. His marriage was over in every way but legally. He would just focus on the event, on helping Mila, and then on running the vineyard in a way that would have made his parents proud.

He *would* focus on that, Jordan told himself when the hope inside him twinged.

There was no point in hoping after all that had happened between them.

CHAPTER EIGHT

SHE NEEDED TO THINK.

She couldn't turn to the usual activities that helped her to do so since they all involved staying in the house with Jordan, so Mila decided to go to the place that always did.

She grabbed her jacket and walked out into the sunshine that was growing rarer the closer it got to winter. Though the cold air reminded her of the season, it brought a beauty to the vineyard that was underappreciated. *Especially from here*, she thought, standing atop the slope that overlooked the vineyard, just as she had the previous day with Jordan.

It felt as if it were a lot longer than that. So much had happened since then. She'd done a lot for the event, yes, but she had also learned a lot about herself. About how much she wanted to look worthy, and how she had sacrificed her relationships in pursuit of that. About how much what people thought about her affected her behaviour—and how she couldn't bring herself to acknowledge that to herself, or to the people who cared about her.

Perhaps it was because there hadn't been many people who cared about her when she was growing up. She'd had ten different foster families over her years of being in foster care, and she couldn't remember even one of them fostering because they actually *cared* about the children they were looking after.

It meant that she desperately wanted to feel loved, to

feel needed. But it also meant that she didn't know how to turn to people when she needed *them*. Her conversation with Lulu had shown her that those were opposing desires, since the people she wanted to feel loved and needed by needed to feel that, too. And, since she struggled to do that, she only succeeded in pushing them away. It was a vicious cycle, and if she was being honest with herself, it was another reason the loss of her baby had broken her.

When she'd fallen pregnant so quickly, so unexpectedly, she had let herself hope for a family. She was going to have a child—someone who would need her without conditions. Someone who would know that she needed them, too, without her having to say it. That was what family was, wasn't it?

But she had also been scared that she wouldn't be a good mother. And of the way having a baby would change her life. In some ways it had been a remnant of her fears about marriage. Her pregnancy seemed to have sharpened them, causing her to worry that they'd moved too fast.

So she had clung to her job, working just as hard as she had before she'd fallen pregnant to prove to herself that things wouldn't change that much. She'd ignored Jordan's suggestion that she move more slowly, that she take time to adjust to the changes her body and their lives were going through.

And then she'd fallen down the stairs and her baby had been born prematurely, only surviving for seventeen minutes in the world Mila was supposed to have prepared him for. Her mourning had been part grief at her loss, part guilt at the fact that she hadn't slowed down. That she'd put her selfish fears first.

And in her grief she'd realised how unimportant those fears had been. Having a family—having her son—had always been the most important. She'd pushed Jordan, Greg and Lulu away because that realisation had come too late, and she hadn't wanted to be reminded of how stupid she'd been.

So she'd locked her hopes for a family away, convincing herself that she could survive without one. And she would cling to that belief so no one would get hurt again because of her. It didn't matter what Lulu said about second chances and Mila wanting more. Wanting more didn't matter. Not any more.

Besides, she and Jordan just weren't right for each other. She absently rubbed at the ache that throbbed in her chest at the thought as she remembered their interaction earlier. She'd had no idea he was as affected as she was by their baby's death, and she felt awful about it. She could still see the way the colour had leached from his face when he'd realised Lulu was pregnant, could still remember how erratic his breathing had been.

It always gave her an objective glimpse into what other people felt when she went through her own episodes, and it wasn't good. And, though she still felt guilt about it, knowing that he struggled, too, made her feel a little better about how she was coping. It made her feel, for the first time since her life had imploded in front of her, as if she wasn't alone.

But that didn't mean anything other than shared experience, she thought firmly. She and Jordan hadn't even shared the way they'd really felt about having a baby. And then she had told him about why *she* hadn't, about why *she* was scared, and he had still refused to share *his* feelings with her. It reminded her of how little she actually knew about him…

No, she concluded. They weren't right for each other. And no matter what her heart said she couldn't be with someone who didn't want to let her in.

'Going down?' a voice asked behind her, and she turned,

her heart in her throat until she realised that it was Frank, not Jordan behind her.

'No.' She smiled at him and checked her watch. 'I have under thirty minutes before I need to leave to do some work on the event. There's no time for me to get lost in the fields today.'

Frank nodded and just stood behind her, and his steady presence gave her a feeling of calm.

'Something's wrong,' Frank said, still staring out to the fields.

She bit her lip when Frank's lack of eye contact reminded her of how uncomfortable he was talking about anything personal, and answered him. 'Nothing out of the ordinary.'

Not if you counted a will forcing you to reunite with a not-so-ex-husband as ordinary.

'You sure?'

'Yes.' She turned to him now, and saw the concern on his face. 'I'm not going to break down because Jordan is back, Frank.'

Frank sank his hands into his pockets and shifted his weight. He hated interfering, she thought, and her heart warmed even as she wondered why he thought he needed to.

'I know you're a strong, independent woman...'

This time Mila didn't try to hide her smile.

'But that doesn't mean that your ex being back shouldn't bother you in some way.'

Her smile faded and she shrugged. 'I'm not saying it doesn't bother me. But I can handle it.'

'He hurt you pretty bad the last time.'

'Yeah, he did. But I hurt him, too,' she answered without thinking, and lifted a hand to her mouth when she realised it was true. She *had* hurt him when she'd asked him to give her space. The thought left a feeling of discomfort in her stomach.

'I can talk to him if you like.'

She smiled. 'You would hate that.'

Frank returned her smile. 'I would. But I'd do it.'

'I know you would. For Greg, right?' She said it because she knew it must be true. Especially since Greg had asked her to look after the others at the vineyard in the same way.

'Yeah. But for you, too.'

She brushed a kiss on Frank's cheek because she knew he cared for her, and laughed when the action made him blush.

'I'm okay, Frank. I promise.'

She left after that, the brief interaction leaving her steadier. Perhaps it was because she believed what she'd told Frank. She *could* handle Jordan.

Yes, his being back brought back emotions, memories that she wished she could forget. And it stirred up the anger, the accusations she'd wanted to hurl at him the moment she'd got the divorce papers that had made her realise he had given up on them. But the more time she spent with him now also made her realise that there were things between them that had never really been right. With her, with him or in their relationship.

But Frank's presence had reminded her of the promise she'd made to Greg to look after the vineyard. And for the first time she realised the implications of Greg's will on that promise. If she didn't put aside her feelings, she wouldn't be able to plan the event. That would mean that 50 per cent of the vineyard would be auctioned off, which would mean an uncertain future.

If someone horrible became part-owner, it would affect Frank and everyone else on the vineyard that she'd grown to care about. She *had* to do it for them. She needed to plan this event, make sure that it was a success and then sign her share over to Jordan even if the whole process pained her.

And she would do it for the people she cared about.

It seemed to Jordan that he wasn't the only one who had decided to let his feelings take a back seat. Mila had greeted him cordially when she'd seen him waiting for her on one of the chairs on the patio and asked him to drive them to the school. Her tone had been reserved, but not entirely cold, and Jordan had thought that maybe she had decided cordiality was better than letting the emotions of the past interfere again.

He couldn't agree more, and so an unspoken truce had formed between them. He'd waited for Mila to grab some things from her room, and when she'd returned and walked past him the smell of vanilla had followed her. His body had tightened in response, and he'd wondered how difficult this truce would be.

'What's our plan for this?'

'Well, I have the list of all the vendors we used last time. Most of them will be at this food fair—thank goodness Stellenbosch's event industry is small—so we can split up and ask them about their availability and interest in our event.'

He ran his tongue over his teeth, keeping his eyes glued to the road. 'I don't think we should split up. Didn't the will stipulate we do this together?'

She gave him a wry smile. 'I don't think that's what your father meant.'

'Maybe not, but it would probably be a good idea for me to tag along with you. I didn't do any of this the first time, remember?'

He wasn't sure when it had suddenly become so important for him to stay with her—especially since he was sure he could convince a few vendors to come to an event that they would get great publicity and payment for.

'Fine, we can stay together.'

She said it as though she was conceding millions instead of just her company. Was there a reason she didn't want to spend time with him? Maybe it was because she could also feel the slight sizzle that simmered between them whenever they were together.

'It would probably be best if I introduce you as the new owner of the vineyard. It might give some of them more incentive to say yes.'

'And what happens after this?'

'We speak to Karen—she's supposed to contact me to confirm if she can do it.'

He glanced over at her, saw the pained expression on her face, and smiled. 'Brings back bad memories, does it?'

She groaned, and it made him feel lighter than he had in a while. 'I've always thought about her with both pride and despair. Her performance that night was fantastic, but I could have done without the drama.'

'But if she *can* perform…?'

'We'll have to work with her to figure out a date. And then we market.'

They had just pulled up at the school, and were being directed up a road that Jordan remembered led to a sports field. It was ages since he'd been here, he thought idly, and then turned his attention back to Mila when she spoke.

'Did you know she's playing a concert? Saturday at Westgate Stadium. It would be an excellent way to show our support. You up for it?'

His eyebrows rose. 'You want me to go with you?'

'If I have to suffer through a concert with a load of teenagers, then so do you, buddy.'

He grinned, and found himself relaxing for the first time since he'd arrived back home. 'Sounds fair to me.'

They got out after he'd parked, and he took a moment to appreciate the beauty of the surroundings he'd in no way appreciated in his teens. The field he stood on reminded him of the countless rugby matches he'd played there, and though nostalgia was easy to slip into, he found the scene beyond the school to be more compelling.

The hills made it seem almost enclosed by nature, and had been the backdrop to many of his teenage escapades. Large trees were scattered over the grounds, leaves fading from green to orange with the turn of the season. He thought it might only be in Cape Town that even a school was beautiful to look at.

'This place hasn't changed since I was here,' Jordan said as they stood in line to get tickets, and he watched as Mila turned her head to follow his gaze.

'The swimming pool is new,' Mila pointed out, and he looked over and saw she was right.

He wasn't sure how he had missed that, since the school grounds were built at a much lower level than where they were parked.

'How do you know the pool's new?'

'I went to school here, too,' she said, a light blush covering her cheeks.

He wondered why telling him that would embarrass her. He frowned. 'Why didn't we see each other?'

'You would have been four years ahead of me, so we would have only seen each other if I was there in your last year.' She glanced over at him. 'I wasn't.'

'So you came after I had already matriculated.' The timeline had already formed in his head.

'Yeah, and only stayed for a year.'

'And then what?'

'I got moved to another family and another school.'

Her words left him...disconcerted. Perhaps it was because of the reminder of her childhood. Or perhaps it was because she had never spoken about her schooling before. It highlighted another crack in the relationship they'd had before breaking up. Shouldn't he have known this about her, his wife?

'Why didn't I know this?'

She shrugged, though the gesture was made with stiff shoulders, and the relaxation Jordan had felt only a few moments ago slipped away.

'There were a lot of things we didn't talk about, Jordan,' she said.

Exactly what he'd realised over the past few days, he thought. He took out his wallet before Mila could pay when they got to the front of the line, and turned to her as they waited for their tickets.

'It seems a bit strange that we didn't talk about it, doesn't it…?'

He trailed off when he saw that her face had lost its colour. And then he realised why. Because the school was at a lower level, there was a long staircase that led down to another sports field. It was steep, even for him, and he felt her shake even before he saw it.

'I can't do this,' she said, and turned away, her eyes wide and frightened.

Jordan felt the punch to his stomach even as steel lined it. 'You don't have a choice,' he said firmly, and grabbed her hand, leading her to the stairs slowly.

Every step she took—every uncertain, painful step— sliced at his heart, but he knew he had to do this for her. He knew that if he could redeem himself in any way for the decisions he'd made since the day she'd fallen down the stairs, it would be by giving her back her freedom. And he knew her well enough to know that the only way to do that was through tough love.

'Jordan, please…' she whispered, her hand white on

the railing. She had managed one step down the stairs, but had then frozen.

'Mila, look at me.' He waited as she did so, letting those behind him pass as he stood with Mila. 'You *have* to do this. The event depends on it. The vineyard depends on it. For my father.'

It was a low blow and he knew it, and he saw the responding flash of red in her eyes. But the look quickly fizzled out as he took her hand again, and was replaced by a combination of fear and…trust? he thought, and felt that punch in his gut again.

He couldn't ponder why that look had that effect on him now, though, and instead focused on taking another step down, waiting for her to join him. After taking a breath, she did. He saw the temptation in her eyes to freeze again, and decided that distracting her would soften the tough-love approach.

'Do you think it's because we did everything so fast that we didn't talk about our pasts?' he asked her, and patted himself on the back when he saw confusion in her eyes at his change of topic.

'That was a part of it.' Her voice was shaky, but she had taken the next step with his encouragement. 'But definitely not the biggest part.'

'What do you mean?'

She rolled her eyes, and he thought vaguely that his attempt at distraction was working. Except that she was distracting *him*, too.

'We told each other about the most important parts. You knew that I didn't have any family, and that I grew up in foster care, and I knew that your mom had passed away from cancer.'

'And we were just content with that…' he said, more to himself than to her.

Ever since he had realised that there had been things in

their relationship that were broken even before the accident, the more he saw them. Yes, they'd known the basics—like the fact that her father had died before she was born and her mother had died shortly after her birth—but he'd had no idea how that had made her *feel*. Just as she hadn't known how his mother's death had affected him. And how much he blamed himself for it.

'*You* were,' she scoffed, and took another step down, still leaning on him. 'I wanted to know everything about you. About your father, your mother, your childhood… *Everything*,' she repeated. 'But you didn't seem willing to offer the information…'

She took a deep breath, but he knew it had little to do with the fact that she was going down the stairs.

'And I never wanted to push.'

He frowned. 'You didn't *want* to ask me about my life?'

She was silent for a moment. 'I didn't want to push you to give me any information you didn't want to.'

'Why not?'

She looked at him, uncertainty flickering in her eyes. 'Because I didn't want to tell *you* things either.'

It was a strange conversation to be having while she was facing her fears, he thought briefly, but in that moment the only thing that had his attention was what she was saying.

'What didn't you want to tell me?'

He felt her hand tighten, felt her resistance as she tried to pull away from him, but then she stopped. Maybe because she'd realised that pulling away from him would mean she would have to deal with her fear alone. Or maybe because she had chosen to be cordial and her refusal to answer his question would be going against that. But still she didn't say anything.

'Why did it embarrass you to tell me that you went to school here?' he asked, with a sudden urgency lighting up inside him that made it imperative for him to know. The same urgency that told him that whatever she didn't want to tell him about her life was somehow tied to that.

'It didn't,' she replied quickly. Too quickly for someone who had only a few minutes ago stiffened next to him.

'Mila…' It was a plea—one that came from that urgency—and it seemed to make a dent in that defensiveness she'd always had about her past. One he was beginning to realise *he* had, too.

She let out a huff. 'I just didn't want you to think about my crappy unstable childhood when you'd had the complete opposite.'

'That embarrassed you?' he asked incredulously, and a wave of shame washed through him. Had he said something to her that had made her feel embarrassed about her childhood? Did she really think his had been so wonderful?

'Yes, it did,' she said through gritted teeth. 'You had an amazing home—one you could go to every day. You had a father who loved you. I had none of that.'

'Why were you embarrassed by that?'

'Because…' She had reached the bottom of the stairs, but she didn't seem to notice. She took another breath, and said, 'Because it meant that I wasn't worthy of someone like you.'

CHAPTER NINE

THE WORDS HAD already left Mila's lips when she realised how much they revealed about her. She was annoyed that it was the second time she had disclosed something to Jordan that she hadn't wanted him to know, even if it had made her feel better. Especially since the disturbed look on his face made her think that he didn't feel like what she'd said.

'Did you really believe that?' he asked softly.

'I did.'

Maybe I still do.

'It doesn't matter any more, though, does it?'

'You're wrong, you know.' He shook his head. 'I haven't met anyone else I respect more than you. You didn't have family, but you're more loyal than any family member I can think of. Even me.'

He paused, and she thought that he was sacrificing his own comfort to make her feel better. It melted her heart.

'You looked after my father when I couldn't. Thank you.'

His words made her blush, and she mumbled, 'You know you don't have to thank me for that.'

'I know you don't think I need to—which just proves my point. You *are* worthy, Mila. *I'm* the one who isn't worthy of *you*.' He shook his head. 'I didn't have the childhood you thought I did.'

'What do you mean?'

He stuffed his hands into his pockets and looked down. The gesture made him look so defeated she wanted to hold him in her arms, but as she followed his gaze she realised she was looking at grass. She'd made it down the stairs!

'I did it...' she said to herself, not quite believing this victory, especially after the fear had paralysed her for over a year.

'Yeah, you did.'

Jordan smiled at her, and for the first time since he had returned, she could tell that it was completely genuine, despite the look of disconcertion on his face.

'I did it. I really did it.'

She felt like a fool when her eyes started tearing up, but she couldn't help it. A small piece inside her that had broken after she'd lost her son had become whole, and it gave her a sense of peace. She felt relief, a sense of accomplishment, and so many other emotions she couldn't even begin to put her finger on.

When she looked at Jordan, she saw that his frown had cleared, replaced by a look of satisfaction.

He did this purposely, she thought and, ignoring the voice that screamed in her head, she hugged him.

The comfort of it hit her so hard that she had to close her eyes. But that only heightened her senses. The woodsy smell of him was intoxicating—so familiar and masculine that awareness heated inside her. She was moulded to his body, could feel the strength of the muscles she had admired when she'd first seen him after he'd returned. His arms—which had been still at his sides until that moment—wrapped around her and she was pulled in tighter to his body. Her breathing slowed, her heart sped up, and she had to resist the urge to pull his head down so that she could taste his lips.

And then she lifted her head and met his eyes. The heat of longing there was a reflection of her own, and she could feel the world fade as it always did with him. Gooseflesh shot out on her skin, and she considered for a brief moment what would happen if she kissed him.

It would be magical, she knew. The things inside her that had died when he'd left would find life. She would finally feel alive again. *But at what cost?* a voice asked her, and she took a step back from him, knowing that it would take away everything she had rebuilt if she gave in to this temptation.

'Thank you,' she said, and felt the warmth of a blush light her face. But she'd needed to say it, to make sure that he knew why she had hugged him—as a token of gratitude, nothing else. The physical effect the seemingly innocent gesture had awakened was merely an unforeseen consequence.

'It's the least I can do,' he replied in a gravelly voice, and she knew that their contact had affected him, too.

What was more surprising to her was that he looked as though he genuinely meant the words, that he wasn't just saying them automatically.

She cleared her throat. 'So…we should probably start rallying the troops.'

He nodded his agreement, and she forced herself to shift focus. She could be professional. She prided herself on it, in fact. She began to explain her strategy—she would speak to the vendors first, since they knew her, and then introduce them to Jordan as the new owner of the vineyard. Then they would pitch their event, find out if they were interested and available, and hope for the best. Since the will stipulated that they should give evidence of trying their best to find exactly the same service providers for the event, she would record their interactions and use them to show Mark if they needed to find alternatives.

'You've thought of everything, haven't you?'

'That's the job,' she replied, her neck prickling at the admiration she heard in Jordan's voice.

'Where have I heard *that* before?' he muttered, and she remembered she'd said something similar to him the first time they'd met.

She brushed off the nostalgia. 'We'd better get to it.'

They spent almost two hours there. It was time spent waiting for vendors to find a moment to talk to them in between serving people, and eating to fill that time. She found herself growing more comfortable as the minutes went by, the tension that was always inside her around him easing.

He was a wonderful ambassador for the vineyard, she thought as she watched him, and even though all the vendors remembered her and their event—especially since she had used many of them multiple times before—it was Jordan they responded to. He spoke to them with such warmth, with such praise, that she could almost see their spines straighten with pride. He played up his enjoyment of their food so much that sometimes she found herself giggling.

The sound was strange, even to her, and she wondered why it was so easy to relax around him now. Her determination to focus on the event and ignore whatever was between them had been decided just that morning. A few hours later and she had spoken to him about the past, made herself vulnerable by admitting that she hadn't thought she was worthy of him, and had walked down an intimidating staircase. And now she was laughing with him. *At* him.

She knew that at some point he had gone from entertaining the vendors to trying to make *her* laugh. She wasn't sure how she felt about that, but she chose not to ponder it then. Not when for the first time in a long time she felt…free.

'Ice cream?'

She looked at him when she heard his voice, and realised that she had been staring off into space while she thought about the day.

'I'm not sure it's warm enough for ice cream,' she replied, feeling self-conscious now.

'The sun is shining, Mila. We should thank it by offering it the traditional food of appreciation.'

Her lips curved. 'And that's ice cream?'

'Yes, it is.' He smiled back at her and her heart thumped. It was as if they were on a first date, she thought, and then immediately cast the thought aside.

'Besides, we have one more vendor to see,' he continued, 'and he still hasn't returned from his supply run.'

She shrugged off her hesitation. 'Sure—okay.'

She followed him to the ice-cream stand, where they joined a long line.

'Seems like everyone wants to make a sacrifice to the gods,' she said, and smiled at him when he looked at her.

'I told you so,' he replied, and took her hand as though it was the most natural thing in the world.

And the truth was that on that day, after talking, after laughing together, with the winter sun shining on their faces, holding hands *did* seem natural. But it wasn't, she reminded herself, and let go of his hand under the guise of looking for the notepad where she had written down the names of all the vendors and made notes.

'I think we've done pretty well today,' she said, and pretended not to notice the disappointment that had flashed across his face. 'Of the six vendors here, three are interested and are available for two weeks—the end of this month and the beginning of next. It cuts our time in half. Not ideal, but I think it's doable. And if we speak to the owner of the Bacon Bites food truck when he gets back, we could have four.'

'So that means we only have to replace two or three?'

Jordan slipped his hands into the pockets of his jacket,

and she wondered if it was because he was tempted to take her hand again.

Her hand itched at the thought.

'Yes, but we still need to hear from two vendors who aren't here. Lulu said she would follow up on those. But I think we could substitute any who don't come with some of the other vendors here. I chatted to the woman who owns the chocolate truck over there—' she gestured to it with her head '—and she thought our event sounded great. She told me to come over if we were interested.'

'How did you manage to speak to her?'

'Oh, it was between your moan of delight for the meat pies and your groan of appreciation for the burger sliders,' she teased, and saw the tension that had entered his body after she'd let go of his hand fade.

'They have good food here,' he said, with a shrug and a smile.

Before she could respond they were at the front of the line. Behind the glass casing of the van she could see a variety of ice cream flavours that made her mouth water. After a few minutes of looking, she still couldn't decide between the chocolate hazelnut flavour and the vanilla toffee.

'How about you take the chocolate hazelnut and I take the vanilla toffee?' he said when she told him as much, and she smiled at the proposal.

'Perfect!'

She relayed their order to the patient vendor, and watched with delight at he made the sugar cone their ice cream would be served in from scratch.

Her first lick was deliciously creamy, and the thrill of cold ran down her spine. But then she realised that Jordan was watching her—with amusement and something else in his eyes—and she wondered if the thrill *had* come from the cold.

'This is great,' she said to avoid feeling awkward. 'Want some?'

'Sure,' he replied, and moved closer.

He watched her as he tasted the ice cream, and suddenly it was a year ago, when they'd been on honeymoon in Mauritius and had come across an ice-cream stand. It had been perfect for the hot summer's day after they'd been at the beach all morning.

Sharing their ice creams with one another had been... *sensual*, she thought, just as it was now. Shivers went up her spine at the look in his eyes—the look that told her that even though they weren't together any more he still wanted her.

He offered her a lick of his, and as though she was in a trance she leaned forward and tasted it, her eyes still on his. The flavour was just as delectable as she'd thought it would be, but the thought barely registered. Instead she was wondering if their sharing ice cream would end the way it had in Mauritius—with a passion that could have heated the entire resort for a week.

The thought had her moving backwards so quickly she almost stumbled. She regained her balance in time to realise that there was ice cream on her nose. She spent a few seconds trying to figure out how to remove it, and sighed when she saw that neither of them had taken a serviette.

'Do you want some help?' he asked, and she looked up to see that he was watching her—again—this time with an amused expression. And then she thought that she must have been crossing her eyes to look at the spot of ice cream on her nose, and she flushed.

'No, thanks—I'll manage.' She rubbed her nose with her sleeve and quickly turned to look for the vendor they were waiting for, hoping with all her might that he would be there. Relief swamped her when she saw that he was, and she turned back to Jordan, who was now watching her with a guarded expression.

'We should go over there,' she said, and gestured behind her.

He nodded and started walking, and she took a moment to instruct her emotions to stop fluttering around and get into place. When she was sure she had them under control she followed him—and wished with all her might that the roller coaster the two of them were on would stop.

CHAPTER TEN

'WHERE ARE WE GOING?'

They were in the car and supposed to be heading home from the school. But after spending the entire day with Mila, Jordan didn't want it to end.

Yes, they lived together at the moment—he kept waiting for her to tell him she would be leaving—but as soon as they walked through the front door of his father's house Jordan knew that Mila would erect a fence between them. He would be able to see glimpses of her, but he wouldn't be able to get near her, and the thought of that disturbed him.

He didn't think about why—he didn't need to defend himself for the time he spent with the woman who had once been his everything, did he?—but he couldn't bear being kept at a distance any more. Not after he'd seen parts of her today that he hadn't known existed during their marriage.

And now he knew what he had been missing.

'Did you know the Gerbers?'

'The old couple who used to live behind us?'

Mila turned to him, her brows drawn together in a frown, and Jordan's hand itched to reach out and smooth it over. But he tightened his hands on the steering wheel. Just as he had tightened them into fists in his pockets to keep himself from taking her hand again that afternoon.

He had done that by mistake, but it had felt so right

that he hadn't let go even though his mind had told him to. And then she had done it instead, and disappointment had hit him like water from a burst pipe. He blamed that desire to touch her on that hug she'd sprung on him after making it down those stairs.

His body awoke just at the thought of it.

'Yeah…' He forced himself to speak, forced his body to calm down. 'Did you ever speak to them? Get a look around their property?'

'I… No,' she said, confusion clear in her voice. 'What's going on, Jordan? Where are you taking me?'

He had wanted to keep it a surprise, but he didn't want her to worry. 'I'm taking you to our house.'

'What?'

Was that panic her heard in her voice?

He frowned. 'Is something wrong?'

'No, no,' she replied quickly—too quickly—and looked out of the window. Her hands were clasped so tightly together in her lap that he reached over with one of his.

'What's going on, Mila?'

She blew out a shaky breath and he felt the deliberate relaxation of her hands under his. Taking it as a sign that she didn't want to be touched, Jordan moved his hand away. Even that slight loss of contact made him feel empty.

'It's nothing.'

'Mila…' Again, he found himself pleading.

She sighed. 'I just haven't been there since…since you left.'

'And going back now is…worrying for you?'

She didn't answer, and he glanced over to see her deliberately relaxing again. It made him wonder about why she was reacting this way to something as simple as going back to the house they'd shared. He felt a slight stir in his brain and frowned. He was missing something.

'A reminder of the past,' she finally said softly, and

when he looked at her again he saw that she was still looking out of the window. 'Going back to the house we lived in... Going back together... It's just a reminder of a life that seems worlds away.'

'We were planning to go anyway, weren't we? I have to help you get the stuff out so that you can leave.' Even saying the words sent a flash of pain through his heart.

'Oh, yes, of course,' she said, again more quickly than he thought she needed to, and again he wondered what he was missing.

There had to be something... The stirring in his brain seemed like a distant memory, but he couldn't recall it to verify whether that was the truth, and he didn't know if it had anything to do with what was currently happening between them. But it must—why else did he feel as if he was having a conversation without knowing all the facts?

'It's probably because this is unplanned,' she continued. 'Why are we going there now?'

'I have something to show you,' he replied, forcing himself to ignore the dull thud of unrecalled memories and focus on what his intention had been from the beginning. 'Did you ever see that pathway in the backyard, just next to that huge tree we planned to turn into a tree house for the little grape?'

He heard her sharp intake of breath before he realised he had used the pet name they had given their child after finding out they were having a boy. They had been so happy, he thought, pain tainting the memory. It had been the first time they had considered names for the baby, and he had teased her, calling him 'the little grape' since their child would one day have to take over the vineyard.

Mila had protested, of course, and with each objection had come a splutter of laughter that had warmed Jordan's insides so much that the name had stuck. They'd had a list of real names, of course, but they had never got the chance to decide on what they would call him.

'Yes, I remember,' she said hoarsely, and he reached for her hand, not caring about the unspoken rules that meant he shouldn't.

'I'm sorry, Mila, I didn't mean to—'

'It's okay.' She squeezed his hand. 'I think it's time we weren't afraid to refer to our son.'

He tightened his hand on hers and then let go, unable to keep the contact. His son was always in his thoughts—and always would be. He couldn't escape the way it had felt to hold his dying son in his arms when he'd been barely big enough to fit in Jordan's hands.

But she was right—he *had* been afraid to speak about him. And there was a lot more to it than just the fact that he couldn't bring himself to do it. No, admitting to Mila earlier that he'd been scared when they'd found out she was pregnant was only the tip of the iceberg. It hadn't fully left his mind since their conversation, and he'd realised that, as he'd initially thought, he *had* been scared he would turn out to be the same as his father. And that *was* part of the reason he'd left for Johannesburg.

Jordan knew Greg had loved him, but his childhood had been tainted by his father's grief. Grief that had made Greg into a bitter and sometimes angry man. The years after his mother had died had been filled with tension for Jordan—he'd sometimes felt as if he was walking on eggshells when he was around Greg. As a child, Jordan hadn't understood why his father would never look at him in the eye, or why Greg had spoken *at* him instead of *to* him. If he'd ever spoken to Jordan at all.

He had started behaving badly because of it, which had strained his relationship with Greg even more. It had also led to the night that would be burned in his memory for ever. The night that had changed Jordan—and his father—with only a few words.

Jordan vaguely remembered a time when laughing had been easy for his father. When there had been an open affection between them. But those memories were so faded he wondered if he'd made them up. The memories that were clear were of a steady man—a sombre, reserved and often difficult man. It clearly highlighted the fact that when Jordan had lost his mother, he'd lost his father, as well. And that had led to Jordan not being able to grieve fully for his mother because, frankly, his father had done it for both of them.

He hadn't thought about it until Mila had told him she was pregnant, and then suddenly he'd spent nights worrying about whether that grief for his mother would pop up once Mila had had the baby. Whether that grief would turn him into the kind of angry man his father was and spoil his son's childhood *and* Jordan's marriage.

It had made him worry that they'd rushed into marriage, made him think that he should have considered those possibilities when he'd been able to do something about them.

And when they'd lost the baby his fears had only intensified. He'd lost someone he loved, just as his father had, which surely upped the chances of Jordan turning into Greg. So Jordan had left. Escaped. Or, as he'd recently realised, run away…

'He's not alone, you know,' Mila said suddenly as he pulled into the driveway of their old house. 'The little grape's with our parents.'

He glanced over and saw a tiny smile on her lips. It made her look peaceful, he thought, and a large part inside him settled at the thought. It brought *him* peace, too.

'That's a really lovely thing to think about, isn't it?'

She smiled at him, and something in his heart eased. Was that because she'd smiled at him—a sweet, genuine smile that he had only been privy to that day—or was it because it comforted him to think about two generations of his family together?

'He'll have met your mom,' Mila said softly. 'I always wished I could have met her, you know. Your father used to talk about her sometimes.'

Jordan could tell that Mila was looking at him, but he stared steadily ahead. He didn't want to talk about his mother. That would mean telling her about his father. About his childhood. About his fears.

'She sounded amazing.'

He didn't respond, and then he tilted his head. 'Come on. Before it gets dark.'

He got out of the car, aware of the disappointment that shrouded her, and waited for her to join him as he stood outside the house they'd lived in during their short marriage. The first time he had seen the house he had thought it timeless and elegant—exactly what he had been looking for for his sweet, beautiful bride.

A marble pathway led to large oak doors that looked newly polished yet still antiquated. Large glass windows overlooked the road, and gave the white façade a modern feel. The pathway was lined with palm trees, which had always made him feel as if he was walking into an oasis of some kind. It still looked the same to him now, though all the memories made him feel more than he had the first time he had seen it.

Now he thought about those days when they'd had breakfast on the patio, just as the sun went up. She had always moaned about getting up that early, but the peace on her face when she was curled up on a chair, a cup of coffee in her hand, made him think she'd thought it worth it. He remembered walking hand in hand with her through their garden, where the roses that were planted there were always the perfect gift for her. And he could still see her lying next to the pool, the slight swell of her stomach obvious in her swimming costume. Could still feel the surge of protectiveness that had gone through him when he'd looked at her.

'It looks the same…but it feels different,' she said beside him, and he looked down at her to see a mixture of emotions playing over her face that had him grabbing for her hand.

He could feel that she was shaking, and just like that he realised what he'd been missing in the car—why she'd been anxious about coming back.

'It reminds you of your fall, doesn't it?'

She didn't have to answer him—he could see the truth of his words on her face.

I'm an idiot, he thought, and wondered how he hadn't thought about it before.

His mind had been too focused on showing her the secret he'd kept since he'd found out that she was pregnant. He hadn't wanted today to end, hadn't wanted her guard to come up, and in the process his actions to prevent it had hurt her.

He was a selfish man, he thought in disgust.

'I sometimes still dream about it,' she said quietly, and he immediately wanted to hold her in his arms.

But her words told him that she was forcing herself to face it—it was that fire he'd noticed in her when he'd returned again—and he told himself to be content with holding her hand.

'I can feel myself falling, reaching for a railing that wasn't there for support. And then the impact of rolling down the stairs.' She drew a shaky breath. 'I still feel foolish for falling down five steps.'

'It had been raining,' he said immediately, his heart clenching in pain at the anguish—the guilt—that he heard in her voice.

She ignored him. 'I lay there, my breath gone, with shock keeping me from feeling the true pain of what my body had just gone through, and I felt warmth between my legs and realised…'

Her hand was so tight on his that he could tell there was no blood flowing through it, but that didn't matter to him. Not when he could feel the pain of what she had gone through—what she had never spoken of before. Not when he could hear the quickness of her breath. He drew her in, though she didn't seem to notice.

'I realised that something was wrong…that I had done something wrong…and then I saw you, and your face told me that I was right.'

Tears fell from her eyes and he didn't care this time if he was interrupting her. His arms went around her and she sobbed—heart-wrenching sobs that broke everything inside him each time he heard them.

'I'm sorry, Jordan. I'm sorry I wasn't more careful. I'm sorry I didn't slow down like you asked me to. I'm sorry I didn't look after him like I should have.'

'You didn't do anything wrong, Mila.' He felt his own tears as he said the words. 'I shouldn't have asked you to slow down. It was just…fear. My own. I think I was hoping to slow *us* down.' He paused, held her tightly. 'Everything was happening so quickly.'

He could feel her body shake, knew his words weren't having any effect. So he told her the facts, hoping their simplicity would help her.

'You were walking down stairs we'd both used a million times before. It had been raining—a light summer rain that had come from nowhere. You slipped. It was an accident.'

He said the words over and over again—to himself just as much as to her—until her shaking dissipated and everything went still. They stood in each other's arms longer than was necessary, their grief finally—*finally*—something they shared.

Not completely, a voice reminded him, and he stepped back. His heart thudded painfully in his chest as a reminder of what he needed to tell her—worse now that he knew about the guilt she felt. And the expression on her face—the completely exhausted expression—tempted him to ignore it, to tell her some other time.

But he knew that was just an excuse. He wouldn't ever get to that other time—not when he had been meaning to tell her since the accident. And now she had bared her soul to him he knew he couldn't keep it a secret from her any more.

'There's something I need to tell you.' He said it quickly, afraid that he wouldn't get through it otherwise. 'I had to give them permission to operate on you, Mila. You were bleeding from the abruption, losing consciousness...'

He shook his head.

'Waiting for the bleeding to subside would have put you *and* the baby at risk.' He took a shaky breath, not daring to look at her—not yet. 'I had to approve the C-section knowing there was a chance our baby wouldn't survive. But I couldn't take a chance on losing both of you...'

His voice had gone completely hoarse at this admission of something he had carried with him for what felt like for ever, and he forced himself to look at her before he lost his courage. She was staring at him, those eyes more haunting than ever before, carefully blank of all the emotion he wished he could read in her.

Her hand reached up, and he braced himself for the pain of a slap, but she only brushed away the remnants of her tears from her cheeks. Then she cleared her throat.

'I know.'

He looked at her, his eyes wide. 'What?'

'The doctor told me when I went back for my check-up. And then I asked Greg about it and he confirmed it.'

'Your check-up was…' He sorted through the memories 'I was still here, Mila… Why didn't you tell me you knew?' He couldn't believe that the burden he had been carrying with him for such a long time wasn't a secret after all.

'I was waiting for *you* to tell me.'

The look she aimed at him made him feel like a school-boy.

'I wanted to, but I was afraid—'

'That I would blame you for it?'

He nodded, and she folded her arms.

'I did. I thought it was your fault that I didn't get to see my son alive. Why do you think I asked for space?'

He was dumbfounded, the words of apology, of excuse, he'd prepared were wiped from his mind.

'I thought you would go and stay with your dad for a while, and I would be able to deal with all the feelings. I was raw, hurting and in more pain than I thought possible. I just needed time.'

She looked at him, and he saw her anger.

'But then you left me completely. And instead of space I got divorce papers.'

'You're angry with me…' But he'd known that, he thought. Deserved it.

'Yes, I am. But not about you giving them permission to operate. What choice did you have?' She shook her head. 'We both might not have survived if you hadn't.' She paused, kicked at a stone. 'I *was* angry about it. But only because I wished I could have held him during those seventeen minutes he was alive.'

Her breath caught at that, and Jordan wished he could hold her again.

'And then I thought that if it couldn't be me—and since I was still under anaesthesia then it couldn't have been—

you were the only other person I would have wanted it to be. So after a while I forgave you.' She looked at him stonily. 'It wasn't your fault either, Jordan.'

'I can't believe you've known all along. I've been carrying this with me ever since I…' He trailed off when he saw her jaw set and she looked away. And then he realised that she'd said that she wasn't angry with him about *that* any more. 'Why *are* you angry at me, then?'

'You really don't know?'

He opened his mouth to answer, but she waved him away.

'If you can't figure it out then you don't deserve to know.' She set her jaw. 'Can we just leave now, please?'

'No, we can't.' He felt uncomfortable, but he said it because he'd shared one of his deepest secrets with her, which he wouldn't have done with anyone else, and now she was pulling away. Even though he didn't want to delve any further into emotion—his insides were raw and knotted from what had already been said—he persisted. 'I want you to tell me what else I've done wrong.'

'So you can continue with this victim mentality you seem to have going?'

Anger sparked, deep inside him, and pumped through his body with his blood. 'Excuse me?'

'Every tragedy that's happened to you, you somehow blame yourself for it.'

He could see the anger in her, too, but that only fuelled his own.

'You blame yourself for approving an operation that saved my life—that gave your son his best chance at living—and you blame yourself for your father's death. Oh, did you think I couldn't see the weight of guilt crushing you?'

He kept his face clear of the turmoil he felt—the anger and truth in her words were daggers piercing his insides—

and wondered how she had realised what he felt about his father's death.

'You think that his heart attacks were because you left. Because you didn't keep in touch over the past year. You hate it that he died without fixing whatever was wrong between you.'

'Stop!' he said, his hands clenched into fists at his sides.

'Why?' she demanded, her face flushed from her tirade. '*You* were the one who wanted me to continue, remember?' She didn't wait for his affirmation before continuing, as though she was purging herself of everything that she felt. 'Do you want to know what I'm *really* angry about, Jordan? It's because you ran away when I needed you the most.' She took a shaky breath. 'You made me feel like you left because I had lost our child.'

She was trembling, and he itched to touch her, to comfort her, even as her words shook him. 'Stop saying that! Stop blaming yourself for what happened. It wasn't your fault.' And she'd made him see that it wasn't his either.

'If that's not the reason, then why did you go?'

'I was running—just like you said,' he shot out, and immediately stilled.

'Why?'

'Does it matter?' he said, exasperated. He couldn't deal with the emotion any more. 'I'm back now.'

Her eyes flashed. 'Yes, it *matters*, Jordan. And here's why.'

She grabbed the front of his top, and before he knew it her lips were on his.

CHAPTER ELEVEN

SHE'D DONE IT out of desperation, to pierce through that controlled façade he clung to even though she could see that he felt beneath the surface. She wanted him to feel the earthquake that was happening inside her, to know the emotions that sprang from the hole the quake had opened, and the only way she knew how to do that was to kiss him.

But as she sank into the kiss she thought that she was a fool for being so impulsive, for letting go of the control she'd fought for around him. And then she stopped thinking, pressing her body closer to his as she tasted him.

The same…he tasted the same. Of fire and home and pure man.

Her anger had turned into passion, so there was no gentle sliding back into the heat they had always shared. No, they jumped straight into the fire, greedily taking each other, their hands moving over bodies that had changed yet were somehow still the same.

When he lifted her from the ground she went willingly, her arms around him, refusing to lose contact with him. She barely felt the wall that he pressed her against, her senses captivated by what his hands were doing. He pushed aside the jacket she had on, his tongue playing with hers in a way that had her moaning, and the sound seemed to burn away the last of his patience with her clothing.

He ripped open the shirt she wore, his hands roaming

over her bare skin before she even heard the buttons fall
on the marble path to their home. Though the house was
enclosed, and there was no one who would see them, Mila
didn't think she would have cared if there had been. Her
body was too occupied in being touched by the hands that
had always owned it, her mind too employed by the pleasure only he could make her feel.

She fumbled with his clothes, wanting to touch his skin
as he did hers. Giving up, she slid her hands under his top
and eagerly over his body. The toned, muscular body that
she had wanted since the moment she had seen him. Somewhere she thought about how different touching him felt
now, but the thought was vague, dulled by the passion of
his lips on her skin.

She wanted him, she heard her heart tell her as he kissed
her neck, letting her head fall back to give him better ac-
cess. And she would have let him have her, she thought
later, had her phone not rung.

The sound was muffled, since the phone was in her
jacket pocket, but it was clear enough to give them both
pause. And the pause allowed her thoughts to spin back
into her mind.

Though most were still muddled and hazy, one came
to her with the clarity of a conscience after confession—
she was giving herself to the man who had broken her
heart. And one more occurred to her after that—he was
still breaking it.

She pushed him away, ignoring the desire that clouded
his face, and with one hand held her torn shirt together.
She walked a short distance away from him, took a deep
breath and answered her phone.

The conversation only lasted a few minutes, but it was
enough for her thoughts to clear and her cheeks to flush
with embarrassment. She was a fool! she thought, keeping
the phone at her ear even though Simon, Karen's manager,

had long since said goodbye. Why had she thought *kissing* him would make him *feel*? The only thing it had done was to awaken her body and alert her mind to the fact that she was still alive. That she was still a woman who needed, who *wanted*. And that both those needs and wants had to do with Jordan.

She shoved the phone back into her pocket, and zipped up her jacket, not wanting to feel any more exposed than she already did.

'Who was that?'

She turned at his voice, hating it that she still remembered the effect it had had on her the day they had met. That it still had an effect now.

'Karen's manager.' Mila didn't look at him, not wanting him to see the emotions she couldn't hide nearly as well as he did. 'She's doing a show at the university's conservatorium tonight. She wants us to come through.'

There was a moment that beat between them, and then he asked, 'What kind of show does a pop star do at a *conservatorium*?'

'A performance for her studies, apparently,' she answered him. 'It's formal, and it starts in an hour and a half. We'd better get going.'

She strode past him, determined not to look at him, and braced herself for contact when out of the corner of her eye she saw his hand lift. But the contact never came and she sighed with relief—*not* disappointment, she assured herself—and got into the car.

It was going to be a long trip home.

Mila stood under the shower, angling her head so that the warm water could hit her body directly. She stayed like that, hoping that it would wash away her actions of that day. She cringed every time she thought about it, and the day wasn't even over yet. Now, after nearly tearing Jordan's clothes off, Mila was going to have to spend who knew how long with him at a classical concert by the winner of a pop competition.

There was no way around it, she thought, shampooing her hair. Simon had told her that Karen wanted to speak to her before making a decision about the event, and this was the only time she could spare to do it.

At least it meant that Mila wouldn't have to go to a teenybopper concert with Jordan. She could only imagine how the girls would swoon around him. Hadn't she just had first-hand experience of that? Her body still trembled from his touch, reminding her of how good that part of their relationship had been. But what good did that do when there were other, more substantial cracks between them?

Mila knew she had made progress with him, getting him to admit that he'd had to give permission for her C-section. But at what cost? He now knew more about her than she'd wanted him to know—he knew she didn't want to go back to the house, that it reminded her of the accident. He knew that she still dreamt about it, and that she was angry at him for leaving. It was a miracle that he'd admitted that he'd run away, but she still couldn't get him to tell her why. She couldn't even get him to talk about his mother.

Everything was so *controlled* with him. Sometimes she wondered where the man who had given her a surprise picnic the day they had met had gone. That impulsive, romantic man who had swept her off her feet and convinced her to marry him. He didn't seem to exist any more, she thought, and got out of the shower. No, he had been replaced by the man who had run away when she'd needed him—the man who never wanted to speak to her about the things that mattered.

And still the man who set her body on fire.

Calm down, she instructed herself. She just needed to get through the event and then she would be moving on with her life, away from Jordan and all the problems he created for her. And to do that she needed to get Karen to set a date so that things could finally move ahead.

Mila would ignore the voice in her head that told her that finding out what Jordan didn't want to tell her was about more than just her. The voice that told her Jordan needed to admit it to himself, too, or he would carry the guilt of his past for the rest of his life. It might have been harsh, but she had meant it when she'd referred to him seeing himself as a victim.

It wasn't her problem, she reminded herself. And even if finding out would mean she would have to sacrifice a part of herself that she had carried for a long time, there was part of her that didn't want to ask for what she wanted. That couldn't. There was no way Mila would do that when there was nothing on the line—no relationship, no family—and she had no guarantee Jordan would do the same for her.

So she focused on getting ready. She took out the only two dresses she had kept when she'd moved in with Greg that were formal enough to work for the event. One was a knee-length loose black dress. Pretty enough to wear to a formal event, but demure enough not to draw attention.

She put it in front of her body and realised that it was no longer something she wanted to wear. It reminded her of someone she no longer seemed to be, and she took a moment to figure out whether she was okay with that. When the thought didn't make her feel anxious something settled inside her, and she pressed her hand to her stomach with a small smile.

Maybe she was changing for the better, she thought, and then put the thought away as something she would take with her when she moved on. And when *that* thought unsettled her she dismissed it completely and looked at the second dress.

It was long and midnight blue, with a lace halter-neck

overlay that led down her arms to form sleeves. It covered the sweetheart neckline designed to show off her bust, and though she would have preferred something *completely* covered after her actions earlier, she put the dress on and chose to feel confident in it. *Another change?* she considered.

She fluffed her hair, sighing when her curls wouldn't play along, and decided to leave it loose. She might as well accept all of herself, she thought, and spent a few minutes on make-up. She looked in the mirror when she was done, told herself to be careful around Jordan, and then grabbed her purse and headed for the front door.

Jordan was already there, and her heart screamed in protest at how handsome he looked. He was wearing a tuxedo that showed off his strong body and looked as if it had been designed to make her breath catch. He had shaved—the five o'clock shadow that had brushed her skin earlier was only a memory now—and had smoothed back his hair, and he looked at her with an unreadable expression that reminded her of a celebrity who was preparing to walk the red carpet.

But as his eyes swept over her his expression slipped enough for her to see his appreciation of her outfit, and she blushed.

'You're wearing your hair down,' he said.

'Yes, I am,' she answered, and resisted the urge to fiddle with it.

'That's the way I remember it.'

Her heart rapped in her chest, like someone desperately knocking at a door, and she forced herself to calm down. What did it matter if that was how he remembered it?

'It's the way I like it,' he said softly, as though he had been privy to her thoughts, and she had to fight against the embarrassment.

'Are you ready to go?' she said, instead of responding

to his comment, and almost turned away from him before she saw the look in his eyes.

Gooseflesh immediately shot out on her skin, and she resisted the urge to pull at the material around her neck to get more air. He was looking at her as though he would have liked to continue from where they had left off earlier, and his eyes pierced her right down to her soul.

After a moment his face went back to being unreadable, and she sighed in relief and grabbed her coat from the rack that stood behind the front door.

Jordan opened the car door for her when they reached it, and she carefully got in, trying to avoid all contact with him. Which was in vain, she realised, when the train of her dress still lay outside her door after she'd sat down and they both reached to get it.

Their hands touched for the briefest moment, and yet the feeling reminded her of the way she had felt when she'd burned herself the day before. She snatched it back and let Jordan tuck her dress into the car, and only exhaled when he closed her door and walked around to get in at his side.

'Do you have *any* idea why a pop star would be studying classical music?'

He spoke without looking at her, and she wondered if he knew how tight his hands were on the steering wheel despite his outward calm.

'Your guess is as good as mine,' she murmured, proud of the aloof tone she had managed.

She made an extra effort not to fold her arms, which would, for sure, give away *her* nerves about spending time with him. Because, as much as she didn't want to be affected by him, she inevitably always was.

The rest of their journey was made in silence, and she tried not to use it as an opportunity to spend more time thinking about everything. Relief hit her right to her bones when the car stopped at the university's conservatorium. It was a large white building, with the word *conservatorium* printed boldly at the top, and the glass doors at the bottom were open to the crowds who, for some reason, were pouring into the venue.

She looked up in surprise when her door clicked open, and realised that the time she had spent ogling the building meant she'd been distracted from climbing out of the car by herself. Now she was faced with the hand Jordan was offering to help her out.

She couldn't say no, she thought, even if that had been her immediate reaction. He was offering an olive branch, she realised when she saw his face.

She braced herself for the contact, but in no way did it help when she took his hand. Heat and memories slid through her like a warm knife through butter, from the hand he now held to the top of her head and right down to her feet. She tightened her hand on his in response, saw the feeling mirrored on his face, and got out so that they wouldn't have to spend any more time touching.

Except the pavement they had parked on was not meant for high heels, and after she'd stumbled for the second time Jordan snaked an arm around her waist and pulled her closer. Her body immediately groaned in delight at the feel of him so close, and her mind was fogged by the intoxicating smell of his body wash and cologne.

She ignored the effects it had on her body and pulled her coat tighter around her, as though the action would somehow protect her. She pulled away from him the moment they were inside the building, ignoring the way her heart protested at the emptiness she felt immediately, and gave her coat to a man with an unnecessarily prudish expression on his face.

'Mila, I'm so glad that you made it!'

Mila turned at the familiar male voice, and opened her arms to return a hug when she saw it was Simon.

'I'm so glad that you invited us, Simon! We appreciate Karen taking the time to speak to us.'

She pulled back and smiled, and then her skin prickled and she realised that Jordan had joined them.

'You've never met my...' She'd been about to say *husband*, but that didn't seem right. 'You've never met Jordan, have you? He owns the vineyard where Karen performed at the event where we met. Jordan—Simon.'

They shook hands, and she noted the way Jordan's 'businessman' expression slid easily onto his face.

'I'm glad to see you both. Unfortunately Karen won't have time until after the performance to talk to you two, but can you come backstage immediately after and we'll discuss the event then?'

'Yes, of course,' Mila answered.

'Great! I've given your names to the guys at the door, so you can go straight through.' Simon brushed a kiss on Mila's cheek, nodded at Jordan and then moved on to whoever was behind them in the line.

'I suppose we can't sneak out now,' she whispered to Jordan as they walked towards the door. She looked at his face when he didn't respond, and was treated to the stormy expression she had seen that first day after he had returned.

'What's wrong?' she asked, but there was only silence.

She sighed and pulled him out of the line they were standing in, not wanting to be overheard.

'Look, I know what happened this afternoon was... wasn't ideal...' she rolled her eyes at her description '...but this is work. This is why we're here. Can you put your feelings aside so we can do this?'

His expression grew darker, and she was about to launch into another lecture about keeping the event and their personal feelings separate when his face grew blank. He gave her a curt nod, and then extended his arm for her to hook hers onto. She hesitated for a moment and then slipped her arm through his. If he was going to put his feelings aside then so could she, she thought, and ignored the spread of warmth through her body at his touch.

CHAPTER TWELVE

'YOU'RE HEARING THE same thing I am, right?'

Jordan glanced over at Mila, and saw that her jaw had dropped. She nodded at his question, and then quickly closed her mouth.

'This is ridiculous,' she whispered back to him, her eyes still riveted on the stage. 'Why do they have her doing those awful pop songs when she can sing like this?'

He chuckled—more at Mila's reaction than at the fact that Karen-the-pop-star was actually Karen-with-the-most-incredibly-beautiful-classical-voice. She was standing alone in front of an orchestra, her usual red curls straightened into a sophisticated updo that, along with her green ballgown, made her look a lot older than she was. More mature, too, he thought—which was probably the point, though not entirely necessary. Not when each note sent a wave of appreciation through the audience.

'Maybe this is so that she won't *have* to do "awful pop songs" any more,' he responded, and received a death glare from a woman in front of him, who looked like the kind of woman who always shushed people.

It was effective, though, and he didn't speak again until Karen's performance was over. She had been one of many performers that night, all of them students who were singing as part of their evaluation for a degree. And, although he knew that was why Karen had been performing that night, he had expected the beauty of her voice almost as much as he had expected that kiss he and Mila had shared that afternoon.

He sighed when he realised that he was thinking about it yet again.

Though how could he not? an inner voice asked him, and his mind played back portions of it. Mila coming towards him with passion in her eyes…the feeling of her lips on his…the desire that had shot through him and had him tearing at her clothes—literally—just about ready to take her against the wall of the house they had once shared…

If she hadn't taken that phone call he wasn't sure he would have been able to help himself, although he definitely should have…

He wasn't sure if he was grateful for that call or annoyed by it.

Since his mind kept slipping back to that afternoon, he was grateful when all the performances were over and they could make their way backstage. Jordan saw Simon standing with Karen, and warned himself against the jealousy that still threatened. When he'd met Simon, Jordan had noted the easiness of the interaction between him and Mila. He'd only vaguely been able to remember a time when things had been that easy between himself and Mila—when they'd been married, probably—and that thought had led to the annoyance that Mila had incorrectly interpreted as anger earlier.

But Jordan had shaken it off now, and he forced himself to remember that as Simon waved them over.

'Karen, I can't believe it was you out there!' Mila pulled the smiling girl in for a hug. 'It can't be only two years since that event. You have grown up *so* much since then!'

'It makes a huge difference when I'm not in leather tights singing about boys breaking my heart, doesn't it?' Karen responded, and Mila laughed.

'Yeah—although I can't disregard the value of the tights *or* the songs. They're the reason we're able to see *this* amazing side of you.'

It still impressed Jordan to see how good Mila was at networking, even though he'd spent the afternoon witnessing it. She had made every vendor feel as though they were her friend, he remembered, asking them about details of their lives that he was sure they had only mentioned to her in passing. And then, when they had been buttered up by the personal conversation, she would segue into the professional.

Now she was complimenting Karen on her current performance but still highlighting their need for the other side of her to perform. It wasn't only a testament to how good she was at networking, he realised suddenly, it was smart, too.

'They're the reason she's here, too,' Simon chimed in. 'Some well-placed donations helped her get in, even though she had missed the application deadline.'

Mila smiled at Simon, though Jordan saw the flash of annoyance in her eyes, and he found himself agreeing. Why would Karen's manager undermine her talent like that?

'I'm sure it didn't take that much convincing with your voice, though,' Mila said smoothly, and Jordan felt warmth radiate from the smile Karen aimed at Mila.

She cared, he thought, though he wasn't sure why he hadn't thought about that before. Since he'd come back Jordan had learned all kinds of things about his wife—and was clearly still learning. He knew more than he'd known before. She was feisty, and he was beginning to realise just how much he liked it. It made her a lot more confident, he thought as he watched it first-hand and felt the tug of attraction.

'Oh, I'm sorry!' Mila turned to him and he realised it

was his turn to perform. 'I don't think you met Jordan the night of the first Under the Stars event, did you?'

'No, I didn't.'

Karen held out her hand, and Jordan smiled at the interest he saw coming from her. She didn't try to hide it, which amused him even more. It seemed she'd grown up a lot from the whiny teen who'd cried at a broken heart, he thought.

'It's lovely to meet you, Karen. Mila was absolutely right about that performance. If you don't get an A for that, then I'm not sure the lecturers were listening properly.'

'How very kind of you to say, Jordan.'

He hid a smile at the flirtatious tone of her voice.

'Simon tells me that you're interested in me performing at an event you're hosting at the vineyard?'

'Yeah, Mila and I are hosting it, actually.'

'You mean she's hosting the event *for* you?' Karen's eyes didn't leave his face.

'No, I mean we're hosting it together.'

Karen didn't know they were married, Jordan thought, and wondered how it would change things if he told Karen they were.

But then he saw the slight shake of Mila's head and continued, 'My father grew quite fond of Mila after the last event, and his dying wish was that we plan one more event in his name.'

It wasn't exactly a lie, was it?

'He essentially requested a replica of the event you performed at a couple of years ago, in fact. Said he couldn't remember hearing someone sing as beautifully as you.' That, he thought, *was* an outright lie. But desperate times called for desperate measures.

'Oh, wow…' Karen breathed, and Jordan realised his earlier assumption hadn't been entirely correct.

She was still a teenager—she had just learned to hide it better.

'Well, I can't see myself saying no to such an amazing offer. I have time towards the end of the year, right, Simon?'

'Actually...' Mila interrupted whatever answer Simon had been about to give '... I mentioned to Simon that the concert will have to happen quite soon. Like before the end of next month.'

Karen frowned. 'Why so soon?'

Mila exchanged a look with Jordan that screamed "Help me!" and words came out of his mouth before he had an opportunity to think about them.

'Well, Mila's moving away at the end of next month to teach in Korea. She won't be able to do anything once she's gone, and I'd like to honour my father before she leaves, since we don't know when she'll be back.'

Mila bit her lip, and he could see she was trying to hide a smile.

'Yes, Karen—I'm going to teach English to little children in Korea, and I need to do this before I leave. Can you help?'

Karen looked at Simon. 'Tonight was my last exam, but I'll be going on tour in a few weeks and then I won't be available.'

'The proceeds will be going to charity,' Jordan said suddenly, inspired by his fear of losing Karen's performance and the repercussions that might have on their event. But now that he'd said it, he realised it wasn't a bad idea.

Mila raised her eyebrows at him, but said, 'An event for charity will have an awesome effect on your public image, Karen. And, Simon, I don't have to tell you how much that can do for Karen's tour.'

Simon waited a beat, and then whipped out his phone and tapped on the screen. 'She has a sold-out concert at Westgate Stadium this Saturday, but the following Saturday—

the one before the tour—we don't have anything booked. It was intended to give her some rest before she leaves on tour. Would you be willing to sacrifice that?' Simon directed the question to Karen.

'Yeah, sure.' Karen turned to them in expectation, and all they could do was look at her with stunned expressions.

Mila was the first to recover.

'That's great. Would you mind helping us with the marketing, then? We'll organise the tickets, but support from you on social media will properly ensure that we have an audience for you. *And* enough support for charity.'

'Yeah, of course.' Karen's eyes shifted to someone behind them and she smiled. 'Look, you can chat to Simon about the arrangements—the set, details about soundcheck—and he'll let me know what the deal is. We can take it from there. I'm going to run. It was nice seeing you again, Mila… Jordan.'

Karen fluttered her eyelashes, and then walked over to join a group of giggling girls.

'I'll contact you tomorrow, when I've had more time to look at the schedule, and we can talk about things,' Simon said to them.

'Yeah, that's perfect. Thanks, Simon.'

Mila smiled at him, and Jordan nodded a farewell, his mind too consumed by what Mila had just got them into to be concerned about the interested look Simon threw at Mila as he walked away.

They stood in silence after Simon had left, and then Jordan gathered his wits to ask, 'Did you just agree to holding our event in two weeks' time?'

'I…I think I did,' Mila stammered, not quite believing that it was true. But her instincts had taken over, and the event planner inside her had jumped at the opportunity to secure a performer who would ensure their event was a success.

'What were you *thinking*?' he asked under his breath,

and then gave a polite smile to the man who was returning their coats.

'I was thinking that we need Karen to make the event
a success.'

'But you realise we don't actually need the event to be
a success, right?'

He shot her a frown as he slid his coat on, and then
turned for her to help him when his arm got stuck. Her
hands shook a little, but she forced them to behave and
helped him into the garment, lingering a tad too long at
his shoulders.

'We just need there to *be* an event. Whether we have
five or five hundred people there doesn't matter.'

'*You* were the one who said it was for charity,' she
hissed at him. 'And you heard that she wouldn't be able
to do it before our deadline otherwise. What was I supposed to do?'

'Find another performer?'

'It would have been more of an effort,' she replied, and
he nodded as though he'd thought of that, too.

'You've made this much more difficult for us now,' he
said stonily.

'I know that. But we both knew that this was a possibility when we spoke to the vendors today. It was either
at the end of this month *with* Karen, or the beginning of
next month without her.'

She was trying to convince herself as much as she was
him, but suddenly she knew that she had done the right
thing. That her actions would make the event a success.
She really wanted it to be a success, she thought. And because she had just realised why, she said, 'It'll be the last
thing I do for Greg, Jordan. I want it to go as well as it
possibly can.'

Her stomach knotted at her words. The intimacy of
what she had revealed and the fact that she'd said it out

loud warned her that she was growing too comfortable around Jordan. But up until that point it hadn't occurred to her that she might want to do the event for any reason other than the fact that she had to.

Now she knew she wanted to do it as a thank-you to Greg for all he had done for her—the last one she would be able to give him—and perhaps as a goodbye present to all those she cared about at the vineyard. A successful event would boost the vineyard's image and be a foundation they would be able to use to rebuild everything that had been put on pause over the last year with Greg's illness.

'I'm sorry, I—'

'No, it's fine,' she interrupted him, not wanting his sympathy.

She thanked the man for her coat, and took care to slip it on so that she wouldn't need Jordan's help as he had needed hers. They walked to the car in silence, though Jordan once again put an arm around her waist to keep her steady. She murmured a thank-you when she got into the car, and wondered why the silence was suddenly so bothersome. Maybe it was because she could feel, just beneath the armour she had put around her heart, her need for Jordan become stronger.

And he had only been back for three days.

That was another reason—one that also hadn't occurred to her until now—that she'd agreed to expedite the event. The quicker it happened, the sooner she would be able to get away from the reminder of a life that had never been hers to begin with. She would be free of all the wants and needs that were beyond her grasp, and she would finally be able to move on to a more realistic future, where she would be safe from hurt...

'So, I'm going to teach in *Korea*?' she blurted out, sick of the direction of her thoughts.

Jordan chuckled, and the vibration of his voice sent a

chill up her spine. Or maybe that was just the cold, she told herself desperately.

'One of the fellows at the research institute we started in Johannesburg told me about how his daughter was going to teach there in a few months. For some reason that was what jumped into my head when you sent me the fire signal for help.'

She smiled. 'Fire signal?'

'Your eyes were screaming "Help me!" so loudly I'm surprised no one else heard it.'

'I'm grateful that you came to my rescue—though now I'm wondering if Korea might be a good next step for me.'

She was still smiling, but her words reminded them that she would be leaving after the event. The thought was sobering—for both of them, she thought, when Jordan didn't respond—and again she sought for something to break the tension.

'How did things go with the institute?'

He looked over at her, and she wondered why he seemed to be checking to see if she was asking him seriously.

Because that's the excuse he used to leave the first time, she thought, and shook her head at the fact that everywhere she turned there was a reminder of a life she no longer had and a future that was uncertain.

'It went well,' he said after a moment. 'We had already started the ball rolling by then, so I just went there to finalise the staffing and ensure that the premises were suited for the expected capacity.'

'Was it?'

'Yeah, it was. It's in central Johannesburg, which is a great location, and it has enough space for the research fellows and for research seminars.'

'Worth the hassle of the accreditation process?'

She remembered the hours he'd had to spend on the phone, and the countless meetings when he'd first had the idea for a research institution for wine microbiology. He had wanted to give back—to contribute to the wine industry in some way other than just selling—and setting up an educational institution that would ensure the quality of the wines the Thomas Vineyard made as well as allow continued research into wine production had seemed like the way to do it. But getting accreditation from the Department of Education for some kind of qualification for the fellows had been a mission—as Jordan's facial expression now proved.

'Right now, with twenty fellows, I'm going to say yes.'

'Seems like you did a good thing, then.' She meant it—though she wished it hadn't been at the expense of their relationship. But then again, they'd already established that that hadn't been the real reason—at least not the only one—that he'd left.

'How was living there?' she asked suddenly, thinking that perhaps knowing how Jordan had lived in his year without her would bring her some peace.

He frowned again, his hands still on the steering wheel, and she realised that they were already in front of the house. She waited a few more minutes and then shook her head in disappointment, feeling the cold run through her as she said, 'Don't tell me, then. I'll just add it to the list.'

She opened the car door, happy to escape from the desperate need inside her to know more about him. To know more about the aspects of his life that she hadn't been a part of.

To escape the need to demand to know about them.

'Mila, wait!' he called after her.

But she had already reached the front door and was trying to find her key to get in—to get away from him. The key fell from her hand, and she let out an exasperated breath as he came from behind her and picked it up.

He inserted the key into the door, but didn't turn it. 'I'll tell you,' he said, without looking at her, and she scoffed.

'I'm not pulling your teeth, Jordan. Talking to people is supposed to be natural. Or at least it's supposed to be with your *wife*.'

It was the first time she had referred to herself like that since learning that she *was* still his wife, and it sounded strange—maybe even terrifying—to hear it. But at the same time something came to rest inside her at the term—an acknowledgement of why learning about him had become so important.

She cared about him.

As a friend, she assured herself, not because she had been his wife. But even through her self-assurance she knew she was more hurt than she cared to admit that after all the revelations she'd made to him, he refused to share his own with her.

'I want to tell you,' he insisted. 'I want to talk to you… It's just difficult.'

Her eyebrows rose. 'Why?'

He exhaled sharply, and then turned the key in the lock. He pushed the door open and waited for her to walk through. When she had, she took her coat and hung it on the rack, then looked at him expectantly.

He would tell her this at least, she thought.

He took his jacket off, and then rubbed at his chin, which was already starting to show stubble. She remembered the slight burn on her skin from the friction earlier and her body responded with need.

To combat it, she folded her arms, and waited for him to speak.

'There's a lot I have to deal with. Since I came back here after Dad died…' He stuffed his hands into his pockets. 'It's hard for me to verbalise it. It's…a lot.'

She steeled herself against the softening that inevitably

touched her heart, and said, 'We've both had to deal with "a lot," Jordan.' Her next words were already forming, and she ignored the voice telling her not to say them. 'Don't accuse me of pushing away the people who care about me when *you're* doing exactly the same thing.'

CHAPTER THIRTEEN

SHE HAD A POINT, Jordan thought, even as he wished for the old Mila. The one who would have understood him saying he had a lot to deal with and wouldn't have pushed. But hadn't he, only a few hours earlier, thought about how much he *liked* this new Mila? He couldn't change his mind now, just because she was making him uncomfortable. Especially when she was right.

'Fine—let's talk, then,' he forced himself to say, though he wasn't sure what he was prepared to talk about. 'But let me change first. I'd feel better in comfortable clothes.'

He wasn't sure how true that was, but he wasn't about to bare his soul in a tuxedo. Mila nodded, and he went to his bedroom, already unbuttoning his shirt.

The room hadn't changed much since his childhood, Jordan thought as he pulled on a pair of worn jeans and a long-sleeved shirt. It was still painted the blue his mother had chosen for him when he was younger. It had been one of their last activities together, before she had become too sick to get out of bed.

His memories of her had faded over time, but he still remembered how much time she had wanted to spend with him. He would play in front of the house on the patio, shouting for her to look when he did something that only a four-year-old would find impressive. And she had always sat on those chairs beside the front door, cheering for him, sharing his pride and telling him how happy he made her.

Even when his father had no longer joined her she'd sat there, watching over him. Even when she'd grown frailer, paler, more sickly, with his father hovering around, she'd spent hours with Jordan outdoors. His heart ached at the memories, which suddenly seemed so clear now, and he took a deep breath.

Why was he thinking about this *now*? There was no purpose in rehashing that part of his past. The part that reminded him of his father's anger towards him and, ever since he had learned the truth about his mother's death, his anger towards himself and the guilt he felt.

The thought had already put him on edge, and he forced himself to control it or he knew the conversation he was preparing to have with Mila could only go poorly.

It didn't work, since he found himself considering why he was preparing to have this conversation in the first place. Why had it all of a sudden become so important for her to see him trying? For her to see that he wanted to let her in, to tell her the real reasons behind why he had left?

There was no answer that would pull him away from the edge, and his insides tensed even further.

When he walked into the lounge, he noticed that she had started a fire. And then she walked into the room, a glass of wine in each hand, and his gut tightened.

She had changed, too, into a long-sleeved shirt he recognised as an old one of his. It was worn, and stretched so much that it almost touched her knees, which were clad in tights. She hadn't worn that particular shirt before, but it still reminded him of the times when she would wear his clothes. They smelled like him, she had always said, and he wondered if that was the reason she was wearing the shirt now.

The emotions that thought evoked—and his physical reaction to her—did nothing to make him feel better.

'How was my father before his death?' he asked abruptly, his voice harsher than he'd intended.

Her eyebrows rose in response, and he saw the flash of annoyance before it was replaced with ice.

Back to this again, he thought, but knew he was to blame for her reaction.

She set his glass down on the table in front of him, hard enough that he watched the contents swirl in disruption, and then she said, 'No, I'm not doing this with you when you're in this mood.'

'Mila, I don't have—'

'Whatever you're going to say, I'm sure I've heard it before. You don't feel like talking right now…or you're going through a lot…or can we postpone?' She shook her head. 'We don't have to have this conversation *at all*, Jordan.'

'No.' The word came quickly—something he was sure was a result of the answers he hadn't wanted to consider earlier.

'Are you sure?' She raised her eyebrow, and her sassy look sent a shock of desire through him.

'Yes.'

Both brows rose now, and then she picked up her wine and settled back. 'We can start with something simple. Tell me about your life in Johannesburg.'

'There's not much to say. And I'm not saying that because I don't want to tell you,' he said quickly, when he saw the expression on her face. 'I spent most of my time at the institute. Too much time, probably. But it helped to focus on something other than…'

'Me,' she finished when he trailed off.

He nodded. 'And on everything else that had happened.

I thought that if I could make a success of this, something I could actually control, then my failures at home…'

He was messing it up, he thought. Her finger was tracing the rim of her glass again, so although her face was unreadable he knew she was thinking about what he was saying. But he couldn't tell *what* she was thinking, and it was driving him crazy.

'I get that,' she said finally, and raised her eyes to look at him. 'When your dad got sick and asked me to move in…focusing on him instead of the things going on in my life helped me deal with everything.' She cocked her head. 'Did you have a social life?'

'You mean did I date?'

Her mouth opened slightly at the blunt question, and then she straightened her shoulders. 'I suppose so. Though I was talking about whether or not you had friends.'

His lips curved at the slight blush on her cheeks. But he answered her question,

'No dates, but I did go out for drinks with some of the people from work sometimes. Not often enough to keep in touch outside work now, though.'

She nodded, and sipped from her wine. It gave him a clear view of the line of her throat, and again he felt his need for her run through his blood with the memory of how he had kissed her there that afternoon.

'Can I ask about my father now?' he asked quickly, before the need consumed him and he did something he regretted.

'Of course. What do you want to know?'

'Anything.'

Everything, he thought, but stopped the word before it came out.

'Well, he was devastated about the baby,' she began. 'Not that he would ever have said it. You know how he was.'

Yes, he did. And wasn't that part of why he was absorbing everything she was telling him now?

'I didn't speak to him that first month. Not to anyone, really, as you know. But he eventually told me he'd stayed away because he wanted us to deal with it together.'

Jordan remembered that. His father hadn't visited them much after Mila's fall, and when Jordan had turned up at the vineyard Greg hadn't got involved. Not that Jordan had given him a chance to. Jordan hadn't spoken about it—not the accident, not his wife. The only reason he had been there was because Mila hadn't wanted him around. That was the first time he had noticed the anger seep in, the resentment. The signs that he had it in him to react as his father had after his mother's death.

Jordan reached for his glass of wine at the unsettling thought.

'But then you left.' She looked up at him. 'I'd like to say your father and I helped each other through it, but that isn't true. Like with everyone else…I pushed him away. I wanted nothing to do with him since he only reminded me of you, and of what I'd lost.'

She cleared her throat, as though the admission had taken her by surprise. And since it had surprised *him*, too, he didn't interrupt.

'I was staying at the beach house—I couldn't stay at our place alone, not after what had happened—and I told Greg because I didn't want him to worry. And then I got the divorce papers, and Greg was the only person who would understand…'

She stopped, and he heard her take a shaky breath. He didn't blame her—her story was peppered with anecdotes that he wasn't sure she would have shared with him if they hadn't agreed on having an honest conversation.

'I could see that you leaving had hurt him. I'm not saying that to hurt *you*, Jordan,' she said immediately, and he wondered what it was in his face that had told her he needed reassurance. 'I'm telling you because you need to know to move on. He was hurt, but I think he understood. He didn't blame you.'

'I'm not sure that's true.'

'It is,' she said firmly.

'You didn't know him like I knew him, Mila. And he asked me not to go. Told me I would be destroying our relationship if I did.' He could feel his breathing hitch, and he emptied his wine glass.

'Maybe that's true,' she said when he'd set the wine glass down, and he saw that she was watching him. 'But you didn't know him like *I* did either.'

He wondered what she meant by that—was about to ask—and then she continued, 'He was growing frailer, I saw. At first I thought it was because of everything that had happened over the last months. I'd lost some weight, too, so I didn't think too much of it. And then he had the first heart attack. He was out in the fields with Frank. They had people around them, who rallied round to get Greg to the car, to the hospital, the moment they realised what was happening. He wasn't alone.'

Jordan didn't know if she'd done it purposely, but that piece of information seemed to have settled something inside him.

'I didn't think twice when he asked me to move in after that. It was the only admission of needing help that he would ever give, I knew. So I moved in...helped around the house.'

'How long?'

She took a moment to respond, and then she said, 'The time between his first and second heart attacks was short, and between his second and third even shorter.' She was watching him carefully. 'The whole period was just over seven months.'

Seven months. It was shorter than the time his mother had had to suffer, and that comforted him. They'd found out about her cancer when Jordan was two, and she'd had to suffer for three long, agonising years—two without treatment and one with—before she'd passed away.

He thought of watching his mother suffer, and of how his father had suffered because of the pain he'd seen his wife go through. Felt relief that he hadn't been there to witness what Greg had gone through during the past year, and the overwhelming guilt at the thought. And realised how exactly his childhood had impacted him...

'Was he in pain? My father?'

The words escaped his lips before he'd realised he wanted to know the answer. But knowing the answer would confirm what he had just learned about himself—that he couldn't see anyone he cared about suffer.

The compassion in her eyes sent a blow to his heart. 'Sometimes. It made him miserable, difficult. More so than usual.' She paused. 'But it also made him more honest than usual.'

He raised his eyebrows, but she shook her head. 'I'm not going to tell you about that until you share something with me.'

The calm tone of her voice infuriated him. 'Tit for tat? Are we children?'

'If that's what it takes.' She shrugged, but the gesture was anything but casual.

'You have no right to keep things from me!' he spat, his heart pounding furiously. 'He was my father.'

'And maybe I wouldn't have to keep things from you if you'd been here.'

'Back to this, are we?' He shook his head and thought that he needed to get out of the room.

'Yes, we are. But we wouldn't need to get back to it if you just *told* me why you left,' she shot back.

'Because of *you*,' he said angrily. 'You wouldn't listen to me, just like my mother didn't listen to my father. And where did *that* get her?'

He was breathing heavily, and it took him a moment to compose himself.

'What does that mean?' she asked in a shaky voice when he finally looked at her.

Her face had lost its colour, and it shook him more than he wanted it to. 'It doesn't matter.'

'Yes, it does,' she said, in a voice that twisted his insides. 'Please, Jordan, just let me in for once.'

'You know more about me than anyone else.'

'I don't know *enough*,' she contradicted him. 'There's more—I know there's more. I've shared so much with you,' she said, in a tone that told him that that wasn't necessarily what she had wanted. 'Please, Jordan. I...I...*need* you to tell me.'

'I can't give you more than this, Mila,' he rasped, and pushed up from his seat. He didn't need to see the torment on her face when he had his own to deal with.

He walked out of the room, ignoring the voice that mocked him for running away from her for the second time.

CHAPTER FOURTEEN

MILA WATCHED HIM leave and pain tore through her. She had been honest with him. She had pushed through her reservations about opening up to him and told him she *needed* him.

And he'd rejected her.

She gasped when the pain turned into a burn that consumed her entire body, and sank to her knees. *This* was why she didn't want him back. *This* was exactly what she was afraid of. Showing people the real her, showing *him* the real her, and having them—*him*—reject her.

Though she didn't know how it was possible, this was worse than the first time. Maybe it was because then Jordan hadn't been leaving *her*. Not the real her. No, back then he'd been leaving the person she was pretending to be. The one who didn't believe that she was worth him, who didn't speak her mind, who was waiting—expecting—for him to leave. The one who had failed as a mother, as a wife.

But since he'd come back she had shown him more and more of herself. She hadn't realised how much until right at that moment when she hadn't been able to hide behind the person she showed the world.

A sob escaped, but she clasped a hand over her mouth. She *wouldn't* let him hear her cry for him. She would get through this—she would. She had survived growing up without anyone to care for her.

It didn't matter now that the man she loved didn't care for her enough to be honest with her.

Another sob came when she realised the truth that she'd been running away from since Jordan had come back. She still loved him. She'd never stopped. That was why she had started opening up to him. Why she had told him the truth. Why she had shown him who she was. Maybe even why she wanted the event to go well—so she could show him, prove to him, that she was capable, that she was worthy.

She wanted Jordan to love the real her.

It was a foolish hope, she thought now. Not because she wasn't worthy—she was slowly but surely fighting her way out of *that* pit—but because he didn't want to. She knew he was struggling—she had watched him during their conversation, knew that the information she'd given him about his father had opened up something for him—and now she knew that it had to do with his parents. With his mother. But, whatever it was, he didn't want *her* to be a part of it.

He doesn't need me, she thought, and closed her eyes against the pain.

She'd always thought it was something simple—something childish, even—to feel needed. To want a family who would need her unconditionally. But it wasn't, and she needed to face that. She needed to stop *pretending* that she was okay without having it, and to *really* be okay with it.

The man she loved didn't need her. She wouldn't ever get to have the family she had always wanted. And that was okay, she told herself. She would get through it. She *would* be okay.

But that didn't have to happen right now, she thought as she lowered her head between her knees and let the tears fall silently to the floor.

Jordan got up earlier than he normally would the next day. Not only because he hadn't got any sleep, but because he knew Mila was an early riser and he wanted to be up before her. He wasn't running away, he told himself. He just needed to get out of the house to think.

He sighed when he heard a loud thunderclap, and then the steady pelting of rain on the roof. There would be no walking through the vineyard to clear his thoughts, he thought. But since he was already up he decided to get some coffee. He needed the strength.

He had hurt her. The look on her face when she'd told him she needed him to let her in would be branded in his mind for ever. He wished that he could go back, that he could take it back, so that they could go back to the truce they'd had with one another. But he couldn't, and now all he wanted was to finish the darn event and get it over with so that he could move on with his life.

Because he didn't want to get caught up in the past any more. The last few days had been more than enough for his entire lifetime, and he could do without the memories of his mother, without the regrets he had about his father.

And he could do without Mila.

His hand stilled midway on its path to bringing the coffee mug to his mouth. That *was* what he was saying, wasn't it? She was the one forcing him to face his past. The last few days had been filled with his past because of *her*. And since he wanted the event over and done with, it meant he wanted things with *her* to be over and done with…right?

Except that the very thought sent an unpleasant frisson through his body. And an even worse one through his heart. The last thing he wanted was to say goodbye to her. Though they'd been difficult for him, the past few days had also been great. He'd started to get to know a side of Mila that he hadn't seen before. In fact, he'd thought he was getting to know a whole different Mila. The feistiness, the speaking her mind suited her in a way he hadn't considered before.

But it was more than that. It was the passion that he could see she had for her job. For her family. Because, although she didn't think she had one, the way she cared about Lulu and his father was more familial than anything he had ever experienced.

She was compassionate even when she didn't want to be, he thought as he remembered the way she had cared for him after his run-in with Lulu. As he thought about how she'd had nothing to gain when his father had asked her to move in with him and yet she had still done it.

It spoke of warmth, of the kindness that was naturally *her*. She was the best person he knew. And he cared about her.

But he couldn't *be* with her.

Not when she needed more from him than he could give her. So he would simply have to be without her. And even though the thought sent pain through him, he knew it was the right thing.

But that didn't mean he didn't have to apologise to her. He'd been a bit of a jerk the previous day, walking out on her like that, and she didn't deserve it. Not when *he* had been the person to suggest they have an honest conversation in the first place.

He started taking out things for breakfast. It was an apology, yes, but he also wanted to see her smile again. He wanted to see the smile that made him feel as if he was the only person in the world. The smile that pierced through his defences and reminded him of why he had fallen in love with her...

Before he could ponder why seeing her smile had become so important, she walked in. She stopped when she saw him there, and he could sense her hesitation. And then she turned around.

'Hey, I'm making breakfast.'

She stopped, and then slowly turned back to him. 'Are we just going to pretend last night didn't happen?'

Her voice was a little husky, her hair still mussed from sleep, and the effect was potent. It was as if his body was reminding him about yet another thing he was leaving behind, and it took a moment for him to recover.

'I'm trying to apologise.'

'Why? What's the point?'

His heart dribbled against his chest when he realised he didn't have an answer for her.

'Because we have an event to plan together,' he finally managed.

'If that's the only reason, apology not accepted. I've worked with people I don't like before. This won't be a first for me.'

She turned away from him again, and his heart skidded to a halt when he realised that she was putting barriers up. Barriers he didn't think would ever come down again. It bothered him and he didn't know why.

'We're doing more than just working together, Mila,' he found himself saying.

'Really?' She folded her arms. 'What else are we doing, then?'

'We're saying goodbye to my father.' That wasn't it, he realised as his stomach sank. But it was good enough to appease her.

'You know where to hit, don't you?' she said as her arms dropped to her sides.

She was right, but he couldn't think of anything else to say. Not when he was still stunned by how all his conclusions earlier had been swept aside the minute he'd seen her. How much the thought that she would push him away again had alarmed him. How much he wanted things between them to be okay.

'How about we start with a cup of coffee?' she said

when he didn't respond, and he nodded, turning away from her.

Why was it suddenly so important for him to stay close to her? He had resigned himself to letting go—of her, of the past—but now he couldn't imagine anything worse.

He took his time making her coffee, ignoring the sudden jittery feeling in his body, and then he handed it to her carefully, so that they wouldn't touch. But her fingers brushed against his anyway, and his body responded.

Except that the physical effect she had on him had little to do with desire. It was a way of confirming what he had just realised. He still had feelings for her. It was the only thing that made his reaction to her logical. What else could make his rational thoughts seem like the most nonsensical things in the world?

He had barely acknowledged his feelings before he was striding towards her. He took the mug from her hands, had the pleasure of seeing her eyes widen and hearing her sharp inhalation, and then with her body against his, he touched his lips to hers.

She tasted of coffee and toothpaste…a combination he would have never thought sexy if he hadn't experienced it himself. She didn't move at first, her lips stiff under his, and he prepared himself to pull back—all but had words of apology ready in his mind before he felt her hands tentatively touch his waist.

Immediately he felt heat at their contact, but he resisted giving in to it. Instead he kept it slow, like the afternoon walks they'd used to take on Sundays, and let the fire simmer. It made him more aware of the connection they shared, of how their kiss was more than just a meeting of their lips, more than just something he was doing to sate his need for her.

It made slow and tender feel as satisfying and as passionate as the desperate kiss they had shared—was it only the previous day?

He didn't spend much time thinking about it—was too consumed by the way her body fitted his in just the right way. By the way her hands tightened on his waist, and then slid up under his shirt to touch his skin. Everywhere they moved heightened the sensation in his body, and he sank deeper into the kiss, using his tongue to remind her of their passion, of their love.

She moaned, pressed herself tighter against him, and he felt her shake. It turned the temperature up between them and his hands found her waist and lifted her up, setting her on the kitchen counter without losing contact. She pulled the hoodie he wore over his head, and he barely felt the sting of cold on his bare body. Not when she was kissing his neck, his shoulders, then his mouth again, as if she had discovered she needed him just as much as he needed her.

The thought gave him pause, and he moved away.

'Do you want this?' he asked, and searched her face for the real answer.

His heart was filled by her beauty in that moment—the flush of her cheeks, her untamed curls framing her face, her chest heaving—but he couldn't ignore the flash of uncertainty, of fear that lit her face.

It was gone in a moment and she nodded and pulled his head closer, but with all the self-control inside him, he resisted.

'You don't, Mila. At least, you're not sure,' he forced himself to say, and braced himself against the pain that flashed through her eyes at his words.

'No, I think *you're* the one who isn't sure,' she told him.

'You have no idea what I'm thinking,' he said, his voice sharp. She was too close to the truth.

'Whose fault is that?' she asked softly, before pushing at his chest.

He took a step back, watched as she lowered herself off the counter and pulled at the shirt that had ridden up to her waist during their passion. But not before he had got a good look at her stomach. The skin was slightly loose over the flat surface, with tiny vertical lines leading to the scar from her C-section—evidence that she had once carried his child—and his hands itched to touch, to feel, to remind himself of better times between them.

'I don't know what to do about you,' she said suddenly, and all his thoughts gave way to one single thought that ripped at his heart.

He was hurting her.

With his words, with his actions. He couldn't do this with her again, he realised. Not until he was sure.

'I'm sorry,' he said, because he didn't know what else he could say.

'We should just stick to the event, Jordan. Everything else…'

She looked at him, her eyes shockingly beautiful in their misery, and he saw for the first time that they were a little swollen, a little red, as if she'd been crying. The thought sent another blow to his heart.

'*Nothing* else will work between us.'

She walked away, leaving him alone in the kitchen. It was sobering to think that he had never felt so alone ever before. He no longer had his mother, his father. He no longer had his wife.

He was pushing her away.

Was it worth it? Was his guilt, his regret over what had had happened in his childhood, over his relationship with his father, over his mother's choices, worth risking the woman he loved?

He ran a hand through his hair and then slid it down his face. Who was he fooling? Thinking he had feelings for Mila was just vague enough to make him feel better about himself. But he should have known the truth would catch up with him. He should have known from the moment he had seen her and fallen for her that he couldn't run away from his feelings for her.

His shoulders stiffened even more at the thought. He needed to stop running. He loved Mila—had never stopped—and he needed to step up for her. Except…he didn't know how. Or even if he could. He had been running away all his life. From the moment his father had told him that his mother had chosen to look after him instead of her own health. From the moment he'd realised his father blamed Jordan for her death.

Even the thought sent waves of hurt through him, and only his hope of love with Mila was keeping them at bay. He knew that if he told her those hurts might overwhelm him, and that if he didn't they would keep nudging at him, causing him to run all his life.

He had to make a choice. And, despite all the things he had been through in his life, despite all the difficult choices he'd had to make, he knew that this one would be the worst.

CHAPTER FIFTEEN

SHE KEPT MAKING the same mistakes, and if she continued down that path it would destroy her. So Mila kept to her word and focused on her work, ignoring the kiss that she'd shared with Jordan that morning—*and* its after-effects.

She called Lulu and explained that their event was now less than two weeks away and they needed to make sure there *would* be an event. She confirmed the details with Simon, informed the marquee supplier about the date, and called to tell the vendors the same thing. She soothed complaints, found alternatives, until eventually she was fairly certain that the event would take place.

She updated Mark, as the executor of the will, and emailed him records of all they had done to keep within the conditions of the will.

And then she braced herself for visiting her house again.

She had decided the previous evening that she would move out of Greg's house. She should have done it the day after Jordan had returned. It would have saved her so much heartache. Now her heart pained her with every beat, and her mind was consumed by grief because he didn't want her.

He wanted her physically, maybe, she thought, flushing at the memory of that morning, but not in any other way. And so, because she couldn't live with the man who reminded her of everything she wanted and couldn't have, she was going to live at the house where they'd started their lives together.

It was better that way, she told herself as she began packing a bag. She would start clearing the house, get it on the market, and once it was sold she would use the money to buy offices for her business.

She and Lulu had used to work out of the flat she'd rented before she got married and at Lulu's home before Mila's fall, but now she wanted something more legitimate. Something that would make her feel steady. Something that was her own.

It was also the only thing she could think of to use the money from the sale of the house *for*—taking it to live a lavish life didn't seem right to her. And she knew Jordan wouldn't want it back—it would be a slap in the face to him if she offered, when she knew that he'd done it because he had wanted to give her something. He had hurt her, yes, but Mila had no intention of doing the same thing to him. She was better than that.

That was another reason why she had decided to sort out the house on her own. Before she'd thought she needed him. That she couldn't do it by herself. But as part of her resolution to move on, to only rely on herself, she *would* do it by herself.

Yes, her heart still thumped at the thought of going back to the house where she had lost her baby, but it was also the house where she had found out she was going to have him. It was the place where she had first felt him kick, where she had spent the only time she'd had with him. And although focusing on those positives almost made her reconsider selling—*almost*—she knew it would be for the best if she did.

And then, when the event was over, she would file for divorce.

She *would* move on from Jordan.

She packed the case with her essentials—she had enough clothing to last her until the event at the house—and dragged the case behind her to the front door. It rattled on the tiles, and then stopped. She turned back, giving it a forceful pull before continuing.

And walked straight into Jordan.

'Hey!' he said, steadying her, and she had a flashback to those hands on her waist, lifting her. 'Where are you going?'

'I'm going to stay somewhere else.' She knew it sounded snappy, but it was better than showing the need that heated her belly at her memories.

She looked up at him and saw the carefully blank look in his eyes.

'You're leaving,' he said flatly.

'I am,' she said in the same tone. 'It's what's best, isn't it?'

She could almost see the gears grinding in his head as he thought, and she wondered what there was to think about. He'd made his choice. She'd made hers. That was it.

That was it, she reminded herself when something inside her lit up—just a little—at the thought of him wanting her to stay.

'Where are you going?'

'Back to the house.'

She saw the twitch in his eyebrow before he schooled his features again. 'I'll take you.'

'No, no,' she said quickly, feeling all her bravado fade at the prospect of going back with him. 'I'm calling a taxi.'

'No, you're not.'

She would have been annoyed by his tone if she hadn't seen that twitch in his brow again. She had grown familiar with his facial expressions when they were married—was even more so now, perhaps—and she knew he was upset, but was trying to hide it.

'Please, just let me do this thing for you.'

The tone had softened, and she hated that her heart did the same. 'Okay...'

She didn't protest when he took the case from her hand, and she followed him to the car, getting in before he could open the door for her. She had had too many lingering touches from him in the past when he'd done that, and she wasn't interested in repeating it now. Not when she was already warning her heart to stay behind the wall she'd erected the previous night after she had finished sobbing. That wall had already been threatened by their kiss that morning, and she refused to put it in danger again.

When they pulled into the driveway at the house she immediately turned to get out—and then froze when she felt his hand on her thigh. It was in no way sexual, but heat seeped through her and she turned back in the hope that if she did he would remove it.

'Are you going to miss it?' he asked, and pulled back his hand as Mila had hoped.

He was staring at the house now, avoiding her gaze, so she sat back and looked at it, too. It *was* beautiful, she thought, and felt a pang in her heart.

'I am,' she said carefully.

'But it's not the vineyard?' he replied and looked at her.

She felt pinned by the look—especially since he had said exactly what she was thinking. The house she had lived in for the past year had begun to feel like more of a home to her than this place, where she had lived in with the man she had married. It was going to be hard to leave all that behind, she thought.

'I walked in here for the first time and I thought this would be a great house for you to come home to. Your first real home. I wanted it to be special for you.'

And just like that his words carved another spot in her heart.

'It *was* special,' she said, 'and it will always be my first home. Thank you.'

She wanted to kiss him in gratitude—a simple peck as she would have given him so often before—but she resisted.

'I'd like to show you something.'

He got out of the car before she could answer and she followed quickly, unsure of what was going on.

'I wanted to show it to you yesterday, but we…er…got a little distracted.'

He locked the car, and then held out his hand to her. It was a simple gesture, almost a reflex, but he stood like that until she walked over to him and carefully took his hand with her own. The warmth immediately gave her comfort, and she almost pulled away. She didn't need to be reminded of how much Jordan made her feel at home. But then she looked up, saw the impact simply taking her hand had had on him, and left it there.

You're hopeless, she berated herself.

But still she followed—perhaps because she thought it was for the last time.

'Where are you taking me?' she asked, to escape her thoughts.

'You'll see,' he replied, and she felt him tighten his grip on her hand.

It made her sad, and she wasn't completely sure why. They walked in silence, and when they reached a gate that Mila had never seen before Jordan took a key out of his pocket.

'Wait—this is the Gerber place.' Mila let go of his hand and placed hers lightly on his arm.

'It used to be,' he answered, and then pushed open the gate.

It didn't make any sound as it opened—confirmation to her that it had been recently put there—and Jordan gestured for her to go through. The plot was vast and green, as though completely unaffected by the coldness of the season, and a bridge led over the stream that ran around the whole property.

He held out a hand to help her cross, even though she saw that the bridge was fairly sturdy. And she took his hand, needing the contact to help her soothe the sudden anxiety in her stomach.

'I don't think this is a good idea.'

'Trust me.'

She stood at the base of the bridge, looked at the sincerity in his eyes, and felt the wall she had prided herself on erecting and then maintaining completely disintegrate. She nodded, unable to speak, and they walked over the wooden bridge together.

She ran her free hand over the railing, forcing herself to focus on its design—anything to keep her mind occupied with something other than how much she loved him. It was a perfect example of the traditional charm that all the Stellenbosch properties had—just as the barn they were walking towards now was.

'Are you going to tell me what's going on?' Mila asked softly.

'This is the latest Thomas property.'

'You *own* this place?'

'Yeah.'

'How? It must be recent, because I didn't once see or suspect that the Gerbers were selling their property.'

'They weren't planning on selling it, but I managed to convince them.'

He stuffed his hands into his pockets, and the gesture made him seem less rich-vineyard-owner and more handsome-husband. Though his words implied that he had very much *played* rich vineyard owner to get the property.

'When?'

'About a year ago.'

'A year ago? But that was—'

'Just before your fall?'

She nodded, and he continued.

'Yes, it was. I was going to surprise you with it after you gave birth.'

'With what? Another property? We didn't need that—'

'With the Thomas Events venue.'

Her mind took a moment to process what he was saying, and the moment she did she felt the heat of tears in her eyes.

'The Thomas Events venue?' she repeated, and hated it that it sounded so right. Hated it even more that Jordan had been trying to make another dream of hers come true.

She wished with all her might that things could have worked out between them. Her life would have been absolutely perfect then! She would have had a place to go home to, a husband who loved her and a baby who needed her and to whom she would have given the world.

'I thought it was time your business had a home,' Jordan said when she didn't say anything. 'I had the barn redone so that you could host events there—weddings, conferences, anything you wanted—and I was going to turn the house into an office. You could meet your clients there, do mock-ups—even turn one of the rooms into a baby's room, if you wanted.'

'I...um... Wow... I...' She took a deep breath, and pulled her hand away from his. 'This is... I don't know what to say, Jordan.'

A tear slid down her face and he took a step forward.

'I didn't want you to be sad. I just wanted to—'

'*What?*' she asked, grasping for anger instead of pain. 'You wanted to show me another thing I don't have?'

'*No!* No, of course not,' he said quickly, his eyes wide.

'I wanted to show you this because it's still yours. I want you to have it.'

'I don't *want* it,' she snapped, and another tear rolled down her face. 'I don't want any reminder of the life we will never have together.'

'Mila—' He stepped forward again, opening his arms, but she took a step back away from him.

'No, Jordan! You don't get it, do you? I can't do this with you any more. I can't pretend that we're friends, or whatever we're pretending to be at the moment.' She took a shaky breath and impatiently wiped at her tears. 'I need to move on. I *am* moving on. The minute this event is over, I'm gone. Far away from this place—' she threw a hand out '—from the house I lived in as your wife and from the vineyard that started this whole thing in the first place.'

She looked up at him and choked out her next words.

'I'm filing for divorce and moving on from *you*.'

She bit her lip, trying to compose herself as the words tore her heart into pieces.

And then she said slowly, 'I don't want you to show me things I'll never get to enjoy. And I don't want you to show me a person I'll never get to be with.'

'No, Mila—wait,' he said when she turned to walk away, and she heard anger and something else coating his voice with gravel. 'You had your say, so now I'm having mine. I showed you this because it's *yours*. I don't care what you call it, or if you accept it or not. I bought this for *you*. So that you can understand how much I care for you and how much I believe in you.'

Care, she thought. Present tense. Before she could caution herself against it, she felt hope reignite.

'You can move on, move away, Mila, but this place will still be here when you get back.' There was a momentary pause, and then he said, 'It'll be waiting for you just like I will be.'

He took a step closer and lifted her chin until she was looking at him.

'I don't care whether it's a year or ten years, whether we're married or not, I'll be waiting for you.'

'Why?' she whispered, before her mind could give her permission to speak.

There was barely a moment before he answered, 'Because I love you.'

He slid an arm around her waist and pulled her in, silencing her protests even before his mouth found hers. It was similar to the way she had kissed *him* two days ago, she thought hazily, and she wondered if his reason was similar, too—to show her that they mattered.

But she was already too lost in the taste of him to think any more about it. Her body was thanking her for something—*someone*—it had longed for but never got in the last year. And yet still she could feel a part of her resist—the sane, rational part of her that wanted to protect her poor already broken heart—and in response she felt his arm loosen around her.

He was giving her an out—telling her that she could leave the embrace if she wanted to.

But that only made her want him more, and barely a beat after he'd offered her a way out, she found herself pressed against him again. His arms went around her, tighter this time, and his mouth took hers more deeply, hungry after the possibility of stopping.

She couldn't breathe, couldn't hear, couldn't think in his arms, and she poured all the love she felt for him into the kiss, turning it from desperate into tender.

He eased away, and then looked down at her, his eyes heavy with need. 'I love you, Mila.'

Hearing the words again was like a slap. 'Stop!' She pulled herself away from him completely and felt the tears come back. 'You don't mean that.'

'Of *course* I mean it,' he said firmly, almost angrily. But the look in his eyes was…*fear*.

'If you really meant that, Jordan, you would stop being afraid of sharing with me and tell me about your childhood. About your mother and your father. You would *want* to tell me about it.'

CHAPTER SIXTEEN

JORDAN OPENED HIS MOUTH, ready to retort, but she had hit him exactly where she knew he was most vulnerable. He closed his mouth again, and before he could think of something to respond with she spoke again.

'This is exactly what I'm talking about. *Why* is it so hard for you to tell me about it?'

'For the same reasons you don't talk to me about *your* childhood in foster care.'

Her head snapped back as though he had hit her, and something inside him warned him to stop. But the words kept sprinting out of his mouth.

'It isn't that easy to talk about when you're on the other side, is it?' he said steadily, and watched the emotions run over her face like a movie reel.

Eventually she replied, 'No, it isn't. But when you love someone you have to make a sacrifice and put your reservations aside.' She took a deep breath. 'I didn't have anyone who needed me when I was growing up, Jordan. I lived with ten different families in eighteen years. It was hard.'

She blew out a shaky breath, and he felt himself shake a little, too. Was she doing what he thought she was?

'I didn't have anyone who needed me, and quite frankly no one wanted me. Lulu was the first person I met who cared about me—and I mean *really* cared—and I was sixteen years old when I met her.'

She wiped at tears he hadn't seen, too captivated by what she was telling him to notice before—and even more so by what it meant.

'Growing up like that made me… It made me someone I don't want to be any more.' She shrugged. 'I wouldn't ever say what I felt or what I thought because I wanted people to like me.'

'Even with me?' he asked, needing to know.

She looked at him through wet lashes that made her eyes all the more piercing. 'Even with you.' She bit her lip, and then said, 'I couldn't… I *thought* I couldn't tell you what I felt. There was a big part of me that felt like being married to you was a dream, and I didn't want to wake up. It didn't matter how I felt about our house, our cars…'

All things *he* had chosen for her, he thought in disgust.

'I had you. And that was enough for me.'

She lifted a hand when he opened his mouth to speak.

'Wait, I'm not done yet. I have to get this out before you say anything.'

Something shifted in her eyes, and panic spread through his body in response.

This is the last time she'll do this, he thought, and his heart pounded at the thought of losing her.

'But that also meant I didn't know how to ask you for help when we lost our child. I was afraid that you blamed me—you'd asked me to slow down and I hadn't. And then I fell down the stairs and I thought that you were right—I *should* have slowed down, enjoyed being pregnant. After that…I felt like a failure. Like every fear of mine had come true.'

Tears shone in her eyes and he took a step forward, wanting to be closer to her, to comfort her.

'It was a confirmation of what I'd feared all along—that I wasn't worthy of you. I always expected you to leave me, so when you did—'

'I proved you right,' he finished for her, stunned.

How could he have been so unaware of what his wife was going through? How had he not noticed that she hadn't ever disagreed with him? How had he been so blind? She had it completely wrong, he thought. *He* was the one who wasn't worthy of *her*.

'Mila, I'm so sorry. I didn't know…'

He trailed off as he realised that she had just told him everything he had ever wanted to know about her. And based on that information—based on the completely raw look in her eyes—he knew how much it had cost her.

'You love me, too.'

He didn't need her to say it because it was suddenly so painfully clear to him. It made the fact that he felt as if he was losing her so much worse. He looked at her, saw the truth in her eyes, and the past year of his life flashed through his mind.

He had always been a loner, but he hadn't ever felt alone. As difficult as his relationship with his father had been, Jordan had always known he had somewhere to go to, someone to talk to if he needed it. But after he had left for Johannesburg he hadn't really spoken to his father. His life had felt emptier than he'd thought possible, and he'd felt more alone than ever.

He had missed Mila with all of him, and now he knew—he *knew*—that his grief at losing his son, at losing his chance of a full family, would have been bearable if he had been with Mila.

It was something her words had only just made him realise, and the simple truth of it led him to say, 'My father blamed me for my mother's death.'

When the words were out, he couldn't believe such a simple sentence could convey the thing that had followed him around for his entire life. He stuffed his hands in his pockets and faced the stream. He didn't want to see her face—the compassion he knew would be there—while he told her of his childhood. Not when what he was going to tell her might change her opinion of his father, whom she'd clearly cared about.

He rubbed a hand over his face, wondering where to start, and decided on the part Mila already knew about.

'My mom found out about her cancer when I was two.' He took a steadying breath, then continued, 'She refused treatment. For two years she didn't want to get treatment, even though she was ill most of the time… She wanted to be a normal mother.'

He took another breath, shifted the weight between his feet.

'Her mom had died of the same thing, and they'd caught it earlier. She'd had treatment and it hadn't helped. So she refused. She thought the treatment would only make her sicker, even if only for a little while, and she didn't want to lose any time with me. So she chose to be a mother. She chose *me*.'

Jordan shrugged, the movement heavy with the weight he had been carrying. With the guilt.

'My dad hated her choice. He told me once that he'd begged her every day for those two years to get treatment, until finally he wore her down. And during that time my dad kept me at a distance. He wouldn't sit with her when she watched me play—would only agree to family time if she was there.'

Jordan wondered how his memories of the events he was talking about could be vague, but the feelings they evoked still sharp.

'He helped to take care of me physically—especially when my mom grew weaker, more ill—but he wouldn't be a father to me. Not a real one. But he was the *best* husband, and even at my age I knew that he loved her more than anything. By the time she agreed to treatment it was too late.'

He felt her move closer to him, and welcomed the comfort her presence brought.

'She spent her last year in agony, going through a cycle of chemo and radiation, until finally my dad brought her home and she died in her sleep a few days later.'

'It wasn't your fault,' she said, in a voice thick with emotion.

'I didn't think so until…'

This was probably one of the worst parts, he thought, but he pushed through.

'For years after my mom died, I felt like I was walking on eggshells. My father was testy most of the time, and I just got used to trying to make myself invisible at home. But at school, I acted out. And one day…' He took a deep breath. 'One day I did something I can't even remember any more and my dad got called in to school. I remember he sat there, listening to my teacher, and I saw the tic just above his eye. I didn't know what that meant then, but when I got home…'

He paused, then forced himself to say the words.

'The anger that my dad had built up since my mom had died came spilling out of his mouth.' Jordan's jaw clenched. 'He told me that if it hadn't been for me my mom wouldn't have died. He said that it was *my* fault, that she had foregone treatment because of me, and that it had all been for nothing since I was just a bratty, ungrateful child.'

Jordan stopped for a moment, composing himself.

'He said some other things that night—I think most of them things he blamed himself for. He broke down immediately afterwards and apologised, over and over again. It was grief, mixed with anger and regret, but I've never forgotten how seeing my distant father break down felt. Or…' he turned to her now '…how it affected me.'

He could see the sadness gleaming in her eyes, and he waited for resentment to boil up in him at the sight of it.

But it never came, and he realised that the only thing he felt was her support.

'I always wondered why things were so difficult between you two,' she said after a while, and she walked over until she was next to him and took his hand.

The warmth of her gesture of comfort immediately flowed through him, and he tightened his grip. 'I didn't think you'd noticed.'

She let out a slight laugh. 'It was hard not to. I always thought it was because of him.'

'Why?'

'He was a difficult man, Jordan. He didn't show his emotions, didn't say what he thought, and most of the time when he spoke it sounded like a military command.'

Floored, he looked down at her. 'I thought you *liked* him?'

'I loved him,' she corrected. 'He was kind to me, and in his own way he showed me he cared for me. I *loved* him,' she repeated, and he could hear the grief in her voice, 'but that doesn't mean I didn't see his flaws.'

He nodded, and there was a silence as they both thought about his father. As he thought about the fact that he needed to continue with his story.

'He only became the man you're talking about after that night. But even then he wasn't perfect, and I spent my whole life believing that my mother's death was my fault.'

'Your father was angry, Jordan. He was grieving for a woman he had loved with all of him and for the life he thought he would get to live. He didn't mean what he said, *or* the things he did.'

'But she *did* choose me, Mila,' he said softly.

'Exactly. *She* did. You had absolutely no say over the choices she made, Jordan. Don't keep blaming yourself for something you didn't have any control over.' She wrapped an arm around him. 'It won't help.'

Somewhere in his mind her words resonated, and he said, 'I didn't want to see you suffer like she did.'

She looked up at him, her eyes wide. '*That's* why you left?'

'I didn't think so at first. I thought I was doing the right thing.' He stopped, wondering how he was having all the most difficult conversations of his life within the space of an hour. 'But I've realised over the last few days that that *was* why I left. Why I ran.'

Her arm was still around him, though he could feel it slacken.

You deserve it for being a coward, he thought, but it didn't make the pain of her pulling away any easier.

Still he continued. If she was going to leave—if she was going to move on—it wouldn't be because he hadn't fought for her with all his might.

'It was also because I was…*angry*. I couldn't deal with the loss of our son.'

It was his biggest regret about his father's death—that he hadn't been able to tell Greg that he understood the grieving. He had been too young with his mother, but losing his son… Finally Jordan had understood how irrational grief could be.

'I got angry at you for pushing me away, and it…it scared me. I thought I was turning into my father. Even after the anger had dulled I thought it was for the best that I didn't come back, that I didn't fight for us. Because I didn't want to wake up one day and blame you for something that wasn't your fault. I didn't want to treat you like my father had treated me.'

He paused.

'It wasn't your fault, Mila,' he said again, because he thought she needed to know. 'The fall had nothing to do with you not slowing down. You would have had plenty of time to do that later. We *both* would have.' He turned to her. 'You need to let go of whatever's still inside you that thinks the accident was your fault.'

With eyes full of tears, she nodded, and his heart settled at the knowledge of what they'd just shared. He had finally told her everything, and he hoped he had got her to forgive herself. If she chose to leave now, she would leave free of the weight of the past. But still he wished she wouldn't leave, and his heart sank when she pulled away, convinced that she had given up on him.

So much so that he looked up in surprise when he saw she was in front of him.

She took both of his hands in hers. 'I wish you'd told me about this a long time ago.'

'I couldn't.'

'And I wouldn't have been in the right space to listen,' she agreed, and then took a deep breath. 'It makes sense now. All of it.'

'But does it change anything?' he asked hopefully, and a familiar expression shone in her eyes. One he hadn't seen in almost a year.

'I…I think that depends on you.'

The glimmer of affection in her eyes that he'd seen just before gave way to seriousness.

'Are you still angry at me?'

'No, not any more. I understand why you pushed me away. I understand *you* better, too.'

She gave him a small smile. 'Do you still blame yourself for your mom?'

'I…' He took a breath. 'I think it'll take some time—just like I think it will for you not to blame yourself for the baby—but we'll get there.'

She nodded, gripping his hands tightly. 'You won't turn into your father, Jordan, so I won't even ask if you still believe you will.'

'How do you *know*?'

'Because I know *you*. You're strong, and when you're not afraid...' she squeezed his hand '...you're the most considerate man I know.' She paused, and then dropped his hands to slide her arms around his waist. 'And because you have me, and I will make sure that you don't turn into an angry, bitter person. Our little grape wouldn't have wanted that for his father.'

His heart filled at her words. 'You're staying with me?'

'If you want me, I'd really like to.'

'I don't want you, Mila. I *need* you.' He pulled her in tighter and felt the part of him that had been broken heal. 'I love you so much.'

'I love *you*,' she replied, and when she pulled back her eyes were gleaming with tears.

'Don't cry,' he said gently, wiping her cheeks.

'They're happy tears,' she whispered. 'I didn't dare imagine this was possible when you came back, but my heart hoped it would be.'

'Mine, too,' he said, knowing that his heart was only full when he was with her.

'And we'll face everything we go through now together.'

'I promise.' He stopped, and then said gently, 'I want us to have another baby.'

He watched her, saw the fear.

'Not right now. When we're ready—when we've taken the time to *be* ready. You're going to be a wonderful mother, and I want a chance to be a good father. And a good husband to my pregnant wife.'

He smiled, lifted her chin. Noted that the fear had turned into longing.

'We can be a *family*, Mila.'

Another tear slipped down her face. 'It sounds perfect.' And then she smiled. 'How about we seal this with a kiss?'

He laughed and leaned down to kiss her, vowing that he wouldn't spoil his second chance at love with the woman who had always owned his heart.

CHAPTER SEVENTEEN

MILA FELT JORDAN'S hand tighten on hers and she sent him a grateful smile. It was the morning of their event—just over a week since their reconciliation—and she'd told Jordan that she wanted to visit their son's grave. She'd only ever been to the grave twice—when they'd buried him, and when they'd buried Greg. But after spending the past week talking with Jordan, sharing things that they hadn't shared with anyone else before, rebuilding their trust and fortifying the foundations of their new relationship, she finally found herself ready.

It didn't seem right to go through the event without doing it first, so they'd driven over and were now standing just in front of the path that would take them to the grave.

Except now, of course, her legs felt like lead and she didn't think she could do it.

'We can do this,' Jordan said, and she looked over, wondering if she had spoken out loud.

He threaded his fingers through hers and squeezed again, and she returned the pressure, knowing that he was just as nervous as she was. Probably even more so, since it was the first time he'd been back after his father's funeral, too.

Together they walked down the path that led to the family plot Greg had bought after his wife had died. He'd wanted to make sure that the Thomas family would always be together, even in death.

She slid an arm around Jordan's waist when they stopped in front of the first tombstone—made of the most expensive marble—which told her that Jade Thomas, Jordan's mother, had only lived until she was forty.

Way too young, she thought, thinking about how much time with her Greg had been robbed of…how early Jordan had lost her. She knew from losing her own parents how growing up without them could hurt. Perhaps it hurt even more, she considered, when you actually knew them.

'She would have been proud of you,' she said, leaning her head against Jordan's shoulder.

He lifted his arm and pulled her in closer. 'Even though I didn't look after my dad like she asked?' he said, but it was half-hearted, and she knew it reflected habit more than what he believed now.

'I think she would understand,' Mila replied softly, knowing that the tales she'd told Jordan about his mother—the ones Greg had shared with her in his rare open moments—confirmed her words. Jade had been a lovely woman: stubborn, like all the Thomases, but with just as big a heart as her son.

'I think she would, too,' Jordan said eventually, and they walked a few steps further to the front of Greg's grave. It was identical to Jordan's mother's, except that the words were about Greg.

'"Loving husband and father. You will be missed,"' she read aloud, and smiled. 'It's perfect, Jordan.' Her throat closed, but she smiled up at him. 'He *did* love you. Just in his own way.'

'I know.' Jordan laid a hand on the tomb and she waited, knowing that he needed time. 'I know that you loved me, Dad. I wish we could speak just one more time, so I could tell you I love you, too. So that I could tell you I understand now, and that I forgive you.' He took a shaky breath. 'But I think you already know that.'

Mila's heart broke for him, but she knew that it was healthy. It wouldn't do for him to keep it all in any more.

When he didn't say anything else, Mila said, 'Thank you for everything, Greg.' That was enough, she thought, but then she remembered something else. 'Especially for the will. Seems like your plan was right all along.'

They smiled at each other, and then took a few more moments to say goodbye. The overwhelming grief she had felt since Greg's death dulled to a throb in her heart, and that told her it would be okay. She and Jordan would be okay.

The tiny little tombstone that stood above the grave next to Greg's still broke her heart, though.

The name they'd decided on and had engraved that week was bold in grey against the black marble stone. Below the name was a black-and-white picture of her and Jordan on the day she had given birth—they both had tears on their faces, and were both clearly heartbroken, but she had her son in her arms and it was their only family photo.

The dates on his tombstone were the date they'd found out they were expecting their child and the date they'd lost him. And below that was an inscription.

You were the light of our lives.
A light that will stay in our hearts for ever.

'I still have that image of you in my head—you with our son in your arms...the absolute devastation and love on your face.' He sucked in air, and she felt the sucker punch of his emotions—*their* emotions—right down to her gut.

'Me, too. But with your face.'

She spoke because something inside her compelled her to. Perhaps because it was the first time they could acknowledge it together.

'The dreams I have are about that moment a lot. I had

only just felt him alive inside me, and then when I could see him he wasn't.' She was whispering now, her voice no longer willing to say the words that told her the wound inside her was still fresh. 'I'm so glad you got to hold him while he was still alive.'

They clung to each other, and though she knew she was still healing she felt the glimmer of hope that sharing that moment with the only person who knew what she was going through had brought. Suddenly she was even more grateful for their second chance.

We'll do it right this time, baby, she told her son, and her lips curved even through the tears.

'He knows how much we love him.' Jordan's voice was raw as he spoke, but she saw the hope she felt inside reflected in his eyes.

'He does. I'm sure our parents tell him that every day.'

The thought of their family together made her smile widen.

'Yeah...' He looked down at her. 'I think so, too.'

It was a long time before either of them spoke again, but finally Jordan said, 'We should get going. Karen will probably be there for the soundcheck soon.'

They headed back to the car together, and before she climbed in Mila looked back one more time. 'We'll visit them again soon, won't we?'

Jordan kissed her hair. 'Of course.'

She smiled at him, and couldn't help but think that the people they had visited would have loved it that she and Jordan were a family again.

'I'm sweating like a pig,' Lulu said, and fanned herself with the clipboard that she insisted on using for her tasks instead of the tablet Mila was using.

Mila laughed, grabbing a bottle of water from the ice bucket behind the stage that Karen had walked out onto a few minutes ago and handed it to her friend.

'The perks of growing a life inside you!'

Mila found she could say that now, after that morning, without a piercing pain going through her body. It was more like a dull ache in her heart that reminded her of her child, just like her significantly lowered fear of stairs. The necessity of this event had helped her overcome *that* fear, but she knew it was more than that, too. It was knowing that she *could* do it that helped her do it. And because of the person who had helped her reach that realisation.

'No!' Lulu said after gurgling down half the bottle. 'There is *no way* you can tell me that you're not getting as hot as I am.'

'Honey, it's eighteen degrees. We've spent the past half an hour handing out blankets to our guests and setting up the outside heaters. You *know* it's only you.'

'Maybe it's because I've been running around for the past week.'

'And you know I love you for it. Especially when you look at how amazingly it's turned out.'

She peeped out from the tent they had assembled back-stage—just as they had for the first event—and a smile spread on her face.

The amphitheatre held about two hundred fifty people, which was about a hundred more than she had been ex-pecting. Most of them were only there for Karen, but that didn't matter since they had all still bought food from the vendors, still purchased wine from the vineyard. They had managed to set up the marquee so that it had more than enough space for everyone, and as she looked up she was treated to a stunning view of the stars.

'It seems like a success.'

A voice broke through her thoughts and she turned to see Mark standing there, with a briefcase in one hand and some papers in the other, with Jordan behind him.

Her heart immediately responded to him being there,

and she smiled at him before nervously asking Mark, 'Did we tick all the boxes?'

Mark pulled his glasses down from the top of his head and read from the paper in front of him. 'Well, your event *is* "under the stars"—excellent improvisation, by the way—and you have the same performer, you're screening the same movie, you have most of the vendors from the original event, and you've provided me with all the documentation for those who couldn't make it, as well as for their replacements. And you've done this all within the time limit.'

Mark removed his glasses.

'So I would say, yes. Congratulations, you two, you're officially the owners of Greg's share of the vineyard. I'll send the paperwork through in the coming weeks.'

Mark excused himself, and as soon as he was gone, Lulu let out a hoot.

'This is wonderful news, you guys!' She hugged them both, then waved a hand. 'But, much as I would like to celebrate with you, my bladder is telling me there are things that take a slightly higher priority at the moment.'

She winked at Jordan before she waddled off, and though that puzzled her Mila jumped into Jordan's arms the minute they were alone.

'We did it!' she said, her body sighing in contentment as soon as it touched his.

'We did.' He pulled back, and the look on his face made her heart thud.

'What's wrong?'

'There's just something... Actually, I can take care of it myself. I'll just run up to the house...'

He was already starting up the stairs by the time she'd processed his words, and in a bit of a panic she followed him.

'Jordan!' she called when they were far enough from the concert that they wouldn't be heard. 'Wait!'

She was out of breath when she finally caught up with him, and she rested her hands against her knees when she saw that he'd stopped.

'Why wouldn't you just wait for me?' she puffed, and then straightened. 'What's the problem—'

She broke off when she saw where they were, and a smile spread across her face.

'You are such a sneaky—'

He cut her off with a quick kiss, and then grinned as he pulled back.

'Surprise!' he said, and pushed open the gate to the place where they'd picnicked that very first night.

A blanket was spread out, just as it had been then, but this time there was a fire burning in the pit that had been created just in front of it. A bottle of Thomas Vineyard red wine was placed next to two glasses, and a variety of foods similar to those he'd had there the first time sat next to that.

'It's perfect,' she said with a smile as she turned towards him—and froze when she saw him kneeling in front of her.

'What are you *doing*?' she gasped. 'I've already told you I wouldn't file the papers.'

'I want to begin our second chance together properly, Mila.'

The teasing glint in his eyes was gone, replaced by a sincerity that sent a tear down her cheek.

'I can't live my life without you. I want you—and I need you—by my side for ever. I want to have a family with you, and I want to love you and our family unconditionally. Will you give me the chance to do that?'

She nodded, unable to speak, and he grinned.

'I'm not done yet.'

He pulled a ring from his pocket, and her heart skipped when she saw it was the one he'd proposed with the first time. The one she had put in a jewellery box the day she'd received the divorce papers and tried never to think about again.

'Be my wife again, Mila. And not only because we're still married.' He smiled. 'Marry me again.'

'Yes, of course—yes!' she said, and he slid the ring onto her finger.

She smiled at its familiar weight.

'I know the perfect time and the perfect place,' she said, and hooked her arms around his neck.

He grinned. 'Me, too. But until then…'

He kissed her, and she melted against him.

EPILOGUE

Two days later, on their second wedding anniversary, Mila stood in a long white dress covered in lace. Lulu beamed at her as she lowered the veil over Mila's face and dabbed at a tear that had fallen down her cheek.

'I'm such a mess!' Lulu said with a hiccup, and Mila smiled teasingly.

'The joys of—'

'Growing a life inside you—I know.' Lulu rolled her eyes and then smiled. 'I'm so happy for you.'

Mila laid a shaky hand on her stomach. 'Me, too.'

They walked the short distance from the house to the chapel where she and Jordan had made their vows two years before. And although she was wearing the same ring and the same dress as the first time they'd got married, *she* was a different person. She was someone who was more confident, who only cared about the opinions of those who loved her. And she was standing on her own this time.

Though she would have done anything to be walking down the aisle with Greg again, being on her own was oddly comforting. It represented the fact that she *could* be on her own if she needed to. But now she was walking towards the man who had promised her that she would never have to be alone again.

She didn't take her eyes off him as she walked down the short aisle, her heart thumping at how handsome he looked in his suit. And then it was just the two of them, standing in front of the altar, making their promises to one another.

'I can't believe how lucky I am to have you in my life again,' she began, and tears welled up in her eyes. 'You have shown me how it feels to be loved, to be needed. You have given me the family I've never had. You have helped me grow into someone I didn't know I could be. Into someone who is willing to hope after hurt, who is willing to open her heart to the possibilities of the future when shutting everyone out would be so much easier.'

She squeezed his hands, felt the tears run down her face now.

'We have been through the worst of times together. But because I look at you now and see how much stronger you are—*we* are—and how our love has grown stronger because of it, I know that we can face anything together. And I believe that the best of times are still to come.'

His eyes gleamed, but he cleared his throat and said, 'Mila, I am a different man because of *you*. You've helped me unload the baggage I came into this relationship with. And what I have left I know you'll help me carry.'

He smiled at her, brushed a hair out of her face, and she leaned into his touch.

'I promise to stay with you through good times and bad. I promise to love you with all that is in me and put our relationship first. You mean the world to me, and I can't wait to have a family with you. To show our children what love's supposed to be. No matter what we go through, I will be there for you. Thank you for giving us a second chance.'

They kissed, and she felt it solidify their promises, their declarations of love for each other.

As they walked out of the chapel Mila leaned over to Jordan. 'Do you think this is what your father wanted all along?'

Jordan smiled down at her, and her heart warmed at

the look in his eyes. 'Absolutely. And I can't thank him enough.'

She laughed when he scooped her into his arms, and as she placed her head on his shoulder she knew she was finally living the life she had dreamed of.

* * * * *

If you loved this story, don't miss
THE TYCOON'S RELUCTANT CINDERELLA,
the debut novel by Therese Beharrie.
Available now!

If you want to read about another emotional
second-chance romance make sure to indulge in
THE MARRIAGE OF INCONVENIENCE
by Nina Singh.

"I remember the time your father told me he would skin me alive if he ever caught me with one of his daughters. Scared the living daylights out of me."

A slice of surprise caught at her. "I didn't know he'd warned you off. So that's why you didn't give any of us a second look."

"Oh, I took more than a second look. I just made sure you didn't know it. There were plenty of times I thought about you long after my polite, Jedediah-approved chats with you."

Vivian saw the dark hunger in his eyes she'd been sure she'd imagined all those years ago and her heart started to hammer in her chest while her stomach took a big dip. It was as if she was fifteen again and all she wanted was for Benjamin to look at her. And maybe want her a little so she didn't feel like such a fool.

Benjamin lowered his mouth, inch by excruciating inch. She could hardly breathe and thinking was out of the question. When his lips touched hers, she couldn't stop a soft sigh. He must have taken that as an affirmation because then he slid his hand behind her neck and deepened the pressure, exploring her mouth as if he'd been waiting a long time.

Vivian felt herself sinking into the taste and sensation of his hunger. Her body reacted like lightning, taking her completely off guard.

* * *

Honeymoon Mountain:
Love on a hilltop!

HONEYMOON
MOUNTAIN BRIDE

BY
LEANNE BANKS

First Published in Great Britain 2017
By Mills & Boon, an imprint of HarperCollins*Publishers*
1 London Bridge Street, London, SE1 9GF

© 2017 Leanne Banks

ISBN: 978-0-263-92305-6

23-0617

Our policy is to use papers that are natural, renewable and recyclable products and made from wood grown in sustainable forests. The logging and manufacturing processes conform to the legal environmental regulations of the country of origin.

Printed and bound in Spain
by CPI, Barcelona

Leanne Banks is a *New York Times* and *USA TODAY* bestselling author with over sixty-eight books to her credit. Leanne loves her family, the beach and chocolate. You can reach her at www.leannebanks.com.

This book is dedicated to all of you who
encouraged me to write it and finish it!
You know who you are!

Chapter One

"To Dad," Vivian Jackson said, lifting her glass of cheap wine as she looked beyond the dock to the blue waters of the North Carolina lake. "Peaceful sailing."

"Catch the big one," her sister Temple said, lifting her glass.

"To Dad," her youngest sister, Jillian, said. "Drop that eight-point buck with one shot right between the eyes."

Vivian winced at the image but knew her father, Jedediah Jackson, the son of a son of a sailor, retired navy himself and hunter/fisher extraordinaire, would approve.

Although Vivian had never quite thought she'd measured up to her father's expectations, she felt a painful sense of loss. "I almost can't believe he's really gone. I expect him to come down that hill from the lodge with a bait box and two fishing poles, telling me not to be afraid of worms and insects and not to throw the pole in the water when I get a little bite on the line."

"He didn't always know what to do with girls. I think he was hoping for a son," Temple said.

"I'm as close as he got," Jillian said.

Vivian couldn't help but chuckle at her sister's statement. With a bombshell body, bad-girl-red lips, smoky eyes and wild ways with men, platinum blonde Jilly had caused more than her share of their dear dad's indigestion.

"Not close at all," Temple muttered and moved her glass of wine from one hand to the other. She cleared her throat. "I hate to be a mood-killer, but I think we all know what we need to do with the lodge."

Vivian felt a twinge of pain at giving up the lodge, even though it was the practical thing to do. "I didn't think it would bother me," she said, feeling a flood of memories rush through her. Staying with her father in the summers had meant she could get dirty without her mother becoming upset. Vivian had experienced her first crush here at Honeymoon Mountain Lake. The memory was more humiliating than sweet, but she didn't want to give it all away. "Or maybe I just hoped it wouldn't bother me."

Temple gave her a considering glance from behind her glasses. "But you do agree we should sell it.

As it is, it's a money pit. The cabins and main house are in disrepair, and I don't think any of us wants to sink our life's savings into it. Plus, Dad canceled all reservations once he got truly sick. I'm not sure we'll get our regulars back since they had to find another resort for their vacations."

"He was sicker than we realized," Vivian said, feeling regret that she hadn't caught on to his illness. But she was certain Temple, an accountant and financial planner, had done her homework on the best options for their inheritance.

Jilly nodded and tossed back the rest of her wine. "I'm just glad we all got to see him during that last month he was alive. Makes me believe in fate and luck." She sighed. "I have practical skills in many areas, but not enough money to save the lodge."

"Then we're agreed," Temple said. "We're selling it. We may have to accept a low offer due to the condition of the property."

"I didn't ever expect to get any money out of it, anyway," Jilly said.

Vivian put her arm around her youngest sister. Jilly talked and acted tough, but she had a tender heart about some things.

"I'll find a real estate agent, but someone needs to tell the full-time employees." Temple looked expectantly at Vivian.

Vivian frowned. "Why me?"

"You're the oldest," Temple said.

"What does that have to do with anything? In fact, I think you would be the perfect one to deliver the news since you're so eager to get rid of the lodge."

"I don't like it any more than you two do, but someone has to be practical, and as usual, that someone is me," Temple said. "I don't want to overthink or overfeel this."

Vivian understood what Temple was saying. Even though Temple could seem cold and calculating, underneath it all, she was suffering, too.

Vivian took a deep breath. "Okay, I'll do it," she said. "But it's not going to be fun. Do you think we'll be able to find a home for Jet?" she asked, thinking of her father's hound dog.

"It's gonna be tough. Maybe Grayson will take him." Grayson was the lodge's handyman and bartender. Temple extended her glass toward Vivian. "You want my wine?"

Vivian rolled her eyes. "This is going to be hard." She hated to think about how the permanent workers would receive the news. After all, they'd been more like family than employees.

"Wish me luck," Vivian said, snatching Temple's glass and downing the contents.

"Luck," Temple and Jilly said together, but Vivian felt not a lick of comfort.

Vivian winced at the bittersweet taste of the cheap wine. As much as she wished differently, the alcohol content wouldn't build her fortitude. She would have to find it in herself.

"Here we go," Vivian muttered and trudged up the hill to the lodge. Grayson and Millicent, the housekeeper, had worked at the lodge before her father had taken it over when his father passed away. It didn't seem fair that the two of them should be booted off the property at this point, but Vivian felt it was only right to give them as much warning as possible. She and her sisters could request that Millicent and Grayson remain employed by the new owner for a limited time, but any reprieve would be temporary.

Climbing the steps to the large dock furnished with all-weather chairs and three well-worn tables with umbrellas, she paused and took a deep breath. She could do this, she told herself. She *would* do this.

Vivian's discussion with Millicent and Grayson hadn't gone well. Both had started to cry. Grayson revealed both he and Millie had spent their retirement savings at a casino. Millie grew so restless Vivian feared the woman was going to break down.

Distraught, Millie requested that Vivian drive her into town to provide a diversion. An hour and a half later, Vivian had carted Millie to the new big-box store, a wine shop and a convenience store to buy lottery tickets. "I need as much luck as ever after today," Millie said as she got back in the car. "I just want to make one more stop. A couple of beers with my friends should cheer me up. Honeymoon Bar."

Vivian twitched at Millie's final request. Years and years had passed, but when they were teens, Vivian had once suffered a major crush on the man who now owned the Honeymoon Bar. She remembered the summer she'd done her best to get Benjamin Hunter's attention. All to no avail. She felt the heat of embarrassment as she remembered his rejection.

"You sure you don't want to go back to the lodge?" Vivian asked. "You have wine."

"That won't help me like a visit with friends," Millie said. "I won't be long. Just a beer or two."

Vivian stopped to let Millie out at the front door, then parked along the street. Perhaps she could just sit in the car and kill some time checking her email. Pulling out her cell phone, she answered messages and deleted all the useless, impersonal advertisements. She glanced at the outside of the bar again and drummed her fingertips on her steering wheel.

So, what was she going to do? Hide in her car for an hour because she was afraid of coming face-to-face with Benjamin Hunter? That was ridiculous. She was a grown woman. She'd dated several men since then, even gotten married, although that had been a disaster from which she was still recovering.

Shaking her head at herself, she pulled together a molecule of the gumption she'd inherited from her father, strode into the bar and looked around. Millicent, along with a small group of people, sat at a table. A few men sat at the bar while they sipped their beers and watched the game on the wide-screen television. An older man tended the bar.

No sign of Benjamin. Her twinge of disappointment irritated her. Stepping deeper into the large room decorated with sports photos and memorabilia, she noticed a sign—Outdoor Seating. The idea appealed to her. After the events of the day, she felt as if the walls were starting to close in on her. She wandered outside and approved of the wrought iron tables and still-green plants and small trees, a courtyard at odds with the good ol' boy bar.

Sinking into one of the chairs at a table, she let out the pent-up breath she'd been holding for way too long. She drew in the scent of a moonflower blooming as the sun began to set and closed her eyes to savor the peaceful moment.

"Would you care for something to drink or eat?" a voice asked, drawing out of her reverie.

Vivian blinked and nodded at the female server. "White wine," she said, assuming the choices were minimal. "Whatever you have."

The server proceeded to name an impressive list. "Pinot Grigio and water," Vivian said. "Thank you."

"I'll be right back," the server said, then walked into the bar.

Vivian raised her eyebrows. Benjamin had definitely made the bar more classy. The last time she'd sneaked in here, she remembered the place as rough and rowdy. Not so tonight. Then again, it was Thursday night. Maybe the weekends were different.

No matter, she thought. Maybe she should take the moment to take a breath. Leaning back in her chair, she closed her eyes again and heard the distant sound of the ball game on TV, but also the sound of a soft breeze rippling the leaves. She concentrated on that, enjoying the peacefulness. But then her restlessness grabbed at her again and she stood, wandering around the small courtyard.

"Pinot Grigio," a deep male voice said, and she instantly knew it was Benjamin.

Vivian turned around and stared into the brown eyes of Benjamin Hunter. She took in the whole of him in one glance. Unfortunately, he had not become soft and potbellied. In fact, he was leaner and harder than she remembered, and somehow his shoulders seemed even broader.

"Hi, Vivian," he said, giving her glass to her as he studied her face. "I'm sorry about Jedediah."

She swallowed and tried to find her voice. Why did she suddenly feel fifteen again? "Thanks. I got to see him a week before he passed. None of us really realized how sick he was even though he made sure we all came to see him," she said and took a sip of her wine.

"He told me," Benjamin said.

A slice of resentment cut through her. "He did?"

"Just a few days before he passed. He made me swear not to tell anyone."

She took a deep breath and nodded. "That sounds like him. I'm just glad my sisters and I got to see him one last time. We're here this weekend, too. Since he didn't want any kind of memorial service, we toasted his memory on the dock."

"That's what he would have wanted," Benjamin said.

"I know," she said. "It just feels odd not to have an official service."

"I think he liked the idea of drifting away. People are going to miss him. He taught me a lot about fishing and some about being a man. Since my father wasn't around much, that counted for a lot. Lord knows I could have gotten into a lot more trouble than I did." Benjamin chuckled to himself. "I remember the time he told me he would skin me alive if he ever caught me with one of his daughters. Scared the living daylights out of me."

Surprise caught her off guard. "I didn't know he'd warned you off. So that's why you didn't give any of us a second look."

"Oh, I took more than a second look. I just made sure you didn't know it. There were plenty of times I thought about you long after my polite Jedediah-approved chats with you."

Vivian saw the dark hunger in his eyes she'd been sure she'd imagined all those years ago, and her heart started to hammer in her chest while her stomach took a big dip. It was as if she was fifteen again and all she wanted was for Benjamin to look at her. And maybe want her a little so she didn't feel like such a fool.

"I always regretted not…" His voice trailed off. "No one here to throw me in the lake. I'd say we're overdue. What's one kiss?"

Vivian stared at him in shock. He wasn't really going to—

Benjamin lowered his mouth, inch by excruciating inch. She could hardly breathe, and thinking was out of the question. When his lips touched hers, she couldn't stop a soft sigh. He must have taken that as an affirmation, because then he slid his hand behind her neck, deepened the pressure and explored her mouth as if he'd been waiting a long time.

Vivian felt herself sinking into the taste and sensation of his hunger. Her body reacted like lightning, taking her completely off guard.

"Mr. Hunter," a male voice called from behind Benjamin, throwing cold reality at her.

Vivian stumbled, backing away and staring at Benjamin. She didn't know if she was more surprised by his action or her reaction to him.

Not turning from her, Benjamin responded. "Yeah, what do you need?"

"You got a phone call. Somebody wants to hold a party here," the server said.

Benjamin glanced over his shoulder. "Thanks. Take a message. Get the number. Tell them I'll call right back."

He turned back to Vivian, and she was thankful the darkness would cover the heat in her cheeks. "I—uh, I need to go. I just brought Millicent into town because her car isn't working properly." She tugged at her purse. "I'll just pay for my wine."

"It's on me," he said.

She took another deep breath, still trying to get rid of her jitteriness. "Thank you. I'll be going, then."

"I look forward to seeing you around town," he said.

She shook her head. "No. My sisters and I have decided to sell the lodge."

He lifted his eyebrows. "Sorry to hear that."

"Yeah, no," she said, discombobulated. She needed to get away.

Chapter Two

"I'm glad I stopped in to see my friends at the bar. Cheered me up. I coulda used just one more beer," Millicent said, her words slightly slurred.

Vivian thought Millicent appeared to be quite relaxed, so she tried to make easy conversation. "I haven't visited the bar in years. It looks like Benjamin has made several changes."

"Oh, yeah," Millicent said and hiccupped. "He's a go-getter. He would have made it far if his mother hadn't taken ill when he was in college. And then his sister…"

Benjamin's family was none of Vivian's business. "His sister?" she prodded, because she couldn't resist.

"Well," Millicent said, "she's gotten into trouble a few times."

"Hmm," Vivian said, remembering that Benjamin hadn't talked about his sister much when they were younger. "I saw him briefly at the bar."

"He's nice enough, but he gets one lady friend, then moves on to the next. I heard he was engaged a long time ago and got burned. Never recovered from it. He's handsome, but he's not the kind to rely on. Your father would tell you the same thing," she warned her.

Vivian, however, was filled with more questions and curiosity than ever. What did Benjamin's sister do to get into trouble? What had happened during his engagement? Who were all these lady friends?

And why did she care?

Vivian tamped down her curiosity and drove up the mountain to the lodge. She had enough on her mind. She didn't need to add Benjamin to the mix.

Benjamin returned to the bar, wondering what in hell had possessed him to kiss Vivian like that. She was still beautiful in a classy, natural way. Honey-blond hair, blue eyes, creamy skin that burned far too easily and a full pink mouth that had always tempted him. He shook his head. Must have been all those years of denial and restraint, he told himself, and picked up his messages as he headed for his office.

One message was from the McAllisters. They wanted to hold a party on a Sunday night. That would work, he thought. He just couldn't set aside Fridays or Saturdays unless it was a dead weekend.

The second message was from his sister. His heart clenched. "Please come get me," the voice mail from Eliza said. "I ran out of gas."

Benjamin took a deep breath. She seemed coherent. He could only hope she was okay.

Benjamin immediately responded to his sister's message. His stomach clenched as it always did. "Eliza," he said. "Are you okay?"

"I'm mostly good," she said. "But I decided to go for a ride and ran out of gas."

He stifled a groan. "Where are you?"

"I think I'm about twelve miles south of town," she said. "I'm on Route 33."

"Okay, I'll head out. How much charge do you have on your phone battery?"

"Not that much," she said. "Sorry. I just needed to take a drive. I was feeling cramped."

Benjamin nodded. He had heard this story before. "I'm coming for you. Don't use your phone for anything else."

He walked to his SUV and started toward Route 33. He hoped Eliza was okay, but she didn't seem overly panicked. She struggled with her illness, but she had seemed fairly even lately. Driving freed his mind from busy work enough to also think about his unexpected meeting with Vivian. Although he'd been tempted, he'd never thought he would kiss her. If he had, he'd never thought it would affect him after all this time. But it had. It damn well had.

He continued driving south on 33, but his mind

kept gravitating back to Vivian. Why had her lips felt so good beneath his? Why did he want to kiss her again? No single encounter with a woman had affected him like this in a long time.

He shook off his thoughts. He would wake up tomorrow and put the whole thing aside. Right now, he needed to make sure his sister was okay.

Benjamin saw the headlights of his sister's vehicle on the side of the road and pulled over. He got out of his SUV with the gas can he kept in the back of his car and strode toward her, immediately filling her tank. "Are you sure you're okay?" he asked.

His younger sister was wide-eyed and restless, but she nodded. "I'm okay."

"You don't look it," he said.

She twisted her mouth. "I'm working on it."

"Next time, call me before you leave the house," he said, escorting her to her car.

"You ever just want to get in your car and drive forever?" she asked.

"Yeah, but there are people counting on me," he said.

"You've always been the responsible one," she said as she climbed into the driver's seat.

"You're getting there," Benjamin said. "You told me you're becoming. You're on a journey."

"Getting there?" she echoed with a laugh. "Sometimes I'm not sure about that."

"Becoming," he said. "You're becoming. We're all damn becoming."

She met his gaze and grinned. "You believe in me when you shouldn't."

"I believe in who you are becoming," he said. Someone had to believe in her so she could believe in herself.

"I'll keep working on it," she said. "Thanks for coming for me."

Benjamin took a deep breath, got in his car and followed his sister home. On the way, however, his lips burned as he remembered kissing Vivian. She tempted him now more than ever. More than that time she'd invited him into the lake to skinny-dip with her.

He gritted his teeth and shook his head. Vivian was not in his future. She wasn't for him. She never had been, and she never would be. He had responsibilities, and he'd learned the hard way when his fiancé had ditched him. His obligations and life in this small town would cramp the style of a Southern flower like Vivian.

After Vivian arrived at the lodge, she went to her room and took a shower. In other circumstances, this might have been an opportunity to reconnect with her sisters, but between her outing with Millicent and her encounter with Benjamin, she felt tapped out. All she wanted was a good night's rest. It took mere seconds for her to fall asleep.

A few hours later, a sharp rap on the door abruptly awakened her. Vivian jerked upright in her bed.

"Missy! There's been a fire," Grayson called from the other side of the door.

Panic raced through her. "Oh, no. Please come in. What's wrong?"

The door opened and Grayson lifted his hands in distress. "There's a fire. One of the cabins is burning."

"No! No!" Alarm hit her like icy water. "Did you dial emergency?"

"The fire department is on the way, but I don't know if they'll get here in time."

"Let me get dressed and I'll come right out." Grayson left the room and she traded her pajamas for a pair of jeans, T-shirt and jacket.

Vivian raced down the hall past Grayson and pounded on Temple's room. Within a few seconds, Temple jerked open her door. "What's going on?"

"A fire in one of the cabins," Vivian said. "Get Jillian."

Vivian raced out the back door of the lodge, down the steps and across the back lawn to the cabin that was burning. She stared at it, wishing she could douse the fire. Thank goodness there were no guests. Surely she could do something.

Before she knew it, she felt Temple grab one of her hands. Jillian took her other hand. She stared at the fire and knew her sisters were staring into it, too.

"Why is it taking so long for the fire department to get here?" Jillian asked.

"We're too far away," Vivian said. "Up the mountain, and they're down in the valley."

"They should be able to get here faster," Jilly said helplessly.

She and her sisters clung to each other as they watched the cabin burn. A fire engine finally arrived and sprayed the cabin, but it was too late. The cabin was a smoldering ruin.

Vivian couldn't explain it, but her heart was broken. Grayson came to her and shook his head. "I'm so sorry. I tried to keep everything in the lodge up to code, but the last couple of years, Jedediah didn't want to overspend on the cabins, and he just didn't seem to have the energy."

Vivian took a deep breath. She knew the wiring for the cabins was primitive at best. She put her hand on his. "I'm just glad no one was in there tonight."

Grayson nodded. A fireman approached her and Grayson, asked a few questions, filled out a report and left.

Exhausted, Vivian returned to the lodge with her sisters.

"Let's have something to eat," Jillian said and urged the three of them to the kitchen.

"I'm not that hungry," Vivian said.

"Neither am I," Temple added.

"You will be in a few minutes," Jillian said and placed a pan on the stove top. Soon she was frying potatoes, bacon and eggs. She placed plates in front of Vivian and Temple, then served herself.

Vivian tried but couldn't take a bite. She closed

her eyes and opened them. "I'm not sure I want to sell," she whispered.

"I don't want to, either," Jilly said and shoveled a forkful of food into her mouth.

Temple gaped at both of them. "Are you out of your minds? This place is a money pit."

"Maybe. Probably," Vivian said. "But I can't let it go yet. Especially after tonight. The whole place feels like an elderly relative and I can't stand to see the whole place go down. We couldn't save Dad. Maybe we can save the lodge."

"Even though we may need to fix the wiring in the cabins?" Temple asked.

Vivian's stomach twisted because she knew Temple was the most financially astute of the three of them. "Yep," she said.

Temple groaned. "Everything about this is wrong. I've studied this six ways from Sunday, and we're going to have a very tough trip to make it successful."

"So, you're saying we *can* make it successful," Jilly said.

Temple frowned at her. "It's an outside chance."

"I think it's a chance I have to take," Vivian said.

"Me, too," Jilly said and shoveled another big bite into her mouth.

Temple sighed, looking from one of them to the other. "Well. Against my better judgment."

"You're in," Jilly said, clapping her hands.

"Let her finish," Vivian said. "I want to hear her say it."

Temple sighed. "I'm in."

"Yay," Jilly said, and gave a hoot of victory.

"That said, I'll be watching every nickel and dime," Temple warned. "Every nickel and dime."

"I guess that means I can't write off pedicures," Jilly said.

Vivian snickered, but Temple squeezed her forehead as if she were in pain.

After an extensive discussion with a local electrician, it appeared that all the cabins might require rewiring and possible plumbing repairs. The job of fixing one cabin was growing by the minute. Vivian went into town, concerned because the man she'd called wouldn't commit to putting a priority on the full project if necessary. Plus there was the issue of choosing new fixtures to replace the out-of-date ones.

She walked into the Honeymoon Hardware store and headed toward the electrical section. Staring at the array of fixtures, she felt overwhelmed. There were even more choices here than online.

"Hey, how ya doing?" asked a male voice from behind her.

Vivian's stomach clenched. She knew that voice. She knew it was Benjamin's. She took a deep breath before she turned to face him. "Hello. What are you doing here?" she asked.

"I could ask the same," he said. "I'm picking up some paint for the kitchen at the bar. What about you?"

"I can't decide on anything. And I need a faster electrician."

"I can help with that," Benjamin said. "I've got the fastest electrician in town."

"How did you find him?" she asked. "Everyone wants to charge us extra because we live on the mountain."

"Give the guy a room while he does the work," Benjamin said. "He can enjoy the amenities when he's off the clock."

Vivian blinked. "Why didn't I think of that?"

"Because you don't fish or hunt," he said.

Her stomach took a dip as she looked at him, but she sure didn't want that response. "I guess you're right. But I still need to choose the fixtures."

"Choose the most long-lasting, not the prettiest," he told her. "Just a thought," he added.

Vivian nodded. Sounded like words of wisdom to her. She made notes as she walked down the aisle.

"I heard about the fire. Sorry."

"Thank you. It was upsetting to say the least."

"Tough timing," he said.

She nodded. "So," she said, feeling a bit awkward, "I didn't get to ask you about how you've been. The bar seems to be doing well. What about you?"

"I'm good," he said. "I've purchased a couple of businesses other than the bar, so that keeps me busy."

"What about your sister?" she asked, remembering what Millie had told her.

Benjamin seemed to freeze.

Vivian took a big step backward internally and gave a shrug. "I have two sisters and you have a sister, and I thought it was just considerate to ask about yours. I never met her because I was always at the lake."

His shoulders lowered just a bit. "She's doing okay."

"Millicent told me your sister is creative and artistic. Maybe she could create something for the lodge."

Benjamin tilted his head from one side to the other. "Maybe. So, your sisters are all in about you fixing the lodge? The last time I talked to you, you said you were leaving."

"Jilly and I are in. We are dragging Temple. She's an accountant, but after the fire, it just didn't seem right to abandon the lodge."

"I'm impressed that you're going to try to fix it. Your dad would be proud," he said, his gaze locking with hers.

"I'm scared. Especially financially."

"You can make it happen. I'll help you when I can," he said.

She felt a sense of relief. "I'll accept that offer, and since you're here, help me select fixtures. Yes?"

"Sure, if you'll go for coffee with me afterward," he said.

Her stomach dipped at the intent expression on his face. It was just coffee, she chided herself and shrugged. "Why not?"

Chapter Three

"So, how do you feel about living in such a small town?" Benjamin asked after they sat at a small table in the local coffee shop.

"I'm okay with it for now," Vivian said. "I'm still telecommuting with my firm in Atlanta and will have to return for some major events. Eventually I'll need to cut the ties. I'm actually kinda glad to get away from the big city."

"Really?" he asked and took a long draw from his cup. "You didn't like Atlanta?"

"I did and didn't," she said. "Who would love that traffic? At the same time, I loved the sense of history and culture. I was raised in Richmond, so of course I loved that city."

"Why not go back to Richmond?" he asked.

She shook her head. "Oh, no. No. My mother lives there and that would be an invitation to…well…insanity, in the worst way."

"That bad?" he asked.

She nodded. "Yes. Well, she's quite the perfectionist." She took a breath. "But enough about me. I still can't figure out why you didn't go pro with football."

"My mom was sick."

"I heard about that. I'm sorry. But after that," she said. "Couldn't you have gone pro after that?"

"I had other obligations by then," he said, his expression moody.

"Do you wish you had continued playing?"

He shrugged. "Depends on the day. Mostly not. It would have been physical torture. Why all the questions?"

She laughed. "My first opportunity. I barely got to talk with you when we were teens."

He chuckled and seems to relax just a smidge. "Yeah, that's true. Speaking of getting to know you, I'm glad you're fixing the lodge, but I'm wondering if you decided to take on fixing Honeymoon Lodge out of obligation," he said.

She thought about that for a moment, then shook her head. "No. Not for the most part. I think we're not ready to let go of our memories and what we experienced here. It took the fire to bring back how important those memories are to us. At the same time, we want to make it better for those who are new visitors to the lodge. It's tricky."

"Yeah, I guess so. If you want it to be more than a fishing and hunting lodge," he said.

"We do," she said. "We think you can still enjoy the lake and the scenery even if you don't hunt or fish."

"Because you don't like worms," he added with a mischievous glint in his eyes.

"Or crawdads," she said. "The lake and the mountains are still beautiful. A walk along the lake will rejuvenate you," she said.

"Even if you hate worms," he said.

She glowered at him. "Yes. Even if you hate worms. Or cocky men who need to be taken down a notch."

"You couldn't be speaking of me," he said.

"Of course not," she lied.

He laughed loudly, and she really liked him for it.

"Viv, you have a lot more kick than I thought you would," he said.

She rolled her eyes. "Benjamin, how could you expect anything less from Jedediah Jackson's daughter? My middle name is Monterey after the aircraft carrier. Eleven battle stars. My father was determined we wouldn't be wussy women, and he was big on Navy history. Each of our middle names is from an aircraft carrier. As for me, I've tripped and fallen a few times, but I've gotten back up."

Benjamin's eyes widened. "Monterey," he echoed. "I'm impressed. Does that mean I can call you Monty?"

"Only if you want me to clock you," she said.

"I'm bigger than you are," he said.

"I'll catch you when you're sleeping," she returned.

"I can only hope," he said. "If you catch me when I'm sleeping, that means you'll be sleeping with me."

A shiver rushed through her, all the way through her core. "Well, that's not going to happen," she said, because it couldn't and shouldn't. She might have been playing with the idea of flirting with Benjamin, but something inside her told her Benjamin was trouble for her. He appeared to be a pillar of the community and an all-around great guy, but for her, he could be big, big trouble. He could be a distraction to her and she wasn't ready for that kind of distraction, especially now that she needed to focus on the lodge.

Benjamin walked her to her car. She took a deep breath and searched for her sanity. "Thanks for your help with the fixtures. And especially your recommendation for an electrician who can do speedy work," she said.

"Glad I could help," he said, leaning toward her.

She instinctively held her breath. "Thanks again," she managed.

"Let's get together again. Saturday," he said. It wasn't a question.

Vivian bit her lip and shook her head. "I don't think that will work," she said.

"Monday?" he asked.

Her lungs seemed to compress, and she shook her head again. "I'm not sure this is a good idea," she managed.

"What's not a good idea?" he asked.

"You and me," she said.

"Maybe we could finally get to know each other," he said, lowering his head.

He took her mouth in a kiss.

Vivian pulled back. "You have got to stop this," she whispered and walked away, her body in complete chaos.

Vivian huddled with Temple and Jillian on the screened-in porch. Temple was glued her laptop and Jillian was trying a new yoga pose. "I ordered fixtures with the help of Benjamin," Vivian announced.

"How did that happen?" Temple asked, clearly suspicious. "Did you arrange to meet him?"

"I did not," Vivian said and wished her cheeks wouldn't heat. "He was at the hardware store and I took advantage of his expertise. Should I not have asked for his advice?"

Temple met her gaze. "Of course not. But I must ask, is he as hunky as ever?"

"I'd like to say he isn't, but I would be lying," Vivian said. "It doesn't matter, though, because we have too much to do for me to be distracted by an ex-football star."

"He's more than an ex-football star, isn't he?" Jillian asked. "He's the town entrepreneur."

Vivian frowned. "He is, but we can't be distracted. Right?"

"Right," Temple said.

"So, we have fixtures ordered. I scheduled a consultation with a plumber. And in other good news, we'll offer a room to an electrician. While they are performing repairs, they can go fishing or hunting in their off hours."

Temple mused. "That could work."

"I wish I could claim it as my idea, but Benjamin suggested it," she said.

"Well, perhaps we should consult him more often," Jillian said.

"I think this is enough for a start," Vivian said, because she didn't want Benjamin around to distract her. She and her sisters needed to get the lodge up to code as soon as possible. "In the meantime, I'd like us to work on the decor for the cabins."

"Decor?" Temple echoed. "We don't have money for decor," she said firmly. "I'm looking at our budget, and we're squeezed tight as it is."

"This may require an investment from all of us. I'm willing to contribute," Vivian said.

Temple tightened her lips. "I don't want to go overbudget."

"What budget?" Vivian asked. "We don't even have one yet."

"Well, we need one," Temple said. "And we should stick to it. This could get totally out of hand."

"Let's just look at the cottages and brainstorm," Vivian said, opening the door from the screened-in porch.

"I don't like this," Temple said, but the three of them walked down to the cabins.

Vivian stepped inside the dark, musty interior of

the first. "They need wallpaper, a complete freshening, mold abatement, modern air-conditioning, new minikitchens and beds. Definitely new beds."

"No to the wallpaper," Temple said. "It's just an invitation to more refurbishment."

"I can paint," Jilly said enthusiastically, lifting her hand. "I've even been paid for it."

Vivian looked at her youngest sister and wondered what in the world she'd done for the last five years that included being paid for painting. She nodded and placed that fact in a file to think about at 2:00 a.m. when she awakened as she so often did. Unfortunately insomnia had recently become Vivian's friend. "Thank you. That's wonderful. But the AC, minikitchens and—"

"Whoa, whoa, whoa," Temple said, lifting her hand. "These aren't luxury villas. They're cabins. Rustic cabins."

"Do you want to stay anywhere that doesn't have heat and air-conditioning, the ability to cook some food and a good mattress for sleeping?"

Temple frowned, then sighed. "We can work on the heat and AC. No to the full kitchens. I'll price stove tops and microwaves."

"And mattresses," Vivian said.

"I suppose," Temple said, clearly unhappy.

"Don't forget the paint," Jilly said. "We don't have to make these luxurious. A lot of people are trying to get back to nature.

"Just so you know I may not want to camp, but I can do it," Jillian said and walked out the cabin door.

"That girl worries me. I wonder if she's been in some kind of trouble that we don't know about," Temple said, staring after her.

"Me, too. I'm afraid of what she's been doing the last few years. I should have kept in touch better."

"I should have, too," Temple said. "I think Mom did a real number on her. I mean, more of a number than she did on you and me."

"We should take her into town for lunch," Vivian said. "Lunch with no distractions about the lodge. We could ask her more about what's been going on in her life."

Temple shot her a dark look. "You think *lunch* will fix anything? That almost sounds like Mom."

"That was insulting and unnecessary," Vivian said. "I think you know I'm different than Mom. Although I wouldn't mind having her best strengths without her weaknesses," she said, thinking of how socially adept her mother was.

"You're right," Temple said. "Lunch it is. We can make it a goal after we've painted one of the cabins."

"That's perfect," she said. "Thank you."

Temple met her gaze. "The numbers don't add up for this," she said. "I keep trying, but—"

"I'll add my savings," Vivian said.

"But what about your retirement?" Temple asked.

"I guess I'll just work till I die," she said with a laugh.

"That's how you're different than Mom," Temple said. "She would rather marry money than work for it."

"It might look like she's had a free ride, but I don't think she has always been happy. She's been paying for that second marriage ever since she took her vows with the good doctor."

"I never thought of it that way, but now that you say it… Hmm," Temple said.

"She wanted her girls to be taken care of," Vivian said.

"But Dad wasn't broke," Temple said. "He could have afforded our college education."

"Mostly," Vivian said. "You and I got scholarships."

"Jilly was always a wandering soul." Temple paused. "Oh, Lord, I hope I never feel like I have to marry for money."

Vivian looked at her slim sister with shoulder-length brown hair. She wore baggy jeans, a T-shirt and black-framed glasses she was always pushing up her nose. Temple was too intelligent to suffer fools gladly. Her hair hung in dark strands down to her shoulders.

"I don't think that's in your near future," she said.

Temple seemed to snap out of her reverie. "Are you saying I'm no bombshell?"

Vivian lifted her hand. "You are formidable and beautiful. Most men couldn't begin to handle you."

"Another way of saying I'm not suitable for anyone," Temple said and started toward the door.

Vivian touched her sister's shoulder. "Another way of saying you deserve someone amazing."

Temple's expression softened. "How'd you turn

out so nice when Mom was so sharp she cut you nearly every day when we were teenagers?"

Vivian smiled, but she knew her expression was stiff. "I took the first cuts," she said.

"Why don't you hate her?" Temple asked.

"A little therapy didn't hurt. I think she did her best. Her best wasn't yours or mine or Jilly's."

Temple sighed and left the cabin.

Vivian felt her tight shoulders slump. This was becoming about so much more than saving her father's lodge. Far more than she knew or was ready to face at the moment. All she knew was that she was all in. Vivian wanted her sisters back, and she was growing surer by the day that this was the way she could get them.

Five days later, Benjamin's recommended electrician had arrived and appeared to be fishing far more than he was wiring. Vivian thought about calling Benjamin, but instead conjured her father's spirit and rose early to confront the electrician, Bill, as he was headed out for another fishing venture.

She stepped in front of him. "Good morning, Bill. How are you?"

"Good," he said. "Just hoping to catch a few before I start work on the rewiring for the cabins today."

"How many cabins have you rewired?" she asked, crossing her arms over her chest.

"Well, it's been taking longer than I expected. I've done one and a half."

"Bill, Benjamin Hunter recommended you. He

said you would be a good worker. He said you would do good, fair work." She forced herself to stop. She'd heard that remaining silent was an important tool in negotiations. Vivian chewed the inside of her lip and narrowed her eyes. She hoped she looked vicious and intimidating and Bill didn't notice the nervous twitch in her left eye.

"You wouldn't be trying to take advantage of me, would you?" she challenged.

Bill sighed. "No. I wouldn't want to do that." He rubbed his hand across his face. "I don't gotta fish today. I'll work on that next cabin." He paused. "You're not gonna mention this to Ben, are you?"

"Not at the moment," she said, her ire rising at the realization that he might not have responded to her confrontation unless she'd mentioned Benjamin's name. "You do know who is signing your paycheck, writing your future recommendations and allowing you to live rent-free? My name is Vivian Monterey Jackson…"

Bill took a step back and nodded. "Yes, ma'am," he said and headed back to his room, supposedly to get his toolbox so he could get to work on the cabins.

Vivian tried not to grind her teeth, but she couldn't help it. She heard a sound behind her and turned to spot her sister Jilly, who stared at her with a wide-eyed glance.

"You've got balls," Jilly said in wonder.

"I'll take that as a compliment," Vivian said, although she wouldn't trust Bill's performance until he'd made more progress. She was her father's daughter.

That day, she and her sisters worked their butts off painting and completing work on the first cabin. They'd painted the walls a calming spa green and replaced the ratty scatter rugs. A small sitting area with two chairs and a table along with a new microwave, coffeepot and minifridge occupied the side of the room opposite the bed. New shades on the windows would provide a bit of privacy, and new mattresses were on the way for five of the cabins. The other three cabins could wait until they booked some new guests and started making some income again.

"It looks nice. I wouldn't mind staying here, except for the lack of television," Vivian said as the afternoon sun faded from the open blinds.

"You could probably watch some on your iPad by ripping the Wi-Fi from the lodge," Jilly said as if she had experience ripping.

Vivian exchanged a glance with Temple, then brushed her hands together the same way she would have liked to brush aside her concerns about Jilly. After all, her sister was an adult. She'd appeared to survive whatever she'd been doing for the last several years well enough.

"How about we eat an easy dinner, then roast marshmallows and drink wine by the fire pit?" Vivian suggested.

"Can you start a fire from scratch?" Temple asked, her eyes full of doubt.

"I can!" Jilly said with a huge smile on her face. "Didn't you pay attention when Dad showed us?"

"I must confess I haven't had much practice lately," Temple said.

"I can do it. We could roast hot dogs, too."

"Is there anything you can't do?" Temple asked.

Jilly's face fell. "Graduate from college," she said. "Finish just about anything."

Vivian's heart squeezed tight at the lost expression on her youngest sister's face. Silence stretched between the three of them.

"As we're learning, you don't learn everything at college," Temple admitted, even though Vivian and Jilly knew Temple held two advanced degrees. "You can light a fire, and I wouldn't dream of twisting my stiff body into some of those yoga poses you can do. So let's grab those hot dogs, buns and marshmallows." She glanced at Vivian. "A better version of *lunch with the ladies*?"

Vivian smiled and nodded.

Twenty minutes later, the three of them sat around the fire pit as the sun set over the lake. Vivian doused her burned hot dog with mustard and took a bite of it. "Most delicious thing I've eaten in a long time," she said and took another bite.

"Shows how hungry you are," Jilly said. "The more hungry you are, the better anything tastes."

Vivian nodded. "You're probably right. I've eaten some pretty stale sandwiches that tasted good because I skipped lunch." She took a long draw of wine from her red plastic cup. "You know, I was thinking about the last time the three of us were together, and I had a hard time coming up with it."

"Besides your wedding, four and a half years ago at Christmas," Jilly said without batting an eye. She wiped her face with a napkin.

"Too long," Vivian said. "I know Temple has been buried under accounting spreadsheets, and I've been planning events and failing at romance. What have you been doing, Jilly girl?"

"I've been here and there," Jilly said with a shrug. "I went to school to be a massage therapist but skipped the exam. I took a lot of yoga classes, but I had to move before I could finish the teaching preparation. I've tended bar, painted and almost got a cosmetician's license."

Vivian frowned. "You're obviously smart and have super skills. Why didn't you take the exams?"

Jilly shrugged again. "Just didn't ever work out. Anybody want another hot dog? Or are you ready for marshmallows?"

"Marshmallows," Temple said. "And I happened to find an old chocolate bar and some stale graham crackers," she said with a rare jubilant smile as she held up her finds like trophies.

"S'mores," Jilly said. "Oh, wow. With my sisters, eating s'mores by the fire next to the lake. What could be better?"

Vivian still worried about Jilly. It was her nature. She chastised herself for not pressing Jilly for more details during the last few years. She'd been too wrapped up in her own life and making her messes. But for the moment, Jilly was right. What could be better than s'mores with her sisters?

Chapter Four

Vivian made a quick trip to Atlanta to oversee a business conference she'd booked several months ago. She felt guilty leaving her sisters to continue the backbreaking work of refurbishing the cabins. At the same time, Grayson and Millicent were stepping up their game with repairing and cleaning the lodge. Vivian wasn't all that comfortable with Grayson and Millicent working so hard. If they got hurt, she would feel even more guilt. Still, she couldn't boot them out because they didn't have a retirement plan. If she wasn't painting or telecommuting for her full-time job, she was plotting, planning and blogging about the lodge.

Alternately swearing with worry and trying to escape her troubles by singing as she drove back to the lodge, she turned on some music to distract her. She hummed along to her mom's oldies hits and a few eighties songs followed by more recent hits.

By the time she drove up the hill to the lodge, she was in a much better mood. After parking her car, she grabbed her purse and bag, climbed out and headed to the main building.

She mounted the steps and felt a unique sense of home as she entered the foyer. Her life had been chaos for the last several years. How could an old wooden entryway give her such peace?

She took a deep breath and dragged her luggage up the stairway to her room. Sinking onto her bed, she stared at the ceiling. In any other circumstance, she would have wanted, craved, more square footage. Somehow, tonight it was enough.

Vivian closed her eyes, ready for some rest.

Her door burst open. Temple stared down with a slightly crazed expression on her face. "Your blog went viral. Everyone wants to have a wedding here."

"What?" Vivian asked, unable to rise from her bed.

"That blog post you wrote last week," Temple said, sitting next to Vivian. "It went viral. Since you left, we've received dozens of requests from people wanting to hold their weddings here."

"Oh, you're joking," Vivian said. She covered her eyes and forehead with her hand. "I posted only three photos, two of the lodge and one of the lake. Tell me you're joking. We're nowhere near ready."

"We need to get ready," Temple said. "This could

mean the difference between making it and not making it."

"That's too much to load on me tonight," Vivian said.

"Okay, okay," Temple said. "But tomorrow morning, we're going to have to work overtime."

"I thought we were already doing that," Vivian said.

"Apparently overtime is relative," Temple said. "But sleep tonight. We will all be begging for sleep soon." She patted Vivian's arm. "Rest well. You'll need it."

Vivian stared at the ceiling. After her insane schedule, she should have been dead asleep. Instead her brain was racing. How had this happened? She'd written the blog post on a friend's site as a test, hoping for feedback. She never would have dreamed so many people would have been interested with so little information. She tried to imagine getting the lodge ready within four weeks, and the prospect nearly made her head explode. She sighed. She wondered if she could possibly sleep with her eyes wide open and her brain so busy.

After she tossed and turned most of the night, Vivian gave up on sleep, took a two-minute shower, dressed and took her laptop and a pad of paper downstairs. It wasn't quite dawn and the lodge was quiet. She got the coffeemaker going and decided to work from the couch on the screened-in porch. The scent of late phlox wafted into the porch, and the sound of the lake lapping at the shore took the edge off her anxiety.

Vivian started out by making a list of the condition of the rooms in the lodge, minimum repairs and upgrades to be made, and then wishful thinking upgrades. Next she began a list of bed-and-breakfasts and the very few decent hotels within thirty miles.

"You're up mighty early," Grayson said from behind her.

Startled, Vivian glanced around to find the elderly man holding two cups of coffee. He offered one to her. "Thank you," she said, accepting the cup.

"I didn't know how you take it, so I added cream and sugar. Seems like most young people don't drink it black," he said and wandered toward the edge of the porch. He looked at the lake. "One of the prettiest sights in the world. Sunrise on the lake from one window. Sunset from another isn't too bad, either."

Vivian took a sip of her coffee and rose from her chair. "It is beautiful," she said.

"Never gets old," he said. "It can get a little dreary in the winter, but the lake makes up for all the gray." He took a few draws of his coffee. "What's got you all bothered this morning, Missy?"

Vivian sighed. "We're going to try to hold more events here at the lodge. I put some information out on the internet, and Temple told me we're already swamped with people asking for information. We're not ready."

"Then tell them that," Grayson said.

Vivian heard an echo of her father in Grayson's

words and felt a twist of missing him. She'd been so busy she hadn't had time to dwell on grief, so it seemed as if the feeling came out of nowhere. She took a slow, deep breath to push aside the tight feeling in her chest.

"It may not be that easy," she said. "If we're going to make the lodge profitable, we need to grab these opportunities."

"Hmm," Grayson said thoughtfully. "One of the things I always respected about your father was that he didn't pretend to be anyone other than who he was, and he didn't promise what he couldn't deliver. This ain't the Biltmore."

Vivian chuckled. "You're right about that. Maybe that's how we should advertise. *Not the Biltmore.*"

"I'll be glad to help you with painting and repairs. I'm slower than I used to be, but I'm handy."

Vivian's heart softened at his offer. "You're already doing more than you should."

"Not really," he said. "Millicent and I used to do a lot more, but during the last couple of years, your father wasn't much interested in repairs and improvements."

"Well, I appreciate the offer," she said.

"Millicent and I appreciate having a roof over our heads," he countered. "I see it's your nature to worry, but you and your sisters will make this work. You come from pretty stubborn stock."

"Thanks for the vote of confidence," she said.

She had a powwow with her sisters, but there were too many details to settle before they could put together a brochure with final prices. Instead, each of them selected a room to paint in the lodge. Just after lunchtime, which had been a protein bar and energy drink for her, she heard a loud scream followed by a thump. Another loud wail echoed from down the hall.

Vivian's stomach clenched. That sounded like Millicent. Dropping her paint roller into the pan, she jumped from her ladder and ran down the hall.

"Millicent," she called. "Millicent, is that you?"

"Oh, dear," Millicent cried as Vivian pushed open the door. The woman was crumpled on the floor, holding her leg. "I fell off the chair," she said. "I think I might have broken it."

Vivian rushed to her side. "Oh, no," she said. "Can you move it?"

"I'm afraid to," Millicent said, her face wreathed in pain.

"We need to get you to the doctor," Vivian said.

"What's wrong?" Temple asked from behind her.

"Oh, Millicent," Jilly said, rushing to the old woman's side. She ran her hand gently over Millicent's leg.

"She's afraid to move it," Vivian said.

"She probably shouldn't. Even if she can move it, it can still be broken." Jilly shrugged. "I once temped in a pediatrician's office. We need to get you to the clinic. We just need to figure out a way to transport you from here to the car. I don't think you should hop your way downstairs."

"Should we call an ambulance?" Temple asked.

"That will cost a fortune," Millicent said, shaking her head.

"Insurance will cover it," Vivian assured her.

"Millicent," Grayson said as he entered the room. "What have you done?" He bent down beside her, his hands shaking and his face filled with concern.

"I fell," she said. "The fixtures and curtains needed a good dusting, and like you told me, we need to help these girls as much as possible." Her face crumpled. "And now I'm just causing a heap of trouble."

"Oh, no," Jilly said. "Don't you dare think that. We know you work hard. Right now, we just need to concentrate on getting you treated."

With Jilly's assistance, they reinforced a sun lounger, strapped Millicent into it and carried her downstairs to Temple's SUV. Grayson rode with Temple and Millicent while Vivian and Jilly followed in Vivian's car.

Jilly went into the examination room with Grayson and Millicent because the nurse wouldn't allow all five of them to crowd into the room. Given Jilly's experience, Vivian decided to wait outside. Temple spent the time texting with her firm. After a while, when Millicent was getting X-rays, Vivian took a walk outside.

She paced the sidewalk, worried about Millicent, worried about the lodge, worried about her sisters, worried about everything… She took a deep breath and exhaled. Maybe she should try some yoga, as Jilly had been suggesting.

"Hey, there," a familiar male voice said from behind her.

Benjamin, she thought, her heart beating faster. "Hi," she said, turning around to face him.

"I heard Millicent took a spill," he said. "Is she okay?"

"That news traveled quickly," she said.

"It does around here," he said with an ironic half grin. "So, how is she doing?"

"We're waiting to hear about the X-rays. We were so worried about her when it happened that we all came to the clinic, but the nurse didn't want a crowd in the room during the examination. I can't blame him for that."

Benjamin shook his head. "No. How's everything else going?"

Vivian took in his straightforward gaze and the strength of his shoulders and almost burst into tears. She bit the inside of her cheek, horrified by her reaction. He was just being nice. He didn't want her to fall apart in his arms, even though the prospect was way too inviting.

"It's been a little challenging," she said through a tight throat.

"In what way?" he asked.

"Well, I suddenly feel completely responsible for my sisters and Grayson and Millicent. We've also received interest in booking the lodge for weddings. On the one hand, that's great. On the other hand, I don't want to seize the opportunity too soon, we don't want bad reviews."

"Sounds like a lot," he said. "How can I help?"

She opened her mouth, then closed it. She shouldn't start relying on Benjamin. She suspected it could get addictive, and that wouldn't be good for anyone. "We're okay. Just working it out. I shouldn't have complained."

"Everybody needs a little help now and then," Benjamin said. "Don't be afraid to ask for it."

She took a deep breath. "I don't want to ask too often."

"You sound like your dad."

She shrugged. "That's not all bad, is it?" She tried to shore up her defenses.

He gave a low chuckle that rippled inside her. "I guess not. I'll be in touch, Miss Monterey Aircraft Carrier."

She smiled in return. "Thanks."

She watched him walk away and felt another skip of her heart. Why did he affect her that way?

The good news/bad news was that Millicent's injury was a sprain instead of a break. That said, this sprain required a great deal of recovery time, so everyone in the house would be catering to Millicent.

Vivian and her sisters got back to renovating as well as they could. Jilly kept pushing yoga, and Vivian finally gave in. "Okay, let's do it in the morning," Vivian said. "I'm too tired at the end of the day."

"It would really help in the evening, too," Jilly said.

"So, it won't help in the morning?" Temple asked.

"No, I didn't say that." Jilly nodded. "Let's do mornings." She added under her breath, "It's better than nothing."

Vivian joined in the whole namaste thing for the next several days, despite how distracted she was. As each day passed, she felt more sore. Wasn't she supposed to feel better? Her shoulders were still rising upward in tension.

Tuesday night, she went down to the dock after dark with a glass of wine. She felt achy and discouraged. How was she going to make this work for everyone who was counting on her?

"Vivian," a voice said from behind her. Benjamin.

She glanced over her shoulder as he strode toward her. "What are you doing here?"

"I'm here for the next two weeks," he said. "Your dad gave me a lifetime two-week fishing trip."

"I didn't know that," she said.

"Check his will," he said and sat down next to her. "I could be helpful. I'm decently handy."

Benjamin popped open a beer and offered her the same.

"I'm sipping my wine," she said.

"I'll bring wine next time," he said.

"No need," she said. "There won't be a next time."

"Don't say that," he said. "Anything can happen."

"That's what I thought when I was a teenager," she said. "I tried to get you to join me in the lake, but you said no."

"Well, now I'm saying yes."

Her heart skipped a beat, but she ignored it. "It's a little late."

"Think about it," he said.

She glanced at his too-appealing half grin and strong body. Broad shoulders, muscular arms and lean hips. He had aged quite well. Why was she noticing his body? she asked herself. She needed to ignore it.

"No need," she said and rose.

Vivian successfully avoided Benjamin the next night, but she couldn't stay away from the dock too long. After dark two nights later, she carried her glass of wine to sit and sip under the stars.

Despite Jilly's best efforts, Vivian found evenings on the dock more therapeutic than anything. Hearing heavy steps on the dock, she braced herself. It had to be Benjamin.

Without saying a word, he sat down beside her, his legs hanging over the edge of the dock. He put an open bottle of wine between them.

Vivian picked it up and studied the bottle. "It's white. Well done."

"Good to know. I thought I noticed you preferred white."

She poured a half glass. "I can't drink this whole bottle."

"You could try," he said with a grin.

"You are bad," she said.

"In a good way," he returned. "Wanna go for a swim?"

"No," she said immediately. "It's too cold."

"I could keep you warm," he suggested.

"Why couldn't you have said this when I was fifteen?" she asked.

"Your father would have killed me," he said.

"Coward," she said.

He met her gaze for a long moment. "You're calling me a coward?"

"You turned me down all those years ago," she told him.

"You need to look at the overall picture. I was respecting your father."

"And now?" she asked.

"Now I'm going to get you," he said, lowering his head to hers. "In every way."

Her heart spiked. "Oh, I don't think so. I'm older and wiser."

"But you still feel it between you and me, don't you?" he asked. "It hasn't gone away, has it?"

Vivian frowned at him. "There's a remnant. I'm sure it will go away soon." She grabbed the bottle of wine and stood. "You're a little too cocky for my taste."

Benjamin laughed, and the sound was lusty and full of life. She wished she could laugh that way. "You like your men cocky. You always have," he said as she tramped down the dock, her peace totally destroyed by her interaction with him.

She sighed. He needed to go away. She should check her father's will.

"Hey, Viv, don't forget I'm at the end of the hall on the second floor. You have an open invitation."

Chapter Five

Vivian did some number-crunching in her bed-room. She played HGTV in the background, but watching how all the fix-it people seemed to repair everything at the speed of light made her feel more frustrated.

A knock sounded at her door. "Don't be Benjamin," she whispered under her breath. Then she called, "Who is it?"

"Temple. Let me in. Why is your door—"

Vivian opened the door.

"—locked," Temple finished and studied her. "You look cranky. What's wrong? Are the numbers worse than we thought?"

"Not really. I just wish we had one of those

HGTV teams where they come in and fix every-thing overnight."

Temple shot her a skeptical look. "I'm not sure how long-lasting those overnight jobs are. But we're not doing badly, and now that Benjamin has shown up, things are moving even more quickly. He's a real workhorse."

Vivian frowned. "He wouldn't be here if he hadn't made that arrangement with Daddy."

"Well, maybe we should extend it. The electrician is really starting to hustle, and the part-time plumber is hanging in longer than part-time. Everybody likes Benjamin. He seems to inspire people, and you used to have a big crush on him."

"That was fifteen years ago," Vivian said. "He's just so cocky."

"Aren't most football players? He used to play football, didn't he?" Temple asked.

"Quarterback," Vivian said. "They make the calls."

"I didn't know you watched football," Temple said.

"With Daddy," Vivian said. "I covered football. You talked basketball."

Temple stared at her for a long moment and shifted her glasses, then gave her a sad smile. "We sure tried to fill that son vacancy, didn't we?"

Vivian's throat tightened, but she managed to choke out a laugh. "I still say Jilly pulled it off the best."

"Is there anything she can't do, at least partly?"

"Maybe read well," Vivian said in a low voice. "I

remember Mom taking her for some special lessons. It seemed like she was always frustrated with her."

"I've been so focused on becoming a partner with my firm," Temple said. "I'm not sure what all happened between Mom and her."

"I know what you're saying. I worry about what she has gone through. I asked Mom about it one time and she cut me off at the knees." She paused and took a breath. "I want to take better care of Jilly."

"Even though it looks like she's done a pretty good job taking care of herself?" Temple asked.

"Yeah. I don't want her to have to take odd jobs just to survive. She deserves better than that," Vivian said.

Temple lightly touched her arms. "Careful. You're turning into a mother hen."

"How can I not? Between Grayson, Millicent, Jilly and you putting your life savings on the line…"

"Well, not my whole life savings." Temple adjusted her glasses again. "I'm not that naive. We'll get through this. We each have our own talents. Do yoga. Go to sleep. Can I get you some wine?"

"No. I'm fine."

"You are doing fine," Temple said and put her arms around Vivian in an awkward hug.

"I think I'll take a bath," Vivian said.

"Good idea. Trust me, the numbers will always be there whether you're dead or alive."

"Yeah. Thanks. I guess," Vivian said and mustered a smile. "I'll be better in the morning."

"Sure you will. Jilly will get you all twisted with

yoga," Temple said. "Get some rest, princess. You've always been the working kind of princess."

Vivian stared after her sister as she left the room. She and her sisters had often been so busy surviving that they hadn't had much time for each other. Vivian had tried to keep everyone happy and often felt as if she'd failed. Temple had been brainy, but not all that sociable. They'd both been shuttled off to boarding school at a relatively young age. Jilly had been sent off, too, but she hadn't fit in. She'd struggled. Even now, Vivian wished she'd paid better attention. Maybe things would have turned out easier for Jilly…

Vivian's head throbbed, and she squeezed her temples. Time for a bath and some jazz music to push down her porcupine quills. After turning on the taps to the tub, she grabbed her iPod and stripped off her clothes. Stepping into the tub, she sank into the water up to her chin and focused on the music. The water caressed her skin, reminding her of how little she'd been touched lately. She should get a massage, she told herself, but as the water lapped over her nipples and warmed her all over, her mind wandered to Benjamin. How would his big hands feel on her body? Would he be rough or tender? How would his hard, muscled body feel against hers?

She wriggled in the water, feeling an aching awareness in places she hadn't paid any attention to lately. The jazz music seeped throughout her and she tried not to think about Benjamin, but want grew inside her. She tried to push it aside, yet even after she dried off and went to bed, she couldn't stop thinking about his invitation. If she went to his room, maybe he could ease the ache inside her, and she could get on with what she needed to do.

Vivian knew she wouldn't. She was ashamed to admit even to herself that she didn't have the nerve.

The next morning, she focused on sun salutations with Jilly. The poses were killing her. "Jilly, I don't know about this downward dog. I'm having a hard time with it. Jet doesn't ever do this kind of stuff," Vivian said. "He just stays conked out on that rug in the bar."

"Shh," Jilly said. "Just breathe and give in to the stretch."

"I'm not really feeling the Zen," Vivian said.

Jilly sighed. "That's not a problem. Let's do child's pose. That should help."

Vivian gratefully sank onto her mat. This was one pose she could actually say she loved. "Can I stay this way all day?"

Jilly laughed. "No, but let's do a little meditation."

Vivian rose and tried to focus on Jilly's words, but her mind grew busy. There were too many things to do today and tomorrow. There were too many things that needed to turn out just right. Her body stiffened.

"You're not paying attention," Jilly said. "I can feel it."

"Why do you have to be so perceptive?" Vivian asked. "Stop it."

Jilly chuckled. "We all have our skills. We'll try again tomorrow."

"If we must," Vivian said as she hobbled to her feet. She gave her sister a squeeze. "Thanks, beautiful."

Vivian headed out of the screened-in porch while Jilly worked on harder poses. She brushed her hand over her forehead and nearly walked straight into Benjamin's hard chest. "Oh, my. I didn't see you. Um, good morning," she said and noticed he was carrying two fishing rods.

"Good morning to you," he said, pulling his ball cap into place. "You're just who I was looking for."

Vivian blinked. "Why?"

"So we can go fishing," he said. "Two poles. I'll even bait your hook for you."

"I don't have time to go fishing," she said. "But thank you."

"It won't take long," he said. "It'll do more for you than that yoga with your sister."

"I find that hard to believe," she said.

"You're not sore?" he asked.

"Yes, but that's part of the process," she said.

"I can guarantee you won't get sore from fishing," he said.

"If I don't slice my fingers to ribbons trying to put a worm on the hook," she grumbled.

"I already said I'd do that for you. C'mon. I'll just keep you an hour. If you don't feel better after an hour, then I won't make you do it again."

Make her, she thought. He wouldn't make her do

anything. At the same time, she wondered if it might help her to spend a little time on the lake. "Just an hour," she said, relenting. "I have work to do."

"So do I, but I'll get more done if I start out this way," he said. "Maybe you will, too."

She was skeptical, but something in his gaze offered a temporary escape she wanted or needed. But she wouldn't confess to that. Never. Ever.

Benjamin watched Vivian, sitting in the boat across from him, eyeing the hook with trepidation. She was a girlie-girl who'd always tried her best to be more sporty, probably to please her father, and that was one of the reasons she'd always fascinated him. She was willing to step out of her comfort zone.

Benjamin felt her watching him bait his hook.

"I should at least try," she said.

He put his hand over hers. "Not this time."

"Why?" she asked. "You're so sure I can't do it."

"No," he said. "I just don't want this to be the last time you go fishing with me. One thing at a time. I bet you're good at casting." Casting was like shifting gears. Once you got out of Neutral, you were in good shape. He put a juicy worm on her hook. "Show me your stuff."

She looked at the rod, then at him. "This is embarrassing. I've forgotten how. I never dated a fisherman," she said, clearly exasperated.

"That's your first problem," he said. "It will all come back to you. Use your thumb to hold down the casting reel. Pull it back, then slide it forward and release." He nodded as she followed his instructions. "There you go. Perfect."

"I've never been called perfect," she muttered.

"Then maybe you've been hanging around the wrong people," he said.

Her head snapped up and she met his gaze. She might have been raised in Virginia, but her eyes were Carolina blue. He felt the intense, deeper-than-it-should-have-been connection ricochet between them.

She must have felt it, too, because she looked away. "When are you going to cast yours?" she asked, not meeting his gaze.

"Right now," he said and cast his line over the other side of the boat.

After several moments, she sighed and shrugged her shoulders. "I'm remembering why I didn't love fishing. It takes so long."

"Relax. Take a deep breath. This is your opportunity to slow down."

"I don't have time to slow down," she said. "I need to paint a bathroom."

"You'll do it faster if you fish first. Trust me," he said. "Stop thinking about everything you think you need to do and listen to the lake."

Vivian took a deep breath. A thousand thoughts tried to storm through her mind, but she deliberately pushed them aside. She focused on the sounds of the lake. A bird called in the distance. The water made gentle swishing sounds. Gradually she felt soothed. Just a bit.

Something tugged on her line, and she nearly jumped out of her skin. "Ohmygoodness, I have a bite."

"Good for you. Just hold on. Reel him in," he coached.

Benjamin could feel her concentration. Moments later, she pulled the squirming fish into the boat.

"Oh, no," she said. "Look what I've done. I've killed a fish. Should I throw him back in?"

Benjamin bit his lip. "No. You're going to eat him."

Vivian made a face. "Oh, I don't know."

"I will fix him up for you. He's your trophy meal. You deserve it."

"What about the worm?"

"I'll get rid of the worm," he told her and put the fish in the ice chest. "Can you relax now?"

"I'm not sure," she said. "My heart is racing and I feel like I should be doing something."

"You should," he said. "You should be kissing me."

She shot him a suspicious glance.

"Kiss me," he said. "You'll feel better. I promise."

"You're ridiculous," she said, but after a moment, she leaned forward and pressed her mouth against his.

Benjamin slid his hand behind her neck and took her mouth, deepening the kiss. She tasted sweet, like the girl he'd always wanted but never gotten. The boat began to rock. He reached out one of his hands to steady her, but she pulled back.

"I think that's enough," she said breathlessly.

"Do you really?" he asked, leaning toward her.

Vivian leaned backward. "I do," she said.

Benjamin felt a tug on his line and pulled in the fish. "Dinner for two," he said.

"You can have mine," she said.

He shook his head. "Didn't your daddy tell you that you're supposed to eat what you catch?"

"I guess," she said. "What if I don't like this kind of fish?"

"You will," he said. "I'll use the kitchen at the lodge. We can meet on the dock this afternoon."

"I'm not sure it's a good idea," she said. "You're very distracting."

"Thank you," he said.

After her fishing expedition, Vivian painted a bathroom and a quarter of a bedroom. By the end of the day, she ached from head to toe. "All I want is pain meds and my bed," she said as she slumped down in the hall and took a long sip from her water bottle.

Jilly joined her. "Yoga would help," she told her.

Vivian winced and shook her head. "I don't think so. I've been sore every day since I've been doing yoga."

Jilly pursed her lips. "Maybe I've overestimated you. Maybe you need yoga for older people."

Vivian glanced at her sister, insulted. "Excuse me. I'm not old."

"Well, you're not old," Jilly corrected herself.

"But you're new, and you haven't stretched much. The older you get…"

Vivian gave her sister the death glare. "Don't call me old."

Temple hobbled down the hallway toward them. "I need a pain reliever. Maybe something stronger than over-the-counter."

"You and me both," Vivian said.

"I think the lodge would benefit from a spa," Jilly said. "Especially since many older people will visit."

Temple and Vivian glared at her.

Jilly shrugged. "Tell me you wouldn't benefit from soaking in a Jacuzzi. Maybe we should get more than one."

"Because we have so much extra money," Vivian said.

"I bet it's not that much extra," Jilly said.

Temple cocked her head to one side. "You might be right. We should think about it."

"Really, Miss Penny Pincher?" Vivian asked Temple.

"Yeah," Temple said. "They are not hideously expensive, and they evoke luxury."

"Inside or outside?" Vivian asked.

"Outside. That way we can skip indoor mold," Temple said.

"Can we put up a sign that tells people not to pee in the spa?" Vivian asked.

Jilly giggled.

"We can," Temple said. "But we can't skip chlorine."

"Just think how much you could be relaxing in a Jacuzzi right now," Jilly said.

Vivian closed her eyes and groaned. "I wonder how quickly we can get them."

Hearing heavy steps walking toward them on the hallway, she glanced up to see Benjamin. Her heart skipped over itself.

"Fish is ready. I don't want it to get cold. Come on down to the dock," he said.

"I need a shower," she protested.

"Jump in the lake," he said. "I'm hungry."

Vivian scrambled to her feet and stared after him as he walked toward the stairs.

"You went fishing?" Temple asked more than said.

"It was a dare," Vivian said.

"Hmm," Temple said in disbelief.

"Fishing," Jilly said with a mischievous smile. "You'll have to tell us all about it. Go ahead, now, and enjoy…it all."

"I couldn't turn him down," Vivian said. "He said I only had to do it once."

"Sounds like it went well," Temple said.

Vivian groaned. "Stop it. Stop it. Stop it."

"Bet that fish is gonna be delicious," Jilly said. "And maybe the man, too."

Chapter Six

Benjamin successfully seduced her—into joining him in eating their catch of the day with some great sides.

With her honey-blond hair in a ponytail and her face clean except for a few swipes of paint, Vivian looked almost the same as she had fifteen years ago. Except for her curves. She'd definitely filled out in that department. He'd told himself she wasn't his type, but he couldn't resist the urge to get to know her better. Maybe if he spent some time with her, he wouldn't find her such a source of temptation.

"Hush puppies, fried fish and French fries," she said as Benjamin gave her a full plate. "If I die from this, I'm sending my sisters after you."

"There are cabbage and carrots in the coleslaw.

That counts as a vegetable," he said, sitting beside her on the dock. "If you don't want it—"

"Don't even think about taking away this food now that you've tempted me with it." She took a bite of a hush puppy and moaned in approval. "Did you make all of this?"

"No. Grayson did most of it. He also warned me not to take advantage of Jedediah's daughter."

She slid a sideways glance at him. "I'm sure you'll heed his wise words."

Benjamin chuckled at her sly glance. "You're well past the age of consent."

"Are you calling me old?" she countered with a scowl.

"Not at all. If I didn't know better, I'd probably card you at my bar."

Appearing mollified, she twitched her lips. "Well, I'll take that as a compliment," she said and took a bite of fried fish. "Delicious."

"When was the last time you caught your own dinner?" he asked.

"A very long time ago. My dad insisted I bait my own hook, and I was squeamish about it. That meant I spent a lot of time watching and reading."

"Reading?" he said.

She nodded. "He allowed me to bring a book. Otherwise, he said I talked too much and would disturb the fish. I think my chatter bothered him a lot more than it bothered the fish."

"Probably so. I don't think he always knew what to do with three girls."

"I think he tried hard to counter my mom's influence. Ballet, piano, private school, finishing school."

"You think he was successful?" Benjamin asked.

Vivian sighed. "Depends on the day. I know I made some choices due to my mother's expectations. I remember my wedding day. Daddy and I were just getting ready to walk down the aisle. He had never trusted Robert. Daddy turned to me and said, 'You can still call it off. I've got the keys to my Jeep in my pocket.'" She gave a wry smile. "I still remember hearing the jingle of his keys over the sound of Canon in D by Pachelbel."

"And what did you say?"

"'Mom would die.'" Her lips twitched. "He said, 'Mom doesn't have to sleep with him.' He used other, more colorful language, but you catch my drift."

"I guess he had a point," Benjamin said and chuckled.

"In retrospect, he did, but I was hoping things would turn out different." She took another bite of hush puppy and glanced about him. "No temptations to walk down the aisle for you?"

"Once, but it just wasn't right," he said. "No regrets. It turned out for the best for everybody."

"You never missed her?" Vivian asked.

He shrugged. "Maybe once or twice. I had other things to do. What about you? Do you miss your ex?"

"For a while, I missed the man I'd hoped he was, but he wasn't that man. The bad thing is, it made me lose my trust in myself. You need to look at people for who they are, not who you want them to be."

"True, but some of us make a few improvements along the way. If we're determined. And lucky."

"Maybe so," she said. "I didn't realize how profound you could be."

"You just thought I was all good looks and muscle," he said and winked at her.

"I knew you were smart, too," she protested. "I already told you I was surprised you didn't go pro and never look back at the town."

"There are times when you have to step up. That was one of those times. But enough about me. I see you've cleaned your plate."

"Yes, I did. Shame on you," she said with a sexy little pout. "I'll have to run up and down the mountain for three days to work that off."

"You're doing plenty of labor. How about a swim?" he asked, picking up the paper plates and taking them to the trash can.

"I'm not wearing a bathing suit," she said.

"So?" he asked.

"It's still daylight," she told him. "I'm not swimming in the nude in broad daylight."

"The sun will set soon enough. Meet me here at eight thirty. I'll bring some wine. You can even wear a swimsuit if you're a scaredy-cat."

"The water is too cold. I won't be goaded into skinny-dipping," she said.

"I'm not goading," he told her, extending his hand to her. "I'm just teasing a little."

She shot him a distrustful glance, but accepted his hand and stood. He stared into her crystal-blue eyes and took in her creamy skin and inviting pink lips. Her T-shirt and jeans were casual, but he couldn't help noticing the way her breasts stretched the gray cotton, and there was no denying the curve of her hips in the denim.

Benjamin sighed and lifted his hand to her chin. Vivian's eyes widened slightly, but she didn't pull back. "I wouldn't have ever thought you'd get any prettier than you were when you were a teenager. But you've grown into yourself. You've turned into a beautiful woman, a smart one, too, with a good heart. Your father would kill me for what I'm thinking right now."

Vivian swallowed and her eyelids fluttered downward, hiding her expression from him. "I guess it's a good thing he doesn't know."

"I guess so," Benjamin said. "I've got to make a quick trip into town. Don't forget. Eight thirty here at the dock," he said and headed up the hill.

"I didn't say I was coming," she called after him.

"Eight thirty," he said over his shoulder and grinned to himself. He was going to reel this little beauty in, and she wouldn't have any idea what hit her. He'd make sure of it.

She should just paint another room, Vivian told herself as she eyed the clock. Eight twenty-five. Or indulge in a television binge like Jilly. Or do some paperwork like Temple. None of the prospects appealed to her.

A bath, she suggested to herself. A nice, long bath, read a book, then go to sleep. That would be the best therapy in the world for her since her body was aching and her mind needed to settle down.

Vivian glanced at the clock again. Eight twenty-eight. Shutting down a dozen objections and warnings, she grabbed her swimsuit and jerked it on, then snagged a towel and flew out the door. Benjamin would mock her for the suit, but maybe a dip in lake water would do her some good. Oh, who was she fooling? She just wanted to see him again.

He stood on the dock and lifted the wineglasses as he watched her make her way toward him. She felt his gaze on her every step of the way, and it gave her a little thrill.

"Two glasses," she said, accepting one. "You must have been confident I would join you."

"I'd like to put your presence down to my irresistible manly charms. But you've come down to the dock more evenings than not," he said. "However, this time you're wearing a bathing suit. If I can get you in the water…"

"Don't count on anything else," she said.

He took a deep sip of his wine and set his glass on the dock, then pulled off his T-shirt. "Don't worry."

Then he proceeded to shuck his shorts and underwear with his pretty amazing backside to her and jumped in the lake.

Vivian choked on her wine. He bobbed to the surface and waved for her to join him.

"I thought I'd take it slow—sit down and dip in my feet, slide in a little bit at a time," she said.

"That'll take all night," he said. "Jump in all at once. That's the way to go."

"It must be freezing," she said, suspicious.

"It's not freezing. I would be turning blue if it were," he assured her. He lifted his hands. "Come on, Vivian. I'll catch you."

His words made something inside her soften. Since getting divorced over three years ago, she'd been hesitant in her relationships. She'd wondered if someone was going to pull the rug out from beneath her when she least expected it. Benjamin might be a charmer, but she suspected he meant it when he said he'd catch her.

After taking a couple of big gulps of wine, she set down the glass beside her towel, walked to the end of the dock and jumped. The temperature of the water shocked her down to her bones. She gasped at the cold that not even Benjamin's arms could conceal.

"You lied," she said to Benjamin. "It's freezing."

"Refreshing," he corrected her.

"Freezing," she said, shaking her head.

"All right, it's a little brisk, but I'll warm you up," he said and tugged her along as he swam farther into the lake. "Tell the truth—this is nice. It's quiet and peaceful, with stars up above."

"I'll tell you when I regain sensation. At the moment, I'm still numb from the cold."

"Ah, so you're cranky when you get a little chilly," he said. "I'll have to remember that."

"It's more than a little chilly," she retorted, but his arms did feel nice, and his shoulders were so broad and strong. She took a deep breath and sighed. She might as well enjoy the moment.

"Listen," he said. "Close your eyes and listen."

Vivian did as he asked and heard the sound of a bird. "What kind?" she asked.

"Whip-poor-will."

She opened her eyes and looked at him. With his tousled wet hair and drops of lake water on his face, he was ridiculously appealing to her. It was almost a sin for a man to be so sexy. There should have been something wrong with him. She should focus on finding out what that horrible quality was.

"Stop thinking," he told her and spun her around in the water.

She laughed at the combination of his words and the sensation of spinning. "How do you know I'm thinking?"

"Your eyebrows pull down and you stop smiling," he said and spun her around again.

"This is nicer than I thought it was going to be," she said.

"I could make it a lot nicer," he suggested.

She gave him a sideways glance, but he lowered his head anyway and pressed his mouth against hers. She had the sensation of spinning even though she knew the only movement Benjamin made besides kissing and holding her was kicking his legs to keep them above water. He felt so good, so strong, so delicious. Her heart hammered in her chest, and she kissed him back. She wanted more.

His tongue slid over hers, and she noticed the way his strong chest felt against her breasts. Lower, she felt him between her legs. She couldn't resist pressing against him.

He made a low groan that vibrated in her mouth and throughout her body. "I think we should get rid of this swimsuit," he said.

"Hmm," she said, wanting more of his kisses, wanting not to think. She took his mouth again and indulged herself with his lips. A few seconds later, he pulled off her bathing suit top tossed it on the dock, and she felt her bare nipples, taut and achy, rubbing against his chest.

He took one of her breasts in his hand. "So pretty," he said and rubbed her nipple. "You feel so good." He removed her bottoms and lifted her hips, urging her to straddle him, making her aware of his arousal.

Even though a combination of adrenaline and desire was raging through her, Vivian's brain still worked. Sex in the lake? What if someone saw them? What about protection? What about— "I don't think this is a good idea," she managed breathlessly, tugging her mouth from his.

"Really?" he asked. "Why not? We're adults."

The look in his eyes made her mouth go dry. "Yes, but protection," she said.

"Got it," he said.

"What if someone sees us?"

"Not likely, but we can go to my room. Or yours."
He paused and gave a pained chuckle. "Unless you're
getting cold feet."

"It's not cold feet," she said, then sighed. "Well,
maybe a little. You're just a lot of—" She broke off,
thinking, *You're just a lot of man.*

"That's bad?"

"No," she said. "I'm not sure how to handle you."

"I can help you figure that out," he said. "But no
pressure. If you don't want to go further, we won't."

A big part of her really wanted to go further. Con-
flicted, she bit her lip. "Okay. Thanks."

He swam back to the dock, pulling her along with
him, and lifted her to the dock, following after her.
He returned the top of her swimsuit to her. Embarrassed because she'd forgotten about it, she struggled to tie it.

"I can help," he said and took care of the task
with steady hands.

Vivian climbed the ladder, darted for her towel
and trained her gaze on the shore, away from Benjamin. She heard his feet on the dock as he put on his
clothes. At least, she hoped he was getting dressed.
She felt his hand on her shoulder and jumped.

"It's safe. You can look now," he said with a
twinge of humor.

Vivian rolled her eyes, mostly at herself. She collected her wineglass and headed toward the house.

"No need to rush off," he said.

She thought about denying that she was hurrying

away, then decided it was time to be a grown-up. Turning around, she met his gaze. "I need to clear my head. You have muddled it."

"I think that's one of the nicest things I've ever been told," he said. "See you tomorrow night on the dock."

"I don't know."

"We can talk," he said. "Or I can kiss you all night long. It might drive us both wild, but we will enjoy the ride." He leaned toward her and brushed his mouth against her cheek. The caress made her feel weak all over again.

"'Night, Viv," he said.

"G'night, Benjamin," she said and stiffened her legs and her backbone. Lord help her, that man was distracting.

Vivian tossed and turned again that night. In the wee hours, she wondered again if she should just go ahead and share a night with Benjamin to get him out of her system. At the same time, she wasn't at all sure the one-time tactic would work. But realistically, could he be that good?

By midmorning, she heard a hound dog howling in the distance. The mournful sound wafted through the open window, tugging at her heartstrings. She heard a few more howls and suddenly realized it was Jet.

She went into the hallway. Grayson appeared. "Jet?" she asked.

He nodded. "He sounds like he's in trouble. I'll

go look for him, but someone needs to stay with Millicent."

"No. I'll go. I just need you to tell me where you think he might be."

"Neighbor's property. He got stuck in a barbed fence one other time. I hope he didn't get into that again."

"Should I drive?"

"You'll have better luck walking. It's past the cabins. You sure you don't want me to go?" he asked, clearly worried.

"No. I'll leave right now," she said and wondered why neither of her sisters had heard the howling. Checking in on Jilly, she saw her sister moving her head in rhythm to whatever music she was playing on her iPod as she painted a guest room.

Vivian moved in front of her sister and waved her arms. Jilly removed her earbuds. "What up?"

"Jet ran off. He's howling, so we're afraid he's hurt himself."

"Oh, no," Jilly said, crestfallen. Jilly was so tenderhearted about animals. "We need to find him."

Vivian nodded. "I'll get Temple. Grayson says Jet's wails sound like they are coming from the neighboring property. Take your cell phone so we can stay in touch."

Vivian also found Temple painting and wearing earbuds. She was told Temple had been listening to a podcast on corporate accounting. All three of them ran to the path past the cabins. As they approached the barbed wire fence, Vivian listened for Jet. "No howls," she said.

"I'm not sure whether that's a good thing or a bad thing," Temple said. "And how are we supposed to get over that fence without ripping ourselves to shreds?"

Vivian pulled off her sweatshirt. It was a chilly morning, so she was wearing a tank top underneath. "I'll donate my shirt to the cause. Unless we hear more from Jet, I think we need to split up to find him. Just keep your cell phone ready."

"Even though the coverage up here may not be stellar," Temple said, making the first move over the fence.

"Let's just do our best," Vivian muttered as she watched Jilly tackle the fence next.

Vivian followed, then headed up the hill. Since Jet hated baths, he could be stinky. She wondered if she could smell him if she couldn't hear him. Climbing through the woods and leaves, she thought she heard the soft sound of a whine, but she wasn't sure if she'd imagined it. She moved in the direction of the sound. Breathless from rushing and climbing, she stepped over a series of fallen trees and branches and came upon Jet, whining, and Benjamin standing over the dog with his hands on his hips.

Relief flooded through her as she walked toward them. "Is he okay?"

"Not sure. He stepped into a trap. Looks like his leg is in bad shape."

Jet gave a miserable little whine that tore at her.

She put her hand on his head, and he turned to lick it as if he were saying, *Please help me*. "How do we get him out?"

"Without wire cutters, it's a two-person job," he said. "I've got a rope to fasten to Jet's collar so he won't run away. Not that he'll be able to move too fast. I'll hook it to my belt. Then I'll pull this side of the trap, and you pull the other. If you think you can," he added.

"Of course I can," she said, at the same time wishing she'd done a little more strength training lately. Ideally all that painting would help.

"Okay. You may have to hold your side for thirty seconds. Warn me if you're about to let it go," he said.

"I will. I will," she said and put her hands on one side of the steel trap, frowning at the unforgiving metal teeth. "I hate these things," she muttered. "If they're not catching snakes, they should be outlawed."

"Countdown to pulling," he said. "Three. Two. One."

Vivian struggled to hold her side. Using all her strength, she was appalled to see that she'd separated her side by mere inches.

"It's okay. Almost got him," Benjamin said, holding one end of his side with his foot. He carefully pulled Jet's paw free. The dog yelped and hobbled to a few feet away. "You can let go now," Benjamin said. "Good job."

Vivian let out the breath of air she'd been holding. Sweat trickled between her breasts and she had the oddest urge to cry.

Benjamin was checking Jet's paw as much as the dog would allow. Vivian stepped closer. She saw quite a bit of matted fur and blood. "How bad is it?"

"I don't know. He might lose the paw. We need to get him to the vet."

"I'll call Temple and Jilly."

Her sisters met them at the bottom of the hill. "All of us don't need to go to the vet," Vivian said. "I'd like you two to stay at the house." If something worse happened to Jet, then she wanted to soften the blow for her sisters.

Jilly pouted. "But what if something goes wrong with him?"

"I'll call you. I promise," Vivian said.

Temple gave Jet a quick pat on the head, but Jilly hugged him as if her and his lives depended on it. When she pulled back, she had tears in her eyes.

Vivian hugged her sister. "Go tell Grayson we found Jet and we're taking him to the veterinarian. I'll call you as soon as we know anything."

Jilly nodded. "Thanks, Benjamin."

"Glad I could help. We should get going," he said.

Vivian and Benjamin walked quickly to his SUV. When Benjamin started to put Jet in the back, Vivian stopped him. "Don't you think I should hold him?"

"I thought he would be more comfortable back here," he said.

"If you're sure. Maybe I could ride back there with him," she said and climbed in with the dog.

Benjamin gave a slow nod, then got into the cab and drove into town. Memories of her father and Jet filled Vivian's mind during the drive. Jet had enjoyed going hunting with her dad, but he'd hated being bathed. Her father had insisted and always won the battle. She remembered watching Jet riding in a fishing boat with her father. Her father had loved that dog, and the dog had returned the affection.

Jet had stayed with her father even at the end. The dog wouldn't leave Jedediah's side. At that moment, it struck her that Jet had been the only living being with her father when he died at home. He'd kept the seriousness of his illness from almost everyone. A knot formed in her throat. Vivian stroked Jet's head and chest. The dog closed his eyes as if he appreciated the comfort. It was the least she could do. Jet had been so loyal to her father throughout the years.

She remembered the first summer she'd met the dog. He'd sniffed her and occasionally allowed her to pet him, but he clearly wasn't all that interested in her. Jedediah had been his sole focus.

Jet whined and it tore at her. She and the dog might not have been best buddies, but she didn't want him to die. Suddenly her eyes filled with tears and her chest hurt so badly.

Benjamin pulled to a stop beside the animal hospital. Vivian willed herself to dry her tears. She swiped at her cheeks with the backs of her hands, but she couldn't stop herself.

When Benjamin opened the door, she wanted to hide her face.

"Aw, sweetheart. Come here," he said and pulled her into his embrace.

"I don't understand why I can't stop crying. That dog doesn't even like me very much. And he stinks," she added, sobbing.

"He's a part of your dad you don't want to lose," Benjamin said.

"Kinda like the lodge. And Millicent. And Grayson." She sniffed. "When am I going to stop chasing him when I know he's gone?"

"Nah, he's not gone. There are pieces of Jedediah all over the place. In your sisters. In Jet. You just want as much as you can get. No shame in that."

Vivian felt something inside her crack open just a little bit. It was both a relief and scary at the same time. This whole thing was getting to her. Benjamin was getting to her. Being with him made her feel both exhilarated and at peace. She'd never felt this way about a man and it was becoming more and more difficult to keep her heart safe from him.

Chapter Seven

Jet's paw was shredded from the trap, but the vet seemed hopeful that he would recover. "He just needs to rest and keep the bandage clean," Vivian repeated the vet's instructions under her breath as Benjamin pulled into the driveway to the lodge.

"He spends most every day in a half coma. What got into him today?" she muttered, petting Jet's head.

"A full moon is coming. That can make any creature act weirdly," Benjamin said.

She nodded, wondering if the moon was causing her to act out of character. "The vet looked at me strangely when I asked if he wouldn't mind giving Jet a bath today."

"They just want to wait a day for his wound to

heal a little. Jedediah would turn in in his grave if he thought you were going to pay to get Jet washed. He always did it with the hose."

"I've been thinking about that. Maybe Jet wouldn't hate getting cleaned as much if the water was warmer and the experience wasn't so unpleasant."

"Are you talking about a spa day for Jet?" Benjamin asked doubtfully, glancing at her in the rear-view mirror.

"Hey, it's worth a try. Until then, we'll use this doggy deodorant I bought from the vet."

"Bet Jet will lick it off," Benjamin said, pulling the SUV to a stop. He rounded to the back and opened the hatch. "I'm surprised you haven't said a word about the vet bill."

"I'm still in shock," she said. "But I was so afraid he wouldn't be okay that I was all, 'Here, take my money.'" She shook her head and looked down at the hound. "You're worth every stinkin' cent, aren't you, Jet?"

The dog licked her hand as if to thank her.

"Looks like he's starting to like you," Benjamin said, helping her out of the back of the SUV.

"Gold diggin' sweetie pie," she said, rubbing the dog again. She turned to look up at Benjamin. "Thank you for everything."

"Does this mean I get an extra day of fishing?"

"You can have an extra week. I was a wreck," she said. "I sure couldn't have released him from the jaws of that trap by myself."

Benjamin put his arm around her. "I think you

did pretty well. I'll have a word with your neighbor, although he's allowed to set traps on his property."

Jilly and Temple burst out the door. "Is he okay? How's his paw?"

"We both want to see for ourselves," Jilly said and rushed to pat Jet.

"True," Temple said. "Bet it wasn't cheap."

Vivian lifted her eyebrows at her sister. "Are you saying I should have refused service?"

"Oh, no," Temple said, then lifted her hands. "But I'm an accountant, so I think about this stuff."

"I understand. I think we may need to keep Jet on a leash for a while," Vivian said.

"Leash?" Benjamin echoed. "I don't think Jedediah ever put Jet on a leash."

"No baths, no leash," Vivian said. "This is getting better and better."

She glanced at Benjamin and saw him frown as he read something on his cell phone. "Problem?" she asked.

"I need to go back into town," he said. "I'll carry Jet up to his dog bed, and then I need to leave."

Just like that, Benjamin's whole demeanor changed. He was distracted and unhappy. She wondered what was bothering him so much. She wished he would tell her, but she could see he was shut down tight.

Benjamin pushed the speed limit on the way to the pharmacy in town. Damn insurance. His sister had a hard enough time staying on her medication without the insurance company making it difficult for her.

He pushed open the door to the drugstore and saw his sister squared off with the man at the cash register. "Miss Hunter, it says here that your insurance will not cover this medication. I'm sorry, but—"

"That's a crock," Eliza said. "Why would my doctor prescribe something my insurance wouldn't cover?"

"Doctors don't always keep track of all the rules with insurance. Nowadays it's nearly impossible," the pharmacist told her and adjusted his glasses.

"Well, I can't pay that much," she yelled, balling her fists at her sides. "What am I supposed to do?"

The pharmacist cleared his throat nervously. "Miss Hunter, you know this isn't my fault. I would gladly give it to you if I could."

"Eliza," Benjamin called and put his arm around her stiffened body. "Hey, maybe we can work this out. What's the damage?" he asked, and looked at the bill. "Whoa," he said. "I can see why you're upset." He looked at the pharmacist. "Ken, you gotta call the doctor on this one."

"I'll do that, but he may substitute a different medication. Is that what you want?" Ken asked. Benjamin knew the pharmacist had filled many prescriptions for Eliza and knew that finding the right medication for her condition seemed to be an ongoing struggle.

"He'll put me on that stuff before that made me

feel all cloudy," Eliza said. "I'd rather go without if I have to take that."

Benjamin's gut tightened at the idea of his sister going without any meds. Her lows had turned dangerous more than once. "Let me take a look at that bill again."

"You can't pay that. It's ridiculous," Eliza said.

Benjamin waved his hand. "Ken, how about you call the doctor? We'll come back in an hour."

"The doctor may not call me back, and I close at six tonight," Ken said. "I can stretch it to six fifteen, but my wife won't be happy."

"Okay. Just do your best. We'll be back before you close." Benjamin turned to his sister. "Let's go to the bar. I'll get you a burger and some onion rings. You look like you could use some comfort food."

"I haven't felt hungry lately," she said. "It's a shame you don't serve milk shakes."

"We have ice cream. I'm sure Jimmy can come up with something for you. Come on. You can tell me about the jewelry you've been making," he said, urging her out the door and down the street.

"You must really be desperate if you're asking to hear about my jewelry," she said. "I wasn't ready to jump off a cliff back there. I was just getting anxious. That's why I sent you a text."

"And that's why I'm here," he said.

"I thought you were supposed to be taking your fishing vacation at the lodge," she said.

"I am. Kinda," he said. "Jedediah's daughters are

giving the place a face-lift. I think they're going to try to bring in more paying guests."

"How do you feel about that?" she asked.

He shrugged. "They're trying to keep it running. It may bring a little business my way, too."

"Not that you're hurting since you own the only bar in town," she said as they arrived at the door to his business.

"I try to keep up with what customers want," he said and waved to Jimmy behind the bar. "Two orders of burgers and onion rings. If you can rustle up a milk shake for the lady, that would be great. I'll take water."

"You can have beer," Eliza said. "It won't tempt me. I've learned alcohol and these meds don't mix," she said.

"Glad to hear it, but I'll stick with water for now. So, tell me about your jewelry," he said.

"Tell me about the Jackson girls first. You were older and got to spend time at the lodge when I didn't. Plus, it seemed like they were only here during the summers. I always heard they were high society. Can't imagine them doing any physical labor."

Benjamin smiled, picturing Vivian with paint smeared on her face. "Looks like they're all painting machines right now. They're trying to get the lodge ready for wedding season."

Eliza's eyes widened. "Wedding season? Who would want to get married at a hunting and fishing lodge?"

"You'd be surprised. They've gotten the wiring

and plumbing redone on the cabins. Now they're painting the lodge," he said.

"Why don't they just pay someone to do it?"

Benjamin rubbed his fingers together. "Jedediah left the lodge, but not a lot of cash."

"Oh. I'm surprised they didn't just sell it," she said, smiling her thanks at the bartender when he delivered their meals.

"I think they considered it, but something changed their minds."

"Hmm," she said, munching on an onion ring. "I heard they always wore designer clothes and had perfect hair."

"I think their mother was a perfectionist. They seem pretty nice to me. A little nervous about making it all work, but nice."

"But not pretty," she said.

"I didn't say that."

"Oh."

"Tell me about your jewelry," he said.

Eliza gave him a knowing grin. "I wonder if my brother has a crush on one of them."

"Jewelry," he returned, determined not to bite. Eliza could turn into a real snoop if she wanted. He'd always kept his meager love life private from her, and he didn't want to start stirring up her interest now.

The arrival of her milk shake distracted her slightly, and he told her to hustle with consuming her meal so they could get back to the pharmacy.

A few minutes later, it only took one look at Ken's

face to see they were stuck with either no news or bad news. "I'm sorry," Ken said. "They didn't get back in touch with me. I'll get in touch with them tomorrow for you."

Benjamin could feel his sister fretting, although the only visible sign was the knotting and unknotting of her fingers.

"Can we get half the prescription?" Benjamin asked.

"Benjamin, no—" Eliza began.

"I can cover it. I haven't bought any Maseratis lately," he joked.

"Sure, you can take half," Ken said. "I'll ring it up for you and call the doctor again tomorrow."

After Benjamin paid for the prescription and they left the pharmacy, he walked her to her car. "You want me to come over tonight?"

She shook her head. "No. I'm okay. Burger, onion rings, milk shake and new drugs. I didn't sleep well last night, so I'm hoping tonight will be better." She must've spotted the concern on his face even though he thought he was so good at concealing it. She gave him a light punch. "Stop worrying. I'm going to a support group meeting tomorrow."

"Hey, that's great news. How far do you have to drive?" he asked.

"Just twenty-five miles. I can do that." She sighed, then gave him a big hug. "Thanks for being such a good brother."

Forty-five minutes later, Benjamin walked toward the dock with a beer in his hand. When he saw Vivian seated and leaning against a post, he stopped, wondering if he should turn around and go to his room. After his time with his sister, he felt edgy. At the moment, he wasn't full of easy comebacks or jokes.

"Hey, stranger," she called out.

She must have spotted him. Benjamin walked the dock and slid down to sit opposite her. "Sorry I didn't bring your wine. I thought this might be too late for you."

"No problem. I've got my own," she said, lifting her mostly full glass. "Problems?"

"Just putting out a fire before it gets out of control," he said, popped open his can and took a deep swallow.

"You want to talk about it?" she asked.

"Not really," he said. "How's Jet?"

"Back to comatose," she said. "He's favoring his paw. I can't say I blame him. I gave him some of the pain medication from the vet."

"That's good," he said.

Silence stretched between them.

"Listen, Vivian, I may not be the best company tonight. I've got some things on my mind," he said.

"But you don't want to talk about them," she said.

"No."

"Okay. I guess this also means you don't want to go swimming in the lake," she said, trying to get a smile out of him.

He met her gaze, and she saw a glint in his eye. "Are you offering to go first?"

Her breath hitched at the underlying challenge in his tone. "It's a little chilly tonight," she said. "Even you are wearing a jacket."

"Then why did you suggest it?" he asked.

"To help you get back a little sense of humor." She shook her head at herself. "I'm not helping," she muttered. "I should probably go." She started to leave, but he grabbed her hand.

"No need to rush off," he said. "Unless you mind just sitting for a while."

"I guess not," she said.

"Then come over here next to me. That'll put me in a better mood," he said and almost grinned.

She sank down beside him and rested her back against his arm. She closed her eyes and sighed, and she decided to stop worrying for just a moment. She pushed the dark anxiousness and what-ifs from her mind and listened to the water lap against the dock.

"That's a wonderful sound," she said in a low voice. "The water."

"You have to be quiet to hear it."

"Quiet in your mind," she added and turned slightly to look up at him. "You've been living close to the lake for ages. How often have you sat on a dock and listened to the water?"

"Not often enough. I've been busy growing the bar, and then I bought an auto repair shop. I invested in the bakery/ice-cream shop. Not sure how that last one happened."

"You've been busy building your empire," she said.

He chuckled. "I'm not sure I'd call it an empire,

but it has kept me busy. I always liked taking this break at the lodge. I was close enough for emergencies with people or issues, but I wasn't in the middle of everything. And now that I've talked the new boss into letting me stay longer…" He lowered his head and nuzzled her forehead.

Vivian relished the sensation. This was a practically perfect moment in an imperfect day. Lifting her head, she brushed her cheek against his, which was just a little rough from his slight beard.

Benjamin lowered his mouth to hers and kissed her sweetly, deeply. She savored the sensation of his warmth and strength.

The kiss seemed to go on and on, and Vivian grew warmer. She wanted to push her hands beneath his shirt to feel his bare skin, but she stopped herself. The temptation made her feel a little light-headed.

Benjamin pulled away for a short, breathless moment and held her gaze. The desire she saw rocketed through her. He lowered his mouth again, and this time he slid his hands underneath her shirt. His hands were warm, searching and clever. After releasing the clasp of her bra, her cupped one of her breasts and rubbed his thumb over her nipple.

Vivian couldn't resist the urge to press into his hand.

"Like that, huh? I do, too," he murmured against her mouth. He pulled her on top of him, positioning her so she could feel that he was aroused.

Vivian instinctively rubbed against him and he

groaned, squeezing her hips. Vivian strained toward him. She wanted more. She wanted him.

He pulled back slightly. "Viv, if we keep going like this, I'm not gonna want to stop," he said.

She bit her lip and tried to stick to reason, but she wanted him more than the warning bell clanging in her brain. "I don't want to stop, either," she said and ran her hands over his skin.

He hissed at her touch and pulled her back to his mouth. His kiss spoke of dark, raw need, and something inside her echoed the emotion right back at him. He stripped off her shirt and his, but kept her warm in his arms.

"Cold?" he asked.

Vivian shook her head, reveling in the sensation of her breasts against his chest. The night air was cool, but he was hot and making her hotter with each passing moment. He dropped his mouth to her breasts, and she arched into him.

She couldn't remember feeling wanted this much. She couldn't remember wanting this much. He unfastened her jeans and pushed them down, along with her panties. His hands were warm as he caressed her between her legs and she grew damp and restless.

Moving against him, she pulled his mouth to his and kissed him, drawing his tongue into her mouth. His groan of approval aroused her even more, and she reached down to undo his jeans. He was warm and hard, and she enjoyed touching him as intimately as he had touched her.

"Oh, Viv," he said. "I'm not going to be able to stand much of that."

"I want you to feel the way I do," she whispered.

"Lady, I'm already there," he told her and laid his jacket beneath her on the dock. Shucking his jeans, he pulled protection from his pocket.

A breeze flowed over her body, and for just a second she felt a chill. But he covered her with his warmth.

"How did you just happen to have a condom in your pocket?" she asked, smiling into his eyes.

"I told you. The way you make me feel, I always want to be ready. Now I'm going to make sure you're ready, too."

He kissed and caressed his way down her body and back up again until it was all she could do not to beg him to finish her. She felt as if she were in full sensual bloom and need. She might not be verbally begging, but her body sure was.

Touching him again intimately, she found him even harder with need. "Oh, Viv, I've got to have you." He put on the protection and plunged inside her.

His gaze locking with hers, he moved in a rhythm that took them both higher and higher. Sensation chased emotion, and Vivian felt herself burst into a powerful climax. Seconds later, Benjamin thrust deep inside her and stiffened, groaning in pleasure.

Still bracing himself on his forearms, he sank closer to her, kissing her throat. "How'd you get to be so good and bad at the same time?" he asked her.

"I didn't know I was," she said, trying to catch her breath. She wrapped her arms around his shoulders, holding him close, wanting to stay in his embrace as long as possible.

Benjamin rolled onto his back and pulled her on top of him. "You okay?" he asked in sexy, husky voice. "Wanna go again?"

"Oh, wow," she said, feeling a wicked thrill. "Yes, but I'm starting to feel that cool breeze."

"Can't have that," he said and dragged his jacket from beside them to cover her back.

Vivian snuggled against him, savoring the moment, because she knew it couldn't last forever.

"You're quiet," he said. "Regrets already?"

"None," she told him, meeting his gaze. "But I may be a little sex-drunk."

"I'll have to see if I can keep you that way," Benjamin said.

"That could be dangerous," she said.

"I'm willing to try it," he said and took her mouth.

Vivian felt a combination of thrill and fear. She needed to keep the reins on her heart. She'd learned that when she didn't, things could go badly.

Chapter Eight

Vivian slept so hard she drooled on her pillow and awakened an hour past the time she usually rose. After glancing at her clock, she scrambled out of bed and took a quick shower and dressed. She tried not to think about making love with Benjamin last night, but her body reminded her with subtle aches and awareness. She'd forgotten sex could be a workout, or maybe it never had been for her before.

Grabbing an energy bar and a cup of coffee, she gave a quick greeting to Grayson and checked on Jet. The dog seemed to be resting well. Climbing the stairs, she waved at Jilly and mouthed, "Good morning," since Jilly was wearing her earphones.

"Hello. This is looking great," she said to Temple,

pausing on her way to the room she hoped to finish painting today.

"Thanks," Temple said. "Where have you been?"

"I overslept. I guess some of the stress just caught up with me," she said, even though she knew Benjamin was the reason she'd slept so well.

"You're not sick, are you?" Temple asked, walking toward her, studying her more closely.

"No. I'm fine," Vivian said, feeling self-conscious. Even though she knew Temple couldn't see what Vivian had done on the dock last night, she still felt uncomfortable under her scrutiny. "That extra hour of sleep did wonders. I'll head on to my assigned room since I'm a bit behind schedule."

"Wait a minute." Temple frowned. "What's wrong with your neck? It looks like you have a bruise," she said, lifting her finger. "If you were a teenager, I'd suspect a hickey. Have you been having a little too much fun with Benjamin?"

Vivian felt a rush of heat to her face and prayed it didn't show. "Oh, of course not. It's not as if I have gobs of extra time." She rubbed at her neck. "I must have scratched it when I was in the woods looking for Jet yesterday. I was so frantic to find him, I must not have noticed."

"It doesn't look like a scratch," Temple mused.

"Well, it must have happened yesterday. I can't think of anything else. It's not bothering me, so I imagine it will go away soon. I really should get on with painting if we're going to meet our goal. I'll see you at lunch. Okay?"

Temple nodded. "Okay. Don't work too hard. We don't need you getting sick."

"I'm fine. Thanks, though," Vivian said over her shoulder as she headed down the hallway. As soon as she entered the bedroom she was painting, she darted into the bathroom to look in the mirror. Sure enough, she saw a bruise on the side of her neck. Swearing, she released her hair from its ponytail in order to cover the telltale mark. She would have to give Benjamin instructions to be more careful next time. She caught herself at the thought and swore again. Not that there would be a next time.

Benjamin caught a few fish that morning, but they were either too small or they were carp. Nothing worth eating. His mind was mostly on Vivian. He hadn't expected her to be such a daring lover, but she'd been hot enough to fry him inside and out, and now he wanted more. Not just sex. He wanted more time with her, period.

After he cleaned up, he meandered down the hallway to the room she was painting. With her backside facing him, he couldn't help thinking about how he'd squeezed her last night. He came up behind her and put his hands on her hips.

"Aren't you ready for some lunch?"

Vivian squealed, whirling so quickly to face him that he had to dodge her paintbrush. "Whoa," he said, steadying her hand.

"You startled me. What are you doing, sneaking up behind me like that?" she demanded.

"I wasn't sneaking. You just didn't hear me," he said. "What's got your panties in a twist?"

"I think Temple may suspect you and I—" she hesitated "—got together last night. I don't want anyone to know. I don't want to be teased. I don't want the speculation."

"Why would she suspect?" he asked.

"Because you gave me a hickey!" she said in the most outraged whisper he'd ever heard. She lifted her hair to reveal the mark.

"Oops. I don't remember..." He shrugged. "Gotta tell you, I pretty much wanted to consume you. I guess I shouldn't be surprised."

Color rose to her cheeks. "Well, you need to be more careful when we—" She cleared her throat. "If we," she corrected herself.

"I'll do my best, but you're hell on my control. I'm wondering if I might affect you the same way," he said and pulled back his collar so that she could see the mark she'd left on his neck.

Her eyes widened in shock, and she covered her mouth. "Oh, my, no." She shook her head. "Are you sure I did that? I mean, I've never—not that I can remember, anyway." She closed her eyes, clearly mortified. "I apologize."

"Don't," he said and pulled her into his arms. "If I'm the first guy you gave a hickey, then I'm honored. You can even do it again if the mood strikes," he said and chuckled as he brushed his mouth over her forehead.

She glanced up at him. "It's not funny. I'd like to

keep our relationship secret. I don't want to draw attention."

"I'm not really big on secrets. I've had to deal with a few in my lifetime, and they can turn into a big burden," he said, thinking of his sister and his parents' relationship. "But I get that you want to be discreet. I'll try not to attack you when you're around other people."

That afternoon while Vivian painted and tried not to think about Benjamin, her cell phone rang with an unfamiliar number on the caller ID. She considered not answering because her work calls were filtered through the office, but shrugged and picked up. "Vivian Jackson," she said, surveying her painting job.

"Hello, Vivian, this is Corinne Whitman Jergenson. Your friend Sela Warren mentioned you are opening a lake house as an intimate wedding venue. My daughter is getting married. Third marriage," she murmured in a low voice. "We'd like to do this soon. We've been visiting my mother in Ashville, and I wondered if Olive and I could pop by your lakeside villa for a peek."

Vivian nearly dropped her phone. She'd always thought Sela Warren looked down on her as if Vivian weren't quite good enough, despite the fact that the two of them were active in several charities in Atlanta. Perhaps she did look down on her, if she'd sent *the* Corinne Whitman Jergenson, whose father owned a quarter of the state of Georgia.

"I'm so flattered. I don't know what to say. We are nowhere ready to entertain guests. In fact, I'm pa—I'm supervising refurbishment even at this moment."

"No problem. Olive and I have vivid imaginations. We can picture the possibilities."

Vivian clenched her jaw and took a deep breath. "Well, I fear Sela may have embellished. You know what a positive person she is. Honeymoon Mountain Lake is more of a hunting and fishing lodge with cabins."

The deep sound of silence stretched.

Vivian counted to ten, then decided to rescue both herself and *the* Corinne from continuing discomfort. "I really appreciate your interest, but—"

"We'd still like to visit," Corinne said. "Olive's husband-to-be is a professional bass fisherman. And since it's her third marriage… We'll arrive in two hours. See you soon."

"But. But. But." Vivian realized she was speaking to air. "Oh, crap," she said and darted from the room.

"Corinne Whitman Jergenson is coming," she yelled. "We need to straighten up, clean up, make everything perfect," she said, trying to keep her panic from her voice.

Temple peeked her head outside a room down the hall. "Who is Corinne Whitman Jergenson?" she asked.

"She's big. Very big. High society in Atlanta. If we impress her, she will say wonderful things about us."

"So, why is she coming here?" Temple asked.

"It's her daughter's third wedding. I guess they're hedging their bets," Vivian said. "Start cleaning and straightening, please."

Vivian continued down the hall and found Jillian happily painting. Her sister was wearing earphones and wiggling her butt as she painted. Vivian knew yelling would do no good, so she tapped Jilly on the shoulder.

Her sister jumped, splattering paint everywhere.

Vivian swallowed several swearwords.

Jillian pulled out her earphones. "What? Why did you startle me?"

"How do I not startle you when you're wearing earphones?"

Jillian frowned. "Well." She scowled. "I don't know. What do you want?"

"We have a big-time potential client coming, so we need to clean up as quickly as we can."

"Now?" Jillian asked.

"Five minutes ago."

"Who could be that important?"

"She's a very influential woman from Atlanta. If she praises us, we'll be getting bookings with no problems. Her approval is great advertising."

"And if she doesn't like the lodge?" Jillian asked.

Vivian made a face. "Let's not think about that."

She crammed as much as she could into closets and fluffed the pillows on the sofa and chairs on the porch. As she headed to the bar with a dust rag, a knock sounded at the front door.

Wincing, she stuffed the rag in a cabinet and

raced to the door. Just as she opened the door, she realized her hair was in a ponytail and she might still have paint on her face. *Alrighty.*

Vivian flung open the door and gave her best smile. "Hello, and welcome to Honeymoon Lodge. I wish we could have been better prepared for your visit. Please come in and bear in mind that we're making improvements."

Corrine Whitman Jergenson smiled. Her lips moved, but the rest of her face did not. Neither did her hair. Olive wore so much eye makeup and contouring cream.

Olive smiled, however, and the rest of her face moved, so Vivian felt a smidge of relief.

"This looks so charming and rustic. I just know Bubba would approve of it," Olive said. "He loves hunting and fishing, and I know he loves me for me."

"Yes, dear," Corinne said. "Let's take a look around first. I must ask," she said to Vivian, "where would you hold the ceremony?"

"We have limited space for large gatherings. Some people use the foyer for their weddings. The stairway offers a grand entrance and can be decorated as you wish."

"It's a bit small," Corinne said.

Vivian's stomach knotted. "Yes. I'm not sure what size group you want to accommodate."

"We're not, either," Corinne muttered.

"We also offer two outside venues," Vivian said and led them through the screened-in porch to view the outdoor dock. "If you want a larger group, we can accommodate a wedding by the lake."

"Oh, that's beautiful," Olive said. "Bubba would love it."

"What if it rains?" Corinne countered.

"Tents can be rented," Vivian said.

"But the mud," Corinne said with a frown.

"There is one other option in our bar area," Vivian said, walking back to the lodge. "We can remove seating. It would be cozy. After the ceremony, we could open the bar and other areas to accommodate the guests."

Corinne glanced around the area. "It's a bit dark, but not bad. With a little extra lighting, it could work."

"I like the outside better," Olive said.

"Outside venues get too expensive with the need for tents and temperature control, especially since we'd be at the mercy of the weather," Corinne said. "I can see possibilities here. How many bedrooms are available?"

"We have fifteen rooms in the lodge and seven cabins. I must remind you that our accommodations are more rustic than luxury."

"Does that mean our guests will use outhouses?"

"Oh, no," Vivian said. "Our cabins are furnished with comfortable linens, heat and air-conditioning, bathrooms, and a microwave and minifridge."

Corinne waved her hand. "That's more than many luxury resorts offer. Plus, you have an amazing view." She paused. "And it's only one weekend."

Vivian somehow felt as if she'd been patted and slapped at the same time, but forced a smile. "Well, thank you so much for stopping by."

The back door flung open and Jet ambled into the room with Benjamin behind him, carting a cooler. Jet dumped a dead fish at Vivian's feet.

Benjamin glanced from Vivian to the visitors and shook his head. "Jet got out again. He grabbed one of my fish. I guess he was determined to bring it to you."

Despite the disdainful glare of Corinne, Vivian knew what she had to do. Poor Jet had been depressed for so long. She bent down and petted him. "Sweet boy. You're such a good boy. Jet was my father's dog," she began.

Olive wrinkled her nose. "That smell. Is it the fish?"

Unfortunately not. The *smell* was Jet. Before Vivian could say or do anything, she caught sight of Millicent at the bottom of the stairs, wearing a house robe. "Oh, dear," she said. "Do we have visitors? This is my first day I can take on the stairs by myself."

"Good for you," Vivian said. "I'm so pleased for you." She turned to Corinne. "Mrs. Jergenson, I know you can appreciate overcoming a disabling injury. Everyone is familiar with your charity work."

Corinne lifted her chin with an expression of pride. "Yes, of course I understand. I've volunteered many hours of my time, and my husband has even donated a wing to the hospital." She walked to Mil-

licent and offered her hand. "Congratulations on
your improvement. I'm sure you'll be back to your
old self in no time." She then turned to her daughter. "Olive, we should go. Miss Jackson, thank you
for your hospitality. We'll contact you if we need
further information."

"Thank you for stopping by," Vivian said, and
the door closed behind Corinne and her daughter.

Her sisters appeared suddenly as if they'd been
hiding in the woodwork. "How do you think it
went?" Temple asked.

Vivian glanced down at Jet and the dead fish at
her feet and sighed. "I don't know. It seemed like
Corinne wanted to downsize the wedding this time."

"Well, it is Olive's third time down the aisle, isn't
it?" Temple asked.

"Still," Vivian said, her stomach sinking. "I hope
I didn't blow it."

"You didn't blow it," Benjamin said with a shrug.
"I thought you handled the dead fish very well."

His encouragement eased some of her anxiety. At
the same time, Vivian felt uncomfortable with the
idea of counting on Benjamin. Booking this wedding was on her shoulders, not his. "Thanks. Now,
what to do about Jet's odor?"

"I'll take care of it," Jillian said. "I've been thinking about this, and now is the time. I'm going to give
Jet a bath. Inside."

Vivian winced. "Are you sure that's a good idea?
We don't want him tearing up a bathroom."

"It will be fine," she said. "I'm going to give Jet

a spa experience. You know, I once worked at a spa," she said.

"I didn't know that, but I'm not really surprised because you seem to have become a jack-of-all-trades," Vivian said. "Do you want some help?"

"Nope," Jillian said. "I figure three or four hamburgers should distract him enough to get the job done. I'll go fix them right now."

Vivian, Temple and Benjamin watched as Jillian headed to the kitchen, her shoulders squared with determination.

"She's brave," Vivian said.

"Yes, she is. I'll get back to painting," Temple said and walked away.

"I'd better help her," Vivian said.

"Meet me on the dock later?" Benjamin asked.

Vivian shook her head. She clearly needed to get control of herself. "Not tonight."

Ignoring the terrible longing to escape with Benjamin, she joined Jilly in the kitchen, where her sister was putting frozen burgers in the microwave. "I can do this by myself," Jilly said. "And the great thing about Jet is that he won't care that I microwaved the burgers. Why don't you spend some time with Benjamin? You could use it."

"What do you mean, I could use it?" Vivian asked.

Jilly shrugged. "You just seem a little less tense after you've been with Benjamin. Otherwise, you're kinda…" Jilly broke off as she peeked at the progress of the burgers.

"I'm kinda what?" Vivian said.

"I don't know. Tense, a little cranky," Jilly said and slid a sideways glance at her. "Don't get mad at me."

"I'm not mad," Vivian said. "I guess I just didn't realize it was showing that much."

"Well, we're together 24/7, so the real you is going to leak out sometimes."

"Nice to know the real me is so disagreeable," Vivian muttered.

Jilly shook her head as the microwave dinged. "You're not disagreeable all the time. But you have to admit you're worried. You feel responsible for everything, more than you should."

Vivian sighed.

"My offer for morning yoga is still open," Jilly said.

"I have a hard time concentrating during yoga. My mind wanders," Vivian said.

"See Benjamin, then. He's the reason why your mind is wandering," Jilly said. "Time for Jet's bath."

Vivian didn't call Benjamin, but she kept thinking about him. Jilly set the spa mood in the bathroom with soothing Zen music and dimmed lights for the dog. Despite Jilly's best efforts, when they corralled Jet into the bathroom and hoisted him into the tub, he howled and whined as if they were killing him.

Jilly and Vivian kept encouraging him and giving him bites of burger as they scrubbed away his dirt and stink. After a few minutes, he became distracted by the bites of burger and let Jilly have her way with him.

By the end of the ordeal, he still smelled like a wet dog, but a cleaner wet dog. Drenched and exhausted, Vivian looked at Jilly. "There's got to be an easier way. Next time we'll pay the vet to do it."

Jilly shook her head. "Jet is so difficult that I'm not sure even the vet would be willing to do it," she said. "But we can tell everyone in this house not to let him outside, and maybe that will help."

"And a little powder," Vivian said. "Remember how Dad said a little powder could make everything better?"

Jilly chuckled. "We can hope. I'm turning in early tonight. What about you?"

Vivian nodded and thought again of Benjamin. She reined in her unwelcome longing for him. "Me, too."

Chapter Nine

"Pizza delivery," Benjamin called as he knocked on the door of his sister's townhome.

Seconds passed and the door flung open. Eliza laughed up at him. "What a nice surprise. Why are you here? I've been okay lately."

"Surprise pizza is not dependent on your health. In fact, we all need pizza."

"Well, I'll take it," she said, grabbing the box from him. "But what did I do to deserve this visit?"

"Nothing," Benjamin said with a shrug. "I just wanted to visit my sister. How's everything going?" he asked, glancing at the kitchen table, where she had been creating jewelry.

"Good," she said. "I'm doing shows the next few weeks. But what's going on with you?" she asked.

"Nothing. Just taking some time off and fishing," he said.

"Hmm. Why don't I believe you?"

"I don't know," he said. "Why don't you?"

"I think you're under the spell of one of those Jackson girls," she said.

"I'm not under the spell of anyone or anything," he said, even though he felt Vivian's presence in his brain. "I keep a clear head. I have to."

His sister frowned. "Now I feel guilty because I know you have to keep a clear head because of me."

"Don't feel guilty. I have to keep a clear head for everything in my life. It's not a bad thing," he said. "Now, let's eat some pizza and you show me your new jewelry."

"You're dodging me," Eliza said. "But I'm hungry."

While they gobbled down the pizza, Eliza showed him the bracelets, necklaces and earrings she'd created with multicolored stones and hammered metal. Her enthusiasm and intensity about her art had always warmed his heart. Even when she was a little girl, Eliza had always loved art. One of the first signs that she was on a downward turn was a lack of interest in art.

At the moment, though, she seemed to be doing well.

"You sleeping?" he asked.

"Some," she said. "Are you diagnosing me? Because I don't want it right now."

"Just asking," he said with a shrug, but he wondered.

"Don't worry. I have a lot to get done for these shows, but I'm sleeping. Really."

"Good," he said, although he still worried.

"Good," she said. "I think one of those Jackson girls is on your mind. Don't lie to me. Is she trying to rope you into marriage?"

He laughed. "That couldn't be further from the truth." He hesitated a half beat. "She wants to hide our relationship."

"Whoa." She stared at him in surprise. "That's new. Don't most of your girls want you to marry them?"

He shot her a sideways glance.

"Well, maybe except for that one from college who didn't like the idea of settling down in a small t___. ___ shrugged. "I hope it works out how you want it to. I doubt I'll ever marry. I'm still learning how to deal with all my ups and downs. It's hard enough on my brother and me."

"___ ___ that," he said. "You've got a lot going ___ ___ like you could be a little

___k? No, thank you. I'm not ___t to be pitied."

___ty and sympathy and em- ___ow for a fact that you're not ___uggles."

"How ___ ___ that?" she challenged him.

"I own a bar," he said. "You wouldn't believe all the stories I've heard."

"And just like a therapist or a priest, you never tell," she said.

"I've never liked to gossip," he said and knew the reason. People had gossiped about his father for years. As a trucker, his father had spent most of his time away from home. There'd been talk that he had cheated on his mother. Benjamin didn't like the thought of it but knew it was a possibility. Since his father had died in his teens, there were a lot of unanswered questions. Not the kind of questions he would have wanted to ask his mother, especially given her fragile health.

"Saint Benjamin," she teased.

"You know that's not true. If I were a saint, I wouldn't take the last piece of pizza," he said as he snatched the slice and smiled before he took a big bite.

Benjamin almost didn't go back to the lake, but something drew him. It was a cloudy night, but he spotted Vivian perched on the end of the dock, swinging her legs like a little girl. He could almost swear, however, that he saw the weight of the world on those slim but deceptively strong shoulders. Something about the sight of her made his gut tighten. His response to her still caught him off guard.

As he walked toward her, she turned to look at him. "Hi," she said in a soft voice.

"Hi to you," he said, but didn't sit down to join her on the dock.

"I should apologize for acting so cranky with you," she said.

He swallowed a chuckle. "Does that mean you *are* apologizing? Or just that you think should?"

"I apologize. I freaked and took it out on you. I'm sorry," she said.

"Apology accepted," he said and sat down beside her. "You're still worried," he added, glancing at the lake, then back at her.

She nodded. "I haven't heard from Corinne Whitman Jergenson." She paused. "But I did hear from my mother."

"Not a sparkling experience?" he asked.

She gave a wry chuckle. "Not," she said. "I can usually dodge her questions by steering the conversation back to her and my stepfather. But it didn't work this time. I think she senses that both Temple and I have been avoiding her. Neither of us wanted to tell her that we were at Honeymoon Mountain, trying to repair it and make it profitable."

"It's not like you've formed a crime ring. What's so wrong with the three of you pulling together and making this a successful joint effort?"

"Just everything. My mother has very specific ideas and plans for the people in her life. The best way to describe it is, her life is an engine and we are parts of that engine and must play our roles. Trust me, none of her plans include having her daughters bring a hunting lodge back to life."

"Is that why none of you live near her?" he asked.

"That's one reason," she said and shook her head. "She's still not over the fact that I divorced my husband. She told me I should look the other way and give it another try after he got another woman pregnant."

"You're joking," he said.

"No. She said she didn't know if she would survive the scandal among her friends." She sighed. "It seems like she changed after she left my father and got remarried. Everything was about appearances. I went to a private girls' school. I had a lisp, so the other kids made fun of me. My mother was determined that I make friends with the right people, so I saw a speech therapist. It took a while, but I finally lost the lisp. She was so thrilled when it was gone." Vivian glanced down, then up again. "Of course, I was glad, too, and relieved. I was very fortunate that she had the determination and resources to help me."

Silence stretched between them. "But?" he prompted.

She stretched her neck from side to side to relieve tension. "It's going to sound weird, but I remember visiting my father after I'd finally lost the lisp. He said, 'Your little girl voice is gone.' I nodded. He said, 'I'll miss that, but good job. Good for you.'" She bit her lip. "They were such opposites. She was all about appearances. He couldn't give a rip what people thought."

"And you've got the best of both," he said.

Vivian laughed. "They were both extreme, so I'm

not sure what is the best of both. My biggest fear is that my mom will show up here."

"Why?" he asked. "It's not like she has supernatural evil powers."

Vivian winced. "Sometimes it seems like she does. She can make you feel like the worst thing in the world. Or, on very, very rare occasions, she can make you feel like the best."

He shrugged. "If you let her."

"What do you mean?"

"It's all about power. If you don't give her the power, then she doesn't have it. She can't tell you if you're the worst or the best if you don't let her. I've had coaches who tried to manipulate me in good ways and bad ways. You have to choose who you let influence you."

"You sound so smart and sage," she said.

He laughed. "Sports are about power."

"Sometimes it's still hard for me to believe you left it behind," she said.

"I had something more important to do," he said.

"Maybe you should teach me more about sports," she said seductively.

"I can do that," he said and leaned toward her. She lifted her head toward him.

He took her mouth with his.

At the same time, there was a commotion behind them on the dock.

Vivian drew back. "Oh, my."

Benjamin heard a scream and a splash and instinctively rose. "What—"

"It's Temple. She fell into the lake. She doesn't swim that well," Vivian said, running down the dock. "Temple!" she yelled.

Benjamin raced toward the splash and jumped into the lake. He grabbed Temple and dragged her to shore.

"What were you doing?" Vivian yelled to her sister.

"What were you doing?" Temple yelled in return.

"I didn't dive into the lake at night!" Vivian said.

"I wasn't making out on the dock," Temple countered.

"A vapor was involved, but I'm not in charge of this discussion," Benjamin said.

"You're smoking?" Vivian exclaimed. "What in the world are you thinking? You know better than that. I can't believe you, of all people, are smoking."

"Mom called and grilled me today," Temple said.

"Oh," Vivian said. "I understand." She sighed and turned to Benjamin winced. "I'm sorry you got wet. We can talk another time? Thank you. Temple and I need to go in now."

"By all means," he said, because he truly didn't want to get involved in a sister battle.

"You're shivering," Vivian said to Temple. "We need to get you back to the lodge." She urged her sister up the path to the main building. "I'm sorry Mom called you today. She called me, too. I have been putting her off, but I wasn't as successful today."

"Neither was I," Temple said, her teeth chattering. "My biggest fear is that she'll show up here unannounced."

"I've been worried about the same thing," Vivian confessed, guiding her sister down the hallway. "I was hoping her social activities would keep her too busy."

"If she's calling both you and me, she's clearly not busy enough. I just hope she won't try to call Jilly. Jilly is so fragile after being rejected by Mom."

Vivian grabbed a towel as they trudged into Temple's room. "The great thing about Jilly is that she has changed her contact numbers so many times."

"Yes, but Mom can be a pain when it comes to finding people."

Vivian scrubbed her sister with a towel. "I think you need to get into a hot shower."

"I think you're right," Temple said and went to the bathroom.

Vivian heard her sister turn on the spray. Seconds later, Temple called out, "I haven't forgotten that you were making out with Benjamin."

"I was hoping you had," Vivian whispered under her breath. "Get warm," she called.

A few moments later, Temple emerged wearing a towel on her head and a robe. She shot Vivian a questioning brow. "So, what's up with Benjamin?"

"It's supposed to be a secret," Vivian confessed.

"So, this isn't the first time you had a rendezvous on the dock?" Temple asked.

Vivian frowned. "I really don't like discussing this."

"As I don't like discussing my e-cigarette."

Vivian took a deep breath. "Okay. We're kinda involved."

"How involved?"

"Deep, but not forever," Vivian said.

"How do you know it's not forever?" Temple asked.

"Because I'm too busy for forever. I have to make things happen for the lodge," Vivian said.

"Hmm. I'm not sure it will work that way," Temple said.

"Should we discuss your e-cig?" Vivian asked.

"No. I smoked a little when I was in college. You know I finished my degree in three years. I was tempted when I was getting my advanced degrees, but I resisted. It's just since Dad died," Temple said.

"Is this my fault? I shouldn't have pressured you into helping with the lodge," Vivian said.

"No. I want to do this. I just have to manage my partnership and…"

"Do you need to go back to Charlotte? Go back. Go—"

"And there's Mom," Temple interrupted.

"Oh. Sorry," Vivian said.

Temple took a deep breath. "It's okay. Better now that we both know she's after us. Whatever we do, we need to protect Jilly from her."

"Truth," Vivian said and lifted her hand.

Temple lifted hers and pressed it against Vivian's. "Maybe it would be better if we didn't keep so many secrets from each other. Yes?"

"Yes," Vivian said and pulled her sister against her in a hug.

* * *

The following morning, Vivian and her sisters worked nonstop. Vivian still hadn't heard from Corinne Whitman Jergenson and refused to concentrate on that. If that deal didn't work out, another one would.

By the end of the day, she and her sisters ate cheeseburgers prepared by Jilly.

"Best burger in the world," Vivian said.

"Same," Temple said.

"You're just starving," Jilly said with a laugh.

"No, really," Vivian said. "Grilled onions and cheese."

"Mustard and steak sauce," Temple added.

Jilly laughed again. "Well, I'm glad you enjoyed them. By the way, have either of you heard from Mother?"

Vivian nearly choked. "Mother?"

"Yes," she said as she dipped her burger into a combined sauce of mustard and steak sauce. "I received a strange email. I've changed phones several times, so she can't reach me that way. I was surprised to hear from her because she doesn't contact me very often."

"What kind of email?" Temple asked, wiping her mouth. "There's a lot of spam out there."

"This looked legit," Jilly said. "She mentioned both of you. And Honeymoon Mountain."

Vivian swore under her breath. "Delete it. Please."

Vivian felt Jilly searching both her face and Temple's. "Why?"

"She doesn't like it that we're trying to make Honeymoon Mountain work," Vivian said. "Mom has talents and skills, but she can also be a negative influence. We don't need that right now."

"Hmm," Jilly said. "Maybe she needs yoga."

"Yeah," Temple said. "Good luck with that. Yoga meets the devil." She shook her head. "I didn't just say that."

"Of course you didn't," Vivian said, but she knew Jilly was watching and unfortunately hoping for a happily-ever-after with their mother. Vivian was determined to protect her little sister.

An hour later, Vivian holed herself in her room, working on the webpage for the resort. Although she was tired, she was determined to make headway. A knock sounded at her door. Vivian assumed it was one of her sisters. "Come on in," she called.

"Hello," a wonderfully familiar male voice said.

A delicious shiver raced down her spine, and she spun around to look at Benjamin. "What are you doing here?"

"I'm taking you away. You need to escape."

Chapter Ten

"Escape?" Vivian echoed, feeling a flash of excitement. "What do you have in mind?"

"Just trust me," he said. "Grab a cap and sunglasses."

"It's too dark for sunglasses," she said.

"They're only for emergency purposes," he said. "When you need to pretend you're a movie star in disguise."

She couldn't help giggling. "Movie star? Oh, this sounds fun."

"Are you in?" he asked.

"Yes," she said. "Let me grab my cap and sunglasses."

A moment later, she allowed him to lead her out the door, down the road of perdition. Sitting in his

SUV, she turned to him. "Are we going to a strip club?"

Benjamin stared at her in shock. "What the—" He shook his head. "No. This is mostly good, clean fun."

"Well, darn," she said.

He shot her a quick glance. "Are you serious?"

She laughed. "No. I'm giddy over the adventure. I've been so focused."

"Time to change your focus," he said and turned up the radio.

"I feel a little guilty," she said. "My sisters could use a change of focus, too."

"Tomorrow or the next day," he said. "Tonight is for you."

She laughed again. "I can't wait to see my escape."

He reached over and placed his hand over hers. "I think you'll like it."

Twenty minutes later, he drove into a small town.

"Where are we?" she asked.

"Crackerville," he said. "They hold a multicultural festival every year. Latin, Native American, Scottish, everything you can imagine. Put on your cap and you'll fit right in."

Vivian donned her cap and stepped out of his SUV to the competing sounds of Latin music and bagpipes. "What a combination," she said.

He chuckled and took her hand. "Embrace your escape," he said and led her into the crowd.

Latin dancers were teaching people their movements. "Go for it," he said and pushed her into the crowd.

Vivian glanced back at him, then did her best to follow the dances. She laughed throughout the routine. "Oh, pooh," she said as she stumbled repeatedly, but she made it through. She turned around to find Benjamin smiling as he watched her.

She ran toward him. "Happy now that I made a fool of myself?"

"You were no fool," he said. "You had great rhythm."

"You flatter me," she said and put her arm around his waist. "Where to next?"

"Let's eat something really bad," he suggested.

"That sounds good to me," she said.

After a round of shared brats and a funnel cake, Vivian grabbed her stomach. "I'm so full I can barely walk," she said, then saw a row of arts and crafts vendors. "Oh, wait. Let's go look at the crafts."

"Are you sure you don't want to sit down?" Benjamin asked.

She shook her head. "I need to walk off this full feeling. Might as well shop," she said with a smile.

"If you say so," he said, and they walked toward the vendors.

He watched her slide her fingers over scarves, and she even purchased one and asked for the artist's card. Next she admired pottery but didn't make a purchase. Then she arrived at a row of jewelers. At that moment, he felt an indescribable itch, as if this might not be the best idea. He glanced down the row, saw his sister showing her wares and decided they needed to leave. Immediately.

"Hey, does your stomach feel better? We should probably head back," he said, pulling down his cap and adjusting his sunglasses.

"What do you mean? We're just getting to the good stuff," she said and moved to the next vendor.

Benjamin wasn't sure if he should abandon her for a few moments or stick it out. He just didn't want Vivian and his sister to meet. He didn't welcome the questions that would follow from either of them.

Vivian viewed the jewelry from the first two vendors, then moved to his sister's stall. "Oh, wow," she said. "This is stunning, and you have so much to offer. I love the blue topaz, and the jade is gorgeous."

"Thank you," his sister said. "I've been busy. I'm always trying new ways—" She looked at Benjamin and broke off. "Hey, there," she said. "Are you going to introduce me?"

Benjamin sighed. He was caught. "Eliza, this is Vivian," he said. "Eliza is my sister," he added.

Vivian's eyes rounded. "Oh," she said. "I'm so pleased to meet you."

"Same for me," Eliza said. "I thought you would be more prissy."

Benjamin rolled his eyes. Thank goodness his expression was hidden by his sunglasses.

Vivian opened her mouth, then shut it, as if she was searching for a response. "Well, I've spent a lot of time painting the lodge," she managed.

"Oh, it wasn't a criticism," Eliza said. "You're just so naturally pretty. And nice."

Vivian glanced at Benjamin. "I don't know what you've heard about me, but I do try to be kind. Mean is ugly every language."

Eliza laughed. "So true. I think you and I would get along just fine."

"I love your work, but I'm finding it hard to choose," Vivian said, clearly changing the subject.

"Blue topaz necklace," Eliza said. "It will match your eyes. It's on me."

"Oh, no, you're too generous," Vivian said, pulling money from her pocket. "May I have your card?"

"Sure," Eliza said. She reluctantly accepted Vivian's money, then reached up to press her lips against Benjamin's cheek. "She's nicer than I expected."

"Yeah, great," Benjamin said and gently pulled Vivian away from his sister's jewelry stall.

"She's darling," Vivian said. "A little outspoken," she added.

"That's putting it mildly," he muttered.

"What do you mean?" she asked. "You almost act as if you didn't want her to meet me."

"How quickly we forget," he said. "You didn't want to out me to your sisters."

"Well, that's different. I have to lead. They need to believe that I'm level and unaffected by my hormones."

"So I make you hormonal?" he asked.

She playfully slapped at him. "Times ten."

"But I don't involve your intellect?" he said.

"You involve everything. That's why you're so much trouble," she said and reached up to kiss him.

Benjamin drove back to the lodge and stopped just before the door in case Vivian was trying to go incognito. She turned to him. "This was wonderful. You have no idea how much I needed it." She lifted her head toward him, and his mouth immediately took hers.

Their kiss quickly turned passionate. Vivian squeezed his shoulders. He trailed his hands toward her breasts.

The windows fogged.

Vivian dropped her head to his chest. "I know this sounds strange, but I want us to go a little slower."

Although he was aroused, he ground his teeth to settle down. "Good idea."

"But hard," she said.

"You have no idea," he said.

She stroked his jaw, and that touch made him feel tender and loved. "I'm sorry."

"It's okay," he said. "I'll take a cold shower."

"I will, too," she said and left his SUV.

Somehow, the fact that she would also be suffering gave him a little comfort.

Vivian didn't sleep well that night. Her bladder and hormones seemed to bother her. She couldn't get comfortable. Was she getting ready to start her period? It occurred to her when she rose the next morning that she might have rested much better if she and Benjamin had slept together. Such a forbidden thought, but heaven help her, she felt grumpy.

Pushing through her mood, she took a shower and pulled her hair back in a ponytail. She grabbed her laptop, walked to the kitchen, turned on the coffeemaker and strode to the porch, where Jilly was doing yoga.

"Namaste," Vivian said in a low voice.

Jilly struck a difficult pose. "Yeah," she said in a non-namaste voice.

"Are you okay?" Vivian asked.

Jillian took a deep breath. "I haven't actually spoken to Mother, but I still feel freaked out."

"Welcome to my world," Vivian said.

Jillian made a face. "I don't want to feel that way, so I think we should have a party."

"Excuse me?" Vivian said.

Jillian settled into a cross-legged pose. "I think we should have a party. Invite vendors we may need and include the community."

"It sounds like a lot of work," Vivian said.

"It sounds like a lot of money," Temple said as she walked into the screened-in porch. She shoved her hair out of her eyes and sighed as she sat down in a chair.

"It doesn't have to be a lot of work or money," Jillian said. "We could keep it easy with cakes and lemonade by Duane and Darcy. We could also limit the time, make it short and sweet. It would be good for our PR. You haven't heard back from the uptight Atlanta socialite, have you?"

"Not yet," Vivian said, and she was secretly losing hope.

"So, why not?" Jillian asked.

Temple sighed. "I can think of a million reasons why not, but maybe we should do it. Being static won't move us forward."

"Okay, let's do it," Vivian said. "I'll start compiling a guest list."

"And what's the news about you and Benjamin?" Jillian asked.

"I don't really want to talk about it," she said. "But he's pretty great." She lifted her hand. "Don't ask more."

"Chicken," Temple said.

"I could say something," Vivian said, thinking about Temple's vaping issue.

"Nothing, nothing, nothing," Temple said.

"What don't I know?" Jillian asked.

"Nothing, nothing, nothing," Temple repeated.

"Sounds like a lie to me," Jillian said.

"Namaste," Vivian said. "Trust me."

Jillian smiled. "Okay, namaste."

That afternoon, Vivian began to put together a list. The more she thought about it, the more she agreed that a party was a good idea. They'd done a lot of rehab on the lodge and the cabins. After all this work, they needed to round up the community in hopes of getting support. They would need plumbers, electricians for continuing maintenance and bed-and-breakfasts for support. There may be times when they will have an overflow of guests. This will be a short-notice invite.

Vivian talked with Grayson. "We need to make a signature drink for this party," she said.

"Rye whiskey and bourbon," he suggested.

She shook her head. "No. It needs to appeal to both women and men. We need two drinks so that there are options. Suggestions?" she asked.

"Old-fashioned Honeymoon Mountain," he said.

"Do I need to know what's in it?" she asked.

"Not really," he said. "Rye whiskey, Bourbon and a few other things."

"Okay, option two?" she said.

"Honeymoon Mountain martini," he said.

"What's in it?"

"I don't know. Vodka and sweet stuff."

"Can you be a little more specific?"

"Peach? You want some peach. How about some sparkle?"

"That sounds fabulous," she said. "Prepare it for me before you serve it."

"I can do that," he said and winked. "I'll surprise you."

They put the party together in record time, and invitees responded quickly. She barely had a chance to see Benjamin. He seemed to be just as busy in town as she was at the lodge. In fact, the last few nights he'd spent in town. She'd sent him a message inviting him to the party, and he'd sent a text apologizing that he was slammed and couldn't make it. Maybe that was for the best.

She felt edgy and couldn't quite explain why, but she was determined to remain focused. The day of the party, as she dressed, she realized she was late for her period. She wasn't the most regular, but… Vivian couldn't focus on that. She had a party to host.

Walking out in last year's Lilly Pulitzer, she joined Temple and Jillian. Jillian was sparkling like a bright diamond.

Jilly rubbed her hands together. "This is going to be so much fun. I've planned the music," she said.

"Music?" Vivian asked.

Rap sounded from speakers.

"Really?" Temple asked. "You couldn't choose jazz?"

"This is just to get us revved up," Jilly said.

"Or on edge," Temple muttered.

"Stop being a party pooper," Jilly said and pulled Temple into an impromptu dance.

"This isn't my thing," Temple said, awkwardly moving around.

"Stretch yourself," Jilly said. "It'll be good for you."

"Heaven help me," Temple said, but continued to dance.

The doorbell rang, and Jillian clicked the remote. Frank Sinatra oozed through the speakers. "Show-time," she said and pranced toward the front door.

"I want her to represent me at all times," Temple said. "She's so bubbly and friendly. I just want to hide."

"You have your skills," Vivian said. "Don't diminish them."

"If you say so," Temple said. "How are you feeling? You seem a little quiet."

"I'm just getting primed. I'm glad this will last only an afternoon. Getting my smile on," she said.

"Me, too," Temple said, lifting her lips in a grin that was clearly fake and looked more like a grimace.

"You need to work on that. Think of something funny," Vivian said.

"Nothing's funny at the moment," Temple said.

"Then ask someone to tell you a joke," Vivian said. "It's go time."

Despite feeling physically unsettled in a vague way, she marched toward the front door, planted a smile on her face and greeted guests. She chatted and collected business cards in a fishbowl.

Near the end of the open house, a blonde woman approached her. "Hey, I'm Eliza. I didn't get an invitation, but I hope it's okay that I came."

It took a moment before Vivian recognized Benjamin's sister. "Oh, it's lovely to see you again. I'm glad you came. Have you had a bite of our lemon squares or one of our signature drinks?"

"I grabbed a bite of a lemon square. Delicious. I don't drink, though," Eliza said.

"No problem," Vivian said. "We have other beverages."

"I'm okay," Eliza said. "I can see why Benjamin

is fascinated by you. You're beautiful, and you just seem to sparkle."

"You're very kind. Is there something I can do for you?"

"Well, now that you mention it, I have this idea of opening a jewelry and accessory stall at your resort. And I'd like to be a part of it," Eliza said.

"Well, it's a great idea," Vivian said. "But we're not quite ready for anything that specific just yet, since we don't have any definite bookings."

"That's okay," Eliza said. "I just wanted to get my name in during the planning and preparation stage. I think I could offer some cool local jewelry appropriate for your resort."

"I love the idea. I think I have your card, but give it to me again," she said.

"Thanks," Eliza said. "And my brother really likes you. I hope you like him, too."

"I do," Vivian admitted and wished Benjamin had made an appearance at the party. She hadn't seen him in a few days. She wondered what that meant. If anything.

Chapter Eleven

The next morning, Vivian dragged herself from bed. Heavens, she felt so tired. Why?

She started the coffee and literally waited for the machine to produce a cup for her. Sipping despite the fact that it burned her tongue, she wandered to the porch, where Jilly did yoga.

"Want to join me?" Jilly asked, doing some kind of twisty pose.

"I can't even begin to think of it," Vivian said. "I want pastries, coffee and wine. In no particular order."

"Was yesterday that difficult for you?" Jilly asked.

"It's hard to be on all the time. I want this to be a success," Vivian said.

"It's not up to you," Jilly said. "It's part of what the universe provides."

"I can't wait on the universe," Vivian said. "There are people counting on me."

Jilly sighed. "I wish you would be kinder to yourself."

"Me, too," a male voice said from the doorway.

Vivian's heart skipped a beat, and she looked up at Benjamin. "Well, early good morning," she said.

He moved toward her and dropped a kiss on her forehead. "Good morning to you. I'm sorry I couldn't make it yesterday. I'd been away from the bar, and all hell had broken loose with our orders. It took two days to straighten out."

Some part inside her eased. "Thanks," she said.

"I think I'll grab a shower," Jilly said. "Good morning, Benjamin."

"That was lovely and discreet," Vivian said. "Get a cup of coffee for yourself. I'm too lazy to get it for you."

"No worries," Benjamin said and left the porch, then returned with a full mug. He sat down across from her. "So, how did yesterday go?"

"I think pretty well," she said. "It was mostly an invite for the community, but I think we got a few bites for events. Your sister showed up."

His eyes widened. "Oh, really?"

"I wondered if you had told her about the event," she said.

"Not me," he said.

"I was happy to see her. She presented the idea of a jewelry stall. I like the idea. I just can't promise that I can provide her with any ongoing work here," she said.

"That's okay." He frowned. "I don't want you to feel like you need to sell her stuff. She's an artist and—"

Silence stretched between them. "What do you mean?" Vivian asked.

He shrugged. "Her motivation can come and go. But she's very talented."

"Are you saying she's not always consistent?" Vivian asked.

He paused and shrugged again. "Yeah, maybe."

She smiled. "Being consistent is challenging."

"Yeah, but—"

"Yeah, but don't worry about it. I'll do what I can for her. It may not be much, but I'll try."

"Thanks," he said. "So, what's wrong with you?"

"I don't know," she said. "I just feel yucky. I'm hoping it will pass soon."

"Should you see a doctor?" he asked.

"Nah. I'm just a little *off*," she said. "But I need to move past it. I've been invited to an event at the Biltmore Estate celebrating North Carolina tourism next week."

"Me, too," he said. "I heard from them a few weeks ago."

Vivian laughed. "I must be an also-ran. I heard from them this morning."

"They were slow to catch up," he said. "Wanna go with me? Or are you ashamed to be seen with me?"

"Not at all," Vivian said. "You know that was

never the issue. I just didn't want to be hassled by my sisters or anyone else. Like you don't want to be hassled by your sister."

"Fair enough," he said. "We can go separately."

"Let's go together," she said impulsively.

"Are you sure?" he asked.

"Yes," she said. "Why should it be such a big deal?"

"Exactly," he said and leaned toward her to press his lips against hers.

The following week, both Vivian and Benjamin were so busy that they connected only via phone. Vivian still wasn't feeling great, but she tried to push it aside. Her sisters encouraged her to visit a doctor in town, so she made an appointment.

In the meantime, she prepared for the event at the Biltmore by getting a facial and a mani-pedi. She didn't buy a new dress but wore one of her favorite formal dresses. A jade-blue V-neck cocktail dress that highlighted her rosy coloring. She hoped Benjamin would approve.

Temple and Jillian came into her bathroom as she applied last-minute eye makeup.

"More cat eye," Jilly said.

"Less is more," Temple said.

"Line your lips," Jilly said.

"Gloss. Just gloss," Temple corrected her.

Vivian glanced at her sisters, her mascara wand poised. "I'm not sure you're helping."

"You look gorgeous," Jilly said. "I wish I was going."

"I'll pass the next invite to the Biltmore on to you," she said.

"I'm glad it's you and not me," Temple muttered.

Vivian chuckled and gave her eyelashes one last swipe of mascara, then turned around. "I feel like I'm in costume."

"You look like a princess," Jilly said with a huge smile.

"You're very sweet," Vivian said and hugged both her sisters. "I wish I felt better physically."

"You made an appointment with the doctor in town," Temple said.

"Yes. I think I'm just a little worn down."

"It won't hurt to check, although I told you about my yoga and detox regimen. It has worked for me," Jilly said.

"I may ask you more about that after I see the doctor. Just tell me you can't see too many shadows under my eyes," she said.

"None," Jilly said. "Perfect camouflage."

"Thanks. I hope it will last."

The loud doorbell sounded. Vivian felt an excited jiggle in her stomach. "I guess it's time to go."

Both sisters gave her kisses on her cheeks. "That's so sweet," she said, feeling the threat of tears sting her eyes.

"Don't fuss," Temple said. "You're perfect the way you are. Enjoy your evening. Tomorrow you'll be painting and emptying trash."

Vivian chuckled. "Thanks for the reminder. Later, my darlings," she said and swept down the grand staircase. She almost felt like Scarlett O'Hara meeting Rhett Butler, except she was saving a fishing lodge and didn't need his help. He was just as handsome as Rhett, though, she couldn't help thinking.

"I'm almost speechless," Benjamin said. "You are beyond beautiful. Almost as beautiful as you are when your hair is in a ponytail and the only makeup you're wearing is paint."

Vivian sighed. "I think that was the nicest thing you could have said to me."

"It was just the truth," he said and extended his arm. "Shall we go?"

She accepted his arm. "We shall."

It was a magical evening. They traveled to the Biltmore, listening to country music on the way and chatting off and on. She almost forgot that she didn't feel so great physically. As they arrived, the lights of the historic estate greeted them.

"It's beautiful, isn't it?" she asked.

"Nice during the day, too. My school took me for a day trip," he said.

"Really?" she said. "Very cool."

"Did you go to Monticello in Charlottesville?" he asked.

"Of course," she said. "Most school-aged children took a field trip there."

"A few of us lucky ones in Carolina were able to visit Biltmore," he said and pulled up to the valet service. He got out and helped her from her side of his SUV.

"I feel like Cinderella at the ball," she confessed to him.

"I feel almost like a prince," he said, looking deep into her eyes.

"Let's go have a great time," she said.

"We will," he said.

The evening was full of great food, live music and toasts to businesses within the state. Vivian passed out a ton of cards and hoped the contacts would yield returns for Honeymoon Mountain Lodge.

More than that, though, she loved spending the evening with Benjamin. He was so natural. He didn't put on airs. He just displayed his great sense of humor and sly observations.

Soon enough, they needed to leave. Exhausted, Vivian sank back again the seat of his SUV. "What a fabulous night."

"For me, too," he said and dropped a kiss on her lips before he started the drive home.

Vivian drifted off and was embarrassed when she jerked awake as Benjamin pulled to a stop in front of the lodge. He was frowning as his phone rang. He answered it quickly. "Is there a problem? Where is she? I'll be there as soon as possible."

Vivian stared at him and blinked, wondering who *she* was. "What's going on?"

He shook his head. "Sorry. I can't talk about it. I need to go. I'll walk you to the door."

He helped her from the car, clearly distracted.

"What's wrong?" she asked. "I can tell something is wrong. Tell me. Maybe I can help."

"Not this time," he said. "I'm sorry. It was a great evening," he said. "I'll be in touch."

Vivian stared after him, feeling bewildered. She wanted to help him. She sensed he was in pain. At the same time, it hurt that he wouldn't share what was going on with her. Was this about his sister? Vivian was so filled with confusion, she didn't know what to do.

The next morning, Vivian went to the clinic in town. The doctor took a sample of her urine and blood and examined her from head to toe.

"Good news," the cheerful physician's assistant said to her. "You're quite healthy. And pregnant."

Vivian gaped at the woman. "Excuse me?"

"You're pregnant," the PA said. "We need you to start on prenatal vitamins immediately. Otherwise, you're in excellent health."

Still reeling from the PA's announcement, Vivian shook her head. "Excuse me. You're saying I'm pregnant."

"Yes, indeed," the cheerful woman said. "Now, no alcohol intake and continue to exercise. Come in to be evaluated every month. Any questions?" she asked.

"Well," Vivian said.

"Good," the PA said. "Call with any problems," she said and left the room.

Vivian stared after the PA for several moments. A nurse entered the room. "Can I help you?" she asked, probably because Vivian hadn't moved from the examination table.

"It may be too late for that," Vivian said and slid off the table. "Just give me a couple minutes, please."

"Of course. Just let me know if you need my help," the nurse said.

Vivian dressed and walked slowly from the room. Had she just had an out-of-body experience? Was she really pregnant? She stopped by the exit window.

"Here's a small quantity of prenatal vitamins to get you started," the clerk said and stripped off a piece of paper from a pad. "Here's your prescription for the rest of them. If you need a laxative, let us know. These things can stop you up. Congrats and good luck," the woman said.

"Thank you very much," Vivian said, completely dismayed.

She walked outside the clinic, the sun glaring down on her. Well, what to do next? She was a modern woman. She knew she had options. She would keep this baby. The question was, would she raise it with or without Benjamin's assistance?

Vivian arrived back at the lodge with a plan in mind. As soon as she entered the door, Temple greeted her. "So, did you find out what's wrong?"

"I need some vitamins," Vivian said. "I'm a little low on a few of them."

"So they gave you a script?" Temple asked.

"They did," Vivian said.

"Good," Temple said. "In the meantime, the phone has been ringing off the hook here. Apparently people are all worked up after our party last week and your visit to the Biltmore."

"Do any of them want to hold events here?" Vivian asked.

"I sure hope so," Temple said. "We need customers."

"I'll get right on it," Vivian said.

Temple caught her arm. "Take a nap if that's what you need," she said. "You're still looking a little tired."

Vivian pulled her sister against her for a big hug. "Thanks. Love you."

Temple squeezed her, then pulled back in surprise. "Are you sure you're okay?"

"I'm fine. I'll be fine. I'm all about fine," Vivian said.

"That sounds a little too fine," Temple said.

"Don't question me," Vivian said.

"Okay," Temple said. "No questions. Just take your vitamins, please."

Vivian spent the rest of the day following up on calls. She had several big bites of interest for events at the lodge. Thank goodness, because she still hadn't heard from Corinne Whitman Jergenson, and she was losing hope.

The next morning Vivian dragged herself out of bed, and it took all of her concentration to keep from getting sick to her stomach. She crept to the kitchen, popped open a can of ginger ale and grabbed some crackers. This kinda sucked, she thought. She felt a measure of sympathy for her mother. After all, she had gone through this three times.

Vivian wanted to get in touch with Benjamin, but he had been absent recently. Taking deep breaths and sipping soda, she returned to her room and called potential clients.

Halfway through the day, a knock sounded at the door. She opened it to Temple. "What's up?"

"Mother," Temple said, her eyes wide, her skin pale.

"What do you mean, Mother?" Vivian asked.

"She is here," Temple said in a stilted voice.

Vivian muttered a series of swearwords she never, ever used. "I'll be right out," she said and grabbed her glass of soda and a cracker.

Taking a deep breath, she walked to the living room and nodded toward her spotless, stunning mother.

"Hello, Mother. How are you?" she asked.

Tinsley Ferguson stood in all her stiffly perfect auburn glory and looked at Vivian for a long moment. "You're pregnant, aren't you?"

Vivian silently gaped at her mother.

"Cracker, soda," her mother said. "I've lived through this three times. Who's the father? And why couldn't you make it work with your husband?"

"I couldn't make it work with my ex because he knocked up someone else while we were married," she said. "But I've already explained that to you. To what do we owe the honor of your visit?" she asked in her most Tinsley voice ever.

Her mother lifted both her eyebrows, which was quite a feat given all the wrinkle filler injected in her brows. "I've heard about your endeavors with the lodge. Corinne Whitman Jergenson contacted me."

"I'm sure you recommended us," Vivian said.

"Well, I was quite surprised that all of you were involved. Where is Jillian?"

"I hope in yogaland," Temple muttered.

Her mother shot Temple a sharp glance. "You haven't shown yourself in Richmond for ages," she said.

"It's not her sparkle place," Jilly said as she entered the room. "Hello, Mommy."

Vivian instinctively moved between Jilly and her mother. "Jilly, Mom made a surprise visit."

"We're so lucky," Temple muttered.

Jilly stepped in front of Vivian. "Hello, Mommy. How are you doing?"

"Well. And you?"

"I'm thrilled to be reunited with my sisters," Jilly said. "I've missed them."

"Hmm," Tinsley said.

"And you," Jilly said.

Mother blinked. "I'm quite fine. It's a surprise to see you again."

"Yes. And you should know that I'll never be what you wanted me to be," Jilly blurted out.

Tinsley bit her lip. "I've had some time to think about that. Maybe I'm okay with that."

"Maybe?" Jilly asked, crossing her arms over her chest.

Vivian held her breath. She had pictured this meeting, but in her imagination, it had never gone this way.

Mom took a deep breath. "I am okay with that. It's hard because I always wanted the best for all of you."

"But what you want may not match up with what we want or need," Vivian said as gently as she could because her mother seemed almost more vulnerable than Jilly was.

"I know. It's still difficult for me, but I've missed you all so much. I just don't want us to be so separate from each other anymore."

"I have tattoos," Jilly said.

Tinsley cringed. "Okay. Just please don't show them to me."

Jilly chuckled and raced toward their mother. She embraced her. "I've missed you, Mommy."

"I've missed you, too," Tinsley said. She opened her arms to Temple and Vivian. "Please let me hug you."

Temple and Vivian walked into their mother's loving arms. Vivian's heart overflowed with emotion. She'd never thought this kind of reunion was possible.

"Vivian," her mother said. "You must tell me who got you knocked up. I'll make sure he will pay."

"Oh, Mom, I'm vitamin deficient. Really," Vivian said. "I tested yesterday. I need to beef up my vitamins."

"Really?" her mother said skeptically. "You look tired and bloated to me."

"Well, thank you very much," Vivian said. "You look like you've had a little too much filler."

Her mother lifted her chin in disapproval. "That's entirely inappropriate."

"As is your comment about me looking bloated," Vivian said.

Her mother pursed her lips. "Well, perhaps it was. Shall we have some tea, lemonade or bourbon or all of that?"

"All of that sounds good to me," Temple said.

Chapter Twelve

After a full day with her mother on site, Vivian brushed her teeth and sank down onto her bed. Her stomach was churning. She supposed this was what she should expect for the next few months. As she rested her head on her pillow, she wondered how she would tell Benjamin.

A knock sounded on her door. "Yes?" Vivian said but didn't rise.

Temple stepped inside her room. "I know you're pregnant."

"No. I'm not."

"Yes, you are. But I want you to know that I will be here for you. Even through birthing and delivery, as long you promise to get an epidural."

"Well, thank you very much," Vivian said, opening her arms to her sister. "Just so you know, I am in a full state of denial with Mom."

"Good luck, and I'll fib with you until the bloody end," Temple said, squeezing her tight. "Have you told Benjamin?"

"Not yet," Vivian said.

"It will all be okay," Temple said and stroked Vivian's forehead.

"How can you be sure?" Vivian asked.

"You picked an excellent man," Temple said.

"But what if he doesn't really love me?"

Temple chuckled. "He did a long, long time ago."

"I hope that's at least partly true," Vivian said, but she needed to see Benjamin. She needed to tell him. "I've tried calling him, but he hasn't returned my call yet. I don't want to appear desperate."

"Well, this is pretty important. Knowing you, you told him, 'Get in touch with me when you can,' which doesn't sound like the topic is pressing."

Pretty close, Vivian thought. "I'll wait until tonight. Maybe there's something big going on at the bar, or he's buying a new business. He mentioned something about that lately."

"Don't wait too long," Temple said and dropped a kiss on Vivian's forehead. "Sleep well. You need it."

Vivian waited and debated calling that night. Instead, she decided to try to sleep. When she awakened in the morning, though, and struggled with nausea, she knew it was time to talk to Benjamin. Today she would go into town.

* * *

Benjamin had barely been able to return to the bar for more than thirty minutes during the last couple of days. His sister had been on suicide watch, and he'd known he needed to stay with her as much as possible. She'd run out of her medicine and had hoped she could manage on her own. She'd done the same thing several times prior. He wished she could find and accept the help she needed. The side effects of her medication sometimes made her quit it altogether.

Despite the fact that it was midday, he was so tired he could barely put one foot in front of the other. In his office, he studied spreadsheets and order forms.

A knock sounded at the door. He lifted his head. "Yes? Come on in."

Vivian appeared in the doorway with a questioning look on her face. "Everything okay?"

"Not really," he said and rubbed his hand over his face. "I'm sorry I haven't called you back. I've been tied up."

She gave a slow nod. "New business you're purchasing?"

"No. Not that." He sighed. A long silence followed. "I can't talk about it."

"Oh," she said. "Okay. Well, I need to talk to you."

He closed his laptop. "That's fine. You want to close the door behind you?"

"Yes. I think that's a good idea," she said, pushing the door shut and standing in front of his desk.

"You want to sit down?"

She crossed her arms over her chest. "Not really."

Benjamin felt a strange twist in his gut. What was going on? "Okay. I'm all ears."

She bit her lip. "Well. I'm pregnant."

Benjamin stared at her for several seconds, unable to comprehend her words. "Excuse me?"

"I'm. Pregnant."

Benjamin blinked and glanced down. "Wow. I—uh—I—"

"It caught me by surprise, too," she said. "I didn't think I was particularly fertile because—" She broke off and shook her head. "Well, I just didn't. But I really thought you should know."

"Yes, I should," he said, his mind reeling. How had this happened? He'd used protection. What if this baby also suffered from mental health? He should reveal that to Vivian.

"I thought I should tell you," she said and turned as if she planned to leave.

"Wait," he said, standing. His integrity rose inside him. "I'll be here for you and for the baby."

Her face seemed to fall. "That's good to know," she said in an ultrapolite voice. "I guess I'll see you later."

Benjamin frowned as she left his office. He was still whirling from the news. How had this happened? Of course he knew how it had happened, and he had enjoyed every minute. But…

His mind still slamming from one prospect to another, he raced from the office and caught up with Vivian as she walked toward her car. "Hey," he called and took her hand. "Wait up."

She turned to look at him. "What?"

"We should get married. If we're going to have a baby, you and I should get married."

She stared at him for a long moment and bit her lip. "Is that a proposal?"

"Yeah," he said and smiled, feeling elated at the prospect. "Yeah, I guess it is."

"You think we *should* get married," she said. "I have no interest in a *should* marriage. I've already had a bad marriage. I don't want another one," she said, pulled her hand from his and walked away.

"Wait," he said. "How do you know it would be bad?"

"I don't know much, but starting out with a big *should* isn't good. Thanks for the offer, but no thanks," she said and walked to her car.

Benjamin stared after her, knowing in his gut that he had done everything wrong. He wasn't sure how to fix it. He wondered if he possibly could fix it. His prospects sure didn't look good at the moment.

Vivian's mother had to leave the following day. Thank goodness. Her mother frowned at her.

"Are you sure you're not pregnant? You look a bit green," her mother said.

"No chance," Vivian said, nibbling on a muffin she didn't want.

"Are you sure you haven't been exposed?" her mother asked with a slight smirk.

"Oh, Mother," Vivian said.

Temple entered the room with a yawn. "We may as well be in a convent. No need to worry about us."

"Hmm," her mother said. "Well, I must say the lodge is much nicer than I remembered. I think I'll pass along recommendations to some of my friends."

"Oh, please. Don't feel obligated," Vivian said.

"I'm okay if you do," Temple said.

Jilly poured a cup of coffee and offered it to her mother. "Do what makes you feel whole," she said. "Nothing more. Nothing less."

Their mother stared at Jilly. "I'm not sure how I gave birth to you or how you have any DNA from your father or me, but I'm very glad that you're here and I've gotten the opportunity to see you. I want all of you to come to Richmond to visit."

"Absolutely," Jilly said.

"That sounds lovely," Vivian said.

"And you can come here anytime you like," Jilly said.

"Thank you for visiting, Mother," Vivian said and brushed her mother's cheek with a light kiss.

Temple did the same.

Jilly flung her arms around their mother and pressed her pink lips against her mother's cheek. "Thanks for coming, Mommy."

Their mother blinked. "Well, you're very welcome. I'll be in touch, darlings. Ta-ta," she said and started for the door. "Oh, would one of you bring my luggage to my car? It's a bit much for me."

Jilly eagerly stepped forward for the task.

For the rest of the day, Vivian was torn between worrying about Jilly's hopes for a wonderful relationship with their mother and her own pregnancy. Temple had asked about Vivian's trip into town, but Vivian had waved her aside. She hadn't known what she'd expected from Benjamin, but she knew she hadn't gotten what she'd hoped.

She spent the day sitting on the screened-in porch and updating the website, and Benjamin appeared in the late afternoon. "Hey, there," he said. "I really messed up yesterday, didn't I?"

"You were caught off guard. I was, too," she said, feeling her muscles tighten into hard knots.

"You're being kind," he said, stepping in front of her, his hands shoved in his pockets. "I talked about marriage, but I didn't talk about our feelings for each other."

She took a quick, sharp breath and closed her eyes. Vivian couldn't think about feelings. Her feelings overwhelmed her. She shrugged. "It's okay. It's—"

He sank down beside her and took her hands. "It's not okay," he said. "We've been drawn to each other. This baby happened for a reason. This baby happened because we love each other, because we want a future together."

His words blindsided her, and she searched his

face. *Love?* "What are you saying? What are you feeling?"

"I love you," he confessed. "I think I've loved you for a long time. Longer than I would admit to myself."

She bit her lip. "Are you sure?"

He nodded. "Yes, I'm—" His cell phone rang and he glanced at it. He swore. "I have to take this. I'm really sorry."

He rose from the couch and stepped away.

She couldn't hear what he was saying and felt frustrated by the interruption. What could be so important?

A moment later, he reentered the porch. "I'm sorry. I had to take that."

"What was *that*?" she asked. "What was so important that you couldn't share it with me? How can we get married if you are going to keep things from me? Important things?"

He took a deep breath. "I gave my word to my sister. I need to talk to her about this."

"Sister?" she echoed.

"Yeah. Sister," he said. "Give me a day. It's important."

"I hope she's okay," Vivian said.

"I'm always hoping for that," he said. He paused a half beat, then pressed a hard kiss against her mouth. "Don't count me out."

Her heart was slamming against her chest. How could she?

* * *

The following day, she awakened and lost her cookies. This whole pregnancy was getting real as each day passed. She needed to toughen up. She had months to go. Oh, wait. And years after that.

Fighting off anxiety attacks, she took deep breaths and drank decaf tea. Sipping a cup, she sat on the porch. Jilly sat down beside her. "I can tell you're upset. How can I help you?"

Vivian looked at her sweet bleach-blonde sister, dressed in yoga capris and a tank top, and felt love swell in her heart. "I'm good. It just makes me happy that you are here. But if you need to leave, I'll understand. This isn't a sure deal."

Jilly laughed. "Most of my deals haven't been sure, but now I have a roof over my head, and I get to be with my sisters. My life couldn't be much better."

"I need to warn you that Mom can be a little inconsistent," Vivian said. "I don't know how to say this because your relationship with her may be different."

Jilly nodded earnestly. "She's a bit of a wench, isn't she? I wonder what made her that way."

Vivian tilted her head to one side. "I never thought about it that way. I just don't want you to be hurt."

Jilly smiled. "That's one of the nicest things someone has said to me in a long time."

Vivian smiled, too. "I'm so glad we've reconnected. I just really want you to be careful."

"I will be okay. She has rejected me several times before. I'm stronger because of it," Jilly said.

"I can see that," Vivian said, seeing a spark of strength in her sister's eyes. Maybe she could trust Jilly to set her own boundaries.

"But I'm concerned about you," Jilly said. "I sense something has changed about you."

"Your sense is correct," Vivian said. "But I'd rather talk about it at a different time. Is that okay?"

"You've made me even more curious, but I guess I'll have to wait. I'm wondering if Mommy was right about you being pregnant," Jilly said.

"Can we talk about something else?" Vivian asked.

Later that night, her cell phone rang. She hadn't found the energy to shower, so she just lay on her back on the bed with her eyes half-closed.

Not looking at the caller ID, she automatically said, "Vivian Jackson. Hello."

"Hello to you," Benjamin said.

Vivian's eyes flew open, and she sat up in her bed. "Hello," she repeated. Then she stuttered, "H-how are things?"

"Could be better. Could be worse," he said. "Any chance you can come to the county hospital?"

Vivian blinked. "Umm. Sure. When?"

"Now," he said.

She swallowed over her surprise. "Now?"

"Yeah, Eliza may need to be moved to another facility," he said.

"Oh, no. Has she been injured?" she asked.

"It's complicated," he said. "Can you come?"

"Yes," she said without pausing. "I'll be there as soon as I can."

She got up, brushed her teeth and rubbed the dark makeup from under her eyes. Her mother would be horrified. Thank goodness her mother wasn't here.

Walking out her door, she ran into both of her sisters.

Temple, dressed in jammies and carrying a brownie, looked at her. "Where are you going?"

"Benjamin called. He wants me to meet him at the county hospital."

"Oh, no," Jilly said, also wearing her jammies. "Is he okay?"

"I think he is. Mostly," Vivian said.

Temple frowned. "Then what's wrong?"

Vivian hesitated. "Please don't spread it around, but I think it's about his sister, Eliza."

"Oh," Jilly said. "Please call us and let us know. She seemed nice and talented."

"Drive safely," Temple said. "Should I drive for you?"

"I'm good," Vivian said and shrugged. "Just think good thoughts."

Heading out the door, she got into her car and drove to the county hospital, worrying and wondering all the way. She pulled into the parking lot, went to the front desk and asked for Eliza Hunter.

The attendant seemed a bit reluctant to release any information. "And who are you?" she asked.

"Vivian Jackson," she said.

The attendant gave a slow nod. "She's on the fourth floor. You'll have to check in at the desk."

"Thank you," Vivian said, wondering and worrying even more as she walked into the elevator and punched the button for the fourth floor.

The elevator door opened, and she walked to the desk. "I'm here to see Eliza Hunter," she said.

"Just a moment, please," the attendant said and turned away from her.

Vivian waited. And waited.

"Ms. Hunter's brother will be out to meet you," she said.

A few seconds later, Benjamin appeared.

"What's going on?" Vivian asked.

"It's complicated, but Eliza wants to explain," he said.

Vivian frowned. "Eliza? Why can't you explain?"

He shrugged. "I made a promise. This is a big moment for her."

Vivian took a deep breath. "Okay. I hope she's well."

"We're working on it," he said and led her down the hallway. They entered a room where Eliza lay in a bed with her arms tied to the rails.

She glanced up weakly. "Hi, there," she said.

"Hi," Vivian said, moving quickly to the side of the bed. "Are you okay?"

"I will be," Eliza said. "I stopped taking my medication. I keep hoping I won't need it." She bit her lip. "And then I get depressed. Very depressed."

"I'm so sorry," Vivian said and reached out to touch Eliza.

Eliza glanced up at Benjamin. "I think you got a good one," she said, then turned to Vivian. "I'm bipolar. I didn't want Benjamin to tell you or anyone, but I think, maybe, it's time for me to stop being so secretive."

"Oh, Eliza, I'm so sorry," Vivian said. "You shouldn't suffer this alone! It's terrible for you and anyone you love," she said. "But your disease is like diabetes. You need daily treatment. You need a support group." She shrugged. "I'm sorry you have struggled with this, and maybe you'll always struggle in a way, but you must accept assistance for yourself and Benjamin."

Eliza's chin sank to her chest. "Why is this so hard?"

Vivian shook her head. "I bet you've tried to do too much on your own. All of us need help at times. All of us," she said.

Eliza stared into her eyes. "I've just always felt ashamed."

"There are far worse things. You have so many strengths. You are creative, loving and friendly. The world is blessed by your presence."

Eliza's eyes filled with tears. "I don't know what to say."

"Say you'll be more gentle with yourself," Vivian told her.

Eliza closed her eyes as tears streamed down her

cheeks. "Am I ever going to get over this?" she whispered.

Vivian's heart nearly broke at Eliza's suffering. "I'm not telling you anything you don't know. I suspect it's day by day. And you bring light and pleasure to many people. You just need to allow yourself to bring light and pleasure to yourself. You need to remember that you are quite wonderful. Remembering that every day may take some doing."

"How do you know all this?" Eliza asked.

"I've had friends who struggled with this disease and I've had more than a few moments of self-doubt myself. My life hasn't been perfect," Vivian confessed.

"But you know Benjamin wants to marry you," Eliza said.

Vivian's breath caught in her throat. "We're working on that."

"He's been here with me the last few days. I made him swear he wouldn't tell anyone what was going on with me," she said.

Vivian looked at Benjamin. "That explains a lot."

"I wanted to keep my word," he said. "That's why I brought you here tonight."

She stared into his eyes and saw love, love, love. "We need to talk," she said.

"Tell me the news when it happens," Eliza said. "I'm going into a mental health facility, so I'll be out of touch for a while."

Vivian squeezed Eliza's hand. "Good for you. I'm proud of you," she said.

Eliza shrugged. "It will be a lot of work. Not my first rodeo, but I'm ready for this step."

Vivian stepped closer and kissed Eliza on her cheek. "Call me anytime," she said.

Benjamin did the same. "Thank you for tonight," he said.

"It was the least I could do. Gonna give your baby my middle name?" Eliza asked.

Vivian gaped at Benjamin, and he shrugged.

"I had to tell her. I had to stop keeping secrets from you and from her," he said.

Vivian nodded in understanding. "When can we talk?" she asked.

"In just a few minutes. They're going to limit my visits so she can focus on her treatment."

"I'll wait outside," Vivian said.

Vivian paced in the empty waiting room, her emotions roiling.

Benjamin approached her.

"Do you think she'll be okay?" Vivian asked.

"With proper help and medication, she always comes out of this. It can be a terrifying ride, but I think she would do much better if she would join a support group and stick with it. I haven't had much luck convincing her."

Vivian inhaled, trying to collect her thoughts. "You shouldn't have kept this from me," she said.

"I gave my word to Eliza," he said.

"Well, you should have convinced her to release you from that promise. It's wrong for you to suffer this alone. What if I had kept something like this from you?"

He shook his head. "Totally unacceptable."

"That's the way I feel about you. I thought we had something special, but—"

"We do," he said putting his hands on her arms. "We do. I'm just not used to sharing the load when it comes to Eliza. Even the idea is new to me."

"I may not seem like I'm strong enough to handle this kind of thing, but—"

"I never thought that," he said. "I just thought you might not be interested. Not everyone would be."

"Well, of course, I'm interested. Eliza is an important part of your life. She's precious to you so she would also be precious to me."

Benjamin shook his head in disbelief. "I can't believe I found you. I can't believe you're here right now. You're the strongest, most caring, most fascinating woman I've ever met, and I want you in my life. Forever," he said. "I love you."

The commitment in his words vibrated through her. She could hear and feel the certainty, but a part of her was afraid to believe. "Are you sure?" she asked. "This has happened pretty fast. Are you sure you're not saying this because of the baby?"

"I couldn't be more sure," Benjamin said and took a deep breath. "But maybe you need some time."

Vivian blinked. Sure, she had vacillated at the beginning. Her feelings had been so strong even then. But now, and not just because of the baby, she wanted him more than ever. She wanted his presence in her life. She wanted to be there for him and for him to be there for her. She checked herself. Her heart, mind and soul all agreed. She knew that being with him was right.

"I love you. I've never known a man I trust more. That I love being with more. We've had some tricky moments. Some fun and some scary ones. Life is like that. You're the one I want to be with through all those times."

He shook his head. "I don't even have a ring for you."

"I'd rather have your heart forever," she said, and he lowered his mouth to hers in a kiss that promised everything.

Epilogue

Three weeks and two days later, the first wedding at Honeymoon Mountain Lodge was held between Benjamin and Vivian. Another wedding was scheduled in two weeks. That was the wedding of Corinne Whitman Jergenson's daughter, Olive, and her groom, Bubba.

Vivian and Benjamin had wanted to wait until his sister was out of the mental health facility so that all their important people could join them. The weather was gorgeous, and although the leaves were falling, the clear blue lake provided a beautiful backdrop for the vows they would take on the dock.

The wedding crowd was small with no attendants. Vivian took one last glance in the mirror and walked down the hallway to where her sisters and mother stood.

"You look beautiful," Jilly said.

"You do," Temple said. "Are you sure you want to go through with this? I mean, marriage is challenging."

Their mother shot Temple a sharp glance. "Of course she does. She's pregnant."

Vivian shook her head. "Of course. I do. I love Benjamin and he loves me. Y'all go ahead. I want a moment."

Her sisters and mother exited to the dock, and Vivian closed her eyes. "Well, Daddy, all I can say is thank you for leaving the lodge to us and introducing me to the love of my life. I hope you're happy up there. We sure miss you," she whispered and felt her eyes well with tears.

Blinking furiously to dry her eyes, she walked to the door, which Grayson opened for her. His eyes turned a bit shiny. "You look beautiful, Missy. Your father would be proud."

The strains of a guitar played, and Vivian looked to the front of the small group where Benjamin stood.

Dressed in a dark suit, he looked more handsome than ever. His gaze locked with hers, and he broke tradition by rushing to meet her and pulling her against him. "I love you so much," he said.

"I was thinking the same thing about you," she said and joined him as they walked to the front, where the minister stood waiting. She heard a few whispers but couldn't make out what was said.

She stared into Benjamin's gaze as they repeated their vows. They might have taken the long road to finding each other again, but it had been worth it.

"I now pronounce you husband and wife," the minister said.

Benjamin swooped her up in his arms and kissed her.

The crowd laughed and cheered.

"I knew she was pregnant," her mother said to Temple as she wiped her eyes. "A mother knows these things."

"She looks so beautiful," Jilly said.

"They are so happy," Eliza said.

And nothing else needed to be said, because it was true. Benjamin and Vivian were so happy, at last.

* * * * *

Looking for more Leanne Banks?
Try her other romantic stories:

A PRINCESS UNDER THE MISTLETOE
A ROYAL CHRISTMAS PROPOSAL
MAVERICK FOR HIRE
HAPPY NEW YEAR, BABY FORTUNE!
THE MAVERICK & THE MANHATTANITE

Available now from Mills & Boon Cherish!

Pretending they're lovers for the cameras on a reality TV show quickly has Travis Dalton and Brenna O'Reilly wishing this game of love would never have to end...

Turn the page for a sneak preview of New York Times bestselling author Christine Rimmer's

THE MAVERICK FAKES A BRIDE!,

the first book in the next Montana Mavericks continuity,

MONTANA MAVERICKS:
THE GREAT FAMILY ROUNDUP

Chapter One

Early March, Rust Creek Falls, Montana

It was a warm day for March. And everyone in Bee's Beauty Parlor that afternoon had gathered at the wide front windows to watch as Travis Dalton rode his favorite bay gelding down Broomtail Road.

The guy was every cowgirl's fantasy in a snug Western shirt, butt-hugging jeans, Tony Lama boots and a black hat. One of those film school graduates from the little theater in nearby Kalispell, a video camera stuck to his face, walked backward ahead of him, recording his every move. Travis talked and gestured broadly as he went.

"My, my, my." Bee smoothed her brassy blond hair, though it didn't need it. Even in a high wind,

Bee's hair never moved. "Travis does have one fine seat on a horse."

There were soft, low sounds of agreement and appreciation from the women at the window—and then, out of nowhere, Travis tossed his hat in the air and flipped to a handstand right there on that horse in the middle of the street.

The women applauded. There was more than one outright cry of delight.

Only Brenna O'Reilly stood still and silent. She had her arms wrapped around her middle to keep from clapping, and she'd firmly tucked her lips between her teeth in order not to let out a single sound.

Because no way was Brenna sighing over Travis Dalton. Yes, he was one hot cowboy, with that almost-black hair and those dangerous blue eyes, that hard, lean body, and that grin that could make a girl's lady parts spontaneously combust.

And it wasn't only his looks that worked for her. Sometimes an adventurous woman needed a hero on hand. Travis had come to her rescue more than once in her life.

But he'd always made a big deal about how he was too old for her—and okay, maybe he'd had a point, back when she was six and he was fourteen. But now that she'd reached the grown-up age of twenty-six, what did eight years even matter?

Never mind. Not going to happen, Brenna reminded herself for the ten thousandth time. And no matter what people in town might say, she was not and never had been in love with the man.

Right now, today, she was simply appreciating the view, which was spectacular.

Beside her, Dovey Jukes actually let out a moan and made a big show of fanning herself. "Is it just me, or is it *really* hot in here?"

"This is his, er, what did you call it now, Melba?" Bee asked old Melba Strickland, who'd come out from under the dryer to watch the local heartthrob ride by.

"It's his package," replied Melba.

Dovey snickered.

Bee let out her trademark smoke-and-whiskey laugh. "Not *that* kind of package." She gave Dovey a playful slap on the arm.

"It's reality television slang," Melba clarified. "Tessa told me all about it." Melba's granddaughter lived in Los Angeles now. Tessa Strickland Drake had a high-powered job in advertising and understood how things worked in the entertainment industry. "A package is an audition application and video."

"Audition for what?" one of the other girls asked.

"A brand-new reality show." Melba was in the know. "It's going to get made at a secret location right here in Montana this summer, and it will be called *The Great Roundup*. From what I heard, it's going to be like *Survivor*, but with cowboys—you know, roping and branding, bringing in the strays, everyone sharing their life stories around the campfire, sleeping out under the stars, answering challenge after challenge, trying not to get eliminated. The winner will earn himself a million-dollar prize."

Brenna, who'd never met a challenge she couldn't rise to, clutched the round thermal brush in her hand a little tighter and tried to ignore the tug of longing in heart. After all, she'd been raised on the family ranch and could rope and ride with the best of them. She couldn't help but imagine herself on this new cowboy reality show.

True, lately, she'd been putting in some serious effort to quell her wild and crazy side, to settle down a little, you might say.

But a reality show? She could enjoy the excitement while accomplishing a valid goal of winning those big bucks. A few months ago, Bee had started dating a handsome sixtyish widower from Kalispell. Now that things had gotten serious, she'd been talking about selling the shop and retiring so she and her new man could travel. Brenna would love to step up as owner when Bee left.

But that would cost money she didn't have. If she won a million dollars on a reality show, however, she could buy the shop and still have plenty of money to spare.

And then again, no. Trying out for a reality show was a crazy idea, and Brenna was keeping a lid on her wild side, she truly was. *The Great Roundup* was not for her.

She asked wistfully, "You think Travis has a chance to be on the show?"

"Are you kidding?" Bee let out a teasing growl. "Those Hollywood people would be crazy not to choose him. And if the one doing the choosing is female, all that man has to do is give her a smile."

Every woman at that window enthusiastically agreed.

First week of May, a studio soundstage,
Los Angeles, California

Travis Dalton hooked his booted foot across his knee and relaxed in the interview chair.

It was happening. *Really* happening. His video had wowed them. And his application? He'd broken all the rules with it, just like that book he'd bought—*Be a Reality Star*—had instructed. He'd used red ink, added lots of silly Western doodles and filled it chock-full of colorful stories of his life on the family ranch.

He'd knocked them clean out of their boots, if he did say so himself. And now here he was in Hollywood auditioning for *The Great Roundup.*

"Tell us about growing up on a ranch," said the casting director, whose name was Giselle. Giselle dressed like a fashion model. She had a way of making a guy feel like she could see inside his head. *Sharp.* That was the word for Giselle. Sharp—and interested. Her calculating eyes watched him so closely.

Which was fine. Good. He wanted her looking at him with interest. He wanted to make the cut, get on *The Great Roundup* and win himself a million bucks.

Travis gave a slow grin in the general direction of one of the cameras that recorded every move he made. "I grew up on my family's ranch in northwestern Montana." He was careful to include Giselle's question in his answer, in case they ended up using this interview in the show. Then they could cut Giselle's voice out and what he said would still make perfect sense. "My dad put me on a horse for the first time at the age of five. Sometimes it feels like I was born in the saddle."

Giselle and her assistant nodded their approval as he went on—about the horses he'd trained and the ones that had thrown him. About the local rodeos where he'd been bucked off more than one bad-tempered bull—and made it all the way to eight full seconds on a few. He thought it was going pretty well, that he was charming them, winning them over, showing them he wasn't shy, that an audience would love him.

"Can you take off your shirt for us, Travis?"

He'd assumed that would be coming. Rising, Travis unbuttoned and shrugged out of his shirt. At first, he kept it all business, no funny stuff. They needed to get a good look at the body that ranching had built and he kept in shape. He figured they wouldn't be disappointed.

But they wanted to see a little personality, too, so when Giselle instructed, "Turn around slowly," he held out his arms, bending his elbows and bringing them down, giving them the cowboy version of a bodybuilder's flex. As he turned, he grabbed his hat off the back of his chair and plunked it on his head, aiming his chin to the side, giving them a profile shot and then going all the way with a slow grin and a wink over his shoulder.

The casting assistant, Roxanne, stifled a giggle as she grinned right back.

"Go ahead and sit back down," Giselle said. She wasn't flirty like Roxanne, but in her sharp-edged way she seemed happy with how the interview was shaking out.

Travis took off his hat again. He bent to get his shirt.

"Leave it," said Giselle.

He gave her a slight nod and no smile as he settled back into the chair. Because this was serious business. To him—and to her.

"Now we want to know about that hometown of yours." Giselle almost smiled then, though really it was more of a smirk. "We've been hearing some pretty crazy things about Rust Creek Falls."

Was he ready for that one? You bet he was. His town had been making national news the past few years. First came the flood. He explained about the Fourth of July rains that wouldn't stop and all the ways the people of Rust Creek Falls had pulled together to come back from the worst disaster in a century. He spoke of rebuilding after the waters receded, of the national attention and the sudden influx of young women who had come to town to find themselves a cowboy.

When Giselle asked if any of those women had

found him, he answered in a lazy drawl, "To tell you the truth, I met a lot of pretty women after the great flood." He put his right hand on his chest. "Each one of them holds a special place in my heart."

Roxanne had to stifle another giggle.

Giselle sent her a cool look. Roxanne's smile vanished as if it had never been. "Tell us more," said Giselle.

And he told them about a certain Fourth of July wedding almost two years ago now, a wedding in Rust Creek Falls Park. A local eccentric by the name of Homer Gilmore had spiked the wedding punch with his special recipe moonshine—purported to make people do things they would never do ordinarily.

"A few got in fights," he confessed, "present company included, I'm sorry to say." He made an effort to look appropriately embarrassed at his own behavior before adding, "And a whole bunch of folks got romantic—and that meant that *last* year, Rust Creek Falls had a serious baby boom. You might have heard of that. We called it the baby bonanza. So now we have what amounts to a population explosion in our little town. Nobody's complaining, though. In Rust Creek Falls, love and babies are what it's all about."

Travis explained that he wanted to join the cast of *The Great Roundup* for the thrill of it—and he also wanted to be the last cowboy standing. He had a fine life working the Dalton family ranch, but the million-dollar prize would build him his own house on the land he loved and put a little money in the bank, too.

"I'm not getting any younger," he admitted with a smile he hoped came across as both sexy *and* modest. "One of these days, I might even want to find the right girl and settle down."

Giselle, who had excellent posture in the first place, seemed to sit up even straighter, like a prize hunting dog catching a scent. "The right girl? Interesting." She glanced at Roxanne, who bobbed her head in an eager nod. "Is there anyone special you've got your eye on?"

There was no one, and there probably wouldn't be any time soon. But he got Giselle's message loud and clear. For some reason, the casting director would prefer that he had a sweetheart.

And what Giselle preferred, Travis Dalton was bound and determined to deliver. "Is there a special woman in my life? Well, she's a…very private person."

"That would be yes, then. You're exclusive with someone?"

Damn. Message received, loud and clear. He wasn't getting out of this without confessing—or lying through his teeth. And since he intended to get on the show, he knew what his choice had to be.

"I don't want to speak out of hand, but yeah. There is a special someone in my life now. We…haven't been together long, but…" He let out a low whistle and pasted on an expression that he hoped would pass for completely smitten. "Oh, yeah. *Special* would be the word for her."

"Is this special someone a hometown girl?" Giselle's eyes twinkled in a way that was simultaneously aggressive, gleeful and calculating.

"She's from Rust Creek Falls, yes. And she's amazing." *Whoever the hell she is.* "It's the greatest thing in the world, to know someone your whole life and then suddenly to realize there's a lot more going on between the two of you than you've ever admitted before." Whoa. He probably ought to be ashamed of himself. His mama had brought him up right, taught him not to tell lies. But who did this little white lie hurt, anyway? Not a soul. And to get on *The Great Roundup*, Travis Dalton would tell Giselle whatever she needed to hear.

"What's her name?" asked Giselle. It was the next logical question, damn it. He should have known it was coming.

He put on his best killer smile—and lied some more. "Sorry, I can't tell you her name. You know small towns." Giselle frowned. She might be sharp as a barbwire fence, but he would bet his Collin Traub dress saddle that she'd never been within a hundred miles of a town like Rust Creek Falls. "We're keeping what we have together just between the two of us, my girl and me. It's a special time in our relationship, and we don't want the whole town butting into our private business." *A special time.* Damned if he didn't sound downright sensitive—

for a bald-faced liar. But would the casting director buy it?

Giselle didn't seem all that thrilled with his unwillingness to out his nonexistent girlfriend, but at least she let it go. A few minutes later, she gave the cameraman a break. Then she chatted with Travis off the record for a couple of minutes more. She said she'd heard he was staying at the Malibu house of LA power player Carson Drake, whose wife, Tessa Strickland Drake, had deep Montana roots. Travis explained that he'd known Tessa all his life. She'd grown up in Bozeman, but she spent most of her childhood summers staying at her grandmother's boardinghouse in Rust Creek Falls.

After the chitchat, Giselle asked him to have a seat outside. He grabbed his shirt and went out to the waiting area, which consisted of a bunch of chairs, a few tables with ratty-looking magazines, a row of vending machines and a watercooler, all arranged along what was essentially a wide hallway between soundstages. He put on his shirt and took one of the chairs.

An hour went by and then another. He struck up conversations with some of the other applicants. A crusty old guy named Wally Wilson told stories about growing up on the Oklahoma prairie and riding the rodeos all over the West.

Potential contestants went through the door to the soundstage, stayed awhile and came back out. Some of them emerged from the interview and sat down and waited, like Travis. Some left. Travis took heart from the fact that he was among the ones asked to stay.

It was after six when they called him back in to tell him that he wouldn't be returning to Malibu that night—or any time soon, as it turned out. Real Deal Entertainment would put him up in a hotel room instead.

Travis lived in that hotel room for two weeks at Real Deal's beck and call. He took full advantage of room service, and he worked out in the hotel fitness center to pass the time while he got his background checked and his blood drawn. He even got interviewed by a shrink, who asked a lot of way-too-personal questions. There were also a series of follow-up meetings with casting people and producers. At the two-week mark, in a Century City office tower, he got a little quality time with a bunch of network suits.

That evening, absolutely certain he'd made the show, he raided the minibar in his room and raised a toast to his success.

Hot damn, he'd done it! He was going to be a contestant on *The Great Roundup*. He would have his shot at a cool million bucks.

And he would win, too. Damned if he wouldn't. He would build his own house on the family ranch and get more say in the day-to-day running of the place. His older brother, Anderson, made most of the decisions now. But if Travis had some hard cash to invest, his big brother would take him more seriously. Travis would step up as a real partner in running the ranch.

Being the good-time cowboy of the family had been fun. But there comes a point when every man has to figure out what to do with his life. Travis had reached that point. And *The Great Roundup* was going to take him where he needed to go.

The next morning, a car arrived to deliver him to the studio, where he sat in another waiting area outside a different soundstage with pretty much the same group of potential contestants he'd sat with two weeks before. One by one, they were called through the door. They all emerged smiling to be swiftly led away by their drivers.

When Travis's turn came, he walked onto the soundstage to find Giselle and Roxanne and a couple producers waiting at a long table. The camera was rolling. Except for that meeting in the office tower with the suits and a couple of sessions involving lawyers with papers to sign, a camera had been pointed at him every time they talked to him.

Giselle said, "Have a seat, Travis." He took the lone chair facing the others at the table. "We have some great news for you."

He knew it, he was in! He did a mental fist pump.

But then Giselle said, "You've made the cut for the final audition."

What the hell? *Another* audition?

"You'll love this, Travis." Giselle watched him expectantly as she announced, "The final audition will be in Rust Creek Falls."

Wait. What?

She went on, "As it happens, your hometown is not far from the supersecret location where *The Great Roundup* will be filmed. And since your first audition, we have been busy…"

Dirk Henley, one of the producers, chimed in. "We've been in touch with the mayor and the town council."

"Of Rust Creek Falls?" Travis asked, feeling dazed. He was still trying to deal with the fact that there was more auditioning to get through. He couldn't believe she'd just said the audition would be happening in his hometown.

"Of course of Rust Creek Falls." Giselle actually smiled, a smile that tried to be indulgent but was much too full of sharp white teeth to be anything but scary.

Dirk took over again. "Mayor Traub and the other council members are excited to welcome Real Deal Entertainment to their charming little Montana town."

Travis valiantly remained positive. Okay, he hadn't made the final cut, but he was still in the running and that was what mattered.

As for the final audition happening at home, well, now that he'd had a second or two to deal with that information, he supposed he wasn't all that surprised.

For a show like *The Great Roundup*, his hometown was a location scout's dream come true. And the mayor and the council would say yes to the idea in a New York minute. The movers and shakers of

Rust Creek Falls had gotten pretty ambitious in the last few years. They were always open to anything that might bring attention, money and/or jobs to town. Real Deal Entertainment should be good for at least the first two.

Dirk said, "We'll be sending Giselle, Roxanne, a camera crew *and* a few production people along with you for a last on-camera group audition."

Giselle showed more teeth. "We're going to put you and your fellow finalists in your own milieu, you might say."

Dirk nodded his approval. "And that milieu is a very atmospheric cowboy bar with which I'm sure you are familiar."

There was only one bar inside the Rust Creek Falls town limits. Travis named it. "The Ace."

"That's right!" Dirk beamed. "The Ace in the Hole, which we love."

What did that even mean? They loved the name? Must be it. No Hollywood type would actually *love* the Ace. It was a down-home, no-frills kind of place.

Dirk was still talking. "We'll be taking over 'the Ace'—" he actually air quoted it "—for a night of rollicking country fun. You know, burgers and brews and a country-western band. We want to see you get loose, kick over the traces, party in a purely cowboy sort of way. It will be fabulous. You're going to have a great time." He nodded at the other producer, who nodded right back. "I'm sure we'll get footage we can use on the show."

And then Giselle piped up with, "And, Travis…"

Her voice was much too casual, much too smooth. "We want you to bring your fiancée along to the audition. We love what you've told us about her, and we can't wait to meet her."

Chapter Two

*F*iancée?

Travis's heart bounced upward into his throat. He tried not to choke and put all he had into keeping his game face on.

But…

Fiancée? When did his imaginary girlfriend become a fiancée?

He'd never in his life had a fiancée. He hadn't even been with a woman in almost a year.

Yeah, all right. He had a rep as a ladies' man and he knew how to play that rep, but all that, with the women and the wild nights? It had gotten really old over time. And then there was what had happened last summer. After that, he'd realized he needed to grow the hell up. He'd sworn off women for a while.

Damn. This was bad. Much worse than finding out there was still another audition to get through. How had he not seen this coming?

Apparently, they'd decided they needed a little romance on the show, a young couple in love and engaged to be married—and he'd let Giselle get the idea that he could give them that. He'd thought he was playing the game, but he'd only played himself.

Giselle stood. "So, we're set then. You'll be taken back to the hotel for tonight. Pack up. Your plane leaves first thing tomorrow."

Ten of his fellow finalists were on that 7:00 a.m. flight to Salt Lake City the next day, including old Wally Wilson and the Franklins—Fred Franklin and his twin sons, Rob and Joey. Travis exchanged greetings with Wally, the Franklins and the rest of them, too.

He wasn't sitting near any of them, though. And the guy in the seat next to him dismissed Travis with a nod and spent the flight to Salt Lake City fiddling with his smartphone.

Travis stared out the window and considered his predicament.

A girl.

He needed a girl and he needed her fast.

Without one, he had a really bad feeling he wouldn't make the final *Great Roundup* cut.

At Salt Lake City International, they switched to a smaller plane that took them to Kalispell. Again, he got a seat next to a complete stranger. He stared out the window some more and gave himself a pep talk.

He'd come this far, and he wasn't about to give up now. Somehow, he needed to find himself a temporary fiancée. She had to be outgoing and pretty, someone who could rope and ride, build a campfire and handle a rifle, someone he could trust, someone he wouldn't mind pretending to be in love with.

And she had to be someone from town.

It was impossible. He knew that. But damn it, he was not giving up. Somehow, he had to find a way to give Giselle and the others what they wanted.

Real Deal Entertainment had a van waiting at the airport in Kalispell. The company had also sent along a production assistant, Gerry, to ride herd on the talent. Gerry made sure everyone and their luggage got on board the van and then drove them to Maverick Manor, a resort a few miles outside the Rust Creek Falls town limits.

Gerry herded them to the front desk. As he passed out the key cards, he announced that he was heading back to the airport to pick up the next group of finalists. They were to rest up and order room service. The producers and casting director would be calling everyone together first thing tomorrow right here in the main lobby.

Travis grabbed Gerry's arm before he could get away. "I need to go into town." *And rustle up a fiancée.*

Gerry frowned—but then he nodded. "Right.

You're Dalton, the local guy. You can get your own ride?"

"Yeah." A ride was the least of his problems.

Gerry regarded him, narrow eyed. Travis understood. As potential talent, the production company wanted him within reach at all times. He wouldn't be free again until he was either culled from the final cast list—or the show had finished shooting, whichever happened first.

Travis was determined not to be culled. "I'm supposed to bring my fiancée to the audition tomorrow night. I really need to talk to her about that." *As soon as I can find her.*

Gerry, who was about five foot six and weighed maybe 110 soaking wet, glared up at him. "Got it. Don't mess me up, man."

"No way. I *want* this job."

"Remember your confidentiality agreement. Nothing about the production or your possible part in it gets shared."

"I remember."

"Be in your room by seven tonight. I'll be checking."

"And I'll be there."

Gerry headed for the airport, and Travis called the ranch. His mother, Mary, answered the phone. "Honey, I am on my way," she said.

He was waiting at the front entrance of the manor when she pulled up in the battered pickup she'd been driving for as long as he could remember. She jumped out and grabbed him in a bear hug. "Two weeks in Hollywood hasn't done you any damage that I can see." She stepped back and clapped him on the arms. "Get in. Let's go."

She talked nonstop all the way back to the ranch—mostly about his father's brother, Phil, who had recently moved to town from Hardin, Montana. Phil Dalton had wanted a new start after the loss of Travis's aunt Diana. And Uncle Phil hadn't made the move alone. His and Diana's five grown sons had packed up and come with him.

At the ranch, Travis's mom insisted he come inside for a piece of her famous apple pie and some coffee.

"I don't have that long, Mom."

"Sit down," Mary commanded. "It's not gonna kill you to enjoy a slice of my pie."

So he had some pie and coffee. He saw his brother Anderson briefly. His dad, Ben, was still at work at his law office in town.

Zach, one of Uncle Phil's boys, came in, too. "That pie looks really good, Aunt Mary."

Mary laughed. "Sit down and I'll cut you a nice big piece."

Zach poured himself some coffee and took the chair across from Travis. In his late twenties, Zach was a good-looking guy. He asked Travis, "So how's it going with that reality show you're gonna be on?"

Travis kept it vague. "We'll see. I haven't made the final cut yet."

Zach shook his head. "Well, good luck. I don't get the appeal of all that glitzy Hollywood stuff. I'm more interested in settling down, you know? Since we lost Mom…" His voice trailed off, and his blue eyes were mournful.

"Oh, hon." Trav's mom patted Zach gently on the back. She returned to the stove and added over her shoulder, "It's a tough time, I know."

"So sorry about Aunt Diana," Travis said quietly.

Zach nodded. "Thank you both—and like I was sayin', losing Mom has reminded me of what really matters, made me see it's about time I found the right woman and started my family."

Travis ate another bite of his mother's excellent pie and then couldn't resist playing devil's advocate on the subject of settling down. "I can't even begin to understand how tough it's been for you and your dad and the other boys. But come on, Zach. You're not even thirty. What's the big hurry to go tying the knot?"

Zach sipped his coffee. "You would say that. From where I'm sitting, Travis, you're a little behind the curve. All your brothers and sisters—and more than a few cousins—are married and having babies. A wife and kids, that's what life's all about."

"I'll say it again. There's no rush." Well, okay. For him there kind of was. He needed a fiancée, yesterday or sooner. But a wife? Not any time soon.

Travis's mother spoke up from her spot at the stove. "Don't listen to him, Zach. If a wife is what you're looking for, you've come to the right place. There are plenty of pretty, smart, marriageable young women in Rust Creek Falls. Marriage is in the air around here."

Travis grunted. "Or it could be something in the water. Whatever it is, Mom's right. Marriage is nothing short of contagious in this town. Everybody seems to be coming down with it."

Zach forked up his last bite of pie. "Sounds like Rust Creek Falls is exactly the place that I want to be."

It was almost three in the afternoon when Travis climbed in his Ford F-150 crew cab and went to town. He had less than four hours before he had to be back in his room at Maverick Manor. Four hours to find his new fiancée.

He drove up and down the streets of town with the windows down, waving and calling greetings to people he knew, racking his brain for a likely candidate to play the love of his life on *The Great Roundup*.

Driving and waving were getting him nowhere. He decided he'd stop in at Daisy's Donut Shop, just step inside and see if his future fake fiancée might be waiting there, having herself a maple bar and coffee.

He found a spot at the curb in front of Buffalo Bill's Wings To Go, which was right next door to Daisy's. As he walked past, he stuck his head in Wings To Go. No prospects there. He went on to the donut shop, but when he peered in the window, he saw only five senior citizens and a young mother with two little ones under five.

Not a potential fiancée in sight.

Trying really hard not to get discouraged, he started to turn back for his truck. But then the door to the adjacent shop opened.

Callie Crawford, a nurse at the local clinic, came out of the beauty parlor. "Thanks, Brenna," Callie called over her shoulder before letting the door shut. She spotted Travis. "Hey, Travis! I heard about you and that reality show. Exciting stuff."

"Good to see you, Callie." He tipped his hat to her. "Final audition is tomorrow night."

"At the Ace, so I heard. We're all rooting for you."

He thanked her and asked her to say hi to her husband, Nate, for him. With a nod and a smile, Callie got in her SUV and drove off.

And that was it. That was when it happened. He watched Callie drive off down the street when it came to him.

Brenna. Brenna O'Reilly.

Good-looking, smart as a whip and raised on a ranch. She'd taken some ribbons barrel racing during the three or four summers she worked the local rodeo circuit. She was bold, too. Stood up for herself and didn't take any guff.

But he'd always considered himself too old for her. Plus, he kind of thought of himself as a guy who looked out for her. He would never make a move on her.

But this wouldn't be a move.

This would be…an opportunity.

If she was interested and if it was something she could actually handle.

Brenna.

Did he have any other prospects for this?

Hell, no.

He had less than three hours to find someone. At this point, it was pretty much Brenna or bust.

By then, he was already opening the door to the beauty shop. A bell tinkled overhead as he went in.

Brenna was standing right there, behind the reception counter with the cash register on it, facing the door. She looked kind of surprised at the sight of him.

Before either of them could say anything, the owner, Bee, spotted him. "Travis Dalton!" She waved at him with the giant blow-dryer in her left hand. "What do you know? It's our local celebrity."

Every woman in the shop turned to stare at him. He took off his hat and put on his best smile. "Not a celebrity *yet*, Bee. Ladies, how you doing?"

A chorus of greetings followed. He nodded and kept right on smiling.

Bee asked, "What can we do for you, darlin'?"

He thought fast. "The big final audition's tomorrow night."

"So we heard."

"Figured I could maybe use a haircut—just a trim." He hooked his hat on the rack by the door. "So, Brenna, you available?"

Brenna's blue eyes met his. "You're in luck.

I've got an hour before my next appointment." She came out from behind the counter, looking smart and sassy in snug jeans, ankle boots and a silky red shirt. Red worked for her. Matched her hair, which used to be a riot of springy curls way back when. Now she wore it straight and smooth, a waterfall of fire to just below her shoulders.

She waited until he'd hung up his denim jacket next to his hat then led him to her station. "Have a seat."

He dropped into the padded swivel chair and faced his own image in the mirror.

Brenna put her hands on his shoulders and leaned in. He got a whiff of her perfume. Nice. She caught his eye in the mirror and then ran her fingers up into his hair, her touch light, professional. "This looks pretty good."

It should. He'd paid a lot to a Hollywood stylist right before that first audition two weeks ago. "I was thinking just a trim."

She stood back, nodding, a dimple tucking into her velvety cheek as she smiled. "Well, all right. You want a shampoo first?"

What he wanted was to talk to her alone. He cast a glance to either side and lowered his voice. "Say, Brenna…"

She knew instantly that he was up to something. He could tell by the slight narrowing of her eyes and the way the bow of her upper lip flattened just a little. And then she leaned in again and whispered, "What's going on?"

He went for it. "I was wondering if I could talk to you in private."

Her sleek red-brown eyebrows drew together. "Right now?"

"Yeah."

"Where?"

He cast a quick glance around and spotted the hallway that led to the parking area in back. "Outside?"

She folded her arms across her chest and tipped her head to the side. "Sure. Go on out back. I'll be right there."

"Thanks." He got right up and headed for the back door, not even pausing to collect his jacket and hat. It wasn't that cold out, and he could get them later.

"What's going on?" Bee asked as he strode past her station.

Brenna answered for him. "Travis and I need to talk."

Somebody giggled.

Somebody else said, "Oh, I'll just bet you do."

Travis kept walking. It was okay with him if everyone at the beauty shop assumed he was finally making a move on Brenna—because he was.

Just not exactly in the way that they thought.

Outside, he looked for a secluded spot and settled on the three-walled nook where Bee stored her Dumpster. It didn't smell too bad, and the walls would give them privacy.

He heard the back door open again and stuck his head out to watch Brenna emerge. "Psst."

She spotted him and laughed. "Travis, what *is* this?"

He waved her forward. "Come on. We don't have all day."

For that he got an eye roll, but she did hustle on over to the enclosure. "All right, I'm here. Now what is it?"

He opened his mouth—and nothing came out. He had no idea where to even start.

"I...I have a proposal."

Her eyelashes swept down and then back up again. "Excuse me?"

"This... What I'm about to say. I need your solemn word you won't tell a soul about any of it, or I'll get sued for breach of contract. Understand?"

"Not really." She chewed on her lower lip for a moment. "But okay. I'm game. I won't tell a soul. You have my sworn word on that." She hooked her pinkie at him. He gave it a blank look. "Pinkie promise, Trav. You know that is the most solemn of promises and can never be broken."

"What are we, twelve?"

She made a little snorting sound. "Oh, come on."

He gave in and hooked his pinkie with hers. "Satisfied?"

"Are *you*? Because that is the question." She laughed, a sweet, musical sound, and tightened her pinkie against his briefly before letting go.

"As long as you promise me."

"Travis. I promise. I will tell no one, no matter what happens. Now what is going on?"

"How'd you like to be on *The Great Roundup*?"

She wrinkled her nose at him. "What? How? You're making no sense."

"Just listen, okay? Just give me a chance. I...well, I really thought I had it, you know? I thought I was on the show. But it turns out they want a young couple. A young, *engaged* couple. And the casting director sort of asked me if there was anyone special back home and I sort of said yes—and then, all of a sudden, they tell me there's one final audition, that it will be at the Ace and I should bring my fiancée."

Brenna's eyes were wide as dinner plates. "You told them you were *engaged*?"

"No, I didn't *tell* them that. They assumed it and I, well, I let them think it. And now I need a fake fiancée, okay? I need someone who doesn't mind putting herself out there, if you know what I mean. Someone who's not going to be afraid to speak up and hold her head high when the cameras are rolling. Someone good-looking who's familiar with ranch work, who can ride a horse and handle a rifle."

Brenna grinned then. "So you think I'm good-looking, huh?"

"Brenna, you're gorgeous."

"Travis." She looked like she was having a really good time. "Say that again."

Why not? It was only the truth. "Brenna, you are super fine."

And she threw back her red head and let her

laughter chime out. He stood there and watched her and thought how he'd known her since she was knee-high to a gnat. And that she was perfect, just what he needed to make Giselle happy—and earn him his spot on *The Great Roundup*.

But then she stopped laughing. She lowered her head and she regarded him steadily. "So say that it worked—say I go to the Ace with you tomorrow night and we convince them that we're together, that we're going to get married. Then what?"

"Then you belong to them for the next eight to ten weeks. First while they run checks on you and make sure you're healthy, mentally stable and have never murdered anyone or anything."

"You're not serious."

"As a rattler on a hot rock. And as soon as all that's over, we start filming. That's happening at some so far undisclosed Montana location. We're there until they're through filming."

"But what if I get eliminated? *Then* can I come home?"

He shook his head. "Everyone stays. So they can bring you back on camera if they want to, and also because if you come home early, everyone who knows you will know you've been eliminated. They want to keep the suspense going as to who the big winner is until the final show airs. Also, when the filming's over and you come home, you and I would still be pretending to be engaged."

"Until?"

"The episodes where we've each been eliminated

have aired—or the final episode, where one of us wins. The show airs once a week, August through December. Bottom line, you could be my fake fiancée straight through till Christmas."

She leaned against the wall next to the Dumpster and wrapped her arms around herself. "Wow. I... don't know what to say."

He resisted the burning need to promise her that they would win and that she was going to love it. "It's a lot to take in, I know."

She slanted him a glance. "I'd have to check with Bee, see if she'd hold my station for two months."

He knew Brenna was an independent contractor who rented a booth in the shop, but he refused to consider that Bee might say anything but yes. "I get that, sure."

"And then there's the money. I heard the winner gets a million dollars."

"Actually, once you get on the show, there's a graduated fee scale. The million is the top prize, but everybody gets something."

She leaned toward him a little, definitely interested. "Graduated how?"

"The first one eliminated gets twenty-five hundred. The longer you stay in the game, the more you get. For instance, if you last through the sixth show, you get ten thousand. And if you're the last to go before the winner, you get a hundred K."

She actually chuckled. "Good to know. So, Travis, if we're in this together, I say we split everything fifty-fifty."

He'd figured on giving her something, but he'd been kind of hoping she'd settle for much less. After all, he had big plans for his new house, for the ranch. He cleared his throat. "Would you take twenty percent?"

"Travis," she chided.

"Thirty?" he asked hopefully.

"Look at it this way. If they like me and want me on the show, you double your chances to win. Not to mention, the longer we both stay on, the more we both make." She spoke way too patiently. He found himself wistfully recalling the little girl she'd once been, the little girl who'd considered him her own personal hero and would have done anything he asked her to do, instantly, without question. Where had that little girl gone?

"True, but I'm your ticket in," he reminded her. "I'm the one who worked my ass off getting this far, you know?"

"I see that. And I admire that. I sincerely do. But without me, you won't make the cast."

She was probably right. He argued, anyway. "I'm not sure of that."

Brenna was silent, leaning there against the wall, her head tipped down. The seconds ticked by. He waited, trying to look easy and unconcerned, playing it like he didn't have a care in the world. Too bad that inside he was a nervous wreck.

Finally, she looked up and spoke again. "I'm trying not to be so impulsive in my life, to settle down a little, you know what I mean?"

Their eyes met and they gazed at each other for a long count of ten. "Bren. I know exactly what you mean."

She gave a chuckle, sweet and low. "I kind of thought that you might. The thing is, playing your fake fiancée on a reality show is not exactly what I would call settling down. And what are the odds against us, anyway? How many will end up competing with us?"

"I think there are twenty-two contestants total, so it's you and me and twenty others."

"Meaning that however we split the money, odds are someone else will take home the big prize."

He pushed off the wall, took her by the shoulders and looked deeply into those ocean-blue eyes. "First rule. Never, *ever* say we might not win. We *will* win. Half the battle is the mental game. Defeat is not an option. Winning is the only acceptable outcome."

She got it, she really did. He could feel it in the sudden straightening of her shoulders beneath his hands, see it in the bright gleam that lit those wide eyes. "Yeah. You're right. We *will* win."

"That's it. Hold that thought." He let go of her shoulders but held her gaze.

She said, "We really would be increasing our chances, the two of us together. Together, we can work out strategies, you know? We can plan how to handle whatever they throw at us."

"Exactly. We would have each other's backs. So what do you say, Bren?"

"I still want half the money." A gust of wind

slipped into the three-sided enclosure and stirred her hair, blowing a few fiery strands across her mouth.

He smoothed them out of the way, guiding them behind her ear, thinking how soft her pale skin was and marveling at how she'd grown up to be downright hot. It was a good thing he'd always promised himself he'd never make a move on her. Add that promise to the fact that he'd sworn off women and he should be able to keep from getting any romantic ideas about her.

"Travis?" She searched his face. "Did you hear what I just said?"

"I heard." He ordered his mind off her inconvenient hotness and set it on coming up with more reasons she should take less than half the prize.

Unfortunately, he couldn't think of a single one.

So all right, then. His new house and his investment in the ranch would be smaller. But his chances of winning had just doubled—*more* than doubled. Because Brenna was a fighter, and together they *would* go all the way to the win.

"Fair enough, Bren. Fifty-fifty, you and me." He held up his hand.

She slapped a high five on it. "I'll be right back."

He caught her before she could get away. "There's more we need to talk about."

"Not until I get the okay from Bee, we don't." She glanced down at his fingers wrapped around her upper arm.

He let go. "What will you say to her?"

"That I might have a chance on *The Great Roundup*,

but to try for it, I need to know that she'll let me have my booth back on August 1."

"Good. That's good. Don't mention the engagement yet. We still need to decide how to handle that."

She let out another sweet, happy laugh—and then mimed locking her mouth and tossing away the key. "My lips are sealed," she whispered, then whirled on her heel and headed for the back door.

Five endless minutes later, she returned.

"Well?" he asked, his heart pounding a worried rhythm beneath his ribs.

Her smile burst wide open. "Bee wished us luck."

"And?"

"Yes, she'll hold my booth for me."

He almost grabbed her and hugged her, but caught himself in time. "Excellent."

"Yeah—and is there some reason we need to hang around out here? Let's go in. I'll give you that trim you pretended you needed."

He heard a scratching sound, boots crunching gravel. "What's that?"

"What?"

He signaled for silence and stuck his head out of the enclosure in time to see the back of crazy old Homer Gilmore as he scuttled away across the parking lot toward the community center on Main, the next street over.

Brenna stuck her head out, too. "It's just Homer."

They retreated together back into the enclosure. He asked, "You think he heard us?"

She was completely unconcerned. "Even if he did, Homer's not going to say anything."

"And you know this how?"

"He's a little odd, but he minds his own business."

"A *little* odd? He's the one who spiked the punch with moonshine at Braden and Jennifer's wedding two years ago."

"So?" The wind stirred her hair again. She combed it back off her forehead with her fingers. "He never gossips or carries tales. To tell you the truth, I trust him."

"Because...?"

"It's just, well, I don't know. I have this feeling that he looks out for me, like a guardian angel or a fairy godmother."

Travis couldn't help scoffing, "One who just happens to be a peculiar old homeless man."

"Trav," she insisted, "he's not going to say anything. I guarantee it. Now, let's go in and—"

He put up a hand. "Just a minute. A couple more things. Starting tomorrow night, we're madly in love. You'll need to convince a bunch of LA TV people that I'm the only guy for you."

"Well, that's a lot to ask," she teased. "But I'll do my best."

"You'll need to make everyone in town believe it, too—including your family. They all have to think we're for real."

"Trav, I can do it." She was all determination now. "You can count on me."

"That's what I needed to hear."

"Then can we go in?"

"There's one more thing…"

"What?"

"It's important tomorrow night that you be on. You need to show them your most outgoing self. Sell your own personality." When she nodded up at him, he went on, "I did a lot of research on reality shows before I went into this. What I learned is that the show is a story, Bren. A story told in weekly episodes. And a good story is all about big personalities, characters you can't forget, over-the-top emotions. What I'm saying is, you can't be shy. It's better to embarrass yourself than to be all bottled up and boring. Are you hearing what I'm saying?"

"Yes, I am. And let me ask you something. When have you ever known me to be boring?"

Her various escapades over the years scrolled through his mind. At the age of nine, she'd gotten mad at her mom and run away. She got all the way to Portland, Oregon, before they caught up with her. At twelve, she'd coldcocked one of the Peabody boys when she caught him picking on a younger kid. Peabody hit the ground hard. It took thirty stitches to sew him back up. At sixteen, she'd rolled her pickup over a cliff because she never could resist a challenge and Leonie Parker had dared her to race up Fall Mountain. Only the good Lord knew how she'd survived that crash without major injury.

The more Travis thought of all the crazy things she'd done, the more certain he became that Brenna

O'Reilly would have no problem selling herself to Giselle and the rest of them. "All right. I hear you."

"Good. 'Cause I'm a lot of things, Travis Dalton. But I am *never* shy or boring."

The next night, Real Deal Entertainment had assigned Gerry to drive the finalists to the Ace in the Hole.

All except for Travis. They let him make a quick trip to Kalispell in the afternoon and then, in the evening, he drove his F-150 out to the O'Reilly place to pick up his supposed fiancée.

Brenna's mom answered his knock. Travis had always liked Maureen O'Reilly. She loved her life on the family ranch, and her kitchen was the heart of her home. She'd always treated Travis with warmth and affection.

Tonight, however? Not so much. When he swept off his hat and gave her a big smile, she didn't smile back.

"Hello, Travis." Maureen pulled back the door and then hustled him into the living room, where she offered him a seat on the sofa. "Brenna will be right down."

"Great. Thanks."

She leaned toward him a little and asked in a low voice, "Travis, I need you to be honest with me. What's going on here?"

Before he left Brenna at the beauty shop yesterday, they'd agreed on how to handle things with her parents and his. Right now, Maureen needed to know that there was *something* going on between him and her middle daughter. The news of their engagement, however, would come a little bit later. "Brenna and I have a whole lot in common. She's agreed to come out to the audition at the Ace with me tonight."

"What does that mean, 'a whole lot in common'?"

"I care for her. I care for her deeply." It was surprisingly easy to say. Probably because it was true. He did care for Brenna. Always had. "She's one of a kind. There's no other girl like her."

Maureen scowled. She opened her mouth to speak again, but before she got a word out, her husband, Paddy, appeared in the archway that led to the kitchen.

"Travis. How you doin'?"

"Great, Paddy." He popped to his feet, and he and Paddy shook hands. "Real good to see you."

"Heard about you and that reality show."

"Final audition is tonight."

"Well, good luck to you, son."

Maureen started to speak again, but Brenna's arrival cut her off. "It's show business, Dad," she scolded with a playful smile. "In show business, you say 'break a leg.'"

Travis tried not to stare as she came down the steps wearing dark-wash jeans that hugged her strong legs and a sleeveless lace-trimmed purple top that clung to every curve. Damn, she was fine. Purple suede dress boots and a rhinestone-studded cowboy hat completed the perfect picture she made.

Again, Travis reminded himself that she was spunky little Brenna O'Reilly and this so-called relationship they were going to have when they got on the show was just that—all show. Brenna didn't need to be messing with a troublesome cowboy like him.

And he knew very well that Maureen thought so, too.

Still, he could almost start having *real* ideas about Brenna and him and what they might get up to together pretending to be engaged during *The Great Roundup.*

Brenna kissed her mom on the cheek and then her dad, too. She handed Travis her rhinestone-trimmed jean jacket and he helped her into it.

They managed to get out the door and into the pickup without Maureen asking any more uncomfortable questions.

"It's time," she said in a low and angry tone as he turned off the dirt road from the ranch and onto the highway heading toward town. "Scratch that. It's *past* time I got my own place." Rentals in Rust Creek Falls were hard to come by. A lot of young women like Brenna lived with their parents until they got married or scraped together enough to buy something of their own. "Bee offered me her apartment over the beauty shop. She's been living in Kalispell, anyway, with her new guy. So when we win *The Great Roundup,* I'm moving. I love my mom, but she's driving me crazy."

"*When we win.* That's the spirit." As for Maureen, he played the diplomat. "Your mom's a wonderful woman."

Brenna shook her head and stared out the window. He almost asked her exactly what Maureen might have said to upset her—but then again, it was probably about him and he wasn't sure he wanted to know.

The rest of the ride passed in silence. Travis wanted to give Brenna a little more coaching on how to become a reality TV star, but the closer they got to town, the more withdrawn she seemed. He started to worry that something was really bothering her—something more than annoyance with her mom. And he had no idea what to say to ease whatever weighed on her mind.

The parking lot at the Ace was full. Music poured out of the ramshackle wooden building at the front of the lot. They were playing a fast one, something with a driving beat. Travis drove up and down the rows of parked vehicles, looking for a free space. Finally, in the last row at the very back of the lot, he found one.

He pulled in and turned off the engine. "You okay, Brenna?"

She aimed a blinding smile at him. "Great. Let's get going." She opened her door and swung those purple boots to the dirt and got out.

So he jumped out on his side and hustled around to her. He offered his hand. She gave him the strangest wild-eyed sort of look, but then she took it. Hers was ice-cold. He laced their fingers together and considered pulling her back, demanding to know if she was all right.

"Let's do this." She started walking, head high,

that red hair shining down her back, rhinestones glittering on her hat, along the cuffs, hem and collar of her pretty denim jacket.

He fell in step with her, though he had a scary premonition they were headed straight for disaster. She seemed completely determined to go forward. He was afraid to slow her down, afraid that would finish her somehow, that calling a halt until she told him what was wrong would only make her turn and run. Their chance on *The Great Roundup* would be lost before they even got inside to try for it.

They went around to the front of the building and up the wooden steps. A couple of cowboys came out and held the door for them. Both men looked at Brenna with interest, and Travis felt a buzz of irritation under his skin. He gave them each a warning glare. The men tipped their hats and kept on walking.

Inside, it was loud and wall-to-wall with partiers. Travis had never seen the Ace this packed. He spotted a couple of cameramen filming the crowd. Over by the bar, he caught sight of Wally Wilson talking the ear off one of the bartenders. And another finalist, that platinum-blonde rodeo star, Summer Knight, was surrounded by cowboys. He knew it was her by the shine of her almost-white hair and that sexy laugh of hers.

"Come on." He pulled Brenna in closer so she could hear him. "We'll find the casting director, Giselle. I'll introduce you."

She blinked and stared at him through those now-enormous eyes. What was going on with her? She really didn't look good.

Brenna was nervous.

Well, okay. Beyond nervous. Actually, she was freaking out. Brenna never freaked out.

And that freaked her out even more.

She'd been so sure she knew how to handle herself. She *did* know how to handle herself. She was bold. Fearless. Nothing scared her. Ever.

Except this, the Ace packed to bursting, the music so loud. All these people pressing in around her, a casting director waiting to meet her.

And Travis.

Travis, who was counting on her to win them both a spot on *The Great Roundup*.

Dear Lord, she didn't want to blow this. She would never forgive herself if she let Travis down.

"There's Giselle." Travis waved at a tall, model-skinny woman on the other side of the room. The woman lifted a hand and signaled them to join her. "This way." His fingers still laced with hers, he started working his way through the crowd, leading her toward the tall woman with cheekbones so sharp they threatened to poke right through her skin.

"Wait." Brenna dug in her boot heels.

He stopped and turned back to her, a worried frown between his eyebrows. "Bren?" He said her name softly, gently. He knew she was losing it. "What? Tell me."

She blasted a smile at him and forced a brittle laugh. "Can you just give me a minute?" She tipped her head toward the hallway that led to the ladies' room. "I'll be right back." She tugged free of his grip.

"Brenna—"

"I need to check my lip gloss."

"But—"

"Right back." She sent him a quick wave over her shoulder and made for the hallway, scattering *Excuse me*s as she went, weaving her way as fast as she could through the tight knots of people, ignoring anyone who spoke to her or glanced her way.

When she reached the hallway, she kept on going, her eyes on the glowing green exit sign down at the end. She got to the ladies' room and she didn't even slow down. She just kept right on walking down to the end of the hall.

And out the back door.

Don't miss
THE MAVERICK FAKES A BRIDE
by Christine Rimmer,
available July 2017 wherever
Mills & Boon Cherish
books and ebooks are sold.

MILLS & BOON®

Cherish™

EXPERIENCE THE ULTIMATE RUSH OF FALLING IN LOVE

A sneak peek at next month's titles...

In stores from 15th June 2017:

- **Bound to Her Greek Billionaire** – Rebecca Winters
  and **A Bride, a Barn, and a Baby** –
  Nancy Robards Thompson
- **The Mysterious Italian Houseguest** – Scarlet Wilson
  and **A Second Chance for the Single Dad** –
  Marie Ferrarella

In stores from 29th June 2017:

- **Their Baby Surprise** – Katrina Cudmore
  and **It Started with a Diamond** – Teri Wilson
- **The Marriage of Inconvenience** – Nina Singh
  and **The Maverick Fakes a Bride!** – Christine Rimmer

Just can't wait?
Buy our books online before they hit the shops!
www.millsandboon.co.uk

Also available as eBooks.

MILLS & BOON®

EXCLUSIVE EXTRACT

When Charlotte Aldridge tells CEO Lucian Duval she's pregnant, the handsome billionaire is adamant his child will have the one thing he never did – the love of two committed parents…

Read on for a sneak preview of
THEIR BABY SURPRISE

'I want to be a part of this baby's life on a daily basis.'

The knot of anxiety inside her twisted. 'That's not possible, you know that, I'm moving away from London.'

'Don't move away.'

Charlotte gestured around her apartment. 'I need more space. I need to be near my parents. To have family close by.'

'I agree, that's why I believe you should move in with me…and for that matter, why we should marry.'

She sank down onto the window seat below the open window. 'Marry!'

'Yes.'

A known serial dater was proposing marriage. This was crazy. Lucian had the reputation for being impulsive and a maverick within the industry but his decisions were always backed up with sound logic. And that quick-fire decision making, some would even say recklessness, often gave him the edge over his more ponderous rivals. But he had called this one all wrong. She gave an incredulous laugh. 'I bet you don't even believe in marriage?'

He rolled his shoulders and rubbed the back of his neck hard, his expression growing darker before he answered, 'It's the responsible thing to do when a child becomes part of the equation.'

This was crazy. She lifted her hands to her face in shock and exasperation, her hot cheeks burning against the skin of her palms. 'Have you really thought about what it takes to be a father? A child needs consistency, routine, to know that they are the centre of the parent's life. Have you considered the sacrifices needed? Your work life, the constant travel, all of the partying—everything about the way you live now will be affected. Are you prepared to give up all of that?'

Stood in the centre of the room, he folded his arms on his wide imposing chest, his eyes firing with impatient resolve. 'I don't have a choice. This child is my responsibility and duty, I will do whatever it takes to ensure that it has a safe and happy childhood.'

Don't miss
THEIR BABY SURPRISE
by Katrina Cudmore

Available July 2017
www.millsandboon.co.uk